THE THIRD CHILD

MARGE PIERCY

THE
THIRD
CHILD

PIATKUS

First published in Great Britain in 2003 by
Judy Piatkus (Publishers) Ltd of
5 Windmill Street, London W1P 1HF
email: info@piatkus.co.uk

First published in the United States in 2003
by HarperCollins*Publishers* Inc., New York.

ISBN 0 7499 0665 0

Printed and bound in Great Britain by
Mackays of Chatham Ltd, Chatham, Kent

· CHAPTER ONE ·

Your father is an important man." Rosemary placed her small delicate hands firmly on the ebony surface of her desk, the desk that had followed her through the governor's mansion to the Washington house the Senator had rented at what Rosemary said was an exorbitant price. She had called Melissa and Billy into her office at the back. "You have to learn to behave accordingly. If this gets into the papers, it could damage your father."

Billy was trying to look remorseful, but Melissa worried he was not succeeding. The windows were open onto the narrow yard, where something exotic was in bloom. It was spring vacation and much warmer in D.C. than at Miss Porter's School in Connecticut where Melissa was in her last year. In her father's family, the Dickinsons, the women always attended Miss Porter's—even her, no matter how far down the family hierarchy she was rated. The garden was her favorite part of this new house in Georgetown on a street called P in the block off Wisconsin where her parents had moved after the election. She and Billy sat out there last night smoking dope under a magnolia whose big flowers were just browning and falling on them. A tree with pink flowers was opening, a tree as feminine as if it wore a prom dress. In the twilight after Billy went in, she had lain under that tree imagining a lover—not real sex, with its brutal disappointment, but with a soft dissolve, romantic, like perfect kissing. Her grandmother Susie, whom she never saw anymore, would know the name of that tree. When she was little, she had wanted to be like Grandma Susie—growing tomatoes and peonies, beans and zinnias in the yard in Youngstown. She had started a garden on the grounds of the governor's mansion in Harrisburg, but when Rosemary discovered it, the gardener pulled her plants up and restored it the way it had been. Melissa was supposed to want to be a lawyer or something better, whatever that might be. Her father wanted to be President, and her mother was determined to get him there. Billy had bought the pot on M Street. M and Wisconsin were a different world from the staid block of old houses mostly flush to the sidewalk and always swarming with workers painting, gardening, tuck-pointing the bricks, primping the houses—on Wisconsin and on M it was a world of the young, alive and noisy, racially mixed and of all classes. This house was Second Empire, which sounded sinister, and only a hundred twenty-five years old; Rosemary had wanted a federal house of red brick two hundred years old, but those were even more expensive.

"It was just pot, Mother," Billy said. His forelock had fallen over his eyes. She fought the impulse to push it back. His hair in the sun beaming through the window was that light red gold called strawberry blond, different from anybody in the family—not blond like Father and Merilee. Not ordinary light brown hair like Rich Junior and herself. Mother's hair had been blond for years now; it went with her porcelain skin.

"You're just fifteen. Are you trying to get expelled again?" Rosemary shook her head in annoyance.

He gave Melissa one of those Here-we-go-again looks. Actually Billy did not much care if he got expelled, as he'd said to her when he was waiting to be called on the carpet—the two of them sprawled on her bed as always talking in mutters and whispers. He had friends at prep school, but he made friends easily and one school was like another to him. This was his third. They always let him get away with a lot before they tossed him because he was the Senator's son, and because he was good at every sport he bothered to try.

"I was just going along with the other guys."

Melissa said, "In high school, most guys smoke pot sometimes, Mother. Be glad he's not on Ecstasy or heroin. Let's have some perspective." She always tried to make peace between her mother and her younger brother—if only Billy could manage to seem truly sorry, but he couldn't fake it successfully. He had never taken their mother's reprimands as intensely as she had. She had been a puppyish fool, wagging her tail, fetching slippers, trying, always trying to be someone Rosemary wanted for a daughter. Now her aim with her mother was to be cool. She was an undercover agent playing the dutiful daughter, but they would see. They had no idea who she really was, her deadly skills and her hidden brilliance as she played the part of a too tall, too busty, hardworking high school senior. But under that drab exterior, she was something else, something that would astonish them. Oh, sure.

Rosemary ignored her. "Everything you do is visible, Billy. Everything any of us does can come back to haunt your father."

Melissa sighed and slumped into a chair. It was a weird curvy chair, which she supposed went with the house, upholstered in nubby blue silk. Her father's importance. She could not remember when it did not exist. In retrospect, it gilded even the snapshot of him from his Dartmouth days, holding an oar aloft like a captured trophy—a shot always accompanied by the caption saying that he had gone to the 1968 Olympics with his sculling team. She had learned only two years ago that he had not actually competed—her aunt Karen told her. Karen cultivated the unusual habit in the Dickinson family of telling the truth, not a trait valued by the rest of the family—except Billy and her, the two young misfits. Actually Billy was too handsome to be a real misfit. It was one of the many things she wished for, to be gorgeous like her older, golden sister Merilee or like Billy. Billy was two and a half years younger than Melissa. He had been a cute kid, but he had gone through an awkward period around puberty— an awkwardness she had never grown out of. But he had. Lately they weren't as close. Karen was her favorite relative, but she had only been let out of the sanitarium to attend Grandpa Dickinson's seventy-fifth birthday celebration. For the last five years, she had been shut up there. One of Rosemary's favorite admonitions to her: "Do you want to be like your aunt Karen?" when Melissa had done something her parents viewed as out of line, inappropriate, not supportive of family ambitions and goals.

Daddy's importance was like a family member, bigger and even more visible than her two older siblings, Richard IV, called Rich—to differentiate him from his father, Dick. Rich was already talked about as a candidate for state rep in Pennsylvania—and her perfect sister, Merilee, in her first year of law school at George Washington. When Melissa was little, she had imagined her father a king, a radiant figure out of fairy tales. As a highly visible prosecutor in Philadelphia, he had appeared a hero who put dangerous bad guys in jail. She would sometimes enter a room behind him, behind her mother, and the air would crackle and people would stand and applaud and cheer. It had been years since she had thought of him that way. She did not like to remember that she had been such a sucker for his phony smiles and big hellos and ready laugh. How she had believed in him! She had drawn his portrait in crayons, then in acrylic for art class. She had kept a photo of just the two of them—usually photos were of just him and Rosemary, him and some other politician, one of him and the President, or of the whole family—on her dresser until this year.

The first big event Melissa remembered after her father became governor was an execution. It was actually the second execution, but Melissa had been in bed with one of her frequent sinus infections during the first. Number two was a criminal Daddy had prosecuted himself. One great thing about being eighteen was that she had gradually come to understand things that had been encoded and hidden when she was young and naïve. Her past with her parents rewrote itself as she gathered knowledge, as the landscape of her childhood mutated out of golds and bright sky blues to a landscape with shadows and dark pits and hidden fires burning underground like those anthracite mines under Wilkes-Barre that had been ablaze for decades. Her parents were powerful and she was powerless, but she could try to place them in perspective, she could learn and criticize, silently, stealthily. With them, stealth was everything.

Both parents had been out that night. Daddy was at the execution, and Rosemary was talking with her favorite reporter from Channel Four. Merilee and Rich were away at school. Melissa and Billy were in the upstairs rumpus room of the governor's mansion, supposed to be watching *The Little Mermaid* on the VCR, but both of them wanted to watch TV, where all the people with candles were in the streets singing. It was the same outside. Every so often they would look out the window and see the people gathered on Second beyond the fence that surrounded the governor's mansion. Security cameras would be trained on the crowd, and she could see state troopers standing by, as well as the regular security men she knew by name. Mommy called the demonstrators softheads.

The prisoner's name was Toussaint Parker, and he had killed a policeman. Mommy said it was an excuse for the radicals and the commies and the softheads to make a fuss, but no judge was going to let off a Black troublemaker who killed a cop. Melissa noticed all the African-American staff were gathered downstairs in the kitchen watching too. She was aware that her nanny Noreen did not rejoice in the execution the way Rosemary did. Melissa loved Noreen, who had come to take care of her and Billy when Daddy was first running for governor. She never felt that Noreen was disappointed in her the way her parents were. Sometimes she thought that they forgot about her entirely. "I'm not the oldest, I'm not the youngest, I'm not the smartest, I'm not the best looking, I'm not the best athlete," she wailed to Noreen.

"Then you be the sweetest. You be the sugar in the family tea," Noreen said, ruffling Melissa's too fine brown hair. She loved to be held against Noreen's warm chest, which she could sink into, her nice big lap where she was welcome.

Billy and she thought they would actually see the killer die, but they didn't show it on television. Just the people outside the prison with their candles, the people in Philadelphia in front of the courthouse, and the people outside their own house they could see if they peeked out. It looked more impressive on TV. The guy from the Channel Seven news interviewed Daddy and then a police chief who said that cold-blooded cop killer was going to get what he deserved, to deter other lawless thugs from shooting policemen and leaving their families widows and orphans. She had been so silly, she had imagined that when her father was still prosecutor he went after killers like a lawman in a Western and brought them back.

Both her parents liked to ride. When they all went up to Vermont to Grandpa Dickinson's farm, everybody got on horses and climbed the trails on the mountain. Melissa really loved horses. When she was little, she used to pretend to ride a horse to school, before her father got too important for her to walk. Horses were the best thing about going to Vermont to visit crabby Grandpa Dickinson—especially the big grey horse Legerdemain—so it was easy to imagine her father on horseback bringing the outlaw to jail with hands tied behind his back. Seeing her father on TV that night, she wanted to be worthy of him, the hero who had captured the outlaw and now, as governor, was about to hang him. Except, as her teacher had explained in class, execution was by lethal injection. That made her think of the school nurse sticking a needle in her arm to give her a vaccine so she wouldn't get measles. She and Billy fell asleep on the floor by the TV. When Rosemary got in, she was upset to see them sprawled there and scolded Noreen.

When Noreen went out of the governor's mansion that week, she put on a black armband for Toussaint Parker who had been executed, as did a lot of people on the streets of the predominantly African-American neighborhood surrounding the governor's mansion and its huddled bunch of office buildings; but when she came inside, she took it off. Still, Rosemary must have heard about it, because suddenly Noreen was gone. Her place was taken by a white lady with a weird accent, Mrs. Corniliu, who bossed them around and told them how spoiled they were and how lucky. Melissa tried to feel lucky, to make herself worthy of her famous daddy and her beautiful mother.

Melissa felt as if she abandoned past selves like snakeskins of shame along her bumpy route toward adulthood. Girls in her class said that senior year was the best time of their lives, but she never believed that. No, she viewed herself as a project under construction, the road all torn up, piles of dirt heaped to the right and left, dump trucks coming and going, cranes digging away. She would remake herself, she would, into somebody strong and important.

Melissa jerked to attention, suddenly aware her mother was addressing her. "I hope I never have to worry about you, Melissa. I have to know you'll behave in an exemplary way when you begin college in the fall." Rosemary fortunately had no idea how many stupid stunts Emily and she had pulled over the years, because they were more careful than Billy about covering their tracks, about not getting caught. Together they had gotten drunk endless times, tried Ecstasy, shoplifted sweaters, bought and worn clothes Rosemary had forbidden as too revealing, too slutty, gone to raves, though Melissa was too shy, even on Ecstasy, to pick up guys there.

Rosemary said "college" and not "Wesleyan." Melissa suspected her mother had momentarily forgotten which school had accepted her. Rich had gone to Penn State and Merilee had gone to Penn, but now that Father was a senator, she was allowed to go out of state, even though her mother had been disappointed in her choice. Wesleyan would do her no good, Rosemary said, in terms of important contacts. She could easily fall in with a radical crowd there. But Melissa liked Connecticut, near her best friend Emily's family.

She knew her mother didn't want her to go to Wesleyan because she had hidden outside her mother's office and heard Alison, her mother's factotum, discussing whether Rosemary should insist she go elsewhere. Then later she had listened on the steps while Merilee was arguing with Rosemary. They hardly ever fought, so it was worth spying, especially since it turned out they were arguing about her, Merilee said, "You made me go to George Washington law school instead of UCLA to keep me close by. Don't lean on Melissa that way. She's already kind of damaged."

Her gratitude to Merilee for defending her choice of college vanished when she heard what Merilee really thought of her. Damaged? What did that mean? At that point, she hadn't even done it with Jonah yet.

Reprieve time! Alison came to the door of Rosemary's office. "Millie Hay on the phone for you."

Rosemary picked up at once, motioning them out. When she used what Melissa called her geisha voice, Melissa knew the woman must be important. Normally that coy girlish voice was reserved for notable men who might be useful to Dick. She hung around downstairs just long enough to hear Alison congratulating Rosemary and Rosemary gloating. A Supreme Court justice was going to attend a dinner Dick and Rosemary were invited to.

By her third day home, Melissa realized her mother had managed to keep the story quiet and satisfy the school. Senator Dickinson would give a speech for commencement. Melissa had often heard it said that her mother was the brains behind the Senator. She believed it. Billy was a star hockey player and a reasonable baseball player. Her only athletic achievement was tennis, which Aunt Karen had taught her to play. Everything physical was his gift—even the way he moved made her sigh with envy, wishing she had his natural grace. The only thing he couldn't do was dance—he was tone-deaf, like her father. There was never music in the house unless she put it on. For years, she had given her mother and father CDs she loved, that promptly disappeared. She had thought music was one thing she could share with them, but she had been wrong. Neither was interested. For her, music was escape, another level of reality.

College meant liberation, motivating her to keep her grades up, to do every single pukey extracurricular activity from yearbook to French Club to Ecology Club to Young Republicans. Not that she intended to vote Republican when she was old enough. She'd vote Communist or Green or Vegetarian or anything at all that had nothing to do with her parents. She said that to Billy, who did not care, and her best friend, Emily, who thought it was cool. She'd tried that out on Jonah to make clever conversation, but he told her she was stupid.

She did community service to build up her résumé. Summers, she volunteered to take underprivileged kids on camping trips, to the zoo, to the park, whatever. Rosemary had been disturbed when she went to a movie with Mark, who was Korean and volunteering also. Suddenly Mark was moved to another program and she never ran into him again. Back at Miss Porter's, she joined an after-school program in Hartford. Out where Miss Porter's stood, everything was pretty, handsome houses, manicured countryside. Everybody thought of insurance when you said Hartford. In reality, the center of the city was depressed beyond what she could have imagined. Sometimes when she read the little essays she was teaching her kids to write, she cried. She wanted passionately to help them, but it was ladling out a river with a spoon. The level of misery and trouble and rough stuff in their lives was lacerating. She tried to talk with Rosemary about it, but Rosemary nodded and got that glazed look with a little smile. "Yes, dear, those are the people your father is trying to help." Then her attention focused. "Should you be volunteering in such a dangerous neighborhood? Are there drugs around?"

At least she could share her feelings with Emily. She missed Emily on spring break and wished she could have gone home with her. Emily's parents were easygoing chiropractors who lived in East Lyme—which Emily said had given its name to Lyme disease. Aside from always being on a different diet every time she visited—macrobiotic, microbiotic, high protein, fish and seaweed, high carbohydrate—they seemed jolly and laid-back, both playing recorders in a consort and with music always jingling in the house and not an excess of questioning. That was what Melissa called a real vacation. Emily's home was like a soft airy cocoon with good music.

On the top floor in her dormered room, Melissa escaped to call Emily. "I am just so utterly bored, Em. I could just go up in smoke and drift away."

"I bet if I was there, we'd have fun. It's hot. Georgetown Park, that complex, it looks like a great place to pick up guys." Emily could always hook up. She could walk into a mall and come out with a guy. "Maybe your sister knows someone. Have you heard from Jonah?"

"He's such a pig, Em. I'm done with him. All he wants to do is knock boots. He's barely nice to me anymore. And who would I ever meet here? Merilee's seeing this other law student—" She knew deep down she wished Jonah would call or e-mail anyhow, just to make her feel better about herself, even if she was through with him. He made her feel used.

"Is he cute?"

"He's a dork. He's so straight he can't bend over to tie his shoes. But Mother doesn't like him. She doesn't think he's good enough."

"So is Merilee fucking him?"

"Sure. She practically lives in his apartment."

"Your mother doesn't mind?"

"She's so too busy with Daddy and Rich. Rich is getting married in June and it's like a full-time career, Em. It's this Major Event, like an election. Alison, Rosemary's assistant, makes these endless lists and schedules and charts."

"So it's going to be a big society thingie? Can I go?"

"In my place! I was wondering if I couldn't get out of it by developing some not too debilitating disease like a mysterious fever and maybe I could even waste away some." She loved the idea of wasting away. If only she could lose ten pounds, she knew she would like herself better.

"Like Camille." Emily hummed something. She knew all the operas from her parents.

Melissa had no idea who Camille was. "It just seems like forever till we get to college." Melissa felt safe when she thought of going to Wesleyan with Emily. She would not be lonely, even if nobody else liked her. Emily did not care that her father was a senator, for she only got excited about movie stars and rock singers. "Emily, you're the best!" she said suddenly. Em was the only person with whom she could be completely honest. They understood each other's fears and anxieties and wishes. They knew each other's secrets.

"Sure I am." Emily giggled. "Best in show." Emily barked into the phone, subsiding into giggles. Melissa hated to end the connection. She felt cut off as she sat on the bed with its new Ralph Lauren comforter. Maybe once she had lived someplace real. The governor's mansion in Harrisburg had not been theirs. They just occupied it for two terms, and most of the downstairs held reception rooms and offices. This house too was a showplace for entertaining, with her mother's office, Alison's little office and an enormous livingroom and a diningroom formal enough to choke her on the parlor floor. Downstairs, in a sort of high basement called the subfloor, was a kitchen suitable for a restaurant with an antique of a dumbwaiter connecting it to the diningroom above, her father's at-home office lined with books and military memorabilia, and two rooms used by whatever aides were around plus the drivers, when they were in the house. Her parents' bedroom, dressing rooms and Alison's room plus a guest room were on the second floor. Her parents' room opened onto the roof of the downstairs extension, with a glass table, wicker chairs and potted plants. Upstairs under the mansard roof were her bedroom, Billy's and storage. Nominally she was supposed to share her bedroom with Merilee, but her older sister was living in Foggy Bottom near

George Washington U with two other law students. The row house in Philadelphia that maintained Dick Dickinson's residence in his state was even less a home and didn't even have the excitement of Georgetown—when she could escape Rosemary's scrutiny.

Emily's family lived in a real house, with a black Labrador and an Irish setter, with old food in the back of the refrigerator, with CDs on every table and seat, so you had to look before you sat down. On one couch the setter Finnegan would be snoozing on an old fisherman's sweater. On the other, there would be newspapers and half-read books spread out. The Lab, Othello, had his special cushion by the fireplace. Melissa envied Emily her parents. She wanted warm fuzzy parents who would make her drink seaweed shakes, who played *La Bohème* at top volume and sang along with it while throwing sticks and rubber bones for the dogs to fetch. Emily, of course, resented her parents. She felt they were so into each other and their work that they couldn't really see or understand her. They had no idea what she really did. Emily had been sexually active since fourteen. Melissa admired Emily for her daring. Melissa always hung back, but Emily was always tugging her forward. She was always resolving to be bolder, like Em, to have the courage to take chances. Em had been on the pill for years.

A knock on her door. It opened before she spoke. Alison, in her thirties with a sleek cap of chopped-off auburn hair and thin as a broomstick, marched in. "You have an appointment at the J'ai Promis Spa in half an hour."

"What for? I never made an appointment." Guiltily Melissa took her feet off the new bedspread. Billy and she were convinced Alison reported every small transgression to their mother.

"Rosemary had me make it. Tonight is the first of the bridal showers—Laura's aunt is giving it. Come on, you'll enjoy looking smashing." Alison sometimes affected British phrases. She came from northern Pennsylvania.

"I hate going to that place!" Lacquered ladies, fashionable ladies, debutantes, they would look at her and quietly sneer. They would be gossiping with the hairdressers, the manicurists, the masseuses about Beltway things she didn't recognize. They would make her feel huge and ungainly. "I can't go. I have homework. I have a paper to finish."

"Finish it tomorrow," Alison said. "You'll feel great after a makeover. The Senator's car is waiting." Alison would never side with her. The assistant before had sometimes let slip a word of commiseration, but Alison was loyal to Rosemary to the death. Alison seemed to have no other ambition or desire than to please Rosemary and ease her through her days. Even the way she said "Rosemary" suggested that uttering it was a privilege she never took for granted.

That car reference rubbed it in. Melissa had been asking for a car for a year, but she wasn't allowed to have one. Rosemary was terrified she'd get a ticket or cause an accident that would reflect on the Senator. "Aren't I supposed to buy a present?" she asked as Alison hustled her downstairs. "I'll shop after the salon."

"You got them a lovely silver serving set."

"Did you have to go shopping? I could have." It might even have been fun, buying something stupid and expensive.

"It's no effort, Melissa. The bridal register is on-line and I simply ordered something from Tiffany's. Our presents are downstairs, wrapped and ready to go."

She was relieved it was Ox driving—short for Oxford, his given name—not Smart Alec. Ox was middle-aged and Black and easygoing, although he also was security. Alec was just twenty-two and insisted on chatting her up. He was a gofer for Joe, Dick's chief of staff, who had come to Washington with her father from Pennsylvania. Joe stood a head shorter than Dick, his grey hair receding from his forehead. Rosemary said it was from pulling his hair in frustration. Melissa hated him. She remembered the first time she had wanted to talk to her father and Joe had interfered. Since her father had run for governor, a fence of aides and assistants and secretaries had been erected between Dick and her. She wasn't important enough. They had stolen her father from her.

Alison probably had two hundred gifts in her brain filed away and labeled. Bridal registers sounded dull. It was just as well she hadn't had to buy the present. It was so unreal! Rich and Laura had been a couple for three years. Laura was pretty, soft-spoken, a sort of nothing in perfect clothing who was devoted to Rich and with few interests beyond pleasing him and both sets of parents. Laura had all the personality of a sofa pillow. Even when she was playing tennis or jogging, she was perfectly turned out. Rosemary ought to adore her, but didn't. However, since the wedding had been planned for a year, she was going to be stuck with Laura as a daughter-in-law. Laura was the daughter of one of Dick Dickinson's richest and most generous backers, so Rosemary could do little about the match. Melissa grinned to herself. Rich was getting what he wanted, a wife he could boss around—the opposite of his mother. Her father liked Laura just fine, for she flirted with him a little, just the right amount. Melissa could still remember when her father used to take her on his lap, but that had stopped when she was ten and began to sprout breasts, way ahead of the girls in her class. All of a sudden he wouldn't hug her anymore. Rosemary never did.

The wedding, she decided, was really an advantage, because it kept Rosemary off her back. Up until age twelve or thirteen, Melissa would have done anything for a larger share of Rosemary's time and affection. Then she had plotted to capture her mother by all-A report cards, by making gifts in arts and crafts for Rosemary's birthday—bowls and scarves and pins that promptly disappeared—by writing supposedly brilliant essays, by attempting to paint or sculpt or make something out of clay she could bring home and show off, anything that would make her mother say, Why, Melissa, I never knew how talented you are! But something always went wrong. Her pot was crooked. Her essay did not follow what her mother considered the best line, her report card was marred by one B. Even when she got 1460 on her SATs, Rosemary remarked that those tests were dumbed down. Now Melissa just hoped to creep along under Rosemary's radar. If she did well in college, maybe her father would appreciate her.

Rosemary, Dick and Joe were using the diningroom table to spread out résumés. Rosemary was saying, "But what does Babezi know about farms?"

Joe smirked. "He eats vegetables, doesn't he?"

Dick nodded. "We'll put him in for farm service agency director. Now the U.S. marshal . . ." They were making appointments again, the patronage Dick controlled as Senator. He complained it was much less than he'd had at his command as governor, but Rosemary always soothed him.

Melissa felt stunted in her family. Outside, she would blossom, she would grow into someone different from anybody in her family, someone admirable, someone strong and good and loved by others. She would meet people who would judge her not as the inferior child of superior parents, but as herself—alone, separate and visible. Finally she would stand out so powerfully that her mother would see how wrong she had been. We never knew, Rosemary would say, we never guessed. Melissa would do something important or write a wonderful book or make a discovery. It was only a matter of getting away from them finally, so she could show them and the world who she really was.

Melissa felt superfluous, nothing new. Personally, if she ever did get married, she would just sneak off with the guy and do it on the sly. Quiet and personal was tasteful. This was like an awards ceremony. Rich had been sleeping with Laura since he graduated from Harvard Business School, so why couldn't they just say, Hey, we're a couple. Give us a toaster and call it even. But no, Rosemary and Laura's mother, Mrs. Potts, had been planning this event for a year. Now it was hot as a Frialator in Washington and they all had to continuously change their clothes and run around dolled up like idiots. Every five minutes, there was a crisis about whether some senator or cabinet official or undersecretary of waste management or presidential advisor on office supplies was going to come. It was sickening! As if any of them liked each other. It was just head counting. How many advisors and undersecretaries can you cram into a church on a Saturday in June?

It was lucky Laura's parents had money, because this was an incredible potlatch of the stuff. Laura's father was a relatively new backer of Dick's—had kicked in for his campaign for a second term as governor of Pennsylvania. Mr. Potts owned an interstate trucking firm, a corporation specializing in highway construction, a string of ice cream parlors and several steak and brew restaurants. Mr. Potts had the habit of talking as if over a windstorm, to make himself heard by the very deaf. Perhaps he was deaf himself, for he never seemed to hear half of what people said. He had been calling her Melinda and Marissa and Melody. She noticed he never got Merilee's name wrong. If she had that bellowing man to deal with, she would buy earplugs, but Rich seemed to like Potts just fine. Rosemary was closeted with him half the morning. He wasn't her usual type of flirtation, but he was a backer and thus entitled to some attention. Plus the Pottses were paying a fortune for this wedding. Rosemary felt a lavish wedding might put a freshman senator like Dick on the Washington society map. So Mr. Potts was the focus of Rosemary's charm, along with wives of men she wanted to attend.

When Rosemary wanted to pick the brains of some useful type, when she was buttering up a backer or a supporter or useful connection, she spoke differently than she did any other time. Her voice became soft and girlish. She was deferential and almost coy, but she never concealed her intelligence. That fine-pointed instrument was always available. She was absolutely loyal to her husband. Her world was built on Dick and his career. She did not have affairs. No, she had intense ladylike flirtations, usually knee to knee over coffee or tea or sherry.

Alison was frantically busy with the Wedding. Somewhere a gown as large as Idaho was being sewn by angels with gold thimbles. The Save the Date invitations had been sent out six months earlier, hand calligraphy by a weird woman built like an upended box of tissues who actually wore a pince-nez. Emily and she had giggled over that. The Pottses lived near Bryn Mawr, but they had taken a house in Washington for the year so that Laura and her mother could prepare. Mr. Potts usually stayed in Philadelphia, but occasionally he appeared to roar at them. Dick always made time for him, as did Rosemary. Laura was the only daughter in a family with two boys, one of whom was whispered to be gay. Her parents were putting their all and everybody else's into this wedding.

"If you got married," Melissa asked Alison, staggering by with a load of mail that would tax a healthy elephant, "would you want a big wedding like this?"

Alison looked at her blankly. "Married? Why would I marry?"

"Most women do."

"I don't have time for all that," Alison said. She collapsed at her desk, shaking her head slightly, and began slitting open envelopes. "Your mother needs me. She calls me her right arm."

Melissa was relieved when Emily finally came to visit, so she had somebody to vent to besides Billy, who was off every day with guys and indifferent to the preparations. "So it keeps Rosemary off my back. Great. Besides, there'll be champagne. I never got loaded on champagne. They say it's a gigundo high."

Emily and she lay on her bed listening to the bustle. The doorbell rang constantly. Deliverymen came and went. Alison rushed upstairs and then back down. Laura appeared in tears about jewelry. A popular ambassador who was supposed to come was recalled by his country and Rosemary fumed.

"I don't see why Old Man Potts couldn't just buy them a small country like Luxembourg or Liechtenstein. I don't understand weddings. All that preparation—nonstop for twelve months—then one day and it's over."

"I don't know," Emily said dreamily. "You're like the star. You get to wear an incredibly sexy dress if you want to and everybody has to look at you."

"I'd rather have the money. I'd buy a horse and a convertible."

"I'd rather have a ski chalet, like in the mountains."

Melissa had been off of skiing since Jonah had taken her cherry on a ski weekend they had all gone on, Chandler and Emily, her and Jonah. Chandler was the guy Emily had gone out with the longest, a whole four months. Melissa had been so depressed afterward that she had just about given up skiing. Emily said that was silly. You didn't have to fuck some jerk every time you put on a pair of skis. Melissa hadn't felt she had a choice with Jonah, for they had been dating all year and she had just been blowing him and putting the whole thing off.

Em had been so cool about sex, giving her real pointers from the time she started making out with guys. "Don't ever breathe through your mouth, no matter how excited you get. If you had onions even yesterday, if you mouth-breathe on him, he'll be grossed out." It had been a day like today, but in the dorm at Miss Porter's. Em had spoken in a low voice, so the other girls would not overhear. "Use body English when you're kissing." Em wriggled her body. "It gets them excited. They think you're hot. But never initiate the next step or they'll label you a slut. From time to time, you have to say *don't* or *no* but not like you really mean it. It's pro forma, if you get what I mean." Then when Melissa knew she had to suck off Jonah, Emily showed her, using a roll-on deodorant that was about the right shape, demonstrating what to do with her lips and tongue. "Run your tongue around it. Like this." Without Em, she would have freaked out or made some gross mistake. Emily kept her from making a fool of herself in the savage clumsy world of teenage dating. Emily knew what to do, although she seemed so tiny and demure, Rosemary never guessed what Em was really like.

"By the way, where's Rich himself?" Em asked, leaning on an elbow.

Melissa suspected that Emily had a little bitty thing for her older brother. "He's on a bachelor party weekend. They've gone to the Bahamas, about ten of them. He'll be back Monday." It would be a disaster if Emily really did fuck him, but Rich never paid attention to Emily. He liked tall women.

"Have you got your dress yet?"

"It's being altered."

"So what's it like?"

"Mother calls it dupioni silk. But I have to wear yellow, and I totally hate yellow. Laura's in white off the shoulder with gold touches. Her mother is in gold. Rosemary is in blue, and us bridesmaids are in shades of blue or yellow. The guys all get to wear black, naturally. The dress isn't half bad, really, except for the color. Maybe afterward I'll have it dyed. It's kind of slinky."

"Are yellow and blue Laura's favorite colors or school colors or what?"

"It's got something to do with the color of the walls where the reception is. Don't ask me. I'd rather wear black. I look thinner in black. I look huge in yellow."

"Melissa, don't be an idiot. You're not fat. You have a shape, that's all."

"Next to my mother and Merilee, I'm fat. They think I am."

"Well, they're wrong. You don't look like a model, you look like a cute girl with boobs and a nice ass. So stop complaining. I wish I had your chest." Emily had been overweight around puberty, when they had first become friends. She had started having sex because she was fat, she said, and that made up for it with guys. She had long since gone on one diet after another till she was pretty thin, but she never did like the way she looked. They were the same that way. Emily had been invited; that was the only thing Melissa had gotten her way on. She had come a week early to stay the whole time in Melissa's room. It made the wedding bearable. She had heard Rosemary say to Alison that having Emily there who was after all only a chiropractor's daughter nonetheless kept Melissa from conspicuously sulking, so it was worth it. Billy liked Emily, calling her a hottie. He kept sauntering around the upstairs with his shirt off to show his tan—he had burnt himself lobster red on the Maryland shore last Sunday—and his muscles, which were all right, but only all right. Billy thought they were better than that. Emily paid no attention. Billy was two years younger and Emily couldn't care less.

Emily was curious about Alison. "Does she have a life?"

"Not that I can tell. She has a couple of girlfriends she sees maybe once a month. She never dates. I've never heard her make a personal call."

"God, Lissa, she's like a servant in those nineteenth-century dramas on PBS—like a ladies' maid."

"But she's a whiz with computers. If you get into trouble, she can disentangle you."

"Computers are just modern housekeeping devices." Emily dismissed computers with a wave of her hand, that had, for once, been manicured. They had been sent off to be worked on that morning. Now Melissa was afraid to wash her hands. The polish might come off or chip. Her nails were bright yellow. She was equally afraid to move her head too much or her hair would come undone. "Laura's mom finally agreed we can sit together." Melissa sighed. "Otherwise I'd die of boredom, with Laura's cowsy friends and Merilee and the cousins. I wouldn't have anyone to talk to."

"We can dissect them all like frogs."

"That's something to look forward to." Melissa stood up. "Show me what you're going to wear to the rehearsal dinner. I have two dresses I could wear, and you have to help me choose."

"LET ME SEE how you're dressed." Rosemary charged out of her office. They had hoped to slip out unobserved, but they were ready. What Emily called their slut clothes were in her backpack. Through torrid heat smashing off the brick sidewalks in spite of the shade of the trees and creeping under her camp shirt, they walked slowly to Georgetown Park, stores, cafés and restaurants in a Victorian building with a modern façade—a big hangout scene. They changed in the john. Melissa stuffed the stupid Bermuda shorts Rosemary favored into the backpack, put on real shorts and a tight little top and was ready to stroll around eyeing the local talent. They weren't going to pick up guys—they had to be back at the house in two hours—but it felt so good to escape. They drank iced cappuccinos, then strolled along Wisconsin to an ice cream place. If Rosemary knew she was eating ice cream, she would be executed. She had chocolate fro yo instead. Eating yogurt always felt virtuous. Emily had real ice cream, but she'd probably make herself throw up afterward. She did that a lot.

"You're lucky to live in such a cool place," Em said, spooning in strawberry coconut.

"Cool!" Melissa giggled. "It must be ninety-nine in the shade."

"Lyme is so, like, dull. Here you have these quaint little streets where everything is perfect and manicured and then you just go down to the end of the block and it's teen heaven. Be even better if we could get fake ID and go into the bars. I love sidewalk cafés and those bars with no glass in the windows are so cool. Like you're almost on the street but you're inside drinking lime martinis. I would so love that."

"So would I if I wasn't here with my parents. That blows it for me."

EVERYONE HAD GONE to sleep, even Emily. Melissa didn't understand why she couldn't. It wasn't as if she were excited about the wedding; it was a big bore, and starting tomorrow, she wouldn't have a chance to do anything else except be swept along unwillingly and awkwardly. She had dozed off with Emily but then, an hour later, wakened. Now she crept quietly from her room. Maybe if she had warm milk or snitched some of her father's scotch, she could sleep. As she eased down the stairs, she heard her parents' voices. They were still in evening clothes, sitting exhausted in the livingroom. Soundlessly she approached. All her life, she eavesdropped whenever she could, for some hint of the family secrets and business kept from her.

"I've kept hoping something would occur over the past year to end this," Rosemary was saying.

"Be glad it didn't," her father said. His voice was his private one, less resonant, drier. "I need Potts. This binds him to us."

"With his silly daughter. She isn't the sort of wife Rich needs. Why can't he see that?"

"Oh, Rosie, she's all right. Pretty thing. She photographs well. She has manners and money."

From her seat on the third step from the bottom, she could see her father but not her mother. He had loosened the top two buttons of his dress shirt and his tie and kicked off his shoes. Rosemary's hands were visible rubbing the back of his neck and his shoulders. He yawned, then his tone changed abruptly. "Rosemary, you must never allow your opinion of Laura to register with her family. Do you understand?"

"None of them are the brightest, Dick—"

"Bright enough to be worth three hundred million, conservatively speaking. Laura's all right. She'll be a good mother and the constituents will like her."

She could hear Rosemary sigh. "I hope you're right—that she'll do. At any rate, this is going to be one of the weddings of the year in Washington, and that can't hurt you or Rich. The photos will look just wonderful."

"And so will you."

"And you."

She could imagine the look that passed between them, for she had seen it enough times. Her parents admired and loved one another. They satisfied one another. There were vibes between them. Other kids had never been able to believe their parents had sex, but she had never doubted they did. Would anyone ever look at her that way? Her father moved out of her line of sight and she heard noises that probably meant they were kissing.

"Do you think *he's* coming?" Rosemary asked after a couple of minutes, when her father returned to his previous position and Rosemary's hands once again appeared, massaging his shoulders. *He* in that tone of voice always meant the President.

"He likes to keep his options open. He can always plead an emergency. But he owes me. I delivered Pennsylvania for him, just as I promised. I didn't want a cabinet position—"

"That surprised him."

"I was open about my plans to run for the Senate. Now I'm on his field. If he doesn't come, it means he doesn't think I'm going to be a player."

"Or it just may mean that he really is tied up."

She heard the rustle of Rosemary's skirt and quietly crept up the stairway to her bed. Tomorrow the real razzle-dazzle started.

DINNER WAS AT the Four Seasons. The video man was already taping, even Melissa's stupid little speech that Alison had written and given her to memorize. How Rich had always been an outstanding example, an older brother she could truly admire, who looked out for her and helped her through the small disturbances of childhood and adolescence. And other whopping lies. Other than pulling her hair or her ear, she couldn't remember Rich laying a hand on her. Occasionally teasing her to tears did not exactly stack up to brotherly love. His usual name for her had been Melon-head. Melon-belly. He had not been cruel or abusive, just uninterested. Mostly, she thought, they viewed each other as minor nuisances. Ships that passed on the stairs.

Rich was even taller than their father, but more solid, more muscular. He worked out. Dad just watched his weight, playing golf and tennis. People often said Rich was a carbon copy of his father. The family resemblance was strong—as it wasn't in her or Billy. He had a dark tan already from being on the boat the Pottses had brought down from the Chesapeake and from the bachelor weekend in the Bahamas. His eyes were blue like Dick's and Billy's, striking against his tan. He looked successful, that's what it was with Rich. Before he had ever done anything, and really he had never done anything much—unlike Merilee, his grades and accomplishments were just average—but he looked like a winner. Big guy, handsome, dazzling smile, lots of the right friends. Those friends were telling stories about him now, a legend in the making.

"I remember when Rich got the dean's golf cart and put it on his roof!"

"You should have seen him shooting three-pointers."

"I'm the one who introduced the happy couple. I knew they were going to click, but I had no idea that, three years later, they'd be marching down the aisle. We were all at the Westminster Dog Show that day. My mother's trainer was showing her shar-pei and Laura's mother had a chow in the show. I can't even remember why Rich was there—to keep me company? I think we had something planned for that evening. That's how it all started—going to the dogs. Neither of our dogs won, but we all went out together afterward—except the dogs, of course. If they'd won, we would have taken them to the restaurant too."

Actually Rich disliked animals, as Rosemary did. The family never had pets, even though Dick's campaign manager had urged him to get a dog to improve his image. Then a backer had given them a cocker spaniel when Dick was running for governor the first time. It was a female who had become Melissa's and she had named her Floppy. Floppy had been hers to walk and care for and brush until one day about two months after the election, Melissa had come home from school and Floppy was gone. Rosemary had given her away. Rosemary said she was living on a farm where she could run free, but Melissa had never seen her again and had always suspected something much worse. The excuse given the backer was that Rich was allergic to dogs.

Now Alison had a tropical fish tank in her office, because she said the water sound soothed her: that was the closest to animal life that entered the family. The girls had been allowed to go horseback riding, one of the few enthusiasms Melissa shared with Merilee. Melissa loved animals: cats, dogs, horses, any creature at the petting zoo where she remembered Noreen taking them. Rosemary considered animals unsanitary. Anything that might shed was dangerous. Laura had grown up with dogs. Even if they were show dogs, they were real; they ran around the house and played and sat up and rolled over. If Melissa ever got rich, she would keep horses. A paddock with horses. Or at least one horse, a bay gelding, who would come and eat sugar cubes and apples and carrots from her hand. All right, that wasn't going to happen soon, but eventually, eventually. Maybe she would move out west and own a ranch. That would be really far from her family and really different. She saw herself on horseback leading a line of tourists up a canyon. A rattlesnake rose before her. She reined in her horse, soothing it with her touch, drew her gun and shot. Actually she didn't like to kill anything. Anyhow, when she finished college and moved into an apartment with Emily, she would at least have a dog. Her own, as she had always dreamed. Not a breed. She was sick of pedigrees. No, a mutt rescued from a shelter, who would be all and entirely hers. She could almost see, almost smell her dog. She had dreamed about dogs and horses hundreds of times. She sighed so loudly a woman turned and stared. Senator Frost's new wife, thirty years his junior. Melissa felt herself blushing. She did not belong with these people. Tomorrow would be even worse.

It was. She looked around the church as the guests filed in, before she was hustled off to the room where the wedding party was gathering. She felt more alone than usual in the spate of preparations and congratulations. Occasionally she recognized a face from TV, journalists who covered the White House or the Senate, senators, congressmen, bureaucrats. The secretary of the interior, whatever that meant. She would never let such a gilded ostentatious fuss be created around her, even if she ever did find somebody who would love her, her as she was. But once she escaped from her family, surely she could find a man who would care for her, not a user like Jonah but somebody with heart. She could love, she knew it. She could love with her whole being, if only she ever had the chance to prove it.

The President did come, which meant secret service, as if things weren't complicated enough. But Rosemary was ecstatic. She flirted with the President, who kissed her on the cheek. Melissa stared at him. She had seen him with her father a couple of times, but she had never been this close. There was something about famous men, they had a kind of gleam as if lights shone only on them. Sometimes Dick looked that way. Up close, they looked as if they were ads for themselves, shiny, no longer made of flesh.

Finally, late but not too late, the ceremony started. Laura had a long train. The bridesmaids had smaller trains. They were, fortunately, detachable, or the dress would have been useless afterward. She felt huge in the yellow off-the-shoulder dress, teetering on yellow satin shoes. She hardly ever wore heels, and if she did, they were sturdy platforms or big clunky heels that made her even taller but were easy to walk on. These were little strappy contraptions designed to pinch the feet, raise her on stalks. Besides, pale yellow shoes were bound to get in trouble, and she already had some kind of stain on hers—as Rosemary, resplendent in blue, had pointed out. Rosemary could do anything on heels. She always wore them. Some of Melissa's pleasanter memories were of her mother sprawled on the couch rubbing her sore feet after a long day, relaxed for once and watching CNN or a movie on the VCR. Rosemary could even run in heels: Melissa had seen her do that a hundred times. Melissa could barely get up and down a staircase in these torture devices. She was so tall she had never wanted to wear heels, fearing she might loom over any guy she was interested in.

She was the tallest bridesmaid. That made her feel conspicuous as they congregated, sorted themselves out, usher to bridesmaid, ring bearer, flower girl, Rosemary and Mrs. Potts, Dick beaming and, like her and Rich, towering. They lined up in order, then stood around waiting for the Episcopal priest to get to them. Okay, the Wedding March from *Lohengrin*. Emily had told her what it was.

Music was a place she could go and her family couldn't follow. Since she was eleven she had her own favorite singers, her own CDs nobody else liked, world music that her family called primitive noise. She loved Middle Eastern music, Greek, African, fusion, Haitian. It was her own special ambience. She could not even share that with Emily, who liked rap, boy groups and opera. Her music was like a foreign country she could run away to, where sounds and rhythms enveloped her and she could imagine herself dancing in veils or sequins, in a costume that would make her suddenly glamorous as she never had been. For a while she had taken dance lessons, but she was so much taller than the other girls, she felt ungainly and too visible.

It was hard to walk so slowly. She was halfway down the long aisle through the ornate church with its multicolored windows staining the air when it happened. Her dress began to slip down her shoulder. She lunged to fix it and hike it back up before her tits fell out in front of everybody. She stepped on Merilee's pale blue train and then her ankle twisted. She lurched to the right and the little stilt on the stupid strappy shoe broke right off. Her face burned. Sweat broke out on her back. She had to limp the rest of the way down the aisle. Rosemary must have eyes in the back of her head—Melissa had often suspected that—because at the altar, her mother glared at her. She felt torrid with shame, sweat trickling down her back. She was sure she smelled of sweat. She had never been so humiliated—oh, yes she had. Dozens of times. It was her fate to be the clumsy one, too tall, too busty, too nervous. She wished she was in the hospital having an operation. She wished she was in a coma. She wished she was dead and buried with a nice small stone over her that nobody would ever notice. Here lies Melissa the fuck-up. The unnecessary. The lame one. If only she could run away and hide and change her name and be somebody, anybody, else.

fterward, she wanted to believe that she had noticed Blake that first day in Creative Nonfiction—basically a comp course—that an aura of premonition had surrounded her first glimpse. But the truth was, she felt wound taut. Everything was new. She was afraid of standing out in some awkward, foolish way; she was afraid of fading into the background and never meeting anyone or making a friend. She wished Emily could be in every class, but they shared only Intermediate French. Campus was confusing. Students swirled around her who all seemed to know what they were doing, where they were going, how to behave, what to say.

Because she had turned down the wrong corridor, she was late to class. All period she scribbled furiously to take down every word Dr. Romfield said. He was a big man, tall and hefty with a ginger beard, middle-aged, probably forty. His voice boomed, and when he called her name, she jumped and stammered her answer. Afterward she could not remember what she had said. Probably something stupid. She so wanted to do well and fit in. This was her real life, she kept telling herself, this counted. She was in charge here and it was up to her to shape a new Melissa, stronger and more confident. But there was too much to adjust to. Too much to take in. She had thought herself sophisticated, for she had been through four elections and witnessed a hundred press conferences and been to Europe and Japan, but this felt like the first day of kindergarten.

After class, she stood reading notices on a kiosk: Psychic Fair, Private Lessons in steel pans. Cuba in 2004. Summer jobs to save the Environment. Discover the Buddhist path to understanding, faith and love. Bike for sale. Their first assignment was in response to an essay they read about teenage drinking. Some dean had decided that all freshman classes should address this issue. "Personally," as she said to Emily, "I think it's just bogus. As if we all don't drink at parties. What are you supposed to do? If we didn't, nobody would ever get up to dance except two or three girls who like to show off. I mean, what would we do for all those boring years?"

Emily was rooming just down the hall from her in Nic 5, one of a cluster of nondescript dormitories on Foss Hill. When she came into Emily's room and saw her friend's dark brown bangs and hair just brushing her ears, with her neat little body Emily would always consider too fat no matter how thin she managed to be, with the palest smattering of freckles and her honey-framed glasses, Melissa felt safe. She could say anything to Emily and be understood. They were twin souls. But Em wasn't alone. She was with her roommate they called Buttercup when she wasn't around, a total twit and perfect snob: Whitney from an old New England family, as she told everyone within five minutes of meeting them. Melissa did not bother telling her that the Dickinsons were also an old New England family, but Buttercup found out and tried to cozy up. They both hated her because Whitney was perfect except for a weak chin: blond, stick thin with mountains of clothes.

"I don't know if I can make it here," Fern said plaintively when Melissa took refuge in her own room. Fern was as tall as Melissa but thinner. Her hair was blue-black and shiny but hacked unevenly short as if she had done it herself. She had a waif air, a natural shyness. Melissa was so relieved that someone was even more lost feeling than herself that she immediately warmed to Fern. They played tennis together. Even though Fern had played only a couple of times, she picked up fast. Like Billy, she was a natural athlete, at ease in her lanky body.

Melissa liked her writing instructor. Dr. Romfield was kind, he was brilliant, he remembered her name. She began to enjoy a little crush on him, no matter if he did have a silly ginger beard. She wondered what it would be like to kiss someone with a beard: would it tickle? She adored conferences with him. He gave her a B plus on her second paper, on immigration policy. She wanted an A. She made Emily walk past his office.

"But he's old," Emily wailed.

She didn't care. She wanted to shine in his eyes. She wanted to have endless conferences with him while he fixed his marvelous blue-grey eyes on her and saw into her soul and listened with the force of great music. The way he listened drove her into infatuation. She had to be pried out of his office. She hated the next student who would usurp his pungent attention.

"You can't want to fuck him," Emily said.

Of course not. She never wanted to fuck anybody. She'd done it because she was expected to after she and Jonah had gone steady all senior year. Before that she had just sucked guys off, which was okay. A girl who did that wasn't a skank, but still a virgin. No, she didn't want to fuck Dr. Romfield, just to write essays that she worked really, really hard on, then have conferences where he discussed what she wrote for him. He made her feel visible and bright. He greeted her intellect to intellect, a novelty she reveled in.

The third assignment was to write about an experience that had seemed one way at the time, but that in retrospect seemed the opposite. He spoke of it as an epiphany. She loved that word. She vaguely remembered it from church, but she always spaced out there and, since she turned fourteen, had refused to go. Now she would get to write directly about herself and he would read it. Excited by the assignment, she paced in her dorm room trying to pick out the thing in her life that would be best, that would show a lot about herself, that would impress Dr. Romfield. His first name was Gregory. Greg.

"I was the third child in my family," she wrote. "I was born seven years after my older sister and have always suspected I was an accident. My parents were very busy when I was little and even busier as my childhood progressed. My father was the district attorney in Philadelphia, and my mother was preoccupied with the lessons and sports activities of my older brother and sister and also the political support she always gave my father. People said she was the brains behind him, and I have come to believe they are correct. At that time, she still wrote his speeches and she certainly recruited and trained his staff.

"Thus when I was nine and my father and mother took me and my younger brother Billy"—she used his name and only his in the narrative—"on a prolonged vacation trip all around our home state of Pennsylvania, I was thrilled. I had never spent so much time with them. Time was the rarest thing in our household. Not my time, of course. Time went by like a glacier of lard when I was little and often alone, except for Billy and the various au pairs who lived with us during this period. I always had the feeling I was on the tail end of a very long list of tasks to be attended to, people to be dealt with, events to arrange.

"My mother was busy and my father was important. That thing, my father's importance, was something that occupied the center of all our lives since I can remember. As a child, I thought of my father's importance as a big object, like the armoire Grandfather Dickinson had given our family, which my mother disliked and considered hideous, but which she always pointed out to visitors, making sure they knew that it had been in the Dickinson family for six generations. Mother was big on tradition, since her family had none. They were the likeable ones, of no importance. Importance was important, I learned early.

"I was crazed with anticipation. I suppose if we had been given a choice, we might have asked to go to DisneyWorld or Yellowstone or California. But to go anyplace for weeks with our parents was like being promised heaven—the best gift in the world. I remember looking at the map of Pennsylvania and getting so excited I couldn't sit still. I felt suddenly special. It was our turn, Billy and I. Maybe they had just been waiting till we were old enough to share things with them. I couldn't sleep for two nights before we left. I kept being afraid something would happen and the trip would be cancelled, like so many other promises when a crisis arose. It would be just the four of us, together on an adventure, a vacation like other families enjoyed and I had always envied, without my older brother and sister who usurped most of the attention my mother could spare. My father's mentor, Uncle Tony, as we had always been taught to call him, kept appearing and every time Billy and I were scared that meant no trip. He was closeted with first our father and then our mother for hours. He had been mayor but now he was a judge. I was always told to sit on his lap and he would rub his stubble into my sore cheek.

"But no crisis intervened and we left on time, car packed to the roof. We drove all over the state. It was incredible to me, that suddenly we had all this time together, days and nights staying in motels, in hotels, once in a lodge in the mountains, but often with acquaintances of my father's. Some of them I had seen before, but most I hadn't. It wasn't like staying with relatives. I didn't like those nights, because there would be long suppers, then my father and mother would go off and have even longer conversations, leaving Billy and me to amuse ourselves in a strange house where we were supposed to be very, very good. Often a family member would be assigned us, playing cards or games with us or just sitting there, resenting it. Mostly we watched television. We had brought a couple of our favorite movies along, but after we'd seen them six times, even we were tired of them.

"Between every stop, my mother would read my father notes about some guy he was going to see, his interests, his political history, his family. My father was always a quick study, and when he arrived, he would always ask the politician about his family in detail right away. 'How's your wife Ellen doing after her operation?' 'Did Congressmen Portocelli help your son into West Point finally?' 'How's that sewage study going?' It wasn't even fake, you have to understand: he loved them, he wanted to possess them. He was genuinely fascinated not only with those in power but with those who had lost elections. He sought them out and stroked their egos. He recruited them to his cause. He flattered them, asked them for favors and made them his own.

"I remember the first time I walked into a room where my father was having one of those political conversations. There are times when some cliché strikes home to you. A watched pot really does seem to take longer to boil. And this really was a smoke-filled room. That summer, there were plenty of smoke-filled rooms all over Pennsylvania.

"We went to county fairs, and even though once you have seen five prize hogs in five different counties and five prize jars of strawberry jam and five different midways on which to throw up after rides that toss you around like buttered popcorn, you get a little jaded, still that was at least some kind of fun. The other thing we did a lot was walk up and down outside courthouses and office buildings, waiting for my father. Sometimes we would be parked at an ice cream place or coffee shop or in the lobby to wait, when our mother was needed also.

"I don't mean to give the impression we did nothing normal tourists do. We drove around Pennsylvania Dutch country and ate shoofly pie. We visited the chocolate factory at Hershey. We went to a baseball game in Pittsburgh. We toured Gettysburg with the assistant mayor, a tall skinny man who kept telling us that everyone said he resembled Abraham Lincoln, even though he didn't have a beard and his hair was grey. Billy and I ran among those mostly hideous monuments whooping and pretending to shoot each other. The other thing I remember is chicken potpie. A park restaurant there served chicken potpie, which I had a passion for at nine. I'd eat it every chance I got. It was not something we ever had at home. Too fattening. I was proud that most of the mayors and other pols we met treated my father so well. It confirmed my sense of how wonderful he was, that he cut a ribbon at a mall in Johnstown and gave a speech about the importance of coal in Wilkes-Barre. Everybody seemed to like my dad, and that made us feel as if we were important too.

"Mostly, we were happy, Billy and I. We felt special. Our older brother and sister were not along because they had summer jobs Daddy had found for them. Our parents' attention was enough to make us giddy. We would have stayed in that car forever—an Olds only a year old, dark blue—and never complained. We never whined, Are we almost there? We were so glad to be away and with them that we didn't care. When we arrived, they would have to deal with our hosts and my father would be off doing something we didn't understand.

"Of course, eventually we did. He was lining up backers and feeling out other politicians with an eye to running for governor. That was the sole purpose of our vacation, and Billy and I were along for window dressing. Until he had a firm base of support across the state, he didn't want publicity, he didn't want attention, he didn't want to tip his hand to possible rivals for the Republican nomination. There were other politicians thinking of running, since the two-term governor's time was running out. The old man was retiring from politics back to the family business of ski runs and lumber. Besides, he had just bought himself a minor league hockey team.

"Unlike the outgoing governor, Daddy was not a millionaire and he relied on other people with money to help him on his way." She wasn't going to explain that Rosemary actually had built them a decent fortune since then over years of careful investing but didn't believe in using their own money for campaigns. "He and Mother were recruiting that summer. That was why my parents had suddenly taken an interest in their two youngest children, taking us on a wonderful journey we both thought meant something else. It wasn't until I was twelve that I figured it out. Until then, that trip was the time I always thought about when I wanted to make myself feel cared for. It hasn't worked since."

She hoped that Dr. Romfield would like her essay. She wanted to explain herself to him, and so she was honest about her family, something she had been carefully trained never to do. She had not had a real home since that year of the traveling together. She found out Gregory Romfield wasn't married—he was said to be divorced from another faculty member—so she imagined marrying him and living in Middletown, far from her parents, far from Washington. She wanted to get married young and have a house and the hell with the rest of them, except Billy, who could come and visit. She would elope and not even tell them till afterward. Then she would have a baby as fast as possible, so that her new family couldn't be taken from her. And dogs. At least two dogs.

Dr. Romfield liked the essay all right, but then he had her read it to the class, and she almost died. It had never occurred to her anybody but "Gregory" would ever know what she had said—except of course Emily. He kept telling her to speak up, as her voice kept fading into her throat thickened with embarrassment. She was so very sorry she had taken the assignment seriously and written about her family and herself—and now to read it aloud to all those indifferent, bored faces was a terrible punishment. Every sentence sounded ridiculous to her, silly, naïve. Maybe they would think she was boasting, mentioning that her father had been a governor. Maybe they would imagine she was proud of him.

Then she had to endure the criticism. "Be more specific," that suck-ass Celia Hodges said. She always said that. "We want sensory details."

"It's just self-indulgent," Florette said. "At least they took you all over. You had a vacation. You're just going back and trashing it."

"Where's the epiphany?" the guy beside her complained.

After class that day, a student fell into step beside her. "Your father's Dick Dickinson?" he asked.

She was even more embarrassed. "Yeah, that's him." She forced herself to look at him. He was tall, with dark golden skin and black hair. She had vaguely noticed him because he was exceptionally attractive in an exotic way, but she had been too focused on Dr. Romfield to pay attention to her classmates.

"You don't sound as if you admire him as much as you're supposed to."

"I don't admire him at all. I did when I was little, but not since I reached the age of reason—say, twelve?"

He was silent for a few steps. "It must be kind of hard, being someone like that's daughter. Someone so public. It would probably be a lot easier if you did believe in him."

"When I did, it wasn't any easier, believe me. . . . Are you close to your father?"

"I'm adopted, so he's not my real father. But yes, I admire him. I took his name and his religion."

"Because you were grateful?"

"Yeah, partly. Partly 'cause he's a good man. He's kind of visible too, in a minor way—not like your father. But he's a well-known criminal lawyer."

"That sounds as slimy as being a politician."

He leaned over her, grinning slightly. "What sharp teeth it has. He could be. But isn't. Does a lot of pro bono work, death appeal cases, political persecution, that sort of thing." She liked his voice. It was mellow, silky. She wondered if he sang.

"I envy you. I wish I could admire my father."

"But you can't?"

"No, I can't."

"Don't envy me too much. I'm not the real offspring. They have their own flesh-and-blood children. I'm the add-on. I'll never be a real son."

"I know what that feels like."

"Thought you might."

She turned off toward her dormitory, where she was meeting Emily. "I live in Hewitt. Just across the path," he said.

"I'm in Nic five." The dormitories clustered on the hill all looked more or less the same, like aging three-story motels.

She told Emily about having to read the paper, but she forgot to mention the guy who talked to her about her father. But the next time class met, two days later, he waited for her afterward. She noticed other people looking at them. It wasn't her they were looking at, she was sure. They walked into Mocon, the big circular echoey building where all the freshmen ate their meals. He took her elbow and steered her toward an empty table on the outer rim. "Let's sit here."

She was so surprised she could not answer for a moment. That stupid essay had not made Dr. Romfield fall in love with her, but it seemed to have intrigued this guy. She could scarcely believe it. Her track record with guys was not exactly super. She blamed her awkwardness on having gone to a girls' school, but Emily knew how to walk into a party and be flirting in five minutes. Maybe he was just lonely. After all, he was a freshman too and away from home. She realized she had not answered and bleated, "Sure . . . sure."

He had a turkey burger and she had the same, so she wouldn't have to think about it and waste time in separate lines. She was looking at him carefully now, and her first impression of his startling good looks stood up to scrutiny. He had straight swept-back black hair and intense dark eyes, long lashes brushing his cheek when he looked down, an aquiline nose and high sharp cheekbones. Although he sat with the African-American students in class, he looked more like an Indian, a Native American, she mentally appended. She knew from class that his name was Blake.

"Where are you from?" she asked. Oh, brilliant opening.

"Philadelphia. And you live in Georgetown." He gave her that cocky crooked grin she already liked.

"You've been asking about me."

"I do my homework." Then he began to talk about class.

She spent most of the next day wondering if on Friday he would ask her to lunch again. In class Friday, she no longer stared at Dr. Romfield but rather kept glancing at Blake. He was sitting with the two African-American kids. Why would she expect him to eat with her again? He was gorgeous and cool and tall. There was something about him, as if there were a zone of silence surrounding him even when he was chatting with his friends or laughing. A shield, she thought, something she could sense but never describe, not even to Emily. She almost hoped he would ignore her, because she felt out of her depth with him. A guy that good looking could never be interested in someone like her. At least he was four inches taller than she was, so she would never have to stoop with him the way she had with Jonah, kind of shuffling so as not to tower over him. Blake was the right size for her, but he could never really be interested. Probably that girl Florette he sat with was his girlfriend. . . . But then he wouldn't have asked her to lunch by herself, right?

Friday after class he hurried out with his friends, Florette taking hold of his arm intimately to check his watch. She noticed then he had a shoulder bag with him, a kind of duffel bag, and his friends had bigger backpacks than usual. They were running to catch the bus, she guessed, going into New York for the weekend. He told her he came from Philadelphia, but that didn't mean he wasn't going to New York with his friends—or maybe just to New Haven to catch the train home. She tried to put Blake out of her mind, but Dr. Romfield had lost his charisma, just a middle-aged man with a ginger beard and a nice speaking voice. She would go on working hard on her essays for him, but she no longer imagined living with him in a nice brick house in Middletown with two babies and a dog, or a baby and two dogs. Instead she imagined herself with Blake. They were dancing in a big room lit only by candles. No, there would be a fire in a high fireplace, like at the lodge of the ski resort. They would dance together just perfectly and gradually he would hold her tighter, closer to him. Her breath caught in her throat as she imagined their bodies touching. He would never be interested in her, but he was perfect for her fantasies. That night and the next, she put herself to sleep having long conversations with him.

Emily brought her along with a group of students she had already managed to meet at some mixer, out for pizza, then a movie, then for ice cream. She was glad to be with them, even though this guy Reed kept hitting on her. He reminded her of Jonah: in fact he had the same squared-off blond looks, the same too-thick eyebrows, the same smirk. No, thank you! She had not come to college to replace one man who felt superior to her for no good reason with another who felt the same. All he could talk about was football and TV and the hundred he had won on last week's Patriots game. There was no mystery, no romance in him.

Emily went off with a guy whose name Melissa never caught. Melissa returned to their dorm by herself, but she would rather be alone with her fantasies than with a man who would treat her the way she knew Reed would. She'd prefer to be alone forever than with a man who did not care for her, a man she could not love with her whole being. She would wait, she would look for love but accept no substitute. Fern greeted her enthusiastically, as if she had been afraid Melissa would never return. "Everyone has so much stuff," Fern said. "I'm on scholarship. I've never seen your friend Emily's roommate in the same outfit twice. She must have come to school with a trailer."

"Think of her as upper-class trailer trash."

But Fern didn't smile. "I could never call anybody that."

"She's just a twit, Fern. The brains of a canary. Em can't stand her."

Fern perched on her bed looking forlorn, her eyes lowered. "Everybody here has gone to summer camp and Europe and I've never left home before. . . ."

"Fern, we're all out of our depths. Every time a professor calls on me in class, I jump. I'm terrified of saying something stupid. But we'll survive. You'll see. You're going to go out for sports, right? So once you're on some team, you'll make friends there too and you'll feel like you belong."

"If it wasn't for you, I don't know what I'd do. Thank you."

She ought to thank Fern for making her feel secure by comparison. She patted her roommate's shoulder and basked in being big-sisterly. It helped. Fern was actually pretty, with her blue-black hair and large melting brown eyes, but she didn't seem to care. She was more interested in using her body than in looking at it or adorning it. However awkward and out of place Fern felt in college, she was at home in her body in a way that neither Emily nor Melissa herself had ever been or probably ever would be. Buttercup had social confidence, but Fern had jock confidence, the belief that whatever she saw any other woman do physically, she could match or better. Already her tennis game was competitive. Melissa envied her. She would love to relax into her body and her life and just live, just plain live.

onday Em and she were walking into the Center for the Arts complex, all white and modern and squarish, to see an old Hitchcock movie.

"Okay, I've made some inquiries. . . . Here I am, your private private eye."

Emily raked her hand through her cropped hair and put on a serious glower, pressing her glasses against her nose. Emily was nearsighted and could not endure contacts. "He hangs with the African-American kids some, but he's a loner. He has a bike, a Honda. Believe it or not, he's Jewish. He had a girl come up and see him once. Nobody paid her enough attention for me to get any dirt. So can't size up the competition."

"Emily, nobody's competition. He's just in class with me. He was curious because of my father. I'm used to people being curious."

"We'll see about that," Emily lilted. "I want you to wear your blue sweater Wednesday. Your tit sweater. I do so well that I'm giving you advice." Emily had gone to a beer party Saturday with the guy from the movie group, but he got drunk and puked on her shoes. "I'm off him. He wasn't much in bed."

"I just have no skill or luck with men. Better without."

"A Black Jew. That would curl your mother's hair. Go after him! It'd drive them up the wall."

"He isn't Black, Em. His skin is barely darker than mine. It's more like Middle Eastern or Mexican or Indian. Anyhow, that'd be just pitiful to try to snag him with a sweater." But she wore it. Her mother sent her an e-mail to watch C-SPAN. Father was in the paper Tuesday with his maiden speech in the Senate, in favor of an amendment to an appropriations bill. It was too complicated for her to figure out, but the amendment had something to do with trucking. Melissa would pretend she had seen it, to save a quarrel. He was always wanting to deregulate something. Probably he wanted truck drivers not to have to bother with licenses, like that. She could imagine the world her father would create, black water spurting out of faucets, air thick as pudding in cities, planes falling out of the sky like dead birds, trucks caroming all over the turnpike.

Wednesday was warm, even for October—the temperature at seventy, the wind abated, the sky blue porcelain. The leaves were still brilliant on the hills around Middletown, since no storm had ravaged them yet. It was one of her favorite times of year. Her siblings and friends would say summer was their favorite season, but in summer, she always felt inadequate. Not as slender as Merilee, apt to burn rather than develop a mahogany tan. Summer was the time she was cast back on her family, separated from the fragile support group school offered. Fall was the time life cranked up and everyone went their own way. Today she was happy—happy to be away from home, happy to be living with Fern right near Emily, happy to be doing all right in school. She and Emily had buddies in the dormitory and both had been to parties a reasonable number of times. Ronnie next door, a sophomore from Texas, often dropped in to chat and one evening taught them the two-step so they could line dance. Em and she were not only surviving, they were flourishing, even if they hadn't been asked out much or found a boyfriend. But who needed a boyfriend? What would she do with one, with all her effort going into making friends and trying to excel in her classes? When they had any time, there were free movies and lectures and cheap events and plays every single night.

Her first class on Wednesdays was Ecology of Plant Populations, to satisfy her science requirement. She had not the least interest in plant ecology, but had taken it because she couldn't get into the more interesting sounding classes. Except for the boredom and the difficulty of making anything out squinting through a microscope, it was not difficult. The microscope was a problem. The first time Melissa had drawn something, it had turned out to be her own eyelash, not the plant cells they were supposed to be studying.

Then she had French with Emily. They were reading Zola's *Germinal*. Melissa was quicker at French than Emily, who had trouble with languages. Melissa liked the sound of her own voice talking French, and she was always trying to get Emily to talk French—but then they never knew the words for what they really wanted to say, so it was always too much trouble after the first few sentences.

She felt like cutting her writing class today. Her crush on Dr. Romfield had evaporated, and the day was so gorgeous, she could imagine taking a long walk down into town under the brilliant maples or just lying on the sun-warmed grass. However, she was not secure enough to cut. She was still afraid she might miss something vital, and she was bound to get one of her sinus infections that winter and miss classes. She wanted to do well in college. She would never be brilliant like Merilee, but at least she could avoid fucking up. She saw herself Phi Beta Kappa, she saw herself taking honors in whatever she finally decided to major in. She lifted her head as she walked along, moving in her cap and gown onto a platform to wild applause.

An instant later, as she trotted along College Row with its weathered brownstone buildings toward her class, she felt overwhelmed by indecision. She still didn't have any idea what she was going to major in. Every Friday when her mother e-mailed her, Rosemary asked her. Government, maybe. After all, that was what she knew the most about. She would be a crusading reporter, investigating men like her father and unmasking their insincerity and corruption. She was doing well in American Government and Politics. She had a lot of knowledge of how politics really worked and what went on that the public never saw. She could tell Rosemary journalism next time her mother pestered her. But Rosemary would ask why, and she could hardly say, In order to prevent people like you and Daddy from running the country and lying to people.

Someone else was in the hot seat today, a football player who had probably cribbed his essay off the internet. That guy really did steal it, she thought, because he was doing a crappy job of answering questions about what he was supposed to have written. It took nerve to copy an essay, or maybe only a lack of imagination. She never cheated, because she was always sure she would be caught; or maybe because she wanted to please, to be deemed worthy. If she did not do her own work, how could she prove herself?

It really was stupid to imagine Blake had felt any boy-girl type interest in her. That girl, Florette, he was sitting with, she was much prettier. Enormous doe eyes. Emily missed her dogs, and Melissa herself was going around like a homeless dog looking for some guy to attach herself to. She felt ashamed. She just wanted someone to care about, someone to care about her. They weren't allowed to have pets in the dormitory. Every day she alternated between thinking she was doing really well at college and suspecting she was a complete misfit and people ignored her or laughed at her. Florette's eyes reminded her of one of the kids she had tutored in language skills in Hartford, Robert, whom the other kids called Pup. He had been writing about his lost mama—he lived with his grandma and his mama was in prison for drugs—and then one day he wasn't in class and Sonya, who always sat with him, was crying. Drive-by shooting. They were aiming at somebody else, but Pup was dead. She would never forget the kids she had tutored, she thought, never. Nobody in her family understood—only Emily, who had an enormous heart for everything living that hurt. Maybe sometime she could tell Blake about it all and how it had changed her. Would he think she was putting it on? Trying to come off liberal and cool? She walked out of class thinking how inept she was at relations with guys, when Blake fell into step with her. "So, want to pick up a sandwich and grab some countryside?"

"What do you mean?"

"You can ride with me. We'll go up into the hills. Looks pretty today, doesn't it? You have afternoon classes?"

She had an aerobics class, but she could cut that. "I was thinking all the way here how gorgeous it is today and how much I'd love to be outside."

"Great. Come on, we'll pick up something at Mocon. My bike's just by Hewitt."

"I've never been on a motorcycle," she said when they came up to where he had chained it to a wrought-iron fence around a little cemetery there weirdly in the middle of campus, by the dorms. Fern said she had heard it held the bodies of students who had killed themselves. Melissa hoped that was a legend.

"You'll love it," he said confidently. "You can't help loving it."

She knew she was supposed to wear a helmet, so it felt clandestine, vaguely wicked and a little dangerous to climb on behind him, holding on to his leather jacket. She thought as he sped through town that they must look tough and very cool. They could not talk, which made things easier. Talking with guys was always skipping along a tightrope. Of course, plastered to his jacketed back, she could see little and only to the right side. They were climbing now, riding the curves up and out of town. She was a little scared but excited. How often did she do something as unlikely as go off with a guy on his bike up into the hills? It was something other girls did, like Emily (not Merilee, never Merilee), and she would envy them their adventures. Even if he just wanted to talk about class or even if they had nothing to say and it was a complete fiasco, she would have a story to tell. She would have an experience of her own. She would say to Ronnie, the redhead in the room next door, that she had cut her afternoon classes and gone up in the hills on a motorcycle. He turned off the pavement. They bumped far more slowly along a dirt road through the woods.

When he finally stopped and she got off, her legs felt funny—tingly and stiff. She misstepped and he caught her arm. "Takes getting used to, but you did fine."

"I liked it."

"Of course you did. Riding the wind. And this was just a little run. But it got us up here, didn't it?"

They were in a clearing near the edge of a cliff—the valley with the college and Middletown below them. "It's beautiful. Thank you."

"Yeah, I arranged it just for you." He pulled a blanket from the saddlebag and spread it out. "I'm hungry."

They ate the sandwiches they had bought, sitting face-to-face on the blanket, with the cliff falling away to their side. A hawk circled over them and then off in spirals across the cliff face. A second hawk spiraled way up and the birds called back and forth, sharp high cries, a couple sharing the sky. There had been no frost yet, and the crickets were shrilling in the shaggy grass of the clearing. She felt a fierce joy that was rare to her, a sense of having escaped from her life, her usual self, her prison of expectation and disappointment. No one knew where she was. No one would guess that she was here and with Blake, an attractive cool guy with a motorcycle. It was her own private, her own secret experience. No matter why he had asked her to come along—maybe he was lonely, maybe he was still curious—she was here and not anybody prettier or smarter or more popular shared a blanket with him.

All her life she had tried to keep little things to herself, often unsuccessfully, the way she had hidden away her diary, the way she hid things like a cobalt blue bottle about four inches high she found in a cabinet in the governor's mansion and quietly appropriated; like a special red rock she had come upon hiking in Vermont with her aunt Karen. Like a blue jay feather that had floated down on the lawn. Silly treasures. If she had something of her own, she was real, she was protected from others' scorn, others' judgments. This afternoon with Blake was such a secret, a treasure all her own. No matter if it was singular and accidental, it was hers to take home, mull over, relive.

"Today you seem happy, full of life," he said, as if he could read her mind, or perhaps her face.

"I am. Thanks for asking me to come with you."

He smiled slightly. "It wasn't a favor. It was an opportunity."

"What do you mean?" She had a moment of apprehension. But he couldn't be a mugger, a rapist, something bad. He was a fellow student.

"Why are you usually so down? I'm right about that, aren't I?"

She shrugged, embarrassed. "I'm less depressed here at college than I usually am at home, that's for sure."

"Escaping?"

"In a way. But escaping to my own life. Me. Not them."

"*Them* is your family."

"My parents, mostly. My younger brother, Billy, he's okay. He's a charming fuck-up. We've always been close."

"But you aren't close to your mother?"

"Rosemary? She doesn't bother much with me, unless I do something she thinks is bad—mostly in the sense that it could reflect poorly on my father. I mess up in any way, and she goes, 'Oh, what will your father say?' or more often, 'What will people say?'" She felt embarrassed talking so much about herself. "What about your parents? Are you close to them?"

"I never knew them. I'm adopted."

"Yeah, I remember you said that. But don't you know who your mother was?"

He shook his head. "It's a blank. A mystery."

"I used to have fantasies I was adopted," she said softly, afraid he would laugh at her.

"Why?" He lay down on the blanket, staring up into the sky. "Believe me, you wouldn't want to be."

"So I wouldn't belong to them. I'd have real parents who would swoop down someday and carry me off and love me the way I am. Just for being me."

"That's what we all want, isn't it? To be loved for being just ourselves. Not for being smart or winning scholarships or playing some stupid game well—just for being us."

"Exactly," she said. "But how well do you get on with your adoptive parents?"

"I respect them," he said. "They've been good to me, and they're good people. But we're different. I'm different from everyone else."

"I always felt that way too."

"Why? You know who you are. You're white, you're affluent, your daddy is important."

"But that isn't me. And it's like I don't really belong in the same family with my older sister, Merilee, and my older brother, Rich. They do everything right. I never did, I never will."

"Doesn't that depend on who's looking? Who's judging? What's right for you may be all wrong for them."

"Yes!" She found herself laughing and didn't know why. He hadn't said anything funny. Maybe she was laughing with pleasure, because she loved talking with him. "I really like being with you. You're easy for me to talk to. Talk with, I mean."

"Yeah," he said. "Isn't that a shocker. Because it's the same with me. I can talk with you. You're not with anybody, are you? Or is there someone at home?"

"Not anyone real. Just guys." She decided to be bold. "I thought you had a girlfriend."

"Been checking me out? There's a girl I was seeing last summer. She came up from Philly one weekend. It's nothing special. Not what I really want."

"What do you really want?" There was a kind of tension now between them that made it almost hard for her to breathe. She must be imagining this gathering sexual tension, she must be projecting it. She tried to rein herself in. Stop imagining silly things. He's just chatting you up.

"I don't know. It could be you, couldn't it?" He was grinning as he rolled on his elbow to face her where she sat cross-legged on the blanket. "Want to find out?"

Her breath caught in her chest and she could not speak. He was staring intensely into her eyes, his dark, almost black, and burning. How he stared. She felt dizzy. He had not touched her, and yet she knew she was more excited than she had ever been with the boys she had fumbled with, sucked off, Jonah, who had taken her cherry. Her skin was almost crawling with the desire to be touched. She tried to make herself breathe normally so he would not guess how he affected her.

He put up a lazy hand to stroke her cheek. Tangle in her hair. Caress her neck, gently, barely touching her. Then the hand tightened on her nape and he pulled her down to him. She fell into him, and it was she who first kissed him, crushing her mouth against his. Then he rolled on top of her. His hands were on her breasts. They were grinding together. She had imagined passion but she had never experienced it. Sex was something she did because boys wanted it, because the dating game required it when you reached a certain stage. Desire was new, a pain furrowing her body. She could feel him hard against her and his hands burned into her wherever he could reach under her clothing. She was not even surprised when almost immediately he pulled at her panties and thrust into her. They were locked together madly pounding at each other. They were someplace else, some hidden intense place of fierce sensations. Her eyes were clenched shut, her nails dug into him and she strained against him. The pleasure that swept through her almost hurt. She heard herself moaning and her eyes burned and a tear leaked out. When he had come, he spoke against her ear softly. "I'm only taking what's mine."

"You didn't use anything," she said a few minutes later, as they lay slack, spent, side by side, still entangled.

"You aren't on the pill?"

"I didn't have any reason to be."

He was silent for a moment. "There's a morning-after pill. Go to health services."

"Okay," she said. "Does it work?"

"I'm told it does. And get them to put you on the pill."

She nodded against his shoulder. Did that mean he wanted to see her again? That this wasn't an aberration? She remembered after she had finally done it with Jonah, he had climbed out of their common bed in the ski lodge, lit a cigarette and turned on a bowl game. She had gone into the bathroom and briefly cried, but she could not even work up a real regret. It felt too insignificant. This had been something else, a completely differ-ent act. She did not want him to turn away and yawn.

"I . . . I feel confused," she said finally.

"About what?" He pulled her head down on his shoulder. "Whether I was just scoring?"

"Yes."

"And the answer is no. Things happen sometimes between people. Explosions. Coming together. I accept it. So should you."

"Okay," she said very softly, liking the way it felt to lie with her head in the crook of his shoulder. It felt safe. She worried about what it would be like when they had to stand up, for she could feel the air growing cooler. She worried about what she had done with him, but she did not regret it. She could not regret it, for it felt too strong. It felt as hard and real as the red rock she had picked up so many years ago on the mountain behind her grandpa's farm and hidden away in her dresser drawer. This afternoon was hers.

or the first time since she had come to Wesleyan, Melissa was not overjoyed to have Emily's company. Emily went with her to health services but would not stop saying that Melissa had gone stark raving crazy.

"Here you are, you kept your cherry till senior year, and this dude doesn't even use a condom. What got into you—besides the obvious."

"It was different, Em, completely different."

"Must have been. Like did he give you something to drink?"

"It wasn't that way. I felt so close to him. He could see right into me. We could just communicate, like I do with you, the way it used to be with Billy."

They were walking back to the dorm. Melissa had the morning-after pill and a supply of birth control pills. "Did they give you a hard time?" Emily asked, finally easing up.

Melissa shook her head. She still felt light-headed. "They're glad if you come in, instead of getting pregnant. They know everybody fucks." She took Emily's arm. It always startled her, how tiny and fragile Emily was: bird bones.

"Did you, like, feel you had to? You think the guy won't look at you if you don't do him. Besides, sometimes it just breaks the ice. Sometimes it makes it worse." Emily squeezed her arm back in a gesture of affection. "Are you going to keep going out with him? I mean, your parents really will have shit fits."

"I don't know, Em. But I'm not the least bit sorry. I mean, I had a real orgasm. I used to wonder what the fuss was about." She still viewed it as something monumental, a divide in her life with a before and after.

"It just means that he's not a complete klutz like Jonah. Really!"

"I don't know. It's like fate. The wheel stopped spinning and there he was."

"Duh. I think you're in for a big letdown."

She remembered him saying, while he was still inside her, "I'm only taking what's mine." She had no idea what he meant, but it resonated. It had felt like fate to her right then. She wasn't about to tell that to Emily. It was too private.

Besides, she'd have to admit she hadn't the foggiest notion what he meant. "Don't tell Ronnie, okay? Nothing will come of it, probably. I don't want her teasing me about Blake or being nosy."

"Did you tell Fern?"

"I will if anything comes of it."

IT RAINED for two days, so it was not until Saturday that he took her back to their clearing. The evening before, they had supper together, Italian in town. She felt a great relief. They were to go on seeing each other. It was real. With both of them living in dormitories, it wasn't too easy to grab privacy to make love. She thought that after a couple more weeks, maybe she could ask Fern to go study at the library for an hour and give them the room.

They made love in a slower, more sensual way. She felt she had in some way grown up, because suddenly she could enjoy sex. She had always thought of it as a guy thing. Women put out and put up with it. But now she wanted it too. His skin was sleek and warm and almost hairless, like flesh formed of warm honey, of amber, except for his wiry pubic hair. They kissed until she had to draw back to catch her breath, and then they kissed again. He coiled against her, partly around her, lean and supple, rocking against her. She felt her skin, her flesh, her breasts and belly awaken wherever he caressed, wherever her skin brushed his, catching desire from him and burning, liquefying under his touch. She felt as if her body had changed its substance into something radiant. If she could see them, her body would glow from within like a lantern. This was so much more than what she had known previously as sex—those hurried, fumbled encounters, poking through clothing, awkward collisions of bone on bone—that it should have a different name. Maybe it did. Maybe this was love. Again she had an orgasm. It was magical. She felt as if she belonged with him. This was what she had always dreamed of without being able to define it, a man who would really hold her, who would want to please her, who would have the skill and knowledge to touch her and bring her all the way alive.

"I saw Florette looking at me," she said. "I guess she doesn't approve of your going out with me."

"A lot I do they don't approve of. I don't let it get to me. I'm my own man. I walk my own path."

"But you like a little company?"

"Our path is together. Don't you know that yet?"

"I hope so," she said very softly. "But how do you know so fast?"

"I know." He smiled, that inturned smile that never seemed quite a smile but something else, not like his usual grin or open smile. When he looked that way, she felt as if he knew a secret he wasn't yet willing to share with her. She did not mind that. She felt important to him, something that had never happened to her before.

He leaned toward her as if sharing a secret. "The truth is, I started hanging out with the brothers because I like some of them. In high school, most of my friends were white. I don't know what I am."

"You don't know the race of your parents?"

"I don't know anything about my biological parents. My adoptive parents, Si and Nadine Ackerman, never knew. I wasn't adopted through an agency. He's a lawyer and he came across an abandoned baby. That was me. I don't know what my parents were—Indian, Filipino, African-American, Malaysian, Polynesian—I'll never know."

"In a way, I almost envy that. Oh, I mean I understand it has to trouble you. Like you have no idea if high blood pressure or diabetes or sickle cell anemia runs in your biological family. You don't know who you came from, you can't put faces or names to your mother and your father. But you're free too."

"Free to define myself. Yes. You do see."

"You're a man of mystery." She gave a short laugh to indicate she knew what she had just said was too silly.

"To myself, also. But we're all mysterious. We come out of the void, we sink into the void, and in between half the time we don't know what we're doing or why. Events come out of the clouds and knock us off our feet. We're always rewriting our lives because everything keeps changing. Your life can be rolling along feeling normal, and then lightning strikes. A crack in the world. And after that, nothing is ever the same."

"I don't think anything that mattered changed for me until I met you." Immediately she felt her face growing hot.

"That may well be true," he said with mock solemnity. "It's shaped like a thigh, this hill." He was sitting up, his clothes buttoned loosely, put back together after their lovemaking. He liked to wear earth tones, tans and browns and olives, khaki and beige. He didn't wear sweats or superbaggy ghetto pants. Other times he affected all black. "We're on the thigh of a sleeping giant. If we make too much noise, he could wake up."

"But he wouldn't hurt us. We make him feel good."

"That's his food. Couples making love create vibrations he feeds on."

"He's a love giant." It was pure silliness, reminding her of childhood games with Billy, games in which they were astronauts or aliens or spies. "My younger brother and me, we used to play like this together—I don't mean sex, I mean pretending things. Making up little worlds."

"What kind did you like best?"

She frowned, remembering. "I guess when we were spies."

"What kind of spies?"

"We'd go sneaking around the governor's mansion into places we weren't supposed to go and we'd move papers around or read things. We'd pretend to be taking pictures from our tiny wrist cameras of sensitive documents. It felt scary sometimes. Because we really were where we weren't supposed to be."

"It sounds as if it would still be fun." He placed his hand on her belly. "Where do you imagine living, if you could choose anyplace?"

"Not Washington. California, maybe. Seattle. Or London. We all went to England and France and Italy and Spain when Merilee graduated from Penn. Once we went with my father to Tokyo on a trade mission. Have you ever gone out of the country?"

"Sure. I hitched around Europe last summer. I wrote about it for class. You know, an event that made you understand yourself better. A travel piece."

"You mean, you just went on your own? Your parents let you?"

"Well, I'd been before. And they were in France. My father talks about the death penalty—he's an opponent—"

"So am I."

"I'm glad to hear that. Thought I might have to tussle with you about it, being as your daddy is so hot and heavy into executions."

"It's sickening. I don't agree with him."

"I'm surprised your parents didn't travel more. Your father comes from money."

"He comes from old money, but they spent it before he was born. His father lives on a farm up in Vermont and raises cows. Honest." She wasn't about to describe Rosemary's clever investing. Rosemary had her own financial advisor, Stan Wolverton, who had been coaching her for the last fifteen years. Rosemary considered him her real father and doted on him. He was a red-faced man who looked like an ex-athlete, but Melissa had never heard one thing about his past. Yet in the time she had seen him coming to closet himself with Rosemary, he had gone through three wives and was working on number four.

"What about your mother's family?"

"Just lower middle class. Baptists from Youngstown, Ohio. I like them, actually, much better than my other grandfather, but we hardly see them anymore. They embarrass Rosemary. And I think they're scared of her."

"How come?"

"My mother is very smart. Much smarter than my father. They're both insanely ambitious—you shouldn't imagine she pushed him into politics or anything. I think he recognized right away that she could really help him."

"So at least he's smart enough to like smart women."

It was clouding over. A chill wind had sprung up and she shivered. "I think the weather's changing."

"We can only use this as our private place when it's warm and it won't be warm much longer. We'll have to start using my room." He stood up, extending a hand for her. She thought that he had a natural courtesy which was extremely unusual among guys. There was something princely about him. She was already spinning fantasies about his unknown and unknowable parentage. She had loved fairy tales when she was little. Emily had not been permitted to read fairy tales, for her parents thought they supported regressive values, but the nannies who had taken care of Billy and her had provided fairy tales along with daily vitamins. Blake was the son of a king, a prince in exile from some mythical golden kingdom. He was her prince who had wakened her not exactly with a kiss but in that general direction. "If we use your room, what about your roommate?"

"Don't have one. I did, but he bailed in the third week. College was too much for him. He was praying all the time, scared, out of his element. He went back to Oklahoma."

"Do you mind? I might be lonely in a single."

"I'm used to being alone. In one way, I've always been alone. Besides, you'll see, I have a lot of valuable computer equipment I don't want some wiseass monkeying with."

She wondered why he had not brought her to his room already, but then she answered her own question. He was intensely private and his impulse was to carry her away, to go off with her apart from other students, away from the college and classes and daily life.

He mounted his bike and she climbed up behind him, clinging. The sky had turned a dark greenish grey and the wind was strong as he rode the curves down from the hill. She squinted her eyes shut and held tight. There was a scent on the wind that made her think of things dying as if it were bringing a frost, and the scent of what had already gone under blew in with it. She had become much more aware of weather and temperature, wind and rain since she had begun seeing Blake. She thought she was more aware of everything. All her senses were keener, quicker. Girls talked of losing baby fat; she had lost a baby sheathing on her nerves. She felt more alive, from the soles of her feet to the top of her head, where he often rested his hand—reminding her that, gangly as she had always felt, she was smaller than Blake, who must be six two.

Sunday they studied together, their knees touching under a table in the library in a high room lit by tall windows the sun poured through from Andrus Field. Since she arrived, she had done just about everything with Emily. She felt a small nagging of guilt that she so much preferred being with Blake. Emily was her best friend. Em had that group from the mixer. She ate with them or with Fern or Ronnie when Melissa was eating with Blake. Emily liked the group, but only so-so. She had already run through what's his name. Melissa wished Em would meet people she liked better, so that she wouldn't feel she ought to be doing things with her or Fern, when she only wanted to be with Blake. She must be sure not to abandon her friend; that would be sleazy.

She got an e-mail from Billy, all about breaking up with Cheryl because she was just too demanding, and about bruising his knee in hockey practice. She couldn't decide whether to tell him about Blake. Finally she decided she would keep Blake to herself. It was almost superstitious, the feeling that if anyone in her family, even Billy, knew, it might weaken the new relationship, might alert her mother so that Rosemary would be galvanized into action to prevent something so "unsuitable." Finally she wrote Billy the kind of answer she usually did, focused on him, minimal stuff about herself. He wouldn't notice.

Rosemary sent a kind of round-robin e-mail to all her children every Friday, bringing them up to date on Dick's activities and accomplishments, the advice and help of his friends and allies, the dark plots of his enemies.

Your father is going to cosponsor legislation with the senator from North Dakota to strengthen and increase the list of crimes to which the federal death penalty can apply in order to bring more stability to our country. He is thrilled that the President is hosting a brunch for the new Republican senators, and of course Dick will be meeting the President then in a more intimate setting. Naturally, when they met during the campaign, it was rather hurried, and while we were delighted he came to Rich's wedding, it was hardly a face-to-face situation. This will be an opportunity for your father to demonstrate his unique charisma and his breadth of vision to the President.

To each report, Rosemary would append comments and queries specific to that offspring.

Are you making friends? Good contacts?

For what?

I am getting to know some very nice girls in the dorm and in my classes. Yes, I go to bed by eleven most nights.

That was a lie, but so what? Nobody in the dorm went to bed that early. It was too noisy for one thing, with everybody's TV or CD player booming, and they all had classwork. She caught up on sleep weekends.

In general I have enough clothes.

After all, she wasn't a clotheshorse like Rosemary.

What I really could use is a leather jacket. They're very in this year.

She wanted one as much like Blake's as possible. She would love that.

I think I'm doing well in my classes. I like most of them. No, I haven't picked a major yet. My advisor says I have plenty of time. I don't know when I might get to Washington.

She could not even write the lying word *home*.

I am still adjusting to college and think sticking around here and catching up on classwork is a better idea. I want to do well in school. It's important to me to use my time well.

She enjoyed lying to her mother. She had begun doing so around twelve, usually to shelter Billy from the consequences of something he had done or not done. With protecting herself, usually it was not so much a matter of avoiding punishment as of denying visibility. She protected her desires, her true interests, her feelings by pretending they didn't exist. It was one of the ways she felt she was real: because she had secrets. Because she hid a picture of her most recent crush under the paper that lined her drawers. Because she hid sexy books Emily lent her. Other girls went around talking about their rock or movie stars, the hunks on TV they adored. She kept her fantasies to herself. Once in a while she had confided a little crush to Emily, who was blatant about her adorations. Emily had always kept lists: first it was, Men I would marry; then it was, Men I would lose my virginity with; then it was, Men I would go to bed with. Emily had really been into Chandler, who played in a local white rap band, for a couple of months. Melissa could barely call up Jonah's face now. He seemed so callow and crude next to Blake. Still, it was good to have some kind of past, no matter how pitiful.

Sometimes Melissa made such lists, but always she erased them at once, for fear someone might see them. It felt hot and dangerous even to write down who she really liked or desired. Perhaps the core of herself lay in secrets she tried to shelter, to nurture. Blake was her biggest secret now. Her parents would try to break them up the moment they saw Blake. Emily would never tell on her, for she had protected Em's adventures from everyone—family, school—for years. That no one in her family could know about Blake made him even more her own. Except for Emily, this was the first time since Floppy disappeared that she had something of her own, a being she passionately cared for.

Melissa followed Blake into his room, at the end of the dormitory hall. His bed was covered with a southwestern print spread. His desk was laden with computer equipment—a desktop and a laptop, speakers, a scanner, two printers, various zip drives—that overflowed onto the stripped bed of his departed roommate, the top of his chest of drawers and a card table set up making an L with the desk. "You're really into computers."

"They're a tool," he said defensively, placing his leather jacket over the back of his desk chair.

"I wasn't criticizing." She wanted to wander around his room examining everything, looking at his comb, his toothpaste, his clothes—put away far more neatly than hers, she noticed. The major mess was caused by connecting cables stretched here and there. She must be careful not to trip on them and bring down some delicate pricey computer thing.

"I got tired of being called a nerd in high school. If you put time into your computer, you get results. You put time into people, the results are mixed."

"You're not in a good mood."

"I'm in a fine mood. I'm just being honest."

She drifted over to his desk, crammed with machines. "What's this?" She picked up a gadget.

"Don't touch that!"

She snapped her hand back. "If you didn't want me to touch anything, you shouldn't have brought me up here."

"Maybe I shouldn't have. Would you like me to go rummaging through your drawers?"

"I wasn't rummaging! But I can't be in a place where I can't touch anything. Blake, we kiss each other, we fuck all the time. We exchange bodily fluids. Isn't that a little more intimate than looking at your computer equipment?"

"I don't think it is. One is just physical. The other is really personal."

"Oh, it isn't personal to fuck? It is for me."

"I didn't mean that. Of course it's personal. I'm just not used to anyone else in my space."

"What's with you? You invited me here. It's cold outside now, and I have a roommate. If you didn't mean it, you shouldn't have brought me here."

"I just don't like anybody else handling equipment. You don't know what you're doing."

"I sure don't know what I'm doing with you, the way you're treating me." She went to the door and opened it. "I can't stay here like this. If you want me here, then decide you really do, and act accordingly." She paused, but he didn't look up at her. "See you in class!"

She hoped he would come after her, but he didn't. At the end of the corridor she stood waiting for him to appear, but after she had loitered there long enough for various occupants of the floor to pass and look her over, she ran down the stairs. She wasn't sure if they had just broken up. She kept herself from bursting into tears on the way across to her dorm by biting the insides of her cheeks, by inhaling sharply. Then she stopped at Emily's room and motioned her to come away. They went into the stairwell to talk, and at once, she started to cry.

"I told you," Emily said. "He's just too weird." She stroked Melissa's hair and shoulder. "Don't cry over him. He's an asshole. We're surrounded by men here. He isn't your only choice."

"I screwed up, Emily. I screwed up my best chance. I fucked up a relationship with the most attractive man I've ever seen and the only man who ever made me feel anything. I love him, Em!"

"You just met him!"

"We're soul mates. The way it's supposed to be. And now I've lost him. Because I screw up everything in my life. My mother's right about me."

An hour later, he called. "I apologize. I told you, I'm not used to being so close to anyone. I have to learn how." When she was silent, unsure what to say, he went on, "Don't you want to teach me?"

"I don't know," she said, but her voice was already softening. "You made me feel worthless today."

"You aren't worthless to me. You're precious. Don't you know that?"

"Not when you treat me that way."

"I said I'm sorry. I don't want to push you away."

"Don't you?" She knew she was already forgiving him, but she could not resist making him plead a little more. "You did a real good job."

"I want to bring you closer. But I need to learn how. I'm serious, Melissa. Will you teach me?"

She stayed silent a minute, hoping that the suspense was building. "I'll try."

"HE APOLOGIZED," she told Emily. "He told me I'm precious to him."

"He should apologize. Are you going to see him again?"

"Of course," Melissa said. "Where would I ever again find a guy so sexy and he makes a fuss over me? Besides, if I break up with him, I'll probably never have another orgasm in my life."

"I don't know." Emily was rubbing antiseptic ointment into her belly button, where her new ring had given her an infection. "I think it's like riding a bike. Once you learn how to do it, your body remembers."

"I think it's chemistry, Em."

"Yeah, then I've had chemistry with some real losers, believe me. Guys you wouldn't want to spend an evening doing your laundry with."

Melissa was reading her botany assignment when her conscience began to pinch. Hadn't she done the very thing to Billy, not to mention to Merilee and her mother, that had made her so angry with Blake? Hadn't she laid down the law with Fern just last week about not touching her dresser? She was extremely private and possessive about her things. She could not endure having anyone casually poke through her desk or dresser top, even if there was nothing available that might embarrass or reveal her. She was fiercely protective of anything remotely personal. Why couldn't she accept that in Blake? Because of the sex: after feeling so intimate, everything should be open to the other. But maybe in a real adult relationship, there were always off-limits areas.

She had the urge to call him and apologize in turn, but she decided that would be way too neurotic. She would be extra nice to him tomorrow. Still, she felt better, for she understood and truly forgave him. They were more alike than she had realized. Knowing that turned a bad thing into a good thing. She hadn't lost him after all. It was just a little bump in the road. He cared enough for her to apologize, prideful as he was.

She lay in bed that night trying to decide what she should call him to herself—her boyfriend, her lover, her mate? What was her secret word for him? Blake was such a strange name. She must ask him about it. She didn't think there was another Blake on campus, whereas there was even another Melissa in her government class. And another in this dorm. Emilys flourished by the dozen. She had always envied Merilee her name that nobody else had, even though to Emily she made fun of it as cobbled together from her mother's name and her father's middle name, Lee. He claimed to be a collateral descendant of the general. Dick's father kept elaborate genealogies of the Dickinson family. If Dick said he was related to Robert E. Lee, no doubt he was. She had always detested the Civil War. It had far too many battles, and she had been dragged to various battlefields, where her father posed for photo opportunities with his children—herself in every picture on the far end, her more photogenic siblings flanking Dick. They hardly ever got to see much—just arrangements for the photo op, though sometimes when the photographer or the newsmen were setting up, she and Billy got to run around and jump in old trenches or climb embankments and run down.

THAT WEEKEND Blake said he had to go to New York. "I'm seeing this dude who has a program I need."

They were in Mocon having breakfast. She had spent the night with him for the first time—in his room. He had insisted that happen to make up for how he had behaved.

"Can't he just send it to you?"

"I need to see him to get it. It wouldn't be cool for him to send it to me."

"Is it like a hacker thing?"

"Something like. Want some more coffee?"

"What does it do?"

"What it's supposed to, I hope." He got himself more black coffee and hers regular, with skim milk and saccharin.

She liked his remembering how she took her coffee, but she didn't like not seeing him all weekend. "You aren't going to tell me?"

"It's on a need-to-know basis, babes. When you need to know, I'll show you. But I promise, you'll like what it does."

"Blake, I like what you do. I'll miss you. Can't I go along?"

"Not this time. This is kind of a delicate negotiation." He finished his coffee quickly. "Some other time we'll go together."

She had the sense she might be pushing him too hard. He was a prickly guy, ready to pull back into his shell. After all, it was just one weekend, and it wasn't like he was going to see another girl. At least she didn't think so. "You said you wanted me to teach you to be close."

"Close, but not standing on my foot."

She had to back off. Sometimes she had the sense about him that she was out of her depth, that she didn't have the skills and experience necessary to get her way with him. A more sophisticated girl would know what to do. But her experience with boys, even her years of dealing with Billy, was limited and useless in this context. Emily would have known how to handle Blake.

He grinned suddenly. "Don't look like I just killed your puppy. It's only computer stuff. You know I'm into that. Aren't there any computer junkies in your family?"

"We all use them, but no. Rich—that's my older brother, Richard Junior, while Dad is Dick and he's Rich—he's into politics. Merilee is into law. And Billy—he's usually into trouble. Alison is my mother's pet computer nerd."

"Alison? Another sister?"

"She's my mother's assistant. Like secretary, scheduler, errand runner, spy on us kids, sycophant, yes-woman, whatever it takes."

"Your mom isn't computer savvy?"

"She uses one, sure. She gets about a hundred e-mail messages a day. But Alison puts programs on and takes them off and all that stuff. When something's wrong, she can usually fix it."

"A hundred messages a day? You're exaggerating."

"Not by much, believe me."

"Does she send you e-mail?"

"Every Friday she e-mails us kids."

"Why don't you show me? I'm curious. If it isn't too personal."

"There's hardly anything personal about it, believe me. Sure, you can read one if you want to. I usually erase them after I answer them."

"That's no problem. I can retrieve them. But next time, don't."

"How come you're so curious about my mother?"

"I want to know everything about you. Your family's been a big deal in your life. I want to understand them so I can understand you better. You're a complex creature, babes. Did you know Melissa means 'bee'?"

"Yeah. I never thought it was sexy or anything. Like busy as a bee."

"Well, you stay busy while I'm gone. Be good."

"I have to be good. You're the one going to New York."

"Business, little honeybee, a program I want, I need, I got to have."

"TWO STEPS FORWARD and one step back," she said to Emily. "Looks like the movies for us this Saturday night."

"Why couldn't he take you along?"

"I don't think he wanted to. He's been a loner, you know. He hitchhiked all around Europe by himself."

"He's a funny dude," Emily said, but she sounded rather happy about the weekend. "We can go with the guys——" That was what Emily called the little group she had been hanging with. "I might be interested in Kurt."

"I thought he and Amy were an item."

"No longer. Her old boyfriend's coming from Cornell next weekend. We'll all go. It'll be great."

Melissa didn't think it would be so great, but she wasn't going to say that and hurt Emily's feelings. Emily had been out of sorts about the amount of time Melissa was spending with Blake, so she wanted to compensate. Melissa wasn't crazy about "the guys," but she could hardly complain if Emily had found people to hang with. She'd stop feeling guilty about Em and they'd have a good time together. After all, she'd existed for almost her whole life before she met Blake. But that was just existing. Now she was fully alive. She could handle the guys better than she had last time. She had her own boyfriend now. She felt more confident, and she knew she exuded something, because Ronnie had been friendlier of late—before she had treated Melissa as an appendage of Emily—and so had Carol, whom Emily always referred to as Queen of the Hall. Carol had won a beauty contest in high school and been homecoming queen. She was bucking for something here. Now she actually said "Hey" when they passed in the hall. Melissa had more confidence in herself, and it must show.

She also put time aside for Fern, who had taken up serious Frisbee and was also playing soccer with other first-year women. "You know, Fern, it's not like we're trying to build résumés. In high school we all had to accumulate these lists of activities and accomplishments. So long as you keep your grades up, they won't take your scholarship away."

"You told me to go out for sports to make friends."

She was embarrassed. She gave Fern advice freely and forgot it five minutes later. She had to be more careful with Fern—there was a fragility to her that contrasted with her athleticism and physical strength. Fern was thin but wiry. She exercised with free weights four mornings a week. "Is it working?"

Fern bowed her long neck. "I think so. . . ." She looked up after a moment. "Whitney doesn't like me. She calls me Fern Bar and Weed."

"Buttercup? Ignore her, Fern. She's an idiot."

"She's been talking about you and Blake. I heard her. She doesn't think enough of me to lower her voice when she's being vicious. She says you're slumming and that you couldn't get a white boyfriend."

She wished Fern wouldn't repeat the nasties she heard, but Fern was only doing it to show she was on Melissa's side—and when had Melissa begun to have a side? Whitney could just choke on her own malice. "I have exactly the boyfriend I want, thank you very much. I think she's jealous."

Buttercup had a nasty streak that reminded Melissa of girls who had picked on her in grade school, the vicious pretty girls who ran the cliques. They bullied her because she was too tall, too chunky. And because they could. She had been bitterly unhappy then. She would have done anything to be accepted by them, but nothing she did made a difference. God, how unhappy she had been for years. She had suffered a recurring dream where she had gone into the woods with her family, then got lost. Instead of searching for her and finding her, they left her there, as if they had forgotten she existed. They abandoned her like Hansel and Gretel; they left her in the woods and the rest of them returned home without her. She would wake frightened and cold. That nightmare had felt so real; in a way it was.

elissa sat on his bed, with its spread imitated from a Navaho blanket. "Of course I missed you. I don't see why I couldn't go along."

"I don't know how far I can trust you." He was leaning on the edge of his desk, his hands clasped behind his head.

"That's an awful thing to say. Why wouldn't you trust me?"

"First, we haven't known each other that long. Second, you're the daughter of privilege and power. How do I know where your allegiance lies? With me or with them? Third, I doubt if you've ever chosen to break the law in your life, for a reason bigger than the pressure of your high school peer group to smoke a little dope or drink some beer."

Her eyes stung. "How can you say those things? How can you say I'm precious to you and then that you don't trust me?"

"Should I trust you?"

"Yes, you should trust me. I care about you."

"Do you love me?"

"You haven't said you love me."

"I asked you a question."

She felt humiliated. How could she say she loved him when he hadn't said it first? But he wouldn't unless she did, she was sure of that. He was too proud. Suppose she said it, and then he said he didn't. She would die. She would sink into the floor and keep sinking through the next floor and the basement into the mud beneath the dormitory.

"Silence means you don't."

She was sure that if she didn't say that she loved him, she would lose him right then and there. It was a test. "Yes, I love you."

"What do you mean by that?"

She felt stymied. "What people mean. I'm in love with you."

"But I don't know if it came to somebody else, say in your family, if you'd put me first. That's what I mean by trust. That we're a real couple with each other, bonded, mated. Then we mean that we're real before all else to each other."

"Do you feel that way about me?"

"Would I bother if I didn't? I despise dating. I hate the way guys in this dorm talk about girls. Do they put out, don't they. Are they like supermodels or just dogs. It's a sick game. I'm not playing."

"I know what you mean." She wanted to touch him, to hold him, but she could not seem to move, "I don't want that either. I never did. I feel like you're something better, something purer and more intense and far more real than any of the guys here."

"From the first time we were together," he said slowly, coming toward her now and placing his hands on either side of her face, "I've felt there was something special in you. That's why I tell you you're precious. I want us to love each other from our spines, from the core of our being."

"I want that too." She had to convince him. "I never felt anything before you touched me the first time. I wasn't alive. I wasn't real."

He pulled her against him, hard against him, and just held her. When they were together, she felt as if she soared onto another level of being. Everything mundane and trivial filtered away. She did not worry about her classes, she did not worry if Rosemary was going to bug her about not having a major, she didn't care if Merilee was smarter and prettier, she didn't mind that Whitney said to her couldn't she get someone to introduce her to a white boy? Even Ronnie said she understood that some girls just liked it down and dirty. None of that mattered. Only his intense fierce eyes focused on her, making her real, making her burn with a mix of desire and aching love for him. No one in her family had ever felt this way, she knew it. They had accommodations and successes and failures and agendas, but none of them ever knew passion that consumed them to a fine point of painful light. She grasped him back, and for moments that felt forever they just held each other hard and tight, clutching, bound together as if they were alone in a vast cold darkness, alone on an asteroid in the hostile night of space.

EMILY WENT OUT Friday night with a guy from their French class instead of her usual crowd.

"What are you going to see?"

"I forgot to ask. Do I care? I just want to find somebody who's worth hooking up with. Do you think he's cute?"

Actually, until he had stopped Emily after class, Melissa had never noticed him. He was pretty average in all ways, height, weight, with light brown hair and owl glasses. He did have a good French accent, but she couldn't say she had ever thought about him twice. But loyally she said, "Really, yes."

Emily turned to look at her. "So Blake's coming over here? How did you arrange that with Fern?"

"Actually she has a game tonight. Soccer."

"How are you guys—Blake and you—getting on? Sometimes you come back glowing. Sometimes you come back with the gloom on you like black paint."

"He blows hot and cold. He drives me crazy. One day he's passionate about me. The next, he's testing me. Making me prove myself over and over. When will he believe I'm crazy about him?"

"A power trip," Em said, frowning. "Should I wear red or pink? I love my pink sweater, but somehow I don't think I'm the pink type."

She had told Blake she would call him as soon as Fern left. He was going to come over to her room for the first time. She rushed around tidying, lest he think her a complete slob. His room was always neat, except for the clutter of computer stuff. She had the habit of discarding clothes on the floor or the chair. Fern had so little, the mess was just about all hers. She found tights missing for two weeks and a belt she thought she had lost. She found Emily's Swatch watch. She found a coating of dust she wiped up with tissues, the remains of two apples and various cups of coffee and a postcard from Chandler that Emily had tossed at the wastebasket but missed. How little of Fern's was scattered about. Like Blake, she was neat, yet she never complained about Melissa's sloppiness. The only thing to be tidied of Fern's was a crooked pile of books beside her bed.

Blake arrived only twenty minutes late. Tomorrow they were going to a jazz concert at Westco he was interested in, but tonight they would enjoy the rare opportunity to have her room to themselves. They curled up together on her single bed, filling each other in on the fifty things that had happened since the evening before. "I feel as if I'm only half alive until you get here."

"We're one being together. Each of us by ourselves is only half."

She liked that. It made her feel secure with him. How could you lose half of yourself?

"I have a present for you tonight. A surprise."

She patted his pockets, teasing him with her hands. "What is it?"

"First, did you get your regular e-mail from your mother today?"

"Sure. Punctuality is next to cleanliness or whatever. She never keeps people waiting except to make a point—like, they aren't important and she is."

"In photos she looks like a beautiful woman. Is she?"

"Everyone says so. I thought so when I was little. Now I try to find something wrong, to make myself feel less clunky. But she's perfect. Do you understand? Nothing ever out of place, no blemishes, nothing too big or too small. She's always boasting that she's the same size as she was when she married my father. She barely eats."

He took her face between his hands. "I know how insecure she makes you feel. Have you ever wondered what she says to your brothers and sister?"

"Of course. I wonder every week."

"Maybe we can find out. Call up her last message for me on your computer."

She obeyed. He nudged her out of the seat then and faced her laptop. "DSL connection, so she's on a network. Okay. Great. I can do it. Just give me some time." He pulled a disc from his backpack and sat at the computer for half an hour, typing with his eyes locked on the screen. She picked up the book she was reading for French, a play of Sartre's. There was a lot of slang and idiomatic French in it she had to look up or guess at. Emily and she had been working at it over supper, until Emily had to get dressed for her date. The French was hard and she almost forgot to watch him. They were expected to be able to translate a passage on demand in class Monday. When Em got home, she would give her the translation she was working on.

"Okay, babes," he said at last. "We're in. But first I want to send all this to my computer so I can do it more easily for you next week." The download onto a zip drive he had brought took a little more time, but he came and lay on the bed with her while the computer was talking to the zip drive. She loved the way he kissed, not in a hurry, not with his lips hard, not as if it was something to blast through to reach the real stuff, but almost an end in itself. That was part of what got her so excited with him, the kissing. She felt sometimes she could lie with him kissing for hours, for days. The first time had been so abrupt that it had been a pleasant surprise to find out how much he liked just plain kissing. They made love slowly these days, making it last.

"Suppose you hadn't gone to Wesleyan. Or suppose I'd gone to Penn like my sister, Merilee. Then we'd never have met."

"I believe we would have, sooner or later," he said, brushing back her hair. "Okay, everything I need is downloaded." He got up to disconnect his portable zip. Then he motioned her over. "Okay, truth time. Let's see what she wrote to your brothers and your sister."

Dearest Rich, I'm so delighted that you are doing well with your developers, but it's time to start lining up support for your first run. I suggest you attach yourself to Congressman Fuller's reelection campaign. You can learn a lot and make some excellent contacts for your future. You can see what's involved in a successful campaign, so that you won't make some of the mistakes people running for office for the first time are prone to. Also you need to form relationships in your district, so that the right people know you. You have to persuade Laura to join important women's organizations such as the Junior League. I'll append a list of my suggestions, but it's my fervent wish that she get going at once. Select a church carefully. I'll give you three suggestions. Then a country club. Again I have two suggestions. Join as many business organizations as you can manage. In each of them, I don't have to tell you, get to know everyone you can.

You need to look around your district and decide what is going to be your issue when you are ready. Education is always a biggie, sweetheart. Property taxes, taxes in general. Control of schools. See what people get excited about. You can only do that by joining organizations and meeting as many future constituents as possible face-to-face. Even unimportant people can give you insight into your district and its hot-button issues. Start keeping lists of potential supporters and donors. Fortunately, it doesn't cost a fortune to run for state representative. But you want to seek out and cultivate those who will later give you full support when you need it, when you are running for higher office.

What did Laura think of Hallie? She should cultivate her, but be cautious, as she is a dreadful gossip. You must begin to school Laura in reticence. She is lovely and has the knack already for putting people at ease, but sometimes she is a little too much at ease herself. She must understand that whether she is with one person or five hundred, she is representing you. She cannot afford to make idle comments or offer opinions that might differ from those you are espousing. Of course, I have seldom heard Laura offer an opinion on public matters, so perhaps this warning is unnecessary. But she does tend to open up a little too much in conversation with other women.

Merilee has finally stopped seeing that unsuitable Italian boy. I was terrified she might be serious about him. He may be good looking now, but in fifteen years, he'll be potbellied and sunk in martini-land, about as exciting as an old leather chair.

Here's your father's record this week. You should peruse it

quickly, so that you stay abreast of his positions and don't inadvertently contradict them. We must all stand together.

Melissa rose and paced around the small room. "She never writes to me that way. She almost treats him as an equal. It isn't fair. She takes him seriously, you can tell. Me, she just interrogates. What time did I go to bed? Am I eating properly? Am I getting enough exercise? Am I losing weight? That crap."

"Well, let's see what she wrote to your sister—what's her name?"

"Merilee," Melissa said shortly, leaning over his shoulder to see the screen.

Dearest Merry One, I hope that this new young man works out better than the last. I know he adored you, but he simply wasn't of your caliber. There is no worse mistake an intelligent and able young woman can make than that of marrying beneath herself—of not marrying up to at least her own potential, her background, her level of ambition. You want a winner, because that's what you are. Bring Bruce to dinner Sunday and I'll give you my candid impressions. Have him here by seven for cocktails first. You can deduce a certain amount from a man's behavior over cocktails—sometimes more than he wants you to see. I promise to be friendly to him, but you have to permit me to form my own judgment, as I know you are still taking input toward forming your own.

I am absolutely delighted you have made Law Review. I expected as much, and you have come through with flying colors. You want to stay in the top tenth percentile of your class. It isn't that I am urging you to marry, but that when you are considering an involvement with a man, by this time he should be of a sort you could marry. The time for experimentation is over. You want people to be impressed by your escorts, not astounded or scandalized or, at worst, to pity you. It is important not to waste time with the unsuitable, when you have little time to waste. Rich's Laura is certainly acceptable. Her family and connections are top drawer, but she lacks a certain inner drive I wish he had married. He needs someone to push him a bit, and I'm afraid Laura can't or won't take on that role. You need a couple of new suits. The jacket length is longer this year and you could use a few stylish blouses. If you like, I'll have my dresser send them directly to you. We're entertaining heavily Saturday. The Washington hostesses are far pickier than the Main Line ladies, and it is necessary to make the preparations impeccable. Alison is doing her best, which is always admirable, but if you have a little time to spare Thursday afternoon for final planning, I could use the help. I always know when I delegate to you, everything will be done on time and done well. This must be top drawer. We have the secretary of transportation and his wife coming, and two congressmen from our state.

 Your loving mother.

"What's a dresser?" he asked.

"She means the woman who picks out her wardrobe. Rosemary doesn't have time to shop. She has a professional. . . . See how different mine is? I'm not neurotic. I'm not paranoid. I just know she thinks about me at the end of the list."

Dear Melissa, Here's what your father has been doing this week:

"Like that's the most important thing where you're concerned," he said. "I thought you were exaggerating, but this is cold by comparison. Is this the sort of thing you've been enduring all your life?"

"Exactly."

I hope you have settled in at Wesleyan and are putting enough effort in your classes. You have not said anything about rushing. I would like you to rethink your position more rationally. Why should you want to live in a big cold anonymous dormitory when you can live in a nice sorority house, making real friends that might last your lifetime—girls you can be proud of knowing, girls with families and connections that might do you some good for a change.

Remember that you will be judged by your companions and choose your clique wisely. You don't want to appear to be antisocial or a loner, but neither do you want to settle for some group of oddballs and misfits.

Have you been eating your meals in the dormitory?

"Doesn't she know there're no dining rooms in the dorms?" he asked. "And no sorority houses on this campus?"

"They've never been up here."

Have you been taking your vitamins? Is there someone there who can cut your hair adequately, a salon in town perhaps? Your hair grows out so quickly, it can look unkempt in a month. Dorm food can be on the heavy side and you may be tempted to indulge in snacks or fast food. Be sure to watch your weight. You cannot afford to gain any more than you already have.

Have you decided on a major? You spoke when you were younger about being a veterinarian. I don't think you really want to spend your life dealing with animals, but if the healing professions still appeal to you, premed is always a possibility. Being a doctor doesn't have the prestige it did a few years ago, what with HMOs and malpractice suits, but it's still a solid profession. If you do insist on journalism, broadcast journalism is the way to go. Really, hardly anyone reads newspapers any longer except for the sports pages, the financial section and the comics. There are more cable news channels all the time.

Love, Mother.

"Well, I see what you mean about your family, babes. It's not fair to you." He put his arms around her. "She doesn't give you affection, she monitors you. She puts up fence posts and strings barbed wire. She pays so little attention, she doesn't even know we don't eat in the dorms and there are no sorority houses."

She hugged him back, hard. "It means so much to me that you see it too. A lot of the times my friends would just think my mother was wonderful—so put together, so cool, so up on everything. They used to want to catch her attention. Maybe that's why I hardly ever brought anyone home. I'd say there were events going on, but that wasn't it."

"Do you want to see what she wrote to your younger brother?"

"No. She's always lecturing him too, threatening him with military school. She'll write things like, They say every family has a black sheep, is that what you want to be? Is that what you want out of life? To be the silly embarrassing disgrace in a fine family?"

"She can get the digs in."

"Absolutely. Blake, I can't tell you what it means to me that you see, you really see."

"Let's do more than see." He sat down at her computer. "Wouldn't it be cool to send everybody's mail to everybody else? Like those remarks about Merilee's boyfriend and Rich's wife."

"Could you do that?"

"Sure. We'll just send everything to everybody. She'll think she pushed the wrong key."

She kissed his cheeks, leaning forward, around one side and then the other. "Do it! Oh, please, do it for me."

"Absolutely," he said. "You can consider it done." His fingers moved rapidly over her keyboard. "I like to see you get your own back. She doesn't respect you. She doesn't value you the way I do. Embarrassing her is a small step toward reparations, don't you think?"

She grinned with amusement. Rosemary deserved it, she really did. Melissa never got the better of her mother, but with Blake's help, she could for once.

After he had sent the messages, while they were in her bed, he caressed her body and drew back, looking at her. "Your mother's crazy. You aren't fat, you aren't overweight. You got a body to die for, babes. Just what there ought to be where it ought to be. I don't want to fuck a skeleton. I worship your tits. I love your booty. I want you just the way you are, good and plenty and what a woman feels like—soft and adorable and warm and sleek. Don't you let her get on your back about your weight. It's just right for me, and I'm the one in bed with you."

"You make me feel pretty."

"God made you pretty. I'm just appreciating the view."

Melissa was delighted as they slowly learned their way into each other, what they shared, what was new to each of them, what little parts would remain private and odd to the other. They came together in a cocoon of music. They shared an interest in world music, but they often knew different aspects. He loved jazz and began teaching her to enjoy it with him. Making love to music felt special, as if it were a soundtrack to a gorgeous scene in a movie. Besides, it gave them more privacy, not to have to worry if the kid who lived in the next room could hear them. She hated the idea of being overheard, as if someone could steal a piece of their intimacy and carry it off. Her fierce zone of privacy had zoomed out to include Blake.

He was going to study computer science. She decided on political science. Thanksgiving came and they went off to their families, promising each other that soon they would finagle a vacation together, somewhere. She said nothing about Blake to anyone in her family. It was not that she was ashamed of him, as she explained at length to Emily, but that he was too important to let anyone in. They would despoil the precious intimacy. She could not trust even Billy to keep his mouth shut. He would enjoy goading Rosemary about Blake. Let Billy remain the troublesome one. Let Rosemary's focus of anxiety remain fixed on him and not on herself.

Dick was preparing for Senate hearings on the trucking industry, one of his interests, and his staff was running in and out, on the phones, rushing back and forth from the Senate Office Building to the Capitol to the house carrying sheaves of files and memos. The committee was deciding whether to further limit the hours of drivers on interstates and whether to regulate those huge semis that dragged more than one loaded trailer.

Potts was not his only backer whose money came at least in part from interstate transportation. Dick was shaking hands and telling various men in suits, "You can count on me."

Alison was wringing her hands because Rosemary was appearing on a platform with the Vice President's wife at a fund-raiser Saturday and the Veep's wife was going to wear blue, so Rosemary couldn't—and Rosemary would now have to wear something different than they had planned. The Veep's wife's advance man said no blue and nothing that would clash, for the photo opportunity. Alison had planned the accessories; now everything must change.

Rosemary had a new "friend," one of those men she charmed, flirted with, remained closeted with for hours—the ones Dick needed or whose brains she wanted to pick. This new catch was Frank Dawes, the senior senator from North Dakota, a bald-headed man slightly stooped but still six feet tall, a widower who was in his fourth term and no end in sight. He worked very hard, spending long hours in his office, had one of the best attendance records on Capitol Hill, but weekends he was on his own. He was a wealthy man, but Rosemary remarked that he lived like a student or a monk. Dick had fastened onto him. Dawes had a weathered face for a man whose last twenty years had been spent in Washington, but that probably stood him in good stead with his constituents. Rosemary joked that he must have a private wind tunnel he used to maintain his Great Plains farmer look. There was nothing of the hayseed about his mind, however, for he had written most of the farm legislation passed in recent decades. He was powerful and Rosemary pronounced him astute, one of her highest compliments. He had become a regular at weekend suppers and parties. Alison was compiling a list of his likes and dislikes in food and company.

"You're an extraordinary woman," Melissa heard Dawes say in his dry, penetrating voice. "Does the junior senator from Pennsylvania know how lucky he is? A wife like you is one in a million."

Merilee's new boyfriend was around. Rosemary liked him better than the last one, but Melissa couldn't see much difference. They were both tall thin guys, glasses, preppy types, moderately athletic, no word out of their mouth that would surprise. The last one at least knew something about food. They wore nothing that was not what others of their class and group wore, had no ideas not current with their peers, were true to their brand names and little else.

Laura had gained weight since the wedding. Alison told Melissa that Laura had gone to a spa to take off ten pounds. Rich had come up from Philadelphia for Thanksgiving, but would return Saturday for an important meeting. He kissed her cheek when he saw her, making a crack about hoping she wasn't turning into one of those Wesleyan radicals; that was the extent of their interaction. Who needed Rich to pay her attention when she had Blake?

Merilee was more curious, which put Melissa on guard. "So how do you like Wesleyan?"

"Fine. I like it fine."

"Are you rooming with that friend of yours? Emma."

"Emily. No. We were assigned roommates. Mine is called Fern "

"Very seventies. Have you made new friends?"

"A few. You know, Mother puts me through a debriefing every week, so you really don't have to bother pretending to be interested."

Merilee fluffed her shoulder-length blond hair. "Sorry for asking. I just thought you might have changed at college. Opened up a bit."

"I think I'm a lot more open to things than you are."

Merilee quirked an eyebrow. "Oh? What kinds of things?"

"Music, for instance."

"Oh." Merilee picked up her casebook. "Music."

Five minutes later, Merilee put down her casebook again. "Did that time we all got each other's e-mail upset you?"

Cautiously Melissa said, "Well, yeah, a bit. To see how differently she writes to each of us—"

"I just couldn't believe her going on to Rich about my boyfriends. As if Rich is some paragon of partner selection. I mean, Laura has the intelligence of a nice dog—and the personality of one."

Melissa giggled with as much surprise as amusement. She was unaccustomed to having her sister confide. "Some breeds of dogs are very good at learning tricks. Laura's mastered her obedience training."

"I don't think Laura is as teachable as Mother would like her to be. But you met Jerry. He was my friend whose father owned a restaurant. There wasn't anything wrong with him. He was brighter than she gave him credit for and he was a warm, funny guy when you got to know him. But he's Italian—"

"Jerry Green?"

"Family name of Verdi. His grandfather changed it. Mother is a complete snob. Nobody's really white unless they're WASPs. I don't like Bruce nearly as well, but Mother is pushing me at him. She thinks he's a good catch."

"Do you want to get married soon?"

"No! I want to be hired at a good law firm and get on the partnership track. Marriage would be a hindrance. For some reason, Mother can't see that."

"She wants you to be her."

Merilee frowned. "She just can't see that what I want is different. I don't want to marry power. I want to have power." Merilee sat forward, tugging on her straw-colored hair. "Mother's trapped in an older model of women's lives. I can't make her understand I might not want to get married till I'm thirty-five—if ever. It looks like immolation to me." Merilee picked up her casebook to indicate the conversation was over. It was still one of the most real exchanges Melissa had ever had with her older sister. Not that she really liked Merilee—she resented her too much—but it was interesting to catch a glimpse of how she saw their family. It was fascinating to realize that Merilee, contrary to Rosemary's propaganda, did not always agree one hundred percent with her mother. It also confirmed Melissa's fears about her mother finding out about Blake and interfering big time: if her mother objected to Jerry because he was Italian, what would she say about Blake? Melissa did not long to find out.

Blake and she e-mailed each other three times a day. That propped her up, enabled her to blow off her family and remain calm. Rosemary made a remark about her pants getting too tight. Melissa then found a best-selling diet book on her pillow. She closed her eyes, imagined Blake telling her how womanly and attractive she was. The worst thing she could do was start fighting with them. It would call attention to her when she longed to slip effortlessly through the cracks of her family's concerns and return to school without letting anything real slide from her tongue or be revealed by any change of habit or demeanor. She enjoyed her self-imposed attempt at invisibility. Instead of feeling last and lost in the family, the bottom feeder, she felt willfully aloof. It gave her a tiny bit of power. She even kept away from Billy, because she knew he was the person she was most tempted to tell about Blake. It was not hard to avoid intimate conversation with him, for he had a new girlfriend he was instant-messaging with for hours, and the rest of the time he was off with his friends playing some new video game. He ate Thanksgiving dinner with the family because he had to.

They had two of Dick's interns; Loren, Dick's appointments secretary and advance man, a brash young Texan from a large oil family whom Rosemary had taken in tow; his primary speechwriter, Eric, who stammered and blushed easily and just ate and ate, as if he were desperate, and whom Melissa rather liked because he could scarcely make conversation and seemed about to crawl under the table when addressed by anyone he thought important; plus Alison, who was always at Rosemary's left elbow at family events. Her truest daughter, Melissa thought, even more faithful than Merilee. That was what Melissa should have become if she wanted Rosemary's acceptance: her ever-helpful shadow, bending, twisting herself to please and provide whatever was needed. Audrey, Dick's divorced correspondence secretary who had been with him since her daughter was four, and eleven-year-old Annette were there too. Audrey never said much but hovered over her daughter, making sure she behaved and ate well. They were sixteen at table, including Rich; a congressman named Parker from Pittsburgh who sat on Dick's right, while Senator Dawes was on Rosemary's right. Two homeless men were being fed in the kitchen, where Melissa had run into them earlier. Rosemary was to be interviewed on local television Monday, to talk about how she shared her Thanksgiving dinner with homeless people, to stress Dick's charitable and compassionate side. The dinner had been cooked by a woman from Martinique, Yolanda, who with her daughter Yvette, did all their smaller dinners. She mostly came in Thursday through Sunday. The other days Rosemary never sat down to eat, and Dick ate out at one of the restaurants preferred by senators or at his desk. The largest parties were catered.

The food was excellent, as always. It was a traditional dinner, the same things they had every year, including the creamed onions that Dick loved from his childhood and nobody else except Audrey ate. Melissa was seated between Alison and an intern. Alison asked her about college and she answered carefully. The intern had gone to Brown and was full of himself. He didn't even bother to flirt with Melissa, a relief. Interns came and went. Dick was not easy to work with. He wanted things done perfectly but had never learned how to give precise directions. That made for dissatisfaction on his part and bruised feelings on the part of the interns. Melissa hated to be recruited for tasks during campaigns.

Senator Dawes was telling Rosemary all about his dead wife, their Thanksgivings together, the garden they had shared in North Dakota, how she had loved roses but most would not survive the winters there, so he had had a greenhouse built for her, not for tropical plants but for the roses and lilies she had loved growing up in Michigan. Melissa pitied him, a man so lonely he mistook Rosemary's interest for friendship. She gathered he was filling the role of mentor to Dick that Uncle Tony had occupied for years.

She told everyone she had a lot of homework, not completely untrue. This was a good time to catch up and even try to get a little ahead on her reading.

I miss you, I miss you, in my body, in my soul I miss you,

she wrote Blake.

He wrote back,

I don't know if I have a soul, but whatever I have misses every part of you. I'm bored without you. I have this fantasy that we'll have a vacation together someday, maybe in a warm place.

It will happen,

she wrote.

I dreamed of you last night. We were on an island with an enormous moon overhead and parrots flying around. We were naked and very happy.

I'd be happy to be naked with you right now. Instead I just ate a vegetarian Thanksgiving—my sisterette Sara insisted it all be veggie or she wouldn't sit at the table. A dead bird, she says, is gross.

What's a sisterette?

Not blood, not bone, but a lot more than nothing.

The weekend crept. Rich and Dick and Rosemary were closeted. Sometimes Alison sat in with them, sometimes one of Dick's aides, always Joe Czernowicz, Dick's longtime chief of staff, now back from Thanksgiving with his Pennsylvania family. She could swear he had grown balder since September, his dome glistening with light sweat as he trotted out to grab a file. They were plotting Rich's run for state rep. His career was all laid out like the street plan for a subdivision before the houses were built. But she remembered one of those subdivisions outside Youngstown, when she was little and they still visited Rosemary's family. It was all overgrown fields and brambles, but the streets were paved and sidewalks ran alongside, their slabs cracked and tilted. Occasional fire hydrants were rusting in the weeds. The subdivision had been plotted years before, but something had gone wrong—the mills had closed, people were laid off—and houses never were built. When she thought of that, she felt a little less pushed aside. Not all buildable lots got built. Not all subdivisions flourished. Not all careers coasted ahead on smoothly oiled rollers toward their destination. Did she like Rich? Not really. The most he had ever given her was a patronizing nod. He scarcely even bothered to tease her in recent years.

Merilee wasn't around much, off with her study group, and then to George Washington for a meeting of the Law Review. Melissa was surprised to find she was a little disappointed. She had hoped that Merilee might open up again. She wouldn't care if Wesleyan abolished vacations, so she didn't have to leave Blake and Emily. Time passed here like one of those endless freight trains across a road, all that clatter and speed but nothing changed, you just sat there waiting and waiting and waiting for it to be over.

Rosemary took her to the train herself on Sunday. As they sat in Union Station with the tourists swarming around them to all the restaurants and shops, Rosemary fixed that clear beam of attention, that laser of energy and inquiry, on Melissa, who squirmed on the bench and wished for some interruption. A fire, a mugger, a bomb alert, the ceiling could fall in. She would be so much happier if her mother would just take off and let her cruise the shops.

"Have you been seeing any particular boys? You never mention any. Has no one asked you out?"

Melissa pulled at her hair, a habit when she was nervous. Come to think of it, Merilee did that too. Melissa's hair was fine, light brown and straight. She twisted it around her finger. "I've gone out with three different boys. Two of them were nice. But I'm not really interested. But sure, I meet boys. Mostly we go out to movies and pizza and parties in groups."

"Why do you think you weren't interested?"

"Because they weren't interesting."

"In what way?"

"Too average. Too hard to distinguish from all the other similar boys."

"That sounds rather snobbish."

"You think I should settle for someone average, because that's all I could possibly attract?"

"I'm just trying to understand, Melissa. There's no hurry for you to find a boyfriend. How about other girls?"

"Well, of course there's Emily. We have Intermediate French together." She had e-mailed her mother all this information, but she did not expect Rosemary to remember something so trivial as who was in Melissa's classes.

"But surely you've met other girls?"

"Of course. My roommate, Fern—"

"On scholarship, you said. Perhaps you could get them to give you someone more suitable."

"She's fine. Easy to live with. There are some very nice girls in my dormitory. But I'm trying to do well in school, so dating some guy and doing things with other girls are not my priorities yet."

"Grades of course are important . . ." Rosemary was still speaking, but Melissa stopped listening. She knew what her mother was going to say. It was better for both of them if Melissa didn't listen: she would not become depressed and defensive and she would not start fighting with her mother when she was about to get on a train and escape. She could see herself slipping into her seat, plugging in her laptop. She could even call Blake on her cell phone and hear his voice. She had hoped he would get on the same train in Philadelphia, but his parents were driving him back to school. She would sit watching the drab late-fall landscape slide past and she would feel liberated. Rosemary was always warning her about fast food, but on the train, she'd have a hot dog and just relax and read and work on her laptop all the way to New Haven. She was not leaving home, as Rosemary was saying: she was going home.

She felt that strongly as she ran across campus from the bus stop, climbing the hill, crossing Andrus Field and finally lurching into her room, carrying her bag of clean laundry, her backpack and laptop. Home! "Fern! Hey!" She ran over to hug her hard, as if they had been separated six months. "I'm so glad to see you. I'm so glad to be back."

Fern had gone home too. "I guess I am. But I miss my mother. I even miss my cat Ginger."

"Did you have a big Thanksgiving dinner?"

"Mom had to work. But I went to the restaurant and they let her serve me free. And she brought home food for the next day. . . . Oh, Blake called. He thought his parents expected him to have supper with them, but he'll call you when they leave."

Emily was in her room unpacking clean laundry. "My parents are so weird sometimes. They keep talking to me about how to meet guys and make friends, as if I am not your super pickup artist—but what do they know? They think I'm shy. I'm just invisible to them."

"Not the worst thing." Melissa told Emily her vacation and her disappointment at not seeing Blake that evening.

"Yeah, tonight you'll have to put up with me." Emily pouted. She had a way of raising her chin and kind of quivering when she felt insulted or disregarded.

"That's fine, Em. Just great. We'll hang out. I'll unpack and be back."

Melissa started putting away her clean underwear, which someone, probably their cleaning service, had actually folded. She realized she simply didn't know what happened to her dirty laundry in Washington. She took it home dirty and brought it back clean.

What she really wanted to do was cruise by the likely restaurants to see what his parents—his adopted parents—looked like, to spy on him with them. But she recognized that neither Emily nor Fern would be enthralled by this knowledge-gathering activity and also that if Blake saw her, he would think she was crazy.

"Are you okay?" she asked Fern. "I'm planning to go see Emily, but if you want company . . . You could come too. . . ."

Fern looked uncertain, then turned to her desk. "I didn't get to study much over Thanksgiving. There was so much to do in the house. I had to fix things for my mom. So I better knuckle down. I have a paper due."

Melissa went off to keep Emily company. Buttercup had flown to Saint Lucia and would be back tomorrow. "There's no music in my parents' house," she said to Emily, who was playing something with flutes. "It's sterile that way."

"Still? But you've given them CDs for years."

"I don't think they ever listened to anything I gave them."

"Dead air," Emily said bleakly. "I couldn't live without music."

"We are from different species, them and me. I will always wonder if there wasn't a mix-up in the hospital."

"Except you kind of look like them, you know?"

"You really think so?" She was a little annoyed. Blake would understand. He was her best friend now. She could hardly wait for class, when she would finally see him. It was the longest they had been separated since they began, and in spite of all the e-mails and several phone calls, she was nibbled by a dozen different anxieties until she could be with him again. Had he sat in Philadelphia with his adopted family and changed his mind about her? Thought, how could he get in so deep so quickly? Thought that he could do better—find a prettier girl, thinner, less neurotic, less clingy, less dependent on him? Maybe he'd decided he should date a woman of color instead of her. Maybe his parents had questioned him, he had told them about her and come to see everything differently. They could have persuaded him to take a step or many steps backwards. Too much, too soon, they would say, not understanding how their coming together had felt as if it were a force like gravity exerting its irresistible tug on them both. She made up scenarios that frightened her. He was intensely important, her center; their relationship was the one good thing she had that was truly her own. He had made her less ashamed of her body. She didn't tend to wrap herself up in layers upon layers now. But would he still want her? She could not stop inventing stories of disaster until finally she saw him face to face, body to body, and alone together.

CHAPTER NINE

Melissa read the e-mail correspondence every week that her mother exchanged with her brothers and sister. Blake downloaded it all for her. "Sometimes I used to feel," she said, curled up on his lap after reading through the week's exchanges, "as if I was paranoid. But here it all is spelled out. Even Billy gets more from her than I do. There's fussing but there's at least some caring. I'm like this appendage to her real family."

"You don't belong to them. You never did."

"Even when I was little, I was never what she wanted." Now although she was the least of them, she had the power of knowledge, the power that came from monitoring them without their being aware.

"How about your father? Did he care for you more?"

"When I was small, he used to take me on his lap and call me little Miss Muffet. He'd bring me presents from his trips, like taffy or a doll." She felt herself flinching. That her father had seemed to love her once was not something she could stand to think about. It had wounded her so when he withdrew. "But after he became governor, he never had time for Billy or me. I felt like a disappointment—gangly, overgrown, not cute any longer. There came to be this fence of aides and front men and speechwriters between him and us. The only time we ever saw much of him was when a photographer would be taking family pictures. We'd be dolled up and hauled out like props. Or we'd have to sit smiling on a platform or at a banquet. We'd have to show up at some stupid ribbon cutting or old folks' brunch, a prayer breakfast, whatever. You ought to hear Daddy pray. You'd swear he was a preacher. And you should hear how, when he goes down near the Mason-Dixon line, he gets this little drawl in his voice."

"But it has to be painful for you, that you used to be close and now you aren't?" He stroked her fine hair back from her forehead.

She turned away from him, but she could not lie. "Yeah."

"Your father is a powerful man, but you have something to offer him that he doesn't get—obviously—from his wife or his staff or anybody else."

She looked at him. "Like what? That's a joke. A bad one."

"No joke." He took her face in his hands. "You could be his conscience. Don't you see that?"

"No, I don't see that. He never talks to me about anything real."

"But you could inform yourself. You could learn about what he's doing, what he has done. You could surprise him with your knowledge, and then you'd have a new and better relationship—and you'd be able to influence him for good."

"How would I ever be able to do that? My mother is the one he listens to. He'd never listen to me."

"He would if you surprised him by your savvy. If you took the time and trouble to learn all about his career and his politics, instead of just running away from it all." He held her head, making her meet his gaze. "You could become a counterbalance to your mother."

A surge of hope flowed through her. She did not believe she could really do it, fight with Rosemary for her father's attention, her father's soul even. But she could not resist the idea. Blake was always surprising her, the way he took an interest in everything to do with her. With Jonah, if she went on too long about her family, he'd glaze over.

"It just seems impossible. But I could try. . . ."

"We have to find a way in. You mentioned prayer breakfasts. Is your father religious?"

"You'd say so, to listen to him. But it's all a show. I don't think he's ever prayed for anything but help me with my backers, get me points with voters, let me win the election." She stroked his cheek. "You have such sleek skin, it always amazes me. Like satin. Are your stepparents religious?"

"They go to synagogue on High Holy Days. At Passover, we have a seder at my grandma's. But they believe in good works. That's the best thing about them."

"Do you really consider yourself a Jew?"

"I was bar-mitzvahed. I like being a Jew. It takes people aback. It's kind of interesting. I like Hebrew. I like languages. Before I decided on computers, I thought I might be a translator. Languages are like computer code in a way, with their rules. I'd love to know ten, twelve languages."

"*J'étude le français, comme tu sais.* . . . What languages do you know?"

"Spanish pretty well. Some French, German and Italian—enough to have a conversation. I picked up a little Czech. I told you I bummed around Europe on my own—on my bike. I wasn't staying in Hiltons. I had to speak the language."

"I want to travel with you."

"We will, babes, we'll go every place." He took her face in his hands. "Do you believe me?"

Sometimes he asked questions, like Do you believe me? or Do you trust me? with an intensity she found flattering. Who else cared if she trusted them? "Of course I believe you."

"I want you to trust me completely. I don't want any doubt between us, any reservations. Nothing held back." His hands pressed hard into her shoulders.

"You're hurting me."

"I have to know."

She wriggled off his lap. "Why do you doubt me?"

"How do I know, if it came to a choice, that you'd come with me?"

"But we aren't going off to Europe next week."

"It's something I have to know, that you're really mine."

When he said it that way, she thrilled deep in her belly, along her spine. It touched some old feral desire, something she needed like a drug. "I swear I am."

"I have to know." He stood and paced to the window, looking out. "It's snowing." The intensity was gone and he was just a rangy nineteen-year-old. "I'm hungry again. Let's go get a burger or pizza."

"You're still growing."

"Damn right."

AFTER CLASS on Wednesday, they walked out just as they always did and headed for Mocon. Then he sat down with Florette and Jamal, from their Creative Nonfiction class, and motioned Melissa into a seat. She was disappointed, because they hadn't had that much time together since Thanksgiving. She felt shy with Florette, who was meltingly pretty, with a smile that, when it flashed, made Melissa jealous. Florette dressed cool too, and she was African-American, an advantage with Blake. Maybe he was having doubts about the relationship. She was nervous about talking in front of Florette, for fear she'd say something that could be considered racist and really mess up. Two, then three more Black kids sat down with them. They all looked at her, but none of them said anything about her until a guy who looked vaguely familiar—a really tall guy wearing a basketball jersey—plunked himself down. They all sat up as if they had been waiting for him. "God, I haven't been in this pit for two years, and I can't allow as I miss it." He looked straight at her. "What's whitey doing here?"

"She's Blake's bitch, Ironman," Florette said. "He don't cross the street without her."

Jamal said loudly, "They're going to let Alan Foreman go. He's the only dude on the faculty who speaks any African languages and really knows West Africa."

"What's their excuse?" Ironman asked, polishing off a big plate of something with chicken in it.

"Hasn't published enough in academic journals," Jamal said.

Florette waved that away. "No, his bad is he actually writes so folks can understand what he's signifying."

"Demonstration in front of the library?" Blake asked casually, eating his usual turkey burger.

"Rapid response," the basketball forward they called Ironman intoned. "Slam them right away."

"We can mount it by Friday." Blake wiped his mouth meticulously. He was clean as a cat and moved with the same grace. She wondered if it was racist to think of him in those terms, but he was so very physical. The way he moved was like music. A demonstration by Friday. He was so casual. She had read about demonstrations, sometimes against her father, and seen them on television, but she had never imagined being in one or how they could be organized. She had always thought of them as being put on by professional agitators, the way her father said. But here were Florette and Jamal and Blake and five other kids planning such an action, sitting and discussing posters and signs with Ironman.

"What can I do?" Melissa asked when there was a lull.

Florette lowered her chin and looked at her sideways. "Honey, your old man is one of the biggest foes of affirmative action in the whole nasty Senate. Why would you care about Foreman?"

"Well, my father's wrong. I know that."

"Did you know that before you were making it with Blake?"

"Blake and I have never talked about affirmative action. Yes, I wrote a paper in opposition to my father's policies when I was in high school." That was a whopper, but after all, Florette wasn't about to interview her teachers back at Miss Porter's. Blake kept looking sideways at her to see what she would say; she felt he was judging her, whether she was on his side enough, whether she had the courage to support him and the other African-American students.

"Mmmm. You can hold a sign right at the cameras. Oh, and call the TV stations. Including Hartford and New Haven. Say who you are. It'll get their attention," Jamal said.

She glanced at Blake, hoping he would say she didn't have to, but he was nodding. "Cool."

She was scared. Her father would surely hear of it and she would be in deep trouble with her parents. If she backed down, Blake would not trust her. How had she gotten into this? Still, she must behave as if she were willing and hope something would come up so she wouldn't have to go through with it.

"Maybe we could make a list of TV stations? I don't really know them around here. And if anybody knows who to contact for the news?"

Ironman said, "I can get the contact list from Josie. She's in Malcolm X with me." One of the houses upperclassmen lived in. "She has it from last year. Or I'll bring it by. What dorm are you in? I'll make sure you get it by tonight. So when are we doing this? We need to get the word out."

She went very slowly back to her dormitory, wondering how she had gotten in deep so fast. It was just a little picket outside the library and nobody would pay any attention—if she didn't mention who she was. But they wanted her to. She had to prove to Blake that she could be trusted, that she was absolutely on his side. On Friday, they would be there with signs and chants and all the things that demonstrators did on television. Somebody would call her parents for comment. Rosemary would be furious. Could her mother pull her out of school? There would be a reckoning in the family, they would find out about Blake. Disaster hung over her head.

Of course Blake and his friends were in the right. She knew that. Her father wasn't even deeply racist. Although he boasted of being a collateral relative of Robert E. Lee on his mother's side, he also, when it was to his advantage, trotted out an Abolitionist ancestor who had been shot leading a charge in the Civil War. Neither Dick nor Rosemary ever used bad language about people of color, never told racist jokes or permitted them. But Dick did not count Black voters among his constituency, so he had no reason to please them. They weren't going to vote for him, work for him, fund-raise or contribute money, so they and their needs and issues were no more important than the opinions of seagulls or pigeons. They were not on his radar except when he had to make a speech about crime or drugs or welfare mothers or family responsibility, whatever. It was not that he hated African-Americans; rather, they simply didn't exist for him in a meaningful way. But they did for her, ever since Hartford. Rosemary was probably more deeply imbued with racism, because she never took her position in life for granted. She had been born lower middle class in a working-class town to sweet parents she viewed as shameful failures. Rosemary had an edge of quiet terror that she would slip in class, in social position. She could not afford to take chances with people she viewed as dubious assets. And herself, Melissa, what was she? Scared.

Later, when they were alone in Blake's room, she asked him, "How come this is so important to you? I mean, you told me yourself, you don't even know if you're African-American. And you hardly look it."

"But that's how I'm classified by others. The cause is right. Besides, what are the odds that I'm Filipino or West Indian? The odds are my parents were African-American. Does that bother you?"

"Of course not! I assumed you were from the beginning. It's just that my mother's going to kill me."

He raised his eyebrows high. "I doubt that. It wouldn't be good publicity to shoot her own daughter."

But she remained scared. How had she pushed herself so far out front of her friends, her acquaintances? She had not meant to take an active role, just to go along with it. She thought she would turn up and wave a sign toward the back. She should have kept her mouth shut. But Blake had kept looking at her sideways. She had to prove herself to him so he would go on loving her. She could not lose him through cowardice. No matter how scared she was, she had to go through with what she had said she would do, even though it made her sick to her stomach. His loving her was a small miracle. No other guy ever had, and she could not easily believe any other ever would. He was something she did not deserve, and she had to do whatever it took to keep him interested. His friends would never really accept her, but this way, they would not give him such a hard time about her—a constant series of small and large sneers, jokes, remarks, attacks she had suspected all along. She saw the way Jamal and Florette looked at them when they passed their table or saw them together.

Ironman hand-carried her the list of contacts, probably to make sure she was really going to make the calls. Fern looked after him with a surprised, impressed face. Ironman was a local sports hero, a junior who'd been on the basketball team since his freshman year. "What did he want? I mean, is he a friend of Blake's? I didn't know he hung with us lowly freshmen." She was at her desk writing a paper.

Melissa explained to Fern and Emily, who often took refuge in Melissa's room to get away from Whitney. Melissa waited for Emily to tell her what an idiot she was. But Emily was intrigued. "That'll drive your parents wild. It'll be fun, too. I'll go. I'll carry a sign. I can make a good one."

"You'll go too? Really?"

"I'll go too," Fern said. "As long as I don't have to say anything."

Emily tilted her head back, eyes on the ceiling. "I always wanted to be in a demonstration. My parents did all that when they were young, back around the Spanish-American War." Emily straddled the desk chair. Her voice rose in amused excitement. "They get all misty when they talk about the good old days on the barricades. Your parents will want to quarantine you, but my parents will adore me. They'll be thrilled. I bet I get the car I've been bugging them for."

"Wow, I wish you would. That would be great."

"It's worth a try," Emily said, yawning. "I've got to catch up on sleep this weekend. I fell asleep in class today."

If Emily and Fern didn't think what she was doing was insane, it must not be too bad. She would tough it out with her parents. She made most of the phone calls, giving her name but not mentioning her father. Melissa Dickinson was a common enough type of name. If people didn't know who her father was, they never guessed. Why seek out trouble? Emily volunteered to call two TV stations. Emily was such a good friend that Melissa almost began to think of herself as unusually lucky, for she had a great boyfriend and a great roommate and friend. Even if her family despised her, she had Blake and Emily and Fern.

The day of the demonstration loomed. That morning it was raining semifrozen drops when she awoke—if waking meant anything after dozing in brief fits all night. She was relieved. She wished it were a monsoon. Then she got scared all over again. She would be branding herself a troublemaker, one of the weird wanna-bes who hung around the African-American students and imitated their clothes, their language, their style. But Blake's group was in the right, and she should be supporting them.

The sleet kept up. The demonstration was called for noon. The local TV station had driven their truck right onto campus and had lights set up. She felt awkward, conspicuous, out of her element. The African-American students and their supporters trickled into the area, lots of raincoats and ponchos and parkas, two faculty umbrellas, a sea of baseball caps. The sleet made the scene look like bad TV reception. Her teeth chattered, perhaps from cold, more likely through pure nervousness. She saw Blake, taller than most in the crowd and far handsomer, already talking to a reporter under one of the outdoor lights they had rigged up. Florette was beside him, both holding forth. Ironman arrived late, but the camera immediately focused on him. She did not go over to join them. She waited on the edge of the small crowd with Emily and Fern. They huddled together, waving their signs. The printing held, but the drawings that Emily had made were running. Fern looked miserable but held her sign high, waving it occasionally.

She hated to see Blake on the other side of the plaza and not to go to him, but she didn't want to be interviewed, she didn't want to appear on TV. She saw Blake gesturing at one point that she should come over, but she pretended not to understand. Instead she just hoisted her sign higher and waved it harder, as if that was what she understood him to want. They had about forty-five, maybe fifty students taking part. Along the other side of the plaza were some antis, frat boys yelling at them. One heavyset guy was in a shouting match with Jamal. Someone from the dean's office appeared to represent the university. An occasional chant arose, but the real confrontation was between Jamal, Ironman, Florette, the guy from the dean's office. There probably wasn't enough action for the reporters, because they closed down and drove off when it became apparent nothing more exciting was going to happen. No building takeovers, no violence. It would be, she suspected, a thirty-second item on the evening news.

Blake made his way to her. "I wanted you to talk to the reporter."

"Would it be appropriate for a white girl to seem to be speaking for the

African-American students? I thought you just wanted me to show my sign to the camera."

"It's okay." He grinned. "We made our point. And it stirs things up a bit. Gets some people involved. What more can you ask?"

It was over. She felt an immense relief. Blake was turning back to Florette and Jamal, who were waiting for him. Melissa took Emily's arm and Fern's, and they trotted back to the dormitory to change out of their wet clothes. She was chilled through. "Let's have hot chocolate," Emily said. "I have a two o'clock, but there's time. One of those coffee machines has hot chocolate, if I can remember which one."

Fern shook her head, but Melissa said, "My treat." Fern went along then. Melissa had noticed Fern never wasted money.

She felt as if she were slinking away, but at least she had done what they asked of her, almost all of it, and she hadn't appeared on TV herself. She could hope her mother wouldn't hear about it. She learned later that one of the Kennedy cousins had been in an automobile accident that morning, and the crews had rushed to the Boston hospital where he was being operated on. She was vastly relieved. The Kennedy cousin had saved her.

THE NEXT NIGHT, she studied with Blake in his room. They worked for a couple of hours, and then he scooped her up out of her chair and carried her toward the bed. She loved being carried. It felt romantic, like a movie, and she was half sorry he did not have to carry her farther. She reached up to him and they kissed, and then, quite slowly and gently, he lowered her to his bed. Then just as slowly he removed her clothes, kissing the skin he uncovered as he went. "I know you were scared," he said in his softest most velvety voice. "I know you were afraid you'd get in trouble with your family."

"I was a little scared."

He went on uncovering her bit by bit and letting his lips travel across her skin. "More than a little."

"I did it. Everything you wanted." She worried he would bring up the moment when he had motioned toward her and she had pretended not to understand.

As if he could read her mind, he said, "Florette wanted you on camera. But I wasn't pissed that you didn't come over. That would have been begging for trouble. And you're right about it being sleazy using a white spokesperson. . . . So you didn't end up doing anything you didn't want to do, did you?"

"Of course not," she said. "I want to be with you in everything you do."

"I know." He smiled and went on making love to every inch of her. "Because what we do, we do together. We move as one. We act as one."

"That's so sweet," she said, her voice catching. She was aroused to the point of almost finding his kisses painful. "Come into me."

"No, I want to eat you first." He stripped rapidly, as always folding his clothes over his desk chair. He never threw his clothes on the floor the way Emily and she did. Each item was processed.

She bent to suck him, but he pushed her back down. "No. This is for you. Because you were brave in spite of being scared. Because you didn't let your family intimidate you. You dared to go against them and what they stand for. You fought them in your own way. That's real strength, babes."

She was embarrassed to have him laboring over her. She had never just lain there and had a man do oral sex on her. "Baby, you don't have to do this," she murmured, trying to pull his head away.

"Why would you think I wouldn't enjoy it?"

"You know. I mean, I'm not beautiful or anything. I'm too fat."

"Fat? You're up a tree. You have a great body. Who ever told you different? You're built like a woman should be. Now shut up."

She felt as if she were taking too long, but she was beyond a level of excitement when she could make him stop. When she came, she found she had tears in her eyes.

Melissa was disappointed with their lunches. Blake had been sitting down with other people. First it was Florette and Jamal. Now it was a white kid from Philadelphia, Phil. She wondered if Blake was growing bored with her company. Emily warned her not to try to keep Blake to herself, no matter how much she desired it. Em knew much more about guys than she did, so she listened. She fantasized that Blake and she were cast away on an island, sent into space in a two-person rocket ship on a five-year mission. Or just snowbound in a cabin. She longed to pull him away from his demanding friends and acquaintances, from distractions and classes, even from the bike he rode off on by himself, claiming it was too cold for her. She never got enough of him.

Florette and Jamal she could understand: they were his closest African-American friends on campus. But Phil? He was a runty guy with red hair cut roughly punk, as if he had done it in the dark in a fit of pique. He rolled his own cigarettes with a flourish. His fingers looked yellow, and he always seemed to have a cold. Em and she considered him weird. She worried that Blake was growing tired of her, that she no longer commanded his prime attention. Yet at moments she was convinced he loved her passionately. She tried to imagine how to make herself more interesting. Emily told her to take an interest in what Blake was interested in. "Guys always fall for that. Even if it's, like, football."

"You're really into Phil," she said tentatively, ready to back off if the statement bothered him.

"I thought he was someone you should know."

"Me? How come?"

"Well, you want to be a crusading journalist, right? Or you did last week."

"That's what I want," she said. The way he said it, it sounded silly. Her mother would certainly think so.

"So, Phil ought to be useful to you. . . . He knows who your father is. How come you don't know who his father is?"

"Phil Lippett?" The last name was vaguely familiar. She tried to think where she had heard it. Back when Dick was governor, Rosemary had tried to cultivate a Lippett who had been attacking her father and whom she had hoped to win over or at least neutralize. He had been one of her failures. "Roger Lippett. A reporter for the *Philadelphia Inquirer*."

"One of their best." Blake beamed at her, tousling her hair. "Yes, babes, that's his father. Our Phil intends to follow in his footsteps. Linking up with him could be useful for you. He's a junior who spends his summers at the *Inquirer*."

"A junior? Why would he hang with us?"

"We intrigue him, babes. It'd be useful for us if we continue to do so."

She felt a rush of gratitude. No matter how unimpressed she had been with Phil, Blake was charming him for her benefit. He actually took her vague ambitions seriously and was trying to help her. Nobody else had ever done that.

"Like his father, he's fascinated with King Richard. By the way, he was on CNN today, Phil told me. I wish I'd known. I like to see King Richard in action."

That was Blake's new name for her father. She had begun using it when she e-mailed Billy, who picked it up at once. King Richard seemed appropriate for Dick, who had always appeared larger than life but also hollow—like the huge balloons she remembered from the parades of her childhood Noreen had taken Billy and her to watch. Blimpy Mickey Mouse and Bugs Bunny, huge and almost frightening to a child. She had read about a woman killed by one of those balloons that had got loose at a Macy's parade in Manhattan. Dick could seem like that: huge, cartoonish, but dangerous too. Rosemary never forgot a slight, but Dick said, "Keep your eye on the ball. The best revenge is turning an enemy into an asset. Watch for their weaknesses, watch for what they most need. Win them over or neutralize them. Only fight when you have to. Revenge isn't victory."

"Oh." She grimaced. "He just wants to know me to get some dirt on my father."

"He's not a reporter yet. He's learning the ropes, as you must. I thought you could help each other. And this is a start to informing yourself so you can learn to act as a conscience for your father. You can't catch his attention unless you know a surprising amount."

"Why would Phil want to help me?" She had a deep mistrust of those who came at her father. Dick might be a little corrupt, but politicians were under far more scrutiny than businessmen or professors. Her father did what he had to, what he could—the same as the President, the same as every other governor or senator. He was cleaner than the others, she was sure of that. Reporters were no better, willing to do anything to get a story, willing to smear people.

"Because you aren't in your father's pocket. I know how difficult growing up in that household has been for you, and I've told him how independent you are. We won't share with him our real aim—to educate you in the ways of your father's politics so eventually we can influence them. That's our project and he doesn't have to know about it."

He was flattering her. She resented it and she ate it up. "How come you started hanging with him? A junior."

"We met in Philadelphia last summer. My parents know his father."

"So maybe he'll just put up with me because he likes you and he knows we're knocking boots." So far, in the two times they'd had lunch together, Phil had barely spoken to her.

"You haven't been open with him either. You just sit there staring at the tabletop."

"I'll do better," she promised. "You know I'm not real forward with people I don't know."

"That's got to vanish if you plan to be a journalist, babes."

"You're right, of course." She felt as if he were the only person she had ever known who saw what she needed and who pushed her to do what she ought to. Emily was on her side, but she didn't put that much intelligence or forethought into daily life. Blake did. That made her fearful she would not live up to his expectations, that she would fail. She had been failing all her life, but at a game she had not agreed to, where she had been discounted before she began. She did not want to fail with Blake. She could just go along with Phil and Blake and keep her opinions to herself, just pick up pointers on doing research and that would be the extent of it. She would treat it like any other course, something unreal but necessary to pass through. And always, as Blake said, she would keep in mind her real goal: to become someone whose political opinions her father would respect, would listen to. It was a fantasy she could slip into easily. Instead of consulting only Rosemary, instead of closeting himself with Rich and leaving her out in the cold, he would be astonished by her insight. He would once again let her into his attention. Rosemary would be shocked, but she would prove herself. She could see herself in her father's office, consulting with him on some bill he was trying to decide whether to support or argue against. Maybe it would never happen, but just maybe it could.

She looked carefully at Phil when they sat down together the next week, just before Christmas break. He was as runty as she remembered, with hair the color of the poinsettias decorating the food court. His eyes were wary as he examined her in return. She suspected that Blake had been talking up each to the other, trying to persuade them to open up, to form an alliance through him. "Blake said you were doing a research project that I might be able to help with—so I'd learn something about how an investigative reporter works."

"I'm hip deep in the Big Muddy of a project, but I don't know that you'd want to help out," he said. He had a surprisingly deep voice for a little guy. She would bet that anyone he was speaking to for the first time on the phone would think he was tall and robust.

She bridled. "Oh. Why is that?"

"The subject of my investigation is some of Dick Dickinson's activities as governor of Pennsylvania."

She felt as if she had been kicked. She had been set up. For a moment she said nothing at all but looked at Blake to ask him with her eyes, *Why?* But he was beaming at her as if he expected her to be overjoyed. She felt trapped. Blake obviously expected her to get involved in whatever project Phil was working on. Oh, she ought to have guessed, when she heard who Phil's father was. Blake was saying, "But Lissa's no fan of her father's. She's been fighting with him for years."

"Arguing about a pet or a curfew is one thing. Digging up the dirt—and there's plenty—is something else again. How did you guys ever hook up?"

"We have a class together," Blake said dismissively. "What kind of dirt?"

"What he'll do for contributors, what he's done for them. Especially around environmental issues. That's my kick."

Roger Lippett had been trying to embarrass her father for years, with only intermittent success. Why did this stupid-looking kid think he could do better? She drew into herself, fearful that Blake could read her reaction. How could working with this nerd possibly bring her closer to her father and gain his respect? But she had to go along. Blake seemed to think it would do her good, both as a potential journalist and as a potential influence on Dick.

Finally she said slowly, still looking down, "The truth is important to me." That didn't commit her to anything. Rosemary often said that reporters didn't care about the truth, only about their bylines and the circulation of their papers.

"In politics," Blake said, "truth is a malleable thing. Depends on who's telling it. Depends on who's hearing it."

"I don't agree," Phil boomed. "The facts can be uncovered, discovered. People can have different opinions about values, but facts are rock-bottom."

"What do you think?" Blake turned to her. "Are facts like bricks? Or like clouds, that change while you watch them from a lion's head to a running dog?"

"I agree with Phil," she said firmly but softly. "Interpretations differ. But facts if you can get at them are what you can rely on."

"So are you really going to help me get at some facts?"

She might as well meet with Phil a couple of times and see if he had anything to teach her. He wasn't about to uncover anything that would hurt her father. If Roger Lippett hadn't managed to injure Dick for all his years of trying, his ridiculous son didn't have a chance. She would humor Blake by pretending an interest, just as Emily had advised her. Plus she would learn more about her father's political activities. "I don't know how to do that, but I'm willing to learn. I am taking a full load of courses, so I don't have lots of time."

"So am I. So am I. This is just a little project on the side, something we can all three fool around with," Phil said.

THE NEXT EVENING, Melissa asked Blake, "Do you really like Phil? 'Cause you kind of play with him." She was sitting in his desk chair as he sprawled on his narrow bed, both of them studying for finals.

"He's not my bud, if that's what you mean. What he's trying to do is interesting, and he could teach you a lot. Liking is beside the point."

"Sometimes you can be very cold."

"Absolutely. You don't want to be on the receiving end of how cold I can be, babes." His voice was lazy but lined with hard metal. "You don't want to know that." He tousled her hair, almost too hard.

"Well, I'm going to apprentice myself to him. I'll learn what I can. Both method and facts. . . . To learn what I can about my father. I mean, wouldn't you learn about your father if you could?"

"I know all I need to know about my father."

"But you don't know who . . . Oh, you mean your adopted father?"

"Who else?" Abruptly he reached over and pulled her down to him on the bed. "I desperately need a break. Let's tussle."

Sometimes he stopped a conversation that way, by starting to make love to her, but she didn't mind. She would rather have sex than talk about Phil and his dirt-digging mission, for she didn't want Blake to guess her lack of enthusiasm.

CHRISTMAS VACATION loomed. All that time stuck at home. Emily suggested they spend a week together. Melissa would be in Philadelphia. Dick needed to be pressing the flesh with his constituency and backers. Mother wanted to spend time with Rich and Laura. Melissa was a little nervous about Blake. They would be in Philadelphia with their families, but she was in no hurry to introduce him.

"There'll be some family junk to get through, but we should have plenty of time to get together," he said. "Show you my old haunts. We're out in Mount Airy, not that far. Will you have wheels?"

"Not a chance. But I can take a cab or public transport. . . . Do you want me to meet your family?"

"Let's see how the ground lies first. You'll be in Connecticut part of vacation, right?"

"I was going to. Emily and I usually visit during the holidays."

"I told you, there'll be a lot of family stuff. My brother and sister, cousins, grandparents, aunts and uncles, third cousins four times removed, grateful clients of both my parents, other lawyers from the Guild. The place is like an airport with everybody coming and going and yelling at each other, and every five minutes we have a huge sit-down meal."

"It sounds wonderful!"

"If you like that kind of thing." He was noncommittal, but she didn't believe his cool demeanor. She wished she could be a part of his family scene, but then she would have to introduce him to hers—and that would be a declaration of war. It was probably better if, for the time being, they got together without making a fuss—met someplace.

"We can just avoid the family thing," she said, "at least for now, if that's okay with you."

"Don't want me to meet your folks, do you?"

"Well, do you want me to meet yours?"

His eyebrow rose sardonically. "I'm trying to spare you bedlam. But I think you're afraid for your parents to lay eyes on me. Who is that? *What* is that?"

"I just don't know if we want to fight that battle yet."

He sat up, glaring. "You're ashamed of me."

"How could I be? You're handsome and smart and wonderful."

"And not exactly white. . . ." He was still glaring at her.

"Do you want to meet them?"

"When you're really ready," he said. "Time to douse it this evening. I'm leaving tomorrow on the early side and I still have to pack."

She was being punished. They hadn't made love that evening and now they weren't going to. She felt hollow as she strode across campus. Blake wasn't fair to her. He'd been the one who wasn't in a hurry to bring her home, before she let him know she wasn't eager either. Now he was sulking because she hadn't insisted. She didn't want to court trouble with Rosemary and Dick. Blake was her secret. She had always hidden what really counted from them, what she cherished most, the same way she hid her diaries and finally destroyed them for fear they would be found. She could see herself throwing her diary into the Schuylkill River when she was sent away to boarding school, for fear Rosemary would read it. Not that she had much to hide, just secret dreams and resentments, her anger, her fantasies. She imagined herself heroic and daring, all the traits she had never possessed. She was the heroine of her own stories, saving villages, leading charges, a clever and dangerous spy. She could not have endured Rosemary or Merilee reading her stories or even the prosaic narratives in her diary about school, her crushes, her daydreams, her sense of being overlooked and undervalued.

Even though it would mean not seeing Blake all vacation, not even seeing Emily, she wished she could just stay at school, the way she had during spring vacation when she was at boarding school when she was sixteen: then her parents had gone abroad. Her father was on a mission to increase exports from Pennsylvania, to secure lucrative overseas contacts and contracts, and of course Rosemary had gone with him. Melissa had felt a little sorry for herself, but only a little, because she could indulge in fantasies and reading and lying late in bed with no one to berate her for lack of ambition. But now, she must go to Philadelphia and just hope that she and Blake could hook up a few times and that she could keep him under wraps awhile longer.

Emily said, "At least we'll have a great week together. Maybe I'll get to Philadelphia, if the folks approve. It doesn't do to ask them beforehand. They'd say, Don't you want to be home with us? But after I'm home for a week or two, they won't care if I take off. Parents always like you better when you're away, don't you think?"

"I'd have to be on Mars to get far enough away to make them miss me." Melissa was trying to cram her laundry into her backpack along with the clothes she would need for parties and dates and dinners. It wasn't working. She hated suitcases. They were so not cool. She would have to take her backpack filled with laundry and then a suitcase stuffed with clothes her parents would expect her to wear. She hated to drag all that stuff out of the dorm. Maybe no one would look at her. But Whitney and Ronnie and Carol would notice her, loaded down like a pack animal. It was too embarrassing, but at least it wasn't as bad as Fern, who was walking out with a battered old imitation leather suitcase, like something from the fifties. Well, Whitney always had loads of luggage, so she should just relax.

CHAPTER ELEVEN

Melissa had spent little time in the town house in Philadelphia, purchased through Stan Wolverton, Rosemary's financial advisor, to provide a legal residence in Pennsylvania. It was a deep narrow redbrick row house two stories tall, plus a converted attic, a few blocks from Rittenhouse Square. Many of the row houses had been rehabbed, but some hadn't. There were lots of young professionals with babies on their block. Behind their row, a paved alley ran, but it had its own name, as if it were a real street. Most of the tiny backyards were taken up with makeshift garages, but theirs was just paved for parking. She liked the square with its cool places to eat and have coffee, but in the daytime it was full of people with dogs, mommies and nannies airing their babies. Next to Georgetown, this lacked excitement.

She had her own room at the top of the house. Her parents did not require much staff on their visits, although Alison came along. Rosemary always needed her, and besides, Melissa could not imagine with whom Alison would spend the holidays otherwise. Alison had been raised by her father and an aunt, but they were never in evidence. Her mother had died of breast cancer. Her father had a younger family Alison sometimes bought presents for but never seemed to visit. As far as Alison was concerned, Rosemary was her family. Alison needed family; Melissa often felt she had rather too much of it.

Her top-floor room had a dormer window and a sloping ceiling on which she had already cracked her head twice. *Her* room: it felt less hers than the room she shared with Fern in the dorm, more like a hotel room where she was spending a few nights. The entire house felt that way, although Rosemary had brought in a decorator. The diningroom was blue, the livingroom gold, the hallways a faded rose—all colonial colors, the decorator had told Rosemary, in keeping with the age of the building.

Melissa liked being up where she could hear pigeons cooing on the surrounding roofs, a soothing, sympathetic sound, as if they were trying to comfort each other. The room was drafty, so she slept under a feather quilt that had been kicking around the family since she could remember. Her room was a pale pink that made her feel as if she were in a nursery, while Merilee's equally tiny room across the hall was pale gold. She wanted to imprint herself on it, but it seemed a waste of energy. How often would she be here? Still, she had to make it somewhat her own. She found a rocking chair under the eaves in what remained unfinished of the former attic and spray-painted it black. She would buy a black bed-spread if she could find one, a relief from the colonial scheme in the house. She'd get posters. Blake would have ideas. She had not heard from him. He had his cell phone off, and the number of the Ackerman house had been busy every time she tried. She imagined him caught, slowly rotating at the vortex of the whirlpool of extended family, gradually drowning.

Her parents' social life was hectic. That night they had three parties to attend. Between the second and third, her mother rushed in to change out of a pale green chiffon and then dashed out again in midnight blue silk. Rosemary's porcelain complexion was rosy with haste and excitement. She liked parties. She viewed them in the same predatory way Emily did, but Em hoped to find a guy to hook up with and Rosemary was looking for contacts useful to Dick she could create or polish. When Melissa was younger, their affairs had seemed glamorous. Now she just wanted to stay out of sight. Her parents set her teeth on edge. They were a handsome couple with a dazzle to them that magnetized the eyes of everyone around. Dick looked hale and hearty, as if his skin were buffed like his shoes. Rosemary appeared fragile, aristocratic, all planes and angles. Together they gleamed like a new Mercedes. They looked ready to be photographed. Televised. They looked like winners.

Merilee was home for the holidays, mostly studying at the nearest library and sometimes going down to a law library she could use. Rosemary was berating her for breaking up with Bruce. "He's exactly the sort of boy you should be encouraging."

"I don't have time to encourage anybody. In law school, everything counts. Everything matters—except who I go out with, if I have time to go out with anybody."

"There's no more important decision than the man you marry—that will determine the parameters of the rest of your life."

"I set my own parameters, Mother. I have no time for guys."

Melissa was happy that Merilee was getting criticism for once. For years, everything Merilee had accomplished was held up to her as the way to go. Merilee was so feminine, so prissy, so proper, so well-behaved, with scarcely a hair out of place, just like their mother. She had never gotten in trouble in school, never been caught smoking in the john and getting shellacked and puking after a football game, all the things Melissa had done and been punished for. She had a little thrill of pleasure: Now Merilee was getting a bit of Rosemary's Procrustean bed for her girl children. Let's chop off that foot right there. Let's pull on your spine a little. Don't slump. Don't stand like a flagpole. Don't speak too loudly. Speak up, don't mumble. You must excel in school, you must live up to your potential. Don't take grades too seriously, they're not the purpose of your existence. Smile: no one looks her best when she's pouting. Don't smile too freely at people who don't matter, they will get the wrong idea.

Melissa watched her parents at the rare meal they shared around the almost unused diningroom table. She waited for the prickles of guilt because of what she had promised to do with that punk-haired dork Phil. They didn't come. Phil and Blake and she were just kids playing at politics. Her parents were the real thing; anyone looking at them would see they were impervious. She tried to think of something to say from the little she had learned so far about Dick that would attract his attention, would impress him and cause him to turn to her, but her mind went blank and her mouth felt dry. Trying to influence him was only a daydream. She was just protecting herself, as she had always done when she eavesdropped on their conversations, arming herself against ambush, against disappointment, against the worst thing, hope. Dick's secretary, Audrey, who stayed with her mom when she was in Philadelphia, came by with a bunch of constituent requests. Rosemary handled most of them, yes to this, put that one off supersweetly, get Alec on this right away.

She had been home for four days and still Blake hadn't called. She finally got through to his parents' house, but whoever answered said Blake was out and they didn't know where. Another time she got a woman, perhaps his mother, who said Blake was with some old friends from high school. She was furious with jealousy. An old girlfriend? She could hardly question his mother, if it was his mother. She could not sleep that night, imagining that she wasn't pretty enough, smart enough, brave enough, sexy enough to keep him interested. Finally, the day after Christmas, the day before she was to go to Emily's in Connecticut, she got him. "Blake! Why haven't you called me? Are you angry with me?"

"I didn't think it was important to you. After all, you didn't want your family to catch sight of your pet darky."

"You said you were going to be very busy with family. That's not fair."

"Then what are you surprised about?"

"Blake, I have to see you. Please. You have me worried sick."

"Are you sure? After all, someone might catch you with me. Then they would k-n-o-w you've hooked up with a Black boy."

"Do you want to come over tonight? Is that what you want? I'll introduce you."

"I want you to want to." Then, as if he'd lost interest in the argument, "So you want to meet for coffee? What's near you?"

It was a storm blown over. She was still stunned. She felt hollow, emptied out. "There's a coffee shop in the Barnes and Noble in Rittenhouse Square."

"I'll meet you there. I've a couple of errands to run. Say in an hour?"

He was late. She sat with a latte looking every three minutes at the Swatch watch Emily had given her. His anger had not blown over. He was still resentful and he would not appear. She had lost him. She grabbed a book to stare at.

Finally, forty minutes after she had arrived, she saw his leather jacket outside and he came striding in, graceful as ever, beaming as if there were not a problem in the world. He was so beautiful, she felt a pang. She could not deserve him, no matter what she did. "What happened? I thought you weren't coming."

"Train was late. And slow. Holiday schedules. Remember my bike is at school. . . . Now aren't you glad you waited?" He leaned to kiss her on the forehead.

That was almost an apology, and she did not want to start an escalation of temper between them. "I missed you."

"All of me or just part of me?" He gave her a crooked grin.

"You didn't answer my e-mails, you didn't answer my calls."

"Never got a message. It's been a madhouse there. I left my laptop at school. I knew I wouldn't have time to work or check my e-mail."

She didn't believe him. He didn't cross the street without his laptop, bound to him by an umbilical cord of habit, of need, of compulsion. But she had a choice to challenge or let it go by. "So what's been happening?"

"Dad's mounting a last-minute appeal for a death row inmate who got screwed by the so-called justice system. Mom is fighting for a lesbian mother to keep custody of her partner's son—the partner died of one of those weird sudden heart attacks. Grandma is fighting city hall about mandatory drug testing in the schools. Great-grandma just broke her hip on a demonstration against the World Bank. My sister Sara is pregnant, and I went with her to the clinic two days before Christmas to get an abortion. My folks don't know—"

"They wouldn't go along with an abortion?"

"She's embarrassed that she got pregnant—"

"She didn't do it by herself, Blake—"

"She forgets to take the pill. Anyhow, I'm cool about it. I went with her and held her hand and she pretended to have the flu."

"That's why you didn't call me?"

"I told you, it's a madhouse. It's like living in a pot where the water is always boiling and there's always room for one more lobster."

"You don't sound unhappy about it."

"They're good people." He rubbed his cheeks into his hands as if washing his face. "Tiring, though. So what's up with your mishpokeh?"

"What does that mean?"

"Mishpokeh. Family. Group. Your folks." He patted her hand. "I pick up a certain amount of Yiddish at home. It goes away at school. So what's up?"

"Merilee broke up with her boyfriend—"

"No surprise there. She's been really sarcastic about him to all the friends she e-mails."

"Why are you reading her e-mail?"

"You got me interested in the ins and outs of your family life. It's part of understanding you. But it's like a political soap opera. I'm addicted. You want to see what I'm talking about?" He reached in his jacket and pulled out a page of printout.

He is just the kind of dodo Mother adores: completely archaic. She is one of the most sexist people I think I've ever, ever met. It goes all the way to her bones. She simply believes that men are superior and that a woman should devote her life to propping one up, as she does Father. She keeps pushing me to get engaged by the time I get my degree, as if that's the point of all this work in law school. I tell her I want to practice law, that I didn't go after a law degree to kill time, and she says, of course, dear, but in the meantime, haven't you met anyone suitable? She's a wheeler-dealer as accomplished as any in Washington, believe me, but that's all okay because she only does it for Father's sake. I don't think she has a real idea. She is viewed as a true Conservative, but if Daddy were Castro, she'd be a Communist, if you see what I mean. She has no ideas, only strategies and tactics. Sometimes she frightens me.

Melissa put the printout down on the table. "I had no idea she had issues with Rosemary. Maybe I should try to talk with my sister." He did have his laptop. Otherwise, how was he reading their e-mail?

"Be careful. Her issues are pretty precise, and most of the time, she adores them. So watch out." He looked at his watch. "Time for us to head off to see some people my mother knows."

"I was hoping you'd have time to help me pick out some posters for my room here. It's so kind of bleak."

"These are people you ought to meet. I've set it up where to find them. They don't know who you are—they think you're writing a piece for school."

"So are they like celebrities?" She wondered if he was putting her on.

"Your father cut funding for the homeless. Leaving it up to the private sector. I thought you'd be interested in seeing what that means."

She could hardly say she wasn't interested, but she resented his volunteering her for something in which she had never expressed the slightest interest. She had hoped they would find some convenient place to make love, that they would talk intently as they did at school, that he would help her find stuff to fix up her room.

They took a bus through a part of the city strange to her that went on and on for miles, where everyone seemed to be African-American. Finally he stood and they got off in a run-down seedy area where there were lots of boarded-up storefronts and buildings. She was glad if she had to be dragged up here, north-central Philly, where nobody she knew ever went, that she wasn't alone. She was glad too for Blake's height and the air of tough bravado he put on with his leather jacket. She should think of this as an adventure; but she felt inconvenienced and disappointed. How could it not be a priority to him to make love? Unless he had been with someone else, that old girlfriend. She hoped he had forgotten she was going to Emily's for her usual Christmas visit, so that he would be shocked to realize what he had missed.

The funny thing, she thought as she looked around, was that, architecturally, this neighborhood had a lot in common with Georgetown. Lots of Federal row houses, mostly stone here, but run down into serious slums. If this neighborhood ever gentrified, it would be pretty—if there were anything left.

It was one of the boarded-up buildings he was heading for, around the back and down the steps into the dark, dank cellar. She hesitated to follow him, but she had seen tough-looking kids on the street, and she wasn't about to stand out there in her best blue sweater and tight low-rider jeans while he disappeared. She inched down the broken stairs behind him.

"Lacy," he was calling. "Lacy, are you here?"

A kid's head dimly appeared upstairs. "Come on up here. We're waiting."

She followed him up. A woman—maybe she was thirty? Maybe younger? Her hair was dirty and her clothes, shapeless, so it was hard to guess—was squatting wrapped in a torn blanket. They had a fire going in a garbage can in the middle of the floor, so the room reeked of smoke. Two children besides the boy who had yelled down to them were sharing another blanket, sitting on plastic milk delivery crates. Along one wall was a greenish couch with broken springs sticking out and a table covered with cigarette burns. In another corner was a stained mattress. The room was dim and smoky—no electricity, of course, no heat. They kind of smelled as she got close. The woman was Lacy, the kids Sammy, Gina and Terry. She couldn't tell if Terry was a boy or a girl, the littlest kid mummified in a down jacket much too big, held together with a woman's belt so that the child looked like a badly wrapped package. The woman was white, but the kids were mixed.

"I brought you sandwiches from my mother," Blake said. "This is my girlfriend, Melissa."

"You know each other from college?" Lacy asked. "I want my kids to go to college when they get old enough, so they never end up like me." She took the bag of sandwiches Blake had pulled from under his jacket. Using an old jackknife, she cut a sandwich into quarters and gave a bit to each of her children. "You thank your mama for us. She's a good woman." She ate the last quarter.

"How do you know Blake's mother?" Melissa asked, watching the kids gulp down the sandwich sections.

"She tried to help us when they were tearing down our building. She tried to keep a roof over our heads, bless her. But the law, they wouldn't let us stay."

"Mama, give us some more," Sammy said. "That wasn't nothing."

"Anything. Wasn't anything," Lacy corrected him, and cut up another sandwich. "I was almost graduated from high school when I got pregnant with Sammy. I know my grammar."

Silently, seriously the children chewed, and when they had finished, Lacy ate the last quarter of the second sandwich. "Now that's enough for now. We'll have the rest for supper. So how are you doing? You got a girlfriend again, good for you. I bet your mama is proud of you."

"Are you living here?" Melissa asked. She couldn't imagine camping in a building without heat or windows or plumbing or furniture. They might as well be in the alley.

"For a month now. It's a good place. But they're going to tear it down too, pretty soon."

"Wouldn't you be better off with the children in a shelter?" She had heard of homeless shelters.

"We're on two lists. But they say it will be at least another year."

"There's a long waiting list for all the shelters," Blake said. "Too many homeless, not enough funds. Governor Dickinson cut the funding."

"What I really want is for Sammy to be able to go to school. It hurts me that he can't because we don't live anyplace legal, you know?"

As they finally left, she saw Blake hand Lacy something. "What did you give her?" she asked.

"A twenty. I don't have much cash. Fortunately, my parents don't observe Christmas, so I don't have to buy five hundred presents."

He had told her not to buy him anything. She had been very disappointed, because she had wanted to shop for him. She had felt it would make it all more real to her, that she had her lover to buy things for. She had wanted him to give her something, but he disdained the holidays, he made that clear. He wouldn't let her celebrate his birthday either. She loved birthdays. "Why doesn't Lacy get a job and move into an apartment?"

"Are you insane? Who'd hire her, unwashed, in dirty clothes? And what would she do with her kids? She doesn't have money for a deposit, to get electricity turned on, to pay rent. She's screwed, and your father's insistence when he was governor on cutting back social programs keeps her on the bottom. I just wanted you to see what one of these people he dismisses looks like—to make her a little bit real to you. Then, when the time comes, you have some material to use to change his mind about the homeless."

"Well, you did that."

She minded that all their time got used up educating her, giving her a social policy lesson. She was half glad she was leaving for Emily's in the morning.

SHE LOVED BEING at Emily's with her laid-back parents. The dogs came bounding toward them the moment they entered the house that smelled of cinnamon and balsam and dog, filled with music bubbling out of the speakers, some kind of Baroque wind ensemble. Emily's parents made an occasion of holidays, lavishing presents on each other. Emily was wearing a new cabled turtleneck cashmere in dark red that was just gorgeous. The presents Melissa got tended to the dull and preppy. She knew that Rosemary had no time to shop and little interest. Alison figured out what to get each of them and then wrapped the gifts impeccably, beautifully— just like a department store. There was nothing wrong with her presents except that they didn't feel personal. She had a new jacket dress in navy, a Coach purse and shoes and belt, all matching as if anybody cared, a pale pink cashmere sweater set, cross-country skis, which she had mentioned at some point last year and promptly forgotten.

The tree at Emily's was fanciful, almost too big for their livingroom and hung with ornaments made of shells and dried flowers and old jewelry, besides the usual balls and glass creatures from Bloomingdale's. One of the dogs ate part of a wreath and barfed in the hall while they were all sitting around the tree singing carols. Nobody got excited. Nobody freaked. Emily's dad cleaned it up. If only the food wasn't so weird and full of crusty grains that stuck in her teeth, she would think she was in heaven. They had a winter squash soufflé and a salad with seaweed. But there was a lot of wine, and nobody minded if she drank it. She did and got droopy by nine thirty. Emily's bedroom had a view of a saltwater marsh, although it was too dark to see anything. Still, she liked knowing it was there. In summer when she visited, they opened the windows and she could smell its clean funkiness.

"It's a drag, having a beautiful mother," Melissa confided. "Maybe I wouldn't mind it if she just knitted afghans or raised Irish setters. It must be wonderful to have a mother you can hope to excel. I mean, your mother's nice enough, but she isn't Mrs. America. Everybody admires Rosemary. She does everything better. Everyone says, Oh, she's so beautiful, oh, she's so smart, she always knows the right thing to do. Can you imagine living with that? It drives me crazy. I was born fourth best, and I'll feel that way my entire life."

"Nonsense. Your mother isn't a musician, or a painter, or a great humanitarian like that guy who went to Africa, Schweitzer, whatever. She dresses pretty dull. She isn't a great cook. She isn't a famous athlete. She never flew to the South Pole or climbed Mount Everest or swam the English Channel or went around the world alone in a sailboat. She never starred in a porn movie or fucked a rock star. I bet she never fucked anybody but your father. She never got a dish named after her or had a horse at the Kentucky Derby. So she's left you a lot of room, idiot. Take advantage of it. Be *you,* not a second-rate *her.*"

"Em, sometimes you are so wise it gives me a bellyache." Melissa knelt on the bed kowtowing to Emily. "I shall follow your words, O wise and righteous one. I will follow your path to total contentment."

"You should," Emily said. "I wish we were allowed to have pets in the dorm. If we had a dog, we'd both be happier. Dogs make me much happier than guys. Want to hear something gross? I got herpes from that guy Winston I fucked at school. I went to a gynecologist two towns over so my parents won't know. I hate VDs. They're so personal, and they hurt where it counts. . . . So how's your main man?"

"Trying to improve me," Melissa said. "I suppose that's a good sign? That he's really interested?" She told Emily about Lacy.

Emily shrugged. "It would be nicer if he showed it by giving you perfume or chocolates or a pretty bracelet, wouldn't it? Who wants to be improved? Maybe computers. Not me, and I bet not you."

But Melissa was not sure. She remembered the woman that Blake had taken her to meet. Lacy's concerns did not revolve around what was said about her on the evening news. Her father had sacrificed ten thousand and one Lacys in order to reduce the state budget and cut taxes, always popular with the voters until they experienced the impact on roads, schools, water and air quality, monitoring of safety in food and health care. But they never seemed to put that erosion of quality together with the lowering of taxes. Cutting taxes got her father reelected and elected to higher office. Lacy couldn't vote, for she had no address. She didn't count. So Melissa had to make her count, had to remember her, had to act on her behalf.

Maybe if her father had met Lacy, he would change his mind. She wondered if Dick had ever actually met a homeless person. She imagined bringing her father down to meet Lacy, but she had no idea how to manage that. She could fantasize to her heart's content about influencing a more humane policy on her father's part, but secretly she doubted she could ever do it. She would have to explain how she had met Lacy. She would have to claim some of her father's extremely busy time. He had things to do, always, people to meet, important legislation hanging fire, position papers to go over, reporters to see, TV programs to prepare for, fund-raisers to attend. He lived in a different world than Lacy did, and the two just didn't overlap. Was it his fault? How could she imagine for a moment that he wasn't more important? He was a senator. Blake just didn't understand that her father couldn't keep track of every citizen, every detail. Blake wasn't fair to him, just as Dick wasn't fair to Lacy. That was just how it was and how it had always been, after all. What could she do about it? Blake was an idealist and that was sweet and she loved him for it, but her father was a realist first and foremost—the way a man in power had to be, as she had grown up knowing. Power wasn't left lying around in piles in the street. To get something done required a huge amount of politicking, she understood that far better than Blake did—or Phil, that know-it-all. There was a lot she knew, from growing up in her family, that other people just couldn't understand. It took money, it took time, it took years and years of work to get anything done in government. She felt as if she had put things back in perspective.

Didn't Blake admire his stepfather? Lawyers did far sleazier things than senators did. They defended rapists and murderers and thugs and tried to set them free, back into society to do it again. Really, maybe she should suggest to Phil and Blake that they investigate Blake's stepfather. She felt safe with Emily, so that she almost didn't mind being away from Blake for a few days. She should not let him push her around so much, let him manipulate her into things she was uncomfortable doing. She would learn some skills from Phil, but that would be the extent of it. She'd give him a couple of Saturday afternoons, then ease out of the entanglement. Quietly she would regain control. And if she educated herself about politics and her father's career in the process, so much the better. Finally she would manage to grab his attention during one of her visits home and impress him with how much she had learned. Maybe Blake's idea of persuading Dick to change would work, although when she was away from Blake she could not imagine it; but at least she could finally command her father's respect. He never talked politics with Merilee even, only with Rosemary and Rich. But she would change that. She would learn enough to make him listen to her.

A t school, Melissa settled into her comfortable daily routines with Fern and Emily, eating breakfast together and often supper, washing their hair at the same time, doing their laundry, trimming each other's ends. She practiced French with Emily; Fern tried to teach her to play squash. Emily had become friendly with Fern, mostly to escape her annoying roommate. Melissa saw Blake almost every day for lunch, and they spent at least four evenings a week together. She stopped fearing that he would lose interest in her. Home was just overbooked and hectic for him. She began to feel a weak but strengthening confidence, like a pale little seedling groping toward light. Blake loved her, if not as strongly as she loved him, still more than she had ever been loved. It was what she had dreamed about all those misfit years.

One day in early March, the sky opened into blue and the breeze smelled faintly of salt and warmth, all the way up from the Gulf Stream. It promised, *spring*. Blake took her out on his bike, up into the hills, where snow still covered the ground except on south-facing slopes. They did not make love in their old spot—it was soggy with melting snow, the ground underneath frozen hard as a slab of granite. But the exhilaration of traveling behind him with the wind rushing through them as if they rode the clouds came back to her. He was perfect and beautiful, she felt, clutching him, pressing her cheek into his leather.

Fern said to her one evening when they were alone, "There's something I want to talk with you about." She seemed very nervous.

"I know I'm sloppy," Melissa said. "I don't mean to bury the room in dirty or half-dirty clothes."

"It's not that," Fern said. "It's something personal." But just then Ronnie came bounding in to announce a party on the floor Friday night.

The next day, the second Thursday of March, Melissa walked into her room to find Fern waiting to hand her a piece of paper, a message that Rosemary had called. She felt a shiver of apprehension. Her mother e-mailed her weekly, more often if something she considered important occurred or was about to. To call was unusual. She went to her afternoon French class with Emily before she used her phone. Had Rosemary learned about Blake?

She got Alison. "Rosemary is in conference with Senator Dawes at the moment. But she was calling you with bad news—your grandfather has suffered a stroke. Your mother is extremely worried about his condition."

"Grandfather Dickinson? Is he going to die?"

"He's receiving the best possible care. But your parents want you to be ready to go north. Rich and Laura are driving up, and they'll call you en route and let you know when to expect them. Keep your cell phone on, please."

"A friend could drive me up there. . . . "

"It's best to confine this to family. The Senator is very upset. You know he's always been close to his father. I won't be able to accompany Rosemary. She needs me here to keep things running. . . ." Alison sounded devastated. Melissa wanted to beg Alison to go in her place.

Melissa didn't think Grandpa was close to anyone, but she wasn't about to argue with Alison. Oh, god, she really didn't want to go up to Vermont with Rich and Laura. She didn't want to go up there at all. When she was a kid, she had sometimes liked the farm. That wasn't because of Grandpa Dickinson, who let you know at once he was from an old and proud family, even if their money had long ago been squandered. Still, he had 115 acres of partly valley and partly mountain land where he raised dairy cattle, made awful cheese and grew Christmas trees. Every year at Christmas, he sent them a big round of his cheddar, of the flavor and consistency of a huge gum eraser, with the tang of laundry soap. It resembled the harsh yellow soap that she remembered Noreen, her favorite nanny, using on them when they got into poison ivy.

She packed lightly, hoping Rosemary would not make her stay long. She had the excuse of school. They were going to pose for a solidarity portrait, affirming familial devotion. She called Blake to let him know what was happening.

"That's terrible, babes. Are you close to him?"

"Not remotely. It's just a ceremonial thing."

When Rich arrived, he said, "Got to repack, kiddo. Black. The old guy died this afternoon. He had a second massive stroke in the hospital, and he's gone."

She did not know what to feel. She didn't like her grandpa—he was a mean and miserly man who seemed to love only his Guernsey cows, although he certainly had some kind of respect for his son. Now he was dead. She had never before experienced a death in the family. She tried to find some sense of awe or regret. She wanted to feel something; she must be shallow to lack emotion. Some people were close to their grandparents. Emily liked her grandma. She wished Blake could go with her. He would know what she should feel, what she should think about Grandpa's death, even though he had no real, blood grandparents. But he did have adopted family in plenty, and he seemed closer to them than she had believed before Christmas. He had, she suspected, pretended to be more alienated, more distant from his family than he was, perhaps to seem more like her. In a way, that pretense was flattering. She tried to imagine Grandpa Dickinson dead. Did it hurt to die of stroke? Did someone know when they were dying? She closed her eyes and tried to imagine.

She sent Blake a fast e-mail and stuffed her laptop into her backpack. Laura and Rich sat in front; she was in back with luggage. Laura drove silently for the first three hours while Rich talked on his cell phone. Then he took over. While he drove, he talked. "Never expected Grandpa to go so fast. He was only seventy-seven, up with the cows. Skinny and tough as leather."

"Rich, what was Grandma like?" Melissa asked. She was trying to remember something that would make her sad.

A longish silence. "Haven't the faintest idea. Never met her. She died years and years ago of heart trouble."

Laura spoke for almost the first time, except to read the map and give directions. "The way everyone in the Dickinson family talks, you'd think your grandfather gave birth to his three children himself. She's been erased."

"Probably nothing to say about her. The old man was a strong character," Rich said.

"I never heard Father mention her," Melissa said. Three children always startled her. She forgot Edward—a lieutenant who died in Vietnam. He was trotted out from time to time in her father's speeches, along with free enterprise, the market economy, family values and order in our schools and on our streets. A photo of him in uniform was all she knew of Uncle Edward.

"Ask Dad if you want to," Rich said. "So how's school?"

The Dickinson family house was white clapboard on a bumpity drive that led straight up from the main road. They drove past the dark meadows with the moon eerily shining on the snow heaped over everything, to arrive at last on the circle of gravel before the house. The Dickinson home was symmetrical except for the outbuildings that straggled away joined by covered passageways: the barn, the henhouse, the woodshed, the shed that held tools and a tractor. It was clearly an old farmhouse, but it had a row of pillars supporting a semicircular porch, as if claiming to be a mansion instead. She remembered it as being always too hot or too cold.

There were several cars outside, including a rented car her parents must have taken from the nearest airport. Merilee's blue Miata was there. An old pickup that belonged to Grandpa was parked at an odd angle to the drive, to make room for the other cars and perhaps cars yet to come. She wondered where Grandpa's body was. She had been to many political funerals over the years, including "Uncle" Tony's. Rosemary had never liked Tony; she felt an alliance with him reflected poorly on Dick once he became governor. Melissa had eavesdropped on their argument.

Dick said firmly, "He helped me. I never let down someone who lent a hand."

"But he's an old ethnic loser, lucky to be a city judge. Why promote him?"

"Because loyalty is more important than who he is. He promoted me." It was one of the few times she had heard her father disagree vehemently with Rosemary. Rosemary had backed down.

She heard her father's resonant voice as she trudged after Laura and Rich into the entrance hall that bisected the downstairs. "Yes, I remember Mother laid out in the parlor. That was how they did it in those days. The undertaker fetched the body and then brought her back. It was more intimate, but a bit hard on kids, as you might imagine. Having the deceased there in the house. Of course it wasn't that way with Edward. When his remains were flown back, he was buried in Arlington. Full military honors. Rifle salute and all."

"It must have been traumatic for you having your departed mother in the parlor," Rosemary said soothingly. "I think it's a little . . . I don't know, barbaric?"

"It was the custom," Dick said. "Karen was more frightened than I was."

"Rich!" Rosemary trotted to meet them. She always wore heels. Even her bedroom slippers had heels. She was wearing a black suit, looking radiant in spite of the day's travels and what had to be exhaustion, getting everyone on the road, making arrangements. "Laura, you look lovely. Melissa, good, you got here. The viewing will be tomorrow. We have a funeral breakfast the next morning and then the service and burial in the family cemetery. We still have paperwork on that. Then of course the will."

"Where's Merilee?" Melissa asked, looking around.

"She's in the kitchen with Grandpa Dickinson's housekeeper. We've been holding supper till everyone arrives."

"Who else is coming?"

"I think we're all here now. Karen should arrive tomorrow."

"Is Karen out?" Melissa asked. Her favorite aunt had been confined to an institution for the last five years. Melissa understood it had something to do with her drinking.

"Well, she had to be released to attend the funeral," Rosemary said. "I do hope she'll behave herself."

It was hard for Melissa to imagine that Karen drank any harder than her parents or their friends. Even now everyone had a martini or a scotch grasped in their hands.

"Where's Billy? Isn't he coming?"

Rosemary ran her hand over her fine-boned face in a gesture of fatigue. "He went out with the hired man to the cows, who knows why? As if Billy could tell which end of a cow the milk comes from."

Melissa tossed her backpack against a wall until she would be assigned a room, then followed the hall to the kitchen, always the warmest room in the house, with a big old-fashioned coal stove to heat it and a huge equally old propane stove for cooking. Merilee was sitting at the white enamel table slicing carrots, while a woman probably in her late thirties stood at the stove stirring a large pot. "So I told him he should hire someone to make cheese. The cows are good cows. Anybody with some training could make fine cheese, but you know, he was a stubborn old man and he liked best to do things his own way."

"Melissa!" Merilee waved a languid hand to her. She had been drinking beer with the housekeeper. Merilee seldom drank, as far as Melissa knew, and she looked sleepy. Maybe she was just tired from traveling like everyone else. "Come on in. You know Liz Greene? She's been our grandfather's housekeeper for the last three years, since Ellen left."

Liz dried her hands on a big white apron to touch hands with Melissa. "You're the youngest?"

"No, Billy is. I'm the third from the top."

"You probably knew Ellen, then. She worked here twenty years, but she just plain got tired, she said." Liz had a thin horsey face with almost white hair, a natural blond with a little grey in it. Her hand was firm, callused and very warm. She turned to Merilee. "How are those carrots coming?"

"Slowly," Merilee said with a little giggle.

"I can help," Melissa said, and took a seat at the kitchen table. Even when her grandfather was alone, he always took his meals in the din-ingroom under the chandelier that hung a little crooked, as if it had been moved from someplace more grand. She began chopping carrots twice as fast as Merilee. Here was one thing she could do better than her sister. Maybe she should become a cook. "What are you making?" she asked Liz.

"A big beef and vegetable soup to feed the multitudes," Liz said wryly. "I had no idea I'd be cooking for so many, but probably this weekend is the last time I'll cook in this kitchen. What do you suppose they'll do with the house? Put it on the market, I expect."

"Grandpa left a will. He was always rewriting it, but he certainly had one," Merilee said. "He had contempt for people who died intestate."

"Leave it to his son, I expect, and he'll sell it."

"Grandpa was crazy about his cows," Melissa said. "He said they were kinder and more useful than people. He knows my father has no interest."

Liz shrugged. "They're good healthy cows. He's got ten of them now and a calf."

"He used to have a bull," Melissa remembered. The bull had chased her and Billy once. They'd had to scramble over the fence.

"Not while I've been coming here. I expect that was when he had a bigger herd. It wouldn't pay him to keep a bull these days."

Merilee had her head propped wearily on her hand. "I was up all night preparing for an exam today and then Mother called. I was planning to come tomorrow. I hated to postpone the exam. That professor doesn't care who dies, it's unimportant compared to his exam. But Mother wouldn't let me off. . . . He said he'd have his assistant give it to me Monday, so I have to keep studying."

"Do you like law school?" She was making conversation, feeling like an imitation adult. Asking questions she did not care about was a very adult thing.

"I mostly like it, although it would get me killed by my fellow students to admit it." Merilee sat up. Her blond hair, so similar to Rosemary's, gleamed under the overhead bulb. She was the one who had their mother's looks, although they had not come out quite so fine boned and angular on her. Merilee was more of a cheerleader type, Melissa thought, pretty rather than beautiful. Melissa would have settled for pretty. "I like solving problems. I like case law. I may go into litigation." Merilee slumped again. "Did Rich or Laura tell you?"

"Tell me what?"

"Laura's pregnant. They're delighted."

"Already? If I was just married, I'd wait."

"Rich wants a family ASAP. Looks good. He's already running for state rep. A family man always looks better, as Father says."

"Do you think you'll ever run for anything?"

"No! I actually want to practice law. And I'd never, never want to run for anything, not even animal control officer."

"But you did in school. You were class president twice and you were always running for something."

"That's the way I was in high school. Don't hold it against me." Merilee shook her pale hair. "I'm not running anymore."

Finishing the carrots, Melissa decided to go out to the barn and see the cows and Billy. Grabbing her coat from the pile in the hall, she passed through the covered passageway to the barn. It wasn't heated, but it kept the snow off. As she walked into the barn, she smelled hay and manure and cow urine and the sweet scent of smoke. The hired man, who was maybe twenty, was sitting with Billy on a pile of straw passing a joint back and forth. They both jumped. Billy said, "Hey, Sis. How are you doing? Want a hit?"

"Please." She never smoked except with Billy. But with her family, she needed help. Merilee had beer, the adults had scotch and vodka martinis, and Billy, she and the hired man scooched down in the hay smoking. "This is Oscar," Billy said. "He's cool."

"Now I'll be out of a job. I don't know what's going to happen with the cows."

"Everybody seems worried about them." She imagined bringing one back to school for a pet. They weren't allowed pets, not even goldfish. Rosemary hated the smell of cows, but Melissa rather liked it, even though after a while the barn made her sneeze.

THE VIEWING on Friday was weird. Her grandfather was wearing a navy suit and a crisp shirt, instead of his usual costume of overalls, a woodsman's buffalo plaid shirt and the muffler he wore knotted around his turkey neck except in the heat of summer. There was a steady line of people along the coffin saying the requisite things to the family. She was part of the receiving line. So was Karen, looking pale. Her reddish hair was streaked with grey and she had grown plump in the facility. She had always been a horsewoman and an athlete, playing tennis, golf, squash, anything she could excel at. Melissa was struck by a strong resemblance between Billy and Aunt Karen she had never recognized. It was not just that they both had that reddish blond hair that had skipped Melissa and Rich. They were—at least Karen had been—of the same full-bodied highly colored beauty, so different from Rosemary and Merilee. Melissa was glad to see her aunt, who was far less conventional than the rest of the family. She had never married. She had gone out for sports as was expected but too seriously. At one time she had been a professional tennis player, until an injury put a stop to her career. She had given tennis lessons for years, and Melissa played as well as she did because of her aunt.

It had been a wonderful treat to visit Karen alone, as she was allowed to do when she was eleven, taking the train to New York, where Karen was living in Chelsea. They went to Staten Island on the ferry and Radio City Music Hall and the Bronx Zoo and the Museum of Natural History, with its dinosaurs. She had even told herself a tale in which her aunt formally adopted her. It would be just the two of them having adventures, riding horses, taking planes, going to movies and musicals and amusement parks where Karen always hit the target and won the big fuzzy blue bear for her. They were both the third child in their generations.

How often had she thought of Karen since the sanitarium? She had seen her briefly two years before at Grandpa Dickinson's seventy-fifth birthday, but Karen had only been let out for the day, and there had been little opportunity to talk. Since then, her own fraught social life or lack of it had filled Melissa's consciousness. She tried to maneuver closer to

Karen in the receiving line. Finally she got Merilee to change places with her so she stood next to their aunt. "It's great to see you."

"It's great to be seen. I'm waiting to find out what happens."

"Can I come up to your room afterward?" Melissa whispered.

Karen nodded slightly and extended her hand to the next well-wisher. The line was mostly local people, but Vermont officials had shown up in honor of the Senator. Some were Democrats, but Melissa had figured out years before all politicians belonged to the same club. They had more in common with each other than with their constituents; the higher up they were, the truer that was.

Afterward, her parents invited the Republican officials back to the house for drinks, the combination of Washington and local gossip and intense partisan political discussion Dick thrived on. Merilee was studying in the kitchen. Billy had disappeared. Melissa crept off to Karen's room. "Wasn't this Grandpa's room?" It was actually the biggest bedroom in the house, looking toward the mountains in the daytime. Like the rest of the house, it was cold and a little damp.

"Right. I don't know if it's to placate me, or if no one else wanted to sleep in his bed."

"Karen, what happened to you? Did you like collapse or go on a bender and wake up like in Mexico sleeping with a toad?"

"How old are you now, Lissa?"

"Nineteen."

"Do you have a lover?"

Melissa paused, but she had always trusted Karen. She nodded. "But nobody, nobody in the family knows about him."

"Why? Is he Black or Jewish or something?"

"Both."

"Oh my god, you've hit the jackpot. But he is a guy?"

"Yeah. He has a motorcycle. He goes to Wesleyan with me."

Karen was sprawled in the bed in pajamas and an old woolen robe Melissa was sure had belonged to Grandpa. "Keep it to yourself as long as you can. They don't react well to unusual choices. Mine wasn't a guy at all."

"It was a woman?"

"Much of one." Karen blew out a perfect smoke ring. "Eve was not only a lesbian but a leftie and that did it. Dick got my dad to commit me to Mountain View Rehabilitation Center, a facility for misfits from wealthy families."

"That's horrible. Couldn't you get a lawyer?"

"If I didn't agree, they were going to get Eve. With a little help from your friendly FBI and state police, the IRS, you can get almost anyone for something. So I took the rest cure. I thought they'd let me out in six months, but they just parked me and forgot to open the gate. But I'm out now and I'm not, not, not going back. Ever!"

"You need a good lawyer. My boyfriend's father is a famous lawyer in Philadelphia."

"I might take you up on that." Karen yawned. "Now it's way past my bedtime, although it's going to be weird trying to sleep without the nurse handing out the go-to-sleep-little-sheep tabs. I've been so overmedicated, it will be a year before the shit leaves my system. . . . You're looking good, Lissa. You look human, unlike most of the rest of this bunch of cannibals."

They had burned part of Karen away, Melissa could tell, but there was still enough left so she hoped that her aunt could manage to stay free. She would be an ally. She always had been.

The funeral was interminable. Dick was handsome in a finely tailored black suit he had worn at important funerals in Pennsylvania. Dick never put on a pound, any more than Rosemary did. She stood tiny but regal, resplendent in a long black dress, and everyone gazed at them. Dick gave a moving eulogy to his father that Rosemary had written that morning on her laptop in the kitchen. Melissa found it hard to believe that her mother had really liked Grandpa, because he certainly had been nasty to her for the first ten years of her marriage. He pretended he couldn't remember Rosemary's name, addressing her as Mary Rose, Rosalie, Rosamund. He'd introduce his son to local people and pointedly refuse to introduce the wife. But Rosemary believed in breeding, in blood, in all the things that Grandpa too believed in. He was a man prone to dismissing most ethnic groups as the scum of the earth. She had heard Grandpa use the phrase fifty times. Finally after Rosemary had produced a governor out of his son, he must have forgiven her the undistinguished Baptist family from Youngstown, Ohio, and considered her an honorary member of WASP nobility. Rosemary had never been less than respectful and affectionate with him. He was the patriarch, and Rosemary believed in the natural superiority of men. That had nothing to do with intelligence or ability, except for the ability to rule.

Dick liked his father well enough, but Melissa would never have described them as close. She doubted they had ever had a personal conversation except for perhaps the time when Dick announced he was marrying Rosemary and Grandpa exploded in contempt. Yet they seemed to think each other fine. Many times, she had tried to imagine what went on inside Grandpa: all she could come up with was a large cold empty room with a clock on the wall ticking furiously and a calendar on one white wall with a picture of a cow.

Sunday Grandpa's lawyer called them all into the parlor for a reading of Grandpa's will. "To my beloved son Richard Tertius, of whose career I am rightfully satisfied, I hereby bequeath all my personal papers, the family photos including the historical treasures of our legacy, the silver that I received from my own father, any of my personal items he may desire and my horse Legerdemain, as every gentleman should possess a horse. I also bequeath to him the pair of dueling pistols I inherited from my own father, which belonged to my Great-grandfather Lucas Dickinson. Also my silver duck-headed cane. I leave him the contents of my checking account at First National Bank of Montpelier so he may act as executor and carry out the provisions of this will.

"To my beloved grandson Richard IV, I bequeath the sword our Great-great-grandfather wore as an officer in the Union army, along with a copy of the book he wrote about his exploits. I also bequeath to him the pastel of our Great-great-grandmother Malvina, who was a cousin to Robert E. Lee.

"To my granddaughters and younger grandson, they may select something from the house that pleases them, providing that it is not an item desired by their father or needed by the owner of the house.

"To my daughter, Karen Bernice, I bequeath the house and land, the cows and my gelding Lancelot and the mare Guinevere. I ask that she spare the cows the butcher's block and keep them in good health on the land until they may die a natural death. I also leave her the contents of my savings account at First National Bank of Montpelier, so she may be able to pay the expenses of the farm until she is self-sufficient again. I also leave her my stocks, of which my lawyer has a list. They should provide some income. All of the bequeathals to my daughter, Karen, are provisional upon her promise never to see Eve Kalman again so long as she may live."

"Well, that's easy," Karen said dryly, "Eve died piloting her plane three years ago. You all wouldn't let me go to the funeral."

Afterward, the family went out to Sunday dinner without Karen or the local people. Karen was busy trying to inventory the house and go over the books. Merilee had left early, to be back for her makeup exam. "Well, I'm a bit surprised," Dick said, sipping a predinner martini. "The old man had a soft spot for Karen."

"What would we do with the farm, besides sell it? I doubt it's worth much. I did hope he'd leave us the stock," Rosemary said.

"He had to provide for Karen. He'd taken her out of circulation for five years," Rich said. "That or we'd have to pay for Mountain View. I for one would really object to that."

"But really, to leave Rich a rusty old sword and an ill-painted portrait," Laura said. "What could he be thinking of? Personally I wonder if we couldn't have redone the place into a nice summer home."

Rosemary shot Laura a warning look. "Rich can't spend summers in Vermont, Laura. Be sensible. He has a lot of preparation. I'm sure Karen would be pleased to have you come up occasionally once your child is born."

Melissa had picked out a doorstop in the shape of a horse, coveted since she was little. Karen gave her a gold locket she said had been her own mother's, with a dried flower inside. That was more than Melissa had expected from her grandfather, but she could tell, as she looked around the table, that everyone else was tasting a sour disappointment. "What are you going to do with your horse?" she asked her father. Maybe he'd give the horse to her, and she could stable it near Wesleyan. Did Blake ride? She'd ask him. She saw herself riding weekends.

"Still little Miss Muffet, worried about horses and spiders and everything living." He put his hand on her shoulder and squeezed gently, giving her the full benefit of his radiant smile, eyes locked with hers. "We'll leave him here, in his home. Don't worry about the cows or horses. Karen is sentimental about animals too. They'll be fine. You're a sweetheart to care. I remember when you wanted to be a veterinarian. And you loved that spaniel, didn't you?"

"Good idea," Rosemary said. "Karen can feed the horse. After all, she got the stocks. I'm told that in the checking account there is only twenty-two hundred. There has to be more in the savings. He was a frugal man."

Rich and Laura planned to depart from the restaurant and drop her at Wesleyan. Tonight she would sleep in her own bunk, instead of that drafty room in the creaky cold house in a bed that sagged like a hammock. She would see Blake. She would see Emily and Fern, whom she vaguely remembered had wanted to talk to her about something. She would be back in her own life again.

CHAPTER THIRTEEN

Melissa was sitting curled in Blake's arm on his bed.

"So you told your aunt about me?" He sounded pleased.

"I thought she was the least likely to go ripshit. She's very accepting, and besides, I just learned she had a lesbian affair with another woman who may have been a Communist."

"Most lesbian affairs are with women, babes." He tousled her hair. "Let's go see her one of these weekends. It sounds as if she could use the help."

"Really? Would you do that?"

"Providing nobody announces an exam for Monday or a paper due, we could get out of here on a Friday afternoon. Weather permitting, because I want to take my bike out for a good long run."

"Blake, that would make me really happy. She's always been my favorite aunt, but I hadn't seen her for years!"

"Didn't you ever go visit her?"

She shrugged. "It all sounded so depressing. I thought maybe she'd blown it."

"Still, you should have investigated for yourself." He looked disappointed in her. "Taking your family's word for it was the lazy way. You let her down."

That evening she got an e-mail from Phil, Blake's nerdy friend, reminding her that she was going to work with him on some research. She had hoped he and Blake had forgotten. He offered her a grid of possible times to get together, so that she couldn't just fuzz out. Phil was going to teach her the rudiments of researching someone—in this case, most likely her father. She felt a little clammy when she thought of actually going through with what she had promised. She knew it was the correct thing for her to do, but she couldn't quite believe that emotionally. It felt sleazy. But it wasn't real. She had to keep that in mind. Investigating her father was just a time waster, and she would turn it to advantage by using it to help her father change into someone with more conscience, more empathy, more soul. That was her duty. It was her way to make an impact on her family and win her father back. Even Blake could not guess how much she wanted her father's attention, her father's approval. All this investigative stuff was just fodder for her plan.

Blake was so pleased when she told him she had an appointment with Phil that she couldn't allow him to know how little she wanted to go through with it. She would learn what Phil could teach her; after all, they were just kids, just students, so it was all pretend anyhow. Roger Lippett had tried for years to smear her father and never succeeded, so why did she imagine some computer nerd could possibly damage him? This way she could keep an eye on Phil.

Phil was engaged in amassing long lists of contributors to Dick's campaigns and to organizations supporting him—the Clean Government Forum, Taxpayers' Rights for Dickinson, a host of others. Some names she could identify, but he wanted more than descriptions. They were looking for interlocking directorates of corporations and institutions to identify the interests of the men—and it was eighty percent men—who had given and given again, whose pockets were deep for Dick. They were looking for men with positions in institutions or corporations or large holdings in them, in the library and on the computer searching databases, annual reports, *Who's Who,* stock market reports. Progress was slow. It was more boring than she had anticipated, but she would keep at it, since it meant something to Blake. Most Saturday afternoons for the next month she would give Phil a couple of hours, identifying the interests of big contributors. It was boring and disappointing. What in this could possibly help her reach her father, communicate with him? Hey, Dad, guess what, I noticed that GE and Du Pont gave you a lot of money, huh? Way to start a great conversation.

With all that was going on with her family and with Blake, Melissa forgot that Fern had said she wanted to talk with her. It wasn't until Fern had been giving her reproachful looks for days that finally Melissa remembered. "You wanted to talk with me? I've been trying to be less of a slob."

"I feel like I have to talk about this. Because maybe you won't want to room with me?"

"Did I do something?"

"Oh, no." Melissa kept thinking Fern was going to slide off her bed and land on the floor, she held herself so bolt upright on the extreme edge. "It's me. Not you. I mean I think it's me."

"I don't follow."

"It's what I think I am."

"Fern, you're making me feel really really dense. Like a raving idiot. What are you talking about?"

"I think I might be a lesbian . . ."

"Oh." Melissa sat upright herself. "Do you mean . . . like you're attracted to me?"

"God, no. I'm attracted to a woman on my soccer team. It's always in sports. Like you look at each other's bodies and she's so buff and fine."

"Have you talked to her?"

"I haven't had the nerve. I could screw everything up for myself." Fern wrung her hands, twisting, miserable. "And I don't know how to be a lesbian. I've never known any, I mean that I knew for sure. I don't have a clue how you meet women and what you say . . ."

"I'm no expert, but Open House has parties. I think you should go." It was one of the houses that, after freshman year, students could go and live in, in this case to identify as gay or lesbian. There were houses for African-American students, students who were into politics, into service, into the arts, whatever.

"I've been nervous about that. I mean, I was afraid I would be just too naïve and clumsy and make a fool of myself."

"I mean, if I was gay, I'd think that was cute—like you were innocent and I'd want to show you. Don't you think that might happen?"

"You don't want to move out because I told you this?"

Melissa shook her head. She was not about to say it, but the first thing that had gone through her head was that Fern wouldn't be interested in Blake then, since they were not infrequently thrown together. "It's cool. I hope you can get more comfortable with yourself. I think this is a great place to come out. Really! Besides, my favorite aunt is gay."

When she told Emily—Fern had sworn her to secrecy, but she never felt that included Emily—Em said, "You know, I kind of wondered. She never seems to look at hot guys or want to go to parties or mixers or anything."

"I just thought she was shy."

"Well, obviously she is. But now it all makes sense. We have to be careful to keep Whitney and Ronnie from finding out. They won't be down with it." Em smiled slightly. "I wonder what it's like with a woman?"

"I don't think Fern knows any more than you do."

THE SECOND WEEKEND in April was mild. In Middletown and even on the surrounding hills and ledges, the snow had melted. Daffodils were blooming in gardens as they swept out of town. She was excited—this was their first trip together, the longest time on his motorcycle, and she was introducing him to her aunt, a tentative connection beyond the couple. But above all, it was spring. That morning she'd heard geese passing over as she trotted to class. Now she was gripping his back and holding tight and they were rushing north. She was sure she had felt nothing in her life as fully as she felt being with Blake. She was a different person now, her nerves, her body, her heart, her brain all forced into flower like a branch of forsythia brought into the house before the buds had begun to open on their own. From bare dead-looking branches, Alison persuaded flowers to open to adorn Rosemary's desk. Blake had opened her into full bloom.

She wished they were going south on 91 into fuller spring, instead of north. As time and the miles passed, the season regressed. It grew chillier. Her thighs ached from gripping. Her kidneys hurt. Her discomfort grew but her joy remained. They could not talk on the bike, but she felt as if they were in strong and perfect communication, pressed together and riding the wind, as he called it.

They stopped for a late lunch in Brattleboro, not far across the Vermont line. It was a town that still had something of a hippie milieu, so nobody paid attention as they sat in a booth eating hamburgers and home fries. He beamed into her eyes, as happy as she felt. "This is a good thing," he said. "We're moving along together. Is that what you want?" He waited for her emphatic nod. "Because that's what I want. To be blended together. To be one."

She did not know what he meant. It sounded romantic, but they were so different their oneness was hard to imagine. She took it as a pledge of love. Her Blake was a romantic, and that was sweet. She passionately hoped things would go well with Karen, because she just knew he would be bruised if the weekend went badly. Of all her relatives, she trusted Karen most to be up to the situation, not to embarrass or humiliate her. If only they could live their whole lives the way they did at school, invisible to their families and their families irrelevant. That was paradise enough. That was freedom from the intolerable burden of being her parents' third and least-favored child.

They reached the farm by three thirty. The sky was blue, but shadows of the mountains were creeping over the pastures. Snow still clung to the sides of the road, although south-facing slopes were clear. It was full mud season. They bucked and splashed up the road to the columned farmhouse. When Melissa jumped off the bike, her knees buckled. Blake caught her with a grin. "Takes some getting used to. You'll straighten out in a minute or two."

Karen had been out in the barn. She was wearing old green corduroy pants and one of Grandpa's plaid shirts, her red-grey hair loose and her skin wind-reddened. Everybody shook hands awkwardly. Melissa felt like running, fleeing down the steep road. Why had she engineered this? It was going to be stupid and clumsy all weekend. She scarcely knew her aunt after five years, and why should Blake care?

Melissa was surprised to see Liz come out of the kitchen, wiping her hands on a denim apron. She said, "I'm glad to see you."

"Your aunt kept me on."

"I haven't seen a stove in a decade. I'd starve to death on frozen suppers." Karen gestured toward the kitchen, the one warm room in the house. "Come have coffee or tea or whatever. Beer? Liz's husband brews it."

"Nasty stuff," Liz said. "I won't touch it. But Karen likes it. Or she's too polite to say."

"I drink it, don't I? I'm off the wagon, but only for beer. After all these years dry, I'm a cheap drunk. One bottle is my limit."

"Coffee, if you don't mind," Blake said. "We're both chilled."

Liz perked coffee and put out a crumb cake. "I have supper in the oven. Just take it out when you're ready to eat. I'm off. The old man and I are stepping out tonight, over to White River."

"Have fun," Karen said, walking Liz to the door. Things had changed. They were on a first-name basis and seemed relaxed with each other. Only the cows had ever been at ease with Grandpa. When Melissa was little, he had scared her. When she was a teenager, she fled as fast as she could on horseback up the mountain and stayed away from him. Looking in the refrigerator for milk to put in her coffee, she noticed the buff wheels of cheese always filling half of it had disappeared. Karen too must have disliked the huge gum erasers.

"You got rid of the cheese?"

"First thing. The crows ate it. And the raccoons."

"You're keeping Liz on indefinitely, then?" Melissa asked. "It seems like you two get on well."

"Liz didn't always stay here. She took off and lived on the edge for years. Hard drinking. Dancing in bars. Up and down the East Coast all the way to the Keys and then out to Texas. Got really sick, went into rehab, then came back here. We understand each other. Couple of retired hard cases."

"Are you going to stay up here and run the farm?" Blake asked. "You seem more of a city person."

"Used to think I'd shrivel if I got farther up the Hudson than Nyack.

But as I'm sure Melissa explained, I've been incarcerated the last five years. That's like they cut a hunk out of you."

Blake stared at her, sitting down backward on a kitchen chair. "Yeah. I can imagine. Even though I don't guess it was a hard-time place."

"Very genteel. Very dull. Five whole years wasted in the equivalent of high school study hall. It's an old-fashioned sort of redbrick storage device for the sons and daughters and wives of the Establishment who bug their families too much. Alcoholics, kleptomaniacs, addicts of various sorts, cross-dressers, misbehaving wives with too many assets to divorce, the broken and abused—few of the abusers. A real mental institution that depends on state funding or insurance, they kick you out in a week, but there are people from wealthy families there who have been locked up for forty years. They couldn't cross the road by themselves after all this time."

Blake rested his chin on his arms folded over the back of the straight chair. "All because you had a girlfriend?"

"It was who she was."

"Rosemary said she was a Communist," Melissa cut in.

"Not even. Actually she was a believer in democracy. But they thought she was trouble, and she tried to be. She was passionate about the environment. They called her an ecoterrorist, but she never terrorized anybody but Dick and Rosemary's imagination."

"Did you love her?" Melissa asked. "Do you have a photo?"

"I had lots of them, but I suspect they went into the fireplace when I went into Mountain View. They wanted to erase her from the face of the earth."

Blake tilted back and forth in his chair, frowning. "Do you think her death was really an accident?"

"I don't think once I was tucked away that Dick or Rosemary had a motive. Anyhow, they wouldn't go that far. Discredit her, yes. Start rumors, sure. Use their pets in the press, why not. Cook up some legal or financial trouble, sure thing. But what do you think, they went out in the woods with a missile launcher?"

"You can't dismiss the possibility someone was out to eliminate her."

"She liked risk. She loved flying. She had an instrument rating, but often she flew when it made me nervous. Yes, I can believe she went down in a thunderstorm over Illinois. I do believe that."

Melissa was leaning on the big old stove. "You didn't answer me, if you loved her."

"With all my heart, with all my strength. The funny thing about being committed was, I hadn't been drinking so much with her. I started drinking too much after I gave up on tennis. After I met Eve, I didn't need the bottle."

"I'd still like to see the reports on the accident," Blake said.

"I know. You want to see if the family is capable of putting out a contract, when they learn about the two of you." Karen grinned. "They're nasty, but they don't kill people."

"I'm not so sure of that," Blake said very quietly. "Do you suppose supper is warm? I'm ravenous."

MELISSA COULD TELL they liked each other. "He is absolutely gorgeous," Karen said to her as they went riding the next morning.

Blake declined to get on a horse. "Two feet good. Four feet bad."

Karen continued, as they took their horses slowly up the trail, "He seems bright and well-spoken. No matter what blather Dick and Rosemary spout when they finally meet him, you could do one hell of a lot worse. He's a keeper."

Melissa felt blessed. As they took their short ride, turning around when the snow became too deep and the going treacherous, she remembered many summer rides with Karen when she had been eight, ten, twelve. Riding had been an escape for both of them from Grandpa's rigid expectations and the cold unpleasant regimen of the farmhouse. Being in Vermont had been a mixed experience. She felt disregarded by Grandpa, parked here by her parents for convenience. Yet she loved the farm animals, she loved when Karen was around. She adored running up the mountain to sit on a rock and feel herself completely, beatifically alone.

To be alone was a rare pleasure. There were always her siblings. If not always her parents, there were the people who worked for them, did for them, wrote Dick's speeches and press releases, planned his campaigns, raised money and spent it, nannies, tutors, cleaning women, cooks, caterers, secretaries of various sorts, interns, assistants, aides. Eyes were always on her.

To be alone was to stare at everything, feeling herself the only, the private consumer of these mountains, these ledges and firs and brambles, the birds that crossed her path, the animals rustling the underbrush. All for her and her alone, the squirrels, the weasels, rabbits. She loved them with her eyes and ears, she gobbled them, she relished them. Then she would sink into one or another fantasy without danger of being caught daydreaming, a capital offense in Rosemary's eyes. She would spin out elaborate movie plots starring herself, with no one to interrupt, no one to make her lie about what she was thinking. She felt then as if she had really escaped her life, her self, her circumscribed destiny.

She had not been supposed to read comic books: Rosemary was passionately opposed to them. But Billy and she had managed to buy them in secret, for they both liked the adventures of superheroes, sharing them the way they shared an occasional toke nowadays. She had not imagined herself to be a mutant with powers like the X-Men because she liked better to imagine hidden powers that no one would guess until she revealed them. Suddenly she would emerge from her quiet ordinary shell and save everybody. Then they would admire her. Then they would see the powerful and wonderful being she hid inside.

Now she rarely fantasized that way. She had not realized the change until this moment bobbing on the roan mare Guinevere behind Karen, who was riding Legerdemain, the horse that Grandpa had left to her father. She enjoyed on a normal day short piercing fantasies about Blake taking her here or there, sharing something that she had enjoyed, making love in different places, getting married. Having children. She imagined his family embracing her. They would protect her from the scorn of her own.

But these daydreams were fleeting. All those years, as long as she could remember from first grade on, she had carried her stories with her as some girls carried knitting. They were ready to open for her in dull classes, during lectures, during boring concerts and bad movies, when she was supposed to be studying in her room, when she was sitting at agonizingly stiff family dinners that seemed to last a week. What had happened to those fantasies? Blake. Blake had happened in all his real body and strong will and sweet succulent smile. Blake had touched her, and all those heroes of a decade of imagining had turned to powder and blown away. Suddenly the path seemed too long and she wanted to be back in the farmhouse with him.

Karen was talking about Eve. "She was always up for everything, but mostly she led the way. I'd never gone white-water rafting before Eve, and I'm sure I never will again."

"You didn't like it?"

"Only with her. She loved adventure. She loved testing herself. Together we had this illusion we were invincible. . . . Blake said you were researching something about Dick?"

"I want to be a reporter, you know? Like an investigative reporter? So Blake put me in touch with a guy whose father does that, and he's learning to do the same thing. I'm getting the how-tos from him. Daddy is just the obvious subject, that's all."

"You don't have to be defensive with me. Eve and I were pushing on him about his role in the Susquehanna River debacle. . . . You know, we had a lot of material. I wonder what happened to it? Eve probably still had it when she died, but I think when they put me away, she lost heart."

"The Susquehanna River project? I vaguely remember that." She had loved the melody of the name. Dick had a plaque on his office wall honoring his role in the project.

"The Susquehanna River Basin Commission is a tristate effort to clean up the Susquehanna and its tributaries, to control flooding, to develop green tourism and manage water use," Karen rattled off. Obviously at one time she had talked about it a lot. "It was supported by environmental groups—including the one Eve was on the board of—along with fishing and recreational interests and local residents not too fond of cancer and floods."

"I remember Father giving speeches for it. So why do you call it a debacle?"

"Baby niece, he may have given speeches blessing it, but he screwed us. He took the protocols we had worked out and watered them down to suit the big polluters, so that they might have sounded great in a sound bite on the evening news, but little real got done, and that little the people of the state paid for, not the polluters. He had a big contributor who developed golf courses. Now golf courses used to water only tees and greens, but in recent years, they've been watering fairways as well—and thus using one hell of a lot of water."

"I always thought of golf courses as being boring but benign. Just a bunch of middle-aged people walking around banging on balls and then ending up in the clubhouse drinking themselves sodden."

"Not only do they use way too much water, they frequently dump herbicides and pesticides into the drinking water. The Commission had been trying to get golf courses to sign on to the protocols about water use, but your father unilaterally excluded them."

"A golf course, could it really matter that much? That's a big long river."

"It doesn't take a lot in the water to cause cancer. It was during his reelection campaign for governor that Dick got Father to stash me away. I don't imagine Dick had trouble talking the old man into it."

"So why did he leave you the farm, then?"

Karen looked back over her shoulder at her, shaking her head. "Because I'm good with animals. So he left his cows and horses to the one person who would take their well-being seriously. It wasn't to take care of me, Melissa. It was to take care of his beloved cows."

"By the way, my roommate at college is a lesbian," Melissa said. She was feeling proud of herself about how cool she had been when Fern told her, and she figured that might be worth a few points with her aunt.

"Yeah? I hope her family takes it better than ours did." Karen looked back over her shoulder, giving the reins a little shake to move Legerdemain along faster. "Good luck to her. She may need it."

CHAPTER FOURTEEN

Melissa and Blake went up a second time to Vermont, to visit Karen. The snow was gone, the cows, out to pasture cropping grass. Liz had talked Karen into a goat named Thelma, and the chickens were laying madly. Karen said she was settling in. "After Mountain View, this place is buzzing with excitement. It's about all I'm capable of handling. We're putting in a kitchen garden. Even I can pick lettuce and boil beans."

FERN AND MELISSA were watching Emily getting dressed, changing her clothes, tossing them around the room. Whitney had gone to a frat party. Melissa rescued a red silk top from the floor. "I always liked this color on you."

"It emphasizes the sad fact that I have no tits." Em threw it back.

"How about the blue stripe?"

"Makes me look fat."

"You aren't fat," Melissa said plaintively. "You're absolutely skinny!"

When Emily had left and Fern and Melissa returned to their own room, Fern said, "Emily doesn't like her body much, does she?"

"I used to hate mine too."

"It seems too weird. To hate yourself. I mean, she isn't ugly or deformed."

"Do you like your body?"

Fern thought for a moment. "I guess I do. I mean, it works just fine. I like to push myself hard, in practice, doing laps, but that makes me feel good. If I didn't like my body, I'd work out more, that's all."

"It isn't that simple!" Melissa shook her hair back. She was growing it out the way Blake had asked her to. "None of us are really beautiful."

Fern looked at her blankly. "Yeah, but since none of us are, why does it matter? It's like saying none of us are six feet six or double-jointed."

"You are."

"I'm just flexible." Fern could do backflips and not only touch her toes but lay her palms on the ground by her feet.

"I hated my body until Blake liked it," Melissa said.

Fern looked at her with visible pity.

THE NEXT TIME Blake went to New York, he let her come along. They stayed with Slam, a friend of his from high school who was going to NYU and lived off Avenue C in a small dirty apartment whose floors creaked and seemed to sway when she walked across them. Downstairs was a falafel place. The apartment smelled of cooking oil and insecticide. They slept on a mattress on the floor. She had never done that, and it was kind of romantic in a way, like that musical the gay guy on Blake's hall kept playing, *Rent*. But everything was dirty and she hated using the bathroom. She was sorry she had nagged Blake to come.

Slam smoked incessantly. His body was like a half-melted icicle, thin but shapeless. She thought he was as dirty as his quarters. He wore the backwards baseball cap and baggy pants of the rapper wanna-be. Fortunately he was hardly ever there except to sleep and recharge his cell phone.

Saturday afternoon, Blake told her to go shopping or to a museum. "Got to see my hacker friends. I bring anybody along, they'll go bullshit. I need them a lot more than they need my couple of bucks."

"What is it you need?"

"Just some programs. I'll meet you back here at six and we'll have supper in the Village. Then take a long walk all over and have a drink at an outdoor café. Maybe catch some jazz. I promise a great evening. But I have to see them now." He swept from the apartment and she heard him forcing his bike through the hall and out. She knew he was bound for Williamsburg. She left immediately afterward, freaked by the cockroaches that ran all over the kitchen and the bathroom. This was sordid. No wonder he hadn't wanted to bring her before, while she had accused him mentally of infidelity or being ashamed of her. She ought to trust him more. No one thought more about her true well-being. She went to the Guggenheim, soothed by its ambience of clean lines and money. The last time she had been here had been with her aunt.

Blake had an amazing number of acquaintances. She knew no one to stay with in New York—so maybe they could have been in a nice clean hotel—but Blake seemed to know people wherever he might be dropped. He got on with a wide assortment of types. He had a gift for sounding formal with the formal, casual with the casual, and streetwise with the streetwise. The very cadences of his voice would change when he spoke to Slam or to her. It was a chameleon gift he used without being conscious of it. When she called him on his changes, he looked at her blankly. It was just what he did, instinctively, unconsciously, but very well.

She bought a sandwich and ate a late lunch on the concrete rim of the plaza of an office building, watching people go by and studying what the women were wearing. A dude tried to pick her up, but she got rid of him without having to move. She window-shopped, bought herself some nice underwear at Saks—Blake might enjoy the change from her utilitarian kit—then slowly made her way to Washington Square Park, where she sat for an hour near guys playing chess. Finally the shadows grew long and it was time to meet him. She took a cab. The subway was beyond her, puzzling and a little frightening. When she got to the apartment, Blake was there and so was Slam, arguing about whether raves were truly liberating. Blake disliked the chaos, she knew that. She always felt buffeted, invisible except when some creep glommed on. And if you didn't do drugs, it felt pointless.

THE END OF the semester was nearing, making her anxious. Her parents were not going to spend the summer in Philadelphia, although they would surely visit often enough for Dick to fuss over his constituency, pat their heads and tummies, stroke his supporters, milk them if he could. The rest of the summer except for two weeks in August, when they would visit a backer who had a summer house on an island in Maine, they were staying put in Washington. Rosemary had not worked all those years to get there in order to leave it so quickly. Next year, Melissa thought, she and Blake should enroll in some summer program rather than go home. Too bad Wesleyan had no summer semester.

One morning, Blake e-mailed her. "I got it! It came through. I'll be studying intensive Russian in Washington from June 15 to August 15—so we'll be together. My father arranged for me to stay in the house of a lawyer colleague of his in Bethesda, so we won't be that far apart."

"Bethesda? Isn't that in Maryland?"

"I keep forgetting you don't know Washington that well. Look, you just go out Wisconsin, one block from your house, right? And keep going. Let's celebrate! A guy on my floor is going to buy a bottle of champagne for us. Tomorrow night I'll get takeout and we'll hang one on. Now will you be happy? You should have faith I'll manage for us."

Now the crisis with her family would loom. Still, she needed Blake, she needed to be with him. Rosemary would just have to eat it. After all, it wasn't the same as when Merilee brought home some guy Rosemary deemed unsuitable; surely Rosemary didn't expect Melissa to fetch a prize. She couldn't keep them in the dark forever.

Congress was still in session when she got home, well before Blake was to arrive. Alison had a summer job lined up for her as a glorified gofer at one of those organizations that shunted money to her father, Citizens for the Right Way. The Right Way was just an office on K, a reception area with a long counter, leather chairs and potted tropical plants, four executive offices, the harried secretaries of the pool, the mail room and her. Her desk was in a corner of the mail room. She was sent out for coffee, takeout, particular requests from the newsstand two blocks away, sent to deliver papers across town. She spent much time tracking FedEx and UPS packages and missives and taking deposits to the bank. She helped send out fund-raising mailings. Often she sat in the mail room reading. She tried to practice her scanty Spanish on the two guys who worked there, but that was pretty much a lost cause. She would spend five minutes piecing together a sentence. Then either they would look at her as if she were crazy or one would answer and she wouldn't understand. It was irritating for them and boring for her. After the first week, they ignored one another.

As she e-mailed Emily, she was marking time until Blake got there, hanging around the house so that her parents would grow bored with her and be glad when Blake arrived and she would be out more. In the last days of Congress, her father was pushing hard to get his maiden bill voted on, but the chances, she understood, were lessening every day. Rosemary was in high gear. She was mounting a campaign to woo the chairman of the committee that would vote the bill out to the full Senate or decide to let it die ignominiously. It was for Mr. Potts mostly, as far as Melissa could tell, and other backers in the trucking business. It had to do with tonnage. The bill itself was never discussed, only how to get it through. Apparently Rosemary had run into the chairman's wife at some boutique and they'd lunched together. Rosemary was now her bosom pal. They had coffee, they had lunch, they shopped together regularly. Rosemary was working all the angles. Billy was at hockey camp. Merilee was interning for the summer in a law firm in New York. Rosemary was not pleased that her favorite daughter was away. Blake was still forwarding the family e-mail to Melissa. She had gotten accustomed to learning about all of them from Rosemary's notes.

Merilee wrote:

I'm hardly alone. I have three roommates, I work in a windowless office with five other interns. I take the subway with millions of commuters morning and night five days a week. I go to Jones Beach with a million swimmers on the weekends. Alone? That would be heaven. I haven't been alone outside the bathroom since I got here—and sometimes not there.

What Rosemary could not object to was the caliber of the law firm. But Melissa knew that her mother did not like Merilee too far away. She worried about the unsuitable. She was afraid that Merilee would slip from her achieved perch on the glass mountain of unutterable perfection. Melissa knew that Rosemary would love to run up to New York and check out Merilee's scene, interview her roommates and associates—but her duty to the Senator and his maiden bill prevented her from getting away even for a day. So she fretted via e-mail.

Whom are you seeing out of the office? With whom do you associate in the office and after work? I wish you would give me more information about these roommates.

Occasionally Rosemary's eye-beam fixed on Melissa. "Have you made any friends at work?"

"Don't be absurd, Mother. The two guys in the mail room are Puerto Rican and they talk to each other in fast Spanish. The secretaries are years older than me. Nobody's my age. The comptroller and the vice president are not about to hang out with me."

"How about other offices in the same building? I'm sure there are young women in the same situation as yourself working there during the summer."

"They keep me busy. I don't have time to scope out the other offices."

"There's always time to make connections if they're desirable. Use your lunch hours. I suppose you miss Emily, but you can't rely on old contacts forever."

It occurred to her if she invented friends at work, she would have a cover for seeing Blake when he arrived. "I'll try, Mother. I promise I'll make an effort," she said fervently. "I'll use my lunch hours as you suggest. That's a great idea."

Every day she communicated with Emily as well as Blake. Em had gone to New York with friends for a weekend, picked up a musician, and now she had body lice. She had to keep her parents from finding out, so she hid the medicine and tried hard not to scratch in front of them.

How totally gross,

Melissa typed.

Are they big as cockroaches?

Emily wrote back:

No, they're little, but they itch like elephants!

That Thursday, Rosemary made her call in sick to work—as if they would miss her—to drag her off to a committee hearing. This was not a glamorous bill, so only minimal press was present, two photographers—one from some trade journal—and three reporters, sitting in a row on the floor against one wall of the paneled room. Dick was up there behind the long table with his aides hovering. He was questioning some old guy very gently about the needs of interstate trucking. Melissa thought she had seen him once with Joe, Dick's chief of staff, who was present, perched in the audience but in and out of the room. Melissa must have dozed off, because Rosemary poked her sharply. "Sit up!"

She had no idea why Rosemary had insisted on bringing her, but perhaps her mother considered this part of her education. Rosemary had dragged her to the Senate gallery twice before she left for college. The surprise was how few senators were on the floor at any given time. Those who were often were chatting or wandering around. Nobody seemed to be listening to the speeches. Most senators were holed up in their Cloakroom—which had nothing to do with cloaks or even coats but was a working hangout, Rosemary told her—in their offices or roaming the corridors looking for other senators to buttonhole on their pet projects. Today all the committee members apparently were present, but the hearings droned on and on until they broke for lunch.

Dick came over. "No reason to hang around. They're not taking a vote today and this afternoon will be abysmally technical."

"Do you have everything you need?" Rosemary asked nervously.

He looked to Joe, who nodded, a sheaf of papers under his arm as usual. Then Joe took Dick by the arm and steered him off to a group waiting to speak with him. Rosemary and she left. What a wasted morning.

Still, she was determined to prove to her father her new political interest and maturity, so the next time she could catch his attention, Saturday noon as they were picking at leftovers in the kitchen, she began, "I've been trying to understand globalization, Daddy—"

"It's just free markets, sweetheart. Bringing people closer together—"

"But I've been reading about what it does to the poor people in those—"

"If that's what they teach you at Wesleyan, I want my money back." He patted her shoulder. "Leave it to the economists. It's complex, my girl."

The following Tuesday, Dick's bill was voted out of committee, a first step and a victory for Rosemary's diplomacy as well as his own. Now the game was to get the Senate to act on it before they recessed. Melissa was paying more attention to her parents' political maneuvering since she had decided on investigative journalism and since Blake always asked so many questions. She found herself restive, itchy. Finally she realized with a shock that not only did she miss Blake but she missed sex. She masturbated—something she hadn't done since arriving at Wesleyan—but it was not satisfying. She wanted his touch and the feel of his long supple body against her own. She wanted him inside her, not her finger. Sometimes, in spite of her restlessness, she simply quit out of boredom before she could reach orgasm.

She almost hated to leave the house evenings or weekends, when it felt like everybody in Washington her age was out on a date in Georgetown. Everybody was having fun, everybody was arm in arm except her. Finally he arrived. He called her cell phone from his room in the lawyer's house. "I'm getting unpacked. Can we get together tomorrow?"

"With me at home and you at some guy's house, how are we ever going to hook up?"

"They go to the Eastern Shore every weekend. No problem. Plus, don't your parents ever go away?"

"Merilee's in New York. Billy's off at camp. Dick goes back and forth every week to Pennsylvania, to keep in touch. But Rosemary hasn't budged yet. Potomac Fever. Maybe when Congress recesses, she'll go with him to Philly."

The lawyer and his family did take off Friday night for the Eastern Shore, where they had a cottage and a boat. The house was brick, multi-leveled, the downstairs one huge wandering room surrounded by decks, all on a rather small lot. Blake's room was a nondescript guest room filled with his computer equipment. They did not bother with supper but fell into bed, both mumbling how much they had missed each other before lapsing into incoherent sounds of desire and relief. Afterward they dozed. Then Blake went downstairs to order a pizza. Once they had eaten, they fell back into bed. By the time she got home, she was sore but relaxed. They were together again.

A SATURDAY two weeks later, her parents went to Philadelphia overnight for some important function and media stuff. Alison actually scheduled dinner and a movie with a female friend. It was too good to be true. As soon as the house was clear, Melissa called Blake. In half an hour he was with her. Out of his backpack he pulled a Toblerone bar. "Got it for you yesterday. I know you love them."

She thought they would go up to her bedroom, but he wanted to look around. "So what's downstairs?"

"That's my father's study. Some staff offices. The kitchen."

"What's in there?"

"That's Rosemary's sitting room. Alison has the office beside her."

He tried the doors. "They're all locked. They don't trust you, do they?"

"It's just habit. So many people come through here. Aides, interns, speechwriters, his legislative assistants, drivers, caterers, the cook and her daughter, the cleaning service. . . . But if you want to see what the offices look like, I know where Rosemary keeps a set of keys."

He squeezed her shoulder. "Let's go." He was right behind her, bounding up the steps.

"She's so organized, she has a second set for everything, and she keeps them in her underwear drawer." Silk garments, wispy and smelling of Opium, the perfume Rosemary always wore. "Here."

He grabbed the keys and returned to the steps, almost flowing down them. Sometimes the way he moved made her catch her breath. Was it racist to think of big cats, of panthers, of jaguars, of leopards? She did not mind putting off making love for a bit. This was like the games she had played with Billy when they were younger, prowling the governor's mansion, going through their parents' things, finding her mother's birth control pills and filmy negligees. She had no idea what they were looking for, but that only made it more of an adventure.

"Let's look over your father's office first."

"Just remember, he has his primary office in the Senate Office Building and another in the Capitol itself. That's where his interns and aides mostly work. What are you looking for? What's the point?"

"Just to see if I can hack in. Like Everest, it's there. But also to understand him. Isn't that something we need to do? It should give you insight into him—right?" He drew a disc and a portable hard drive out of his backpack. "It needs a password," he announced.

"Try 'Senator' or 'Rosemary.' Dick is not too imaginative."

"No luck. Any more suggestions before I start deriving it randomly?"

"He calls her Pumpkin. Try that."

"We're in."

She sat beside him as he rapidly typed in commands, scrolled through files. "Doesn't empty his recycle bin, does he? Here we go."

"What are you looking for?"

"Just exercising my god-given curiosity. Too bad he hasn't had this computer longer. It's only two years old."

"They change the system every two years. Alison does it all for them." She tried to look over his shoulder, but he was scrolling too rapidly.

"Still, somebody transferred a lot of old files for him. They're on here, even though some of them he thought he erased. People always think when they hit delete that things actually go away. But they don't.

Computers have retentive memories. Everything is there somewhere if you know how to look for it."

"So, I repeat, what are you looking for?" She wanted him to pay at least a little attention to her, and she felt uneasy with him fooling with her father's computer. What did Blake really want?

As if he were reading her thoughts, he turned and kissed her. "A sense of who he is. What he wants. What's important to him. Do you realize that you could go through just about everything on his computer and never know he had a family?"

"You'd know he had Rosemary. Rich has the most contact with him. They can talk shop. He's always been Daddy's favorite. I was golden when I was little, but I grew out of whatever I had. He would make an occasional request—get Billy a haircut before Friday. But us kids were more props than intimates. There are hundreds of pictures of our big happy photogenic family, taken on days when that would be the only time we'd see him. I felt I'd just plain lost him somewhere along the line." She felt blue just thinking about it.

"But he's had a huge impact as governor. If a man can be measured by the shadow he cast, your father is quite the man. It's that impact that fascinates me. And it's the best way for you to figure him out yourself—to understand what he did and what he refused to do."

"But that doesn't tell us what he was thinking, what goes on inside him."

He smiled at her, touching her cheek. "You forget, I was raised a Jew. It's what you do that counts. The intention, the kavanah, is for you and the Eternal. The act is what counts." For a long while, his fingers played over the keys. Sometimes she felt he was really a musician, and the computer was his instrument. She liked that conceit. She half dozed in her chair while he played his keyboard instrument. "Your father seems to be a grateful man. He keeps his promises to those who maintain him in office or help him get there. He's a very giving man to those who give to him." At long last he was done. "Let's put everything carefully back. Then let's go upstairs and try out your bed."

"I thought you'd never ask."

He gave her butt a little squeeze as she preceded him up the three flights of stairs from the ground floor to her top-floor room. "No, you didn't."

It was like the culmination of a daydream to make love in her bed. During the weeks they'd been separated, she had imagined this so many times. Now their cast clothes lay on the floor—or rather hers did. Even now he carefully folded his over a chair. She had the air-conditioning on low to be comfortable naked. She put a towel under them so the sheets wouldn't give her away. His skin was as sleek as she remembered, satiny, honey-colored, warm, always warm. "How long do we have?" he asked.

"Alison's movie began at nine. So she couldn't be back here before eleven thirty. We should figure eleven for a deadline."

"That gives us hours . . . hours." He was tonguing her breast. They made love hard and fast and then again more slowly, making up for lost time. Afterward she dozed off, replete. She could hear him showering in her bathroom. She'd take a shower soon, soon.

She woke with a start. It was after ten. Hurriedly she showered, cleaned up the bathroom, made her bed roughly. "Blake? Where are you?" she called.

"Come down," he called back.

Quickly she got back into her rumpled clothes. He was in Rosemary's office.

"I didn't mean to fall asleep," she apologized. "I don't know how it happened. What are you doing in here?"

"You were tired. Don't feel bad. Come, this is fascinating," he said. "Look at the dossiers she keeps."

She read over his shoulder.

Senator Douglas Bernard McCloskey, New Hampshire. Mother's maiden name Jardin. French Canadian mother. Scottish father. 4th generation American. Grew up in Concord, New Hampshire. Father owned a small plant that manufactured plastic dishes and then plastic cutlery and cases. Bought out in 1974 and went into ski resort development. Mother very active in Church politics. Senator raised a Catholic, attended Holy Cross in Massachusetts. Played lacrosse and hockey.

After B.A. went into father's ski business. Made a name with resort and condo development, combined. Ran for state rep in 1978, lost; won two years later, anti-tax platform. Family values, anti-crime, pro-skimobiles and development. Plays golf fanatically. Proud of his scores. Likes to win. Necessary to lose to him but closely. Elected to Senate in 1988. Reelected in '94 and 2000. Wide margin in '94, slim margin in '00. Likes to eat at Lespinasse; also Celadon; just lately, Red Sage. Comes in around 7:30 and has a vodka martini. Wife Pamela Elizabeth has a kir or a daiquiri. Pamela shops at following boutiques . . .

"Rosemary is nothing if not thorough." Melissa perched on the desk next to the computer. "Where Mrs. Senator McCloskey gets her hair done, the caterer she uses, the names of the children and the baby grandchild. Where she buys shoes. Now I understand how Rosemary got to be pals with McCloskey's wife, what's her name—Pamela. They see each other a couple of times a week. Plus, note, call up Rosemary's schedule. See, they've been eating at the same restaurants at least once a week for the last six weeks. My mother leaves nothing to chance. I bet my father has been playing golf at the right course too. She surrounds her victims. She's relentless." She felt far less queasy about him reading Rosemary's notes.

"It's absolutely fascinating," he said. "Now let's put everything back."

Before eleven, he left. She hastily rinsed their glasses and plates. Then she checked her room again, sniffed at her bed and sprayed it with room deodorizer, got into her pajamas, turned on her TV and waited for the reoccupation of the house. It was good he had left, because Alison returned at eleven twenty and immediately checked on her. She felt like an undercover agent in a movie. She could scarcely wait until they had the house to themselves again. She told herself that it was okay for him to snoop around—he wasn't doing anything bad. It was a crash course in the hidden life of her parents. If it wasn't for Blake, she would be bored to death this summer. She remembered the weeks before he came, with nothing to do but work at her empty job and travel back and forth, fend off her mother's occasional questions, sit around eating and gaining weight and watching TV and writing endless e-mails. Now she was alive again, because she was with him. He even made her house interesting. They would play many games this summer, wonderful games together. It made being trapped here almost fun. She had always adored spying on her parents. The knowledge gained made her feel less weak. Like Blake himself, information was something she had that they did not, could not know about. I am coming to know you, she thought, and you may be my parents, but you don't really know me. I am more than you think I am. It was all just a game, almost sexy in its secrecy. Just a household game.

CHAPTER FIFTEEN

Melissa was delighted that Blake was in Washington, where she could manage to see him two or three times a week, besides occasional brief times for lunch, so glad that she wanted to give him something. "I'm ready to brave my family. We can figure out when to introduce you. We can do it."

"That's sweet, babes. But you're having a hard enough summer. Crappy job. Your mother on your back." He stroked her cheek. "Only brief times we can snatch. Why make trouble? I'd like us to be together more, but as long as we can see each other the way we have been, it's cool. Let sleeping dogs lie."

She was relieved. She did not look forward to the scenes that would follow her parents' discovery of Blake. Her parents were out many evenings, and most weekends they went to Pennsylvania. Sometimes Alison saw a girlfriend. Once Rosemary took Alison to Philadelphia with them overnight. Blake's hosts went to the Eastern Shore every weekend. It was late July already. She said she was going to the library or to the drugstore or sometimes she could just sneak out from the subfloor, unless one of Dick's underlings was working late. With so much staff in the house, slipping out was easy sometimes, hard other times. She stayed in contact with Blake via cell phone till they could hook up and look for a private place.

One night they made love on the far side of the canal, in a dark spot downriver from where the tourist canal boats docked, near where it spilled into Rock Creek, then the Potomac. He padded across a narrow wooden gate that separated two locks. She started out, then panicked. On her left was a drop of fifteen or more feet, with the gate scarcely wide enough for her feet.

"Don't look down!" he said impatiently. "Come on. It's just like walk-ing across a floor."

Slowly, putting one foot in front of the other, she edged across to the dark bank by an office building. The Potomac side of the canal was a dif-ferent neighborhood, the Whitehurst Expressway, the old no-man's-land under it and new office and residential buildings that had been springing up regularly the past few years. On the Potomac side, everything was con-temporary or decrepit.

Another night they walked for blocks along the canal where the tow-path the mules used to pull the replica boats hugged an old stone wall. By the Key Bridge, they descended a rickety wooden staircase from the canal to a small park on the river, by a place that rented canoes. There they made it in the damp grass. That became their favorite spot when their houses were occupied. The smell of somewhat polluted water slowly flowing was coming to mean sex to her.

"NO, I DON'T WANT to go to Maine," Melissa said. She was standing in her mother's office before Rosemary's ebony-topped desk. "This is the first real job I've ever had. I want a good recommendation. To feel I've done what I set out to do. I think it would be good for me to be alone. The house has a security system. I've been here alone overnight this summer, and I wasn't scared."

"But wouldn't you rather go up to Colonel Workman's house? It's on an island. It will be cool instead of the steamy heat we're suffering here. You can go sailing with their grandson."

"He's sixteen, Mother. Anyhow, I don't like sailing. Lower this, raise that. I endure enough orders at work. Billy can hang with him. They'll just ignore me."

Rosemary did not drop the subject. Melissa doubted that her mother was eager to bring her but rather was probing why Melissa did not want to come.

"I'm nineteen, and I've never been alone more than overnight. It's like I'm still a child—"

"You're still our daughter. You're not as much an adult as you seem to think you are. . . . I could ask Alison to stay with you."

"I need to be responsible for myself. I don't even know what it's like to be lonely." She was lying: how often had she been lonely in her own family? "I've never had to manage my own meals, my own time. It's only a couple of weeks, but it could be a real learning experience. I'll be at work every day anyhow. You know how crushed Alison would be if you went off without her."

"We'll see," Rosemary said, but Melissa suspected that she had won. If she were going to quit her job early, she would have to give notice now. Melissa knew better than to push harder. She would just let it rest, hoping for two whole weeks seeing Blake. Whole days, whole nights. Blake was already building up a story about a buddy from school who had an apartment where he could stay. It was like a honeymoon waiting, the promise of precious time together. They were counting the days toward the morning her parents would leave for Maine, where Billy would join them from hockey camp. Melissa knew from her mother's e-mails that Merilee too was trying to skip Maine. She claimed her internship in New York prevented her, but Melissa suspected that Merilee was enjoying autonomy. It would be cool in Maine, crisp by comparison with the jungle fetor that lay over Washington as the temperature edged into the high nineties and hung there, day after day, scarcely cooler by night. She was living in a tropical fish tank, just one more harried guppy milling around with a ragged tail in a swarm of hungry fish, most of them bigger than she was.

THEY HAD BEEN planning to get together Thursday evening, but he e-mailed her that morning before she went to work.

> Got to cancel tonight. Phil is coming to town just for the evening—
> going back on the late train. Of course, if you want to hang with
> him, let me know, and we can all get together. Up to you. I know

you've been learning a lot from him, but it's summer and I also know you're not crazy for his company. It's only this one evening, so I couldn't say no.

Phil had some weird fascination for Blake he didn't have for her. She considered whether she should join them. But Blake and she weren't going to get any private time, and Phil would dominate the conversation the way he always did. He would be pushing her to do something she didn't want to. She would put in time with her family, instead of making a lame excuse for escaping. Gloom thickened the air-conditioned atmosphere in the house these days, as Dick had been handed his first senatorial defeat. His transportation bill had not come to a vote before the Senate adjourned. It would have to come up for a vote in the fall. Senator Dawes would cosponsor.

She had heard her father talking with Rosemary. "In some ways, it's hard to get used to, pumpkin. When I was governor, I could just sign an executive order, give a command, promise some patronage and it was done. Now fifty other egomaniacs have to vote my way. This Senate thing is wasteful."

"But you're in for six years, and incumbents have a huge and measurable advantage," Rosemary said. She was stroking his hair, kneading his shoulders. "You're a freshman. As time goes on, you'll gain power. And the power is very real. You could be in there for life, till you're absolutely dinosaur ancient like Strom Thurmond. You were governor as long as you could be governor. But there's no term limit on senators."

"All that effort, all that kowtowing to McCloskey and his insipid wife . . ."

"It's not wasted. He'll get the bill voted on in the fall, and we'll have the opportunity to work on key people for their votes. Dawes will help."

"Still . . . it felt, I don't know, more important to be governor. Governor was the top of the heap."

"President is the top of the heap, darling."

They were both silent, contemplating the golden mountain of their goal. They would never allow her to overhear anything shady. When they talked in the livingroom, it was vetted by both of them to be safe. She thought that they talked about the dirty stuff in bed—not sexually dirty but ethically, politically dirty. Occasionally when they had been visiting Grandpa at the farmhouse, she had heard the murmur of their voices long after they retired, as well as the rustlings and little soft moans and whispers that, as she entered adolescence, she had identified as lovemaking. No matter what she might think about Rosemary and Dick, they were a real couple, fixated on each other emotionally and sexually.

FINALLY IT WAS time for her parents to leave for Colonel Workman's island. He was always addressed as Colonel, although he had retired from the Army a decade before and gone into oil. His home was in Texas, but he had bought a small island off the Maine coast where his family spent summers and he came for August to host influential friends. It was beautiful, but she would have been closely monitored. Plus, the water up there was way too cold for swimming. She had never appealed to the sons of rich men who backed her father, but now she had her own real boyfriend, and even sailing or playing tennis with those spoiled creatures would be a drag. She didn't dare ask if Alison were going, but she kept an eye on her. Finally she noticed Alison packing her laptop and a bulging briefcase, then bringing down a carry-on of clothes.

Hot and stickily humid as it was in Washington, the house was air-conditioned and so was her job. So was the lawyer's house where Blake was staying. In the meantime, Blake's monitoring of Rosemary's e-mail netted her the information that Merilee had caved. Rosemary had gone over her head to one of the partners who seemed in some way bound to Dick. Merilee would be heading for Maine. Melissa felt superior to her older sister for once, since Merilee hadn't wanted to go but had been out-manipulated by their mother.

"Look at this list," she complained to Blake as they ate Middle Eastern takeout at the kitchen table. Yolanda and her daughter had two weeks off, so Melissa was left to fend for herself. "There's a whole paragraph about the garbage disposal. Two paragraphs about laundry, as if she ever does it herself. One paragraph about the answering machine."

"She's thorough, we've said that. Your mother has a very organized mind."

"And she thinks I'm a blithering idiot."

He grinned, dipping Syrian bread into the hummus. "That too. But to be fair, this is the first time she's ever left you alone longer than overnight. She thinks you haven't the faintest what to do. Remove tissue from box. Blow nose. Wipe carefully. Toss into trash."

Melissa giggled. In spite of her sense of outrage at her mother's five-page list of dos and dont's, she was in bliss. Two weeks together. Two weeks to play. Two weeks away from her mother's judging gaze. Two weeks in which everything in this house was hers and Blake's, theirs alone. It was the most wonderful present of her life. If they never came back, would she bother returning to school? Or would she just stay here with him, living in luxury and working some half-assed job and hanging out? That would be the ideal life.

They saw movies Blake brought from the video store. They sat and people-watched through the windowless windows of cafés on M, nursing cups of cappuccino. They played the music they liked really, really loud, and twice they went out to a club that let underage students in to listen or dance and stayed till two in the morning. They moved overstuffed chairs and the glass coffee table into the diningroom—which they never used— so they could dance in the livingroom. They ate pizza and ice cream and Chinese takeout and burgers. They tried out every bed in the house. "I don't like so much being together in here," she said to him after they did it on her parents' bed. "Instead of feeling like I'm getting off on them, I feel too reminded. I want to put them out of my mind. We've escaped. I don't want to remember they exist."

"Oh, they exist. And a lot of people can't ever forget that."

"Why can't we just let them slip into oblivion for this time we've been given? Dropped in our laps to enjoy."

"Because, Lissa mine, this time is a gift to explore not only each other but all the secrets of your powerful father. At our leisure, we can investigate, we can prowl and examine and learn. When will we ever have an opportunity like this again? Maybe not for a year. Maybe not ever."

"You mean because once they find out about us—"

"You bet. The shit will hit the fan big time."

"I won't give you up, Blake. No matter what they do or say."

"I hope not. I pray not. But we'll see, won't we?"

Alison kept an inventory of the wine cellar on her desktop computer, making it simple for them. Whenever they drank a bottle, they eliminated it from the inventory. Blake made sure that they got rid of any incriminating trash. It was part of the fun of their clandestine life in the house that had never before felt hers. Blake made the neighborhood and even the house someplace she belonged and enjoyed. It was their kingdom of pleasure.

Sometimes she imagined they were married. When she dared to tentatively share that with him, he began to play too. It did not scare him. She was astonished and delighted. They played the Mr. and Mrs. game at supper, when they were loading the dishwasher, when they were doing laundry, when they were shopping. He was Mr. Timothy Flapdoodle. She was Mrs. Gina Flapdoodle. They had two children: Annette was precocious and a ballerina; Edgar was a math genius and a champion chess player. They had three dogs and three cats, a parrot and an iguana. The names of the pets changed almost daily, as did their breeds, or lack of them. The Flapdoodle family expanded or contracted at will. They had a second son, Harley, who played soccer and got in trouble at school; then they dropped him. He was too much like Billy for her to enjoy.

"Everybody needs a future," Blake said. "Even if it only extends to the end of the week."

"But we can have a real future, if we're strong with each other," she said. He was too fatalistic. It went along with his invocation of destiny in their meeting. She didn't believe anything was fated. If Jonah had been a nicer person, she might have followed him to William and Mary instead of going to Wesleyan with Emily. Then she would never have met Blake. But she didn't argue. He was a romantic, and she appreciated that. She was the pragmatist in their couple. "There's no way I'm going to let my parents break us up. I can swear that."

"We'll see" was all he would say. But he promised, "In the fall, when they come up to visit me at school, you can meet my folks. We can get that started."

"Does that mean you want to meet my parents this summer while you're in D.C.?" Her stomach clenched hard on itself.

"I'll be leaving the Sunday they're getting back. No, we'll fight that battle down the pike. Let's deal with mine and get them nice and acquiescent and cuddly before we start on yours."

She had an equally great desire to meet his family and to keep hers at bay. She was too afraid of Rosemary to look forward to the scenes that would surely follow any introduction. She could not imagine a happier time than playing house with Blake. Every weekday morning, she went off to work. He hung around the house until his first class, and then he was home when she got back. She had given him one of the keys that hung downstairs for staff, in Dick's office. She rushed back as fast as she could. He usually picked up takeout on his way from class. She was loving the intimacy, the silences as well as the intense conversations in bed late at night, over supper, on the weekends. Her mother called every two days, always around seven—while it was cocktail hour at Colonel and Mrs. Workman's domicile with its view of the tiny rock-strewn harbor. Her mother would walk down from the verandah with her cell phone clasped to her ear. Sometimes Melissa could hear the clank of rigging hitting against the mast of a sailboat, hear the seagulls' raucous cries and warning mews. At moments, she missed the ocean. Then she thought of herself there with her parents; Rich and his pregnant wife, who had joined them; Merilee, who was obediently onboard; Billy, who would be hanging with the grandson, and she shuddered with relief for her freedom, her precious time with Blake. She would rather be in hell with Blake than in heaven with her parents.

Melissa found actually sleeping with Blake, eating with him, living with him full-time except for her work and his class exhilarating, although not without its occasional abrasions. He had a tendency to drag the covers off her. He liked the bedroom ice-cold. He ate faster than she did. Of course he ate more—he was after all bigger—but if she did not hastily grab what she wanted, he would consume it before she got round to selecting a second helping. He wasted a lot of time downloading stuff from the house computers onto his laptop, an obsession fortunately he did not demand she share. When she asked him what he was doing, he usually had a simple answer: downloading material on how her father was going to vote on various issues, actual bills, and why. If she asked further, he would explain the issues to her at length, sometimes at stupefyingly great length. But that left ninety percent bliss. She had to dig for something to complain about. She felt loved. He brought her little presents, silly things: a statuette of a beagle ("because your mother won't let you have a live dog"), a barrette in the form of a blue beaded butterfly from Bali, a book of computer cartoons. He got her favorite cookie dough ice cream, even if he ate more than half. They took long bubble baths together, then had to mop up the flooded bathroom. The neighborhood was their playground, to run out and mingle with other couples on the sidewalks, in restaurants and ice cream parlors and coffeehouses and hangouts. This was what marriage would be like.

Phil wanted to come to the house, but she refused. "I could never explain him. My parents hate his father. They really see him as a demon from hell." She felt strong drawing that line. It showed that she had scruples, that Blake could not push her around, that she was still protecting her parents.

This was Phil's second trip to Washington. She was not overjoyed, but Blake continued to be fascinated with Phil: beauty and the nerd. Blake was enamored of anything to do with computers and any weird hairy guy who dealt seriously with them. Everybody had hobbies. Her father collected memorabilia about Winston Churchill, displayed in his office along all of one wall in a glass case—everything from first editions to a shaving mug in the form of his head. He also collected World War II paraphernalia, and an assortment of guns, shotguns and rifles that Alison kept in good condition, displayed in a large glass case. Rosemary collected important men. Perhaps there was something wrong with her that she had no hobbies. Maybe when Blake and she were married, she would develop a hobby. She could collect dogs—live ones. None of her dogs would be pedigreed. They would all be mutts who were lonely, deserted and needing a home. Blake liked animals. She felt as if a man who liked animals (unlike her father; unlike Rich) should be trusted.

She learned all about his preferences, his dislikes and weaknesses. Pollution could make him sick. He had asthma, and on bad days he relied heavily on an inhaler he carried with him. He avoided smoky places because they could cause an attack. The nights they went to that club, he was sick the next day.

Her mother's phone calls were unrelievedly annoying. "Have you been taking the trash out to the curb? What have you been eating? I hope the sink isn't full of encrusted dishes and burnt pans. Use only your own phone. We are retrieving the messages daily from the other phone. It can't be tied up."

Melissa did not mention that they too were checking the answering machine daily. Everything about her parents interested Blake. Still, he was disappointed in the phone messages. She had to explain that almost everyone who mattered was out of Washington for the summer, on vacation or in their home districts. Anyone who knew her parents would call them in Maine.

Rosemary was still interrogating her. "Are you lonely? I hope you're not doing anything foolish. You could still come up here."

"Remember, you've never given me a car."

"You could fly into Bar Harbor. We'd pick you up."

"I'm still working this week, Mother. I can't suddenly quit. I'm doing just fine. I'm finding out what it's like to be on my own. But I really would like a car."

"I suppose it's not worth it now. We'll be back Sunday. I hope you aren't playing your music too loudly. You don't want to annoy the neighbors. That's a very nice neighborhood."

She had a momentary qualm, because they were playing music loudly, but then she remembered that the neighbors who shared the walls on either side of the row house were out of Washington too. "Of course I'm not."

"I hope you aren't forgetting to turn the air-conditioning down when you leave for work."

"Yes, Mother." Yes, she was forgetting. Blake stayed in the house after she left for work, before his first class. They almost always forgot to turn down the air-conditioning. His classes were only half a day.

"Be careful what you put down the garbage disposal. You can't—"

"Mother, you left five pages of instructions. It isn't necessary to repeat them on the phone. I haven't had a problem with the garbage disposal, the washer, the dryer, the dishwasher, the air-conditioning, the TV, the music system, the doorbell, the plumbing . . ."

Rosemary was ominously silent for a moment. "There's no need for sarcasm. I hope to find things as I left them."

BLAKE CAME BACK from meeting Phil in a state of excitement. "We're finally on to something." They were sitting in the livingroom on the long overstuffed couch, facing each other, legs up and entangled between them.

"What are you talking about?"

"The problem is that general corruption is just taken for granted. The banks that run credit cards give big contributions and senators vote to make bankrupt people pay off their credit cards no matter what, before child support, before anything. Insurance companies give big contributions and stop health care programs that would cover everyone. Tobacco companies give big contributions and the senators vote that the FDA can't treat tobacco like any other addictive drug. It goes on and on and nobody cares but a few cranks."

"I don't see how any of this is going to help me. And where did you get all this information?"

"To be able to get to him—to demand his attention, to get him to communicate with us—we need something that breaks the rules of the private club he's in. Nowadays that includes sex—it never used to, or half the founding fathers and almost all of the presidents would have gone down. But you don't think King Richard strays."

"He and Rosemary are absolutely bonded. Maybe you'd find some affairs in his college days, but so what? Nobody would care. He can always say he repented. I don't think he has much motivation to stray. They have a pretty active sex life, as near as I can tell. They're faithful because they're totally focused on the same things."

"Pages? Interns? Assistants?"

"Mostly they're guys or homely or both. Rosemary vets them. And she's in and out of his office all the time. I don't see it."

"So much for sex. Drugs? Again, we've found no sign of it."

"He froths at the mouth at the mention of drugs. Once he walked into the room when Billy and I had been smoking dope. He sniffed and said, 'What's that funny smell?' He really didn't know. I don't think he ever smoked. They drink a lot, but no more than anybody else in Washington. He has an amazing tolerance for liquor, I've heard his aides say. He knows exactly how much he has in him. I've never, ever seen him drunk."

"Okay, that leaves us with money. Now there are certain accounts I've turned up that look iffy."

"Accounts? What are you talking about?"

"I've been checking expenditures, instead of only donations. He pays a lot of expenses that are politically motivated—like eating at those expensive restaurants Senator McCloskey frequents—out of an account that seems reserved for that. The money into that account may have been transferred from his war chest in part or come straight from contributions. If so, he's playing fast and loose. You can't use campaign contributions for personal expenses. While he may consider those big restaurant tabs political, it's not legal to use contributions for dining out. It's the first hard little pebble of factoid we've found that might actually do some damage."

He was massaging her foot, sending her into sensual bliss. She jerked her foot away. "I don't like this financial stuff. He'd be furious if that's what you've been downloading. I thought you were trying to find out how he's going to vote on stuff like foreign aid and welfare."

"I'm trying to understand the whole picture. What makes him tick. How he makes his decisions. What he does to implement those decisions. That's the heart of the matter, babes. You've never taken the trouble to understand how he operates, so you have no chance to influence him. We're trying to set you up to have some impact." He took her foot back in his hands and slowly massaged his way up her leg.

"So what do we do now?" She moved her other foot up to his crotch and slowly circled it over the growing bulge. He was trying to help her, even though she didn't like him fooling around with the computers so much. He just couldn't keep his hands off computers. It was like Em coming into a room where there was a dog—even if she was trying to flirt with some guy, she'd forget him and go straight to the dog and start baby-talking it and rubbing its ears.

"Right now, we go upstairs."

"I was hoping you'd say that."

"Pleasure before business. That's us."

If only they could just stay on here together. She had longed to be back at school, but now she just wanted their little sojourn to last weeks, months, years. Their bodies fit so well into each other. She kept the air-conditioning low in her room so that they could rub glistening skin on skin without goose bumps. When it was time to sleep, she turned it arctic, the way he liked it at night.

Now they coiled round each other through the gentle mild air, now her on top, now him. Sometimes she felt as if they were rooting, digging through each other's bodies trying to sink deeper and deeper within, as if they were trying to crawl into each other. She was seldom jealous now. Of course, she scarcely saw him with anyone else. They rushed to the house and each other after work, after classes. Three or four times in the neighborhood, they ran into people they knew and chatted, had coffee, but they did not ask them over, saving that precious time for each other.

Friday was the happy day when they faced a whole weekend together, a little tinged with sadness because Blake would have to go back to the lawyer's house Sunday noon, get his stuff together, then return to Philadelphia that night. She would do a quick runaround and make sure everything was in place. They had kept things pretty tidied up, for fear some hireling might come by to check on the house and her. She would be alone when her parents arrived Sunday.

"Si and Nadine wanted to know why I couldn't come back Saturday, but I gave them some BS about a class party." Blake communicated with his parents by e-mail, so he didn't face the problem of having to be near the phone to take calls from them. They assumed he was safely tucked into their friend's house in Bethesda, where he passed by once a day so that they would not think he had disappeared.

She smiled at him. "I think we covered all bases pretty well."

"Like professionals." He high-fived her and they beamed at each other. They were eating Thai takeout tonight.

"I think we've done better than most couples at sharing space, don't you agree?" She watched his face for a reaction.

"Naturally. It's been how it should be." He beamed at her.

Other girls in the dorm told her that if they made noises about commitment, their boyfriends froze up or took off. Blake wasn't like that. She had a confidence in him that she had never had in anyone, not even Billy when he was still all hers. She had imagined being this desired, this cherished, but never truly believed she would achieve it. She would do anything to hold on to him. She would make herself be brave and tough and smart. Their closeness grew out of their need, that they both felt ultimately alone and as if they didn't belong, although she sometimes wondered why he felt that way, since his adopted family seemed to be more satisfied with him than her natural parents could ever be with her. But his folks might be a bunch of perfectionists. Something made him needy, for which she was grateful, since what he seemed to need most was her.

They were sitting at the kitchen table across the ruins of supper, gazing at each other and going over the minute details of their days, one of those marriagelike moments she reveled in. She could have told anybody except Emily about her day in two sentences. With Emily, there would be dissection and discussion. With Blake too, everything was mulled over. He was fascinated by the differences between Russian and English sentence structure and grammar and the differences between Romance languages and Russian. Russian was his first Slavic language, and in spite of all the distractions, he had done well in the course. He always took time to practice with his language tapes. She liked the sound of him speaking a language she had no clue about, although by osmosis she had picked up hello, good-bye, thank you, I am called, what is your name and other standard phrases.

Afterward she would think again and again how grateful she was that they had lingered at the table that evening. His course was finished and he was showing off his Russian to her. He taught her to say "I love you," and "I want to go to bed with you" and "You are the handsomest man I have ever seen." They were in weekend mood, chilling, just enjoying each other and free time. They were being silly and she was asking him how to say outlandish things. "My dog wears blue pants." "My telephone speaks only Chinese."

They were leaning back in their chairs drinking Chardonnay from the cellar with the remains of supper littering the kitchen table between them when she heard something. They both turned. It came from the parlor floor.

"Melissa! Melissa! Are you here? We're home."

It was Rosemary's voice: her family voice of command, not her geisha voice. Melissa froze. Then she jumped up, grabbed the half-empty bottle of wine and shoved it under the sink. She emptied and rinsed their glasses while Blake rose, glancing toward the outside door to the street—the way she used when she sneaked out to meet him. But he had left his backpack with his laptop and a change of clothes upstairs in the livingroom. They looked at each other grimly. He remained standing at attention and jerked at his clothes, while she patted her hair.

"Down here, Mother," she called.

Blake looked frozen. She must have infected him with her fear. She tried to give him a reassuring glance, but his eyes were fixed on the doorway, waiting.

Rosemary tripped down, carrying her handbag and a package. The driver was helping Dick with the bags, and Alison was managing packages of whatever Rosemary had purchased. "I thought we'd better . . ." Her gaze swung to Blake and remained there. "Hello?" The tone was icy.

"Mother, this is Blake. He was in my writing class at school. We ran into each other this week, and we're having supper together."

"In the kitchen. How romantic."

"Mrs. Dickinson, a pleasure to meet you." His voice rose weirdly, but it was full and resonant. "It was nice to run into someone I know in Washington."

"Are you here as a tourist?" Rosemary was still eyeing him.

"No, I've been in a language program. But it's over. It finished today."

"So you're a student at Wesleyan." Rosemary motioned them to follow her upstairs into the diningroom. "Goodness, what happened here?"

"I moved the furniture out of the livingroom. I've been doing an exercise routine every morning before I go to work. I'm trying to firm my tummy."

"How commendable." Rosemary cast a look over her shoulder at Alison, who was hovering in the doorway. "Could you take my things upstairs, Alison?"

"I'll help you move the furniture back, Melissa," Blake said. He was in control of his voice now. "Just show me where it goes."

Rosemary sat at the foot of the diningroom table (she would never for a moment usurp Dick's chair) watching them carefully. Melissa could feel her mother's scrutiny walking like a long-legged spider over her arms and back.

"Got everything in. I let the driver go. How is— What's going on here?" Dick paused in the French doors, watching Blake and Melissa haul chairs back into the livingroom.

"Melissa introduced her friend from school to me. Blake something. Blake, what's your full name?"

"Blake Ackerman, Mrs. Dickinson."

"Oh, yes," she said with a nod of her well-coiffed blond head. Melissa could feel her mother categorizing Blake. What did they see? She looked at her lover, trying to imagine him through their eyes. His eyes like burning coals, intense, dark, radiant. His black hair, Indian looking, long on his neck. Tall, slender but strong in his build. His honey-colored skin. His shapely hands. "And what are you studying, Blake?"

He hesitated. "Well, I'm a freshman like Melissa, Mrs. Dickinson. I haven't really picked a major. Maybe something toward science. Information theory. I don't really know yet."

"But you must be a devoted student to go to summer school, and in Washington."

"I love languages. Sometimes I think of being a translator. Maybe one of those simultaneous translators like at the UN."

"Fascinating. Thank you for helping Melissa move the furniture back. I'm wondering how she would have done it alone on Sunday."

"I thought Billy could help me when you came home."

"But how did you move it out by yourself?"

"Slowly," she said. "A piece at a time." At that moment she hated her mother. Probing, always probing. That sterling intelligence burning like a laser into her explanation. One of the only times her mother ever paid her first-class attention was when she had to lie, when she was in some kind of trouble, when she was making excuses.

"Well, your family must be expecting you . . . but you said they were in Philadelphia?"

"I've been staying with a friend of the family while my class was on. Tomorrow I'll return. As I told you, my class ended today." He picked up his backpack from the chair, where Dick was staring at it as if he could see into it through the coarse black fabric. "I'll be getting back. They'll be expecting me. Bye, Melissa. Thanks for having me over. I'll probably run into you at school."

"Ackerman. Ackerman," Dick was repeating. His mind was a vast Rolodex.

"Good night, sir." Blake fled.

"I should have asked him if his father is related to that lawyer." He turned to Melissa. "What does his father do?"

"I haven't the faintest idea. If I run into him again, I'll ask him, if it matters to you."

"Pesky fellow, that lawyer. He gets criminals off—or he tries to. We've had several tussles."

Rosemary's gaze was now fixed on Melissa. "Weren't you afraid to invite him back to the house alone? How well do you know him?"

"We had the same writing class and we've studied together in the library. I've had lunch with him and other kids from the class. He's a nice guy. No, I'm not afraid of him. I was glad to run into him. He's very bright."

"Jewish," Dick said. "Looks Spanish. I wonder what his mother is."

"I have no idea. Look, what difference does it make? I just had supper with him."

"Why didn't you eat in a restaurant?"

"You always call around seven. I didn't want you to worry. Besides, takeout is cheaper."

"Is he a scholarship student?" Dick asked. "A poor boy?"

"I don't know! Really, how much am I expected to know about some guy from school just to eat supper with him? He's always well dressed and going to some language school this summer instead of working, like I had to do, so I imagine his parents have money." If she had any guts, she would tell them that he was her boyfriend; but she didn't dare. Besides, Blake had not seemed to want that confrontation yet. Still, she felt as if she had betrayed him. She was proud of him, not ashamed. "Now I'm going upstairs!" She fled before she burst into tears, almost tripping over Alison, who was right outside the diningroom listening.

Her room smelled like sex to her. The bed was not made, and quickly she sprayed air freshener all around and over the sheets, then made it. She wanted to air out her room, but opening the window to the hot humid Washington night would alert Rosemary that something was wrong. She ran around her room looking for signs of Blake's presence. There! He had left a stud from his right ear on her night table. She dropped it into her padded jewelry box, where it would get lost among earrings and bracelets. She checked the bathroom. Shaving cream. His razor. She started to put them in her underwear drawer, then remembered that was where anyone would look first. Instead she put them in the back of her desk drawer. She would dispose of them next time she left the house. His deodorant. That went in the same desk drawer. Then she was satisfied nothing was left, except that she had to wash the basin clear of a sprinkle of black hair from shaving.

Creeping out of her room, she heard her parents' voices downstairs, low, murmuring, and she could imagine what they were saying about her. About him. They were only suspicious, she told herself, because they had walked in on them, although of all the things they might have been doing, eating supper was the most unincriminating. But they did not like her bringing a boy into the house in their absence, and they did not like the looks of Blake. She would be in for direct and indirect interrogation, that was for sure. She stared into the mirror, assuming her blandest, blankest expression. She felt as if her real self was coiled within like a seedling in a peach pit. Hidden. Waiting.

CHAPTER SEVENTEEN

Melissa wished she could pull some other friends out of Washington to parade before her parents. She thought of girls she had not seen since Miss Porter's, at least two in the area. She called them both. The first number, she got an answering machine and no one ever called back. The second number, she reached Jessica herself. They arranged to meet Sunday noon at a coffee shop in Georgetown. Jessica sounded surprised but agreed at once—probably bored silly to be home with her parents. Melissa mentioned the meeting casually as if she had been seeing Jessica all summer.

"Jessica—who's she?"

"You met her at Miss Porter's." To a contemporary she would have described Jessica as a plump blond with butch hair and a talent for drinking quarts of beer without getting visibly drunk. To Rosemary, she said, "She's the daughter of a career bureaucrat in the Department of the Interior. Forestry stuff. Her mother is from Virginia and also claims to be a collateral descendant of Robert E. Lee. We talked about it when she was my friend at Miss Porter's."

"I remember. Your father checked it out, and the claim is legitimate. She's a distant relative. That's the sort of connection you should be pursuing. You didn't mention seeing her this summer."

"You didn't ask. What does it matter? We have a good time together."

"As well you should. That's the type of person with whom you have something in common."

"I have more in common with that guy you didn't seem to care for. We go to the same school. We had class together. We know some of the same people."

"Then perhaps you should meet different people this year."

She had a better time with Jessica than she expected. Since they were in different universities, each seemed to feel she could be frank. Jessica was doing a lot of Ecstasy and in trouble at school, having fallen in love with a townie she'd met at a rave. He had a Harley and an ex-wife with a kid. She had added a lip stud to her previous collection. Melissa told her a few things about Blake, including his Honda. They agreed that parents just couldn't understand and promised to get together over Thanksgiving, provided they both were in Washington.

When Melissa returned, a video crew was occupying the first floor and the backyard, making a promo for the NRA featuring Rosemary, who had been a poster child for them previously. The NRA contributed heavily to Dick's campaigns, and he strongly backed the freedom to pack. Rosemary was speaking to the camera in a forceful yet coy way about the need for women to be able to protect themselves and their families.

When taping was finally over, two hours later, Alison came in and picked up the rifle and the revolver Rosemary had put down as soon as she was done with them, as if they might burn her hands. Rosemary might sing the praises of firearms, but she secretly hated them. She disliked even touching them. Alison cleaned the guns, made sure they were in working order by firing them from time to time at a local range and watched Rosemary's posturing with them to make sure it was convincing. Alison had grown up in the countryside of Pennsylvania in a hunting culture. She had made Dick and Rich more proficient at handling firearms. Rich enjoyed shooting. Melissa at one point had thought she might take it up, but Rosemary had not encouraged her interest. "You'd probably shoot Alison by accident or your own foot. Let the boys play." Not that Melissa had ever wanted to shoot anything; she just liked the image of herself looking cool. After all, even Billy knew how to handle firearms: why not her?

MELISSA WAS tremendously relieved to pack up and head back to school. Alison was driving her, as Dick had been invited to play golf with three influential senators, Rosemary was buttering up Mrs. McCloskey in preparation for Congress's return and Melissa had too much stuff to cart on the train. It was a strain to spend seven hours in the car with Alison, who felt impelled to make conversation. But Alison's questions were easier to deflect than Rosemary's, in part because Alison was not and never had been interested in her and lacked the vocation of a true inquisitor. She mainly ran on about Rosemary and her charm and what a wonderful wife and mother she was, how she personally thought Rosemary would make a great senator herself. "She is on top of every issue," Alison declaimed. "She has an understanding of politics at least the equal of your father's."

Well, duh, Melissa thought. Who do you think tells Dick what his issues should be?

"College towns and campuses are always such a hodgepodge," Alison said as they drove through the small downtown uphill to Wesleyan. "You'd think they'd try to keep things more uniform to be aesthetically pleasing." Melissa didn't answer, wanting to defend her school but also wanting to reveal as little of herself as possible to Alison. Finally she was delivered to her dormitory and Emily, whose parents were helping her settle in. Fern had moved into Open House, having finally decided to come out, and Melissa and Emily would be roommates. Emily's mom and dad looked at each other when they learned that Melissa's parents had not bothered to take her to school themselves. That look she had seen pass between them before, pitying and judgmental. Emily's folks did not give hers high marks in the parenting department. Melissa rather enjoyed their mild pity, and she agreed with them about Dick and Rosemary. She imagined her mother ticking her off on a computer-generated list: get third child returned to college. A check beside it. Emily's folks helped her settle in too. She enjoyed the attention, but she could not tell Emily what had happened until her parents left and finally they were alone.

"They just walked in? Without calling? Do you think somebody tipped them and they were trying to catch you bonking him?"

"I don't think so. I'm not important enough for them to think it mattered to let me know they were returning early." Melissa frowned.

"Although maybe they were suspicious. I asked Billy if they interrogated him, and he said they wanted to know if I was seeing anybody."

"Did he tell them?"

"He couldn't. I never confided in him."

"Still, maybe they liked Blake. He's gorgeous and smart—"

"And Jewish and dark-skinned, of obviously mixed race. Just what they'd order up for me, right? Never underestimate their prejudices." She bounced across the room to hug Emily. "I'm so glad to see you, Em. I can't begin to tell you how glad I am to be back here with you."

"Hey, kid. We're sophomores now. We're not the new kids on the block—"

"I hated that group. Merilee used to listen to them—"

"They say nobody ever likes their older siblings' music. I barely remember them. So, anyhow, your parents finally met Blake so now you can ooze into letting them know he's your steady Freddy."

"No hurry!" She set up her laptop. "So do you still have cooties or whatever? Are they contagious?"

"Only if we have sex. No, I got rid of them with crap from the drugstore. It stung but it did them in. What a scurvy skanky guy to give me bugs, Lissa."

"You always like musicians."

Emily shrugged. Her hair looked shinier. Melissa made a mental note to ask her what she was using on it. "It was something to do."

Melissa logged on to get her messages. "Oh my god! Blake is expecting me to meet his parents tonight. At seven they're going to pick me up— what time is it?"

"You have almost an hour to fuss about it."

"What should I wear? Is my hair all right? Is my skin okay?"

She read his message again. He said, "I haven't told my parents who your parents are, so let it be. Actually I told them you're an orphan like me and you're adopted by a family who lives in Washington. Your father's in trucking."

Now why did he do that? She'd have to remember the made-up part all evening. But in a way she was liberated from Dick and Rosemary, enjoying an imaginary family instead. Often she had felt adopted; or like a changeling left in the cradle when the real perfect Dickinson baby had been abducted by aliens.

Blake was usually late and tonight was no exception. She sat in the lounge downstairs trying not to chew her nails, a habit she had broken while still at Miss Porter's. Now she wanted so badly to bite her nails that she had to cross her arms. Then she started pulling at her hair. She radiated anxiety so strongly that a guy sitting near her moved to another seat. She wanted desperately for the Ackermans to like her, but why should they? They would disapprove. They wouldn't be able to guess what Blake saw in her. What did he see in her? She was never quite sure herself. If only she knew, then she could be more that way, starting immediately.

Finally, at seven twenty-three, she saw him coming in the door accompanied by a wizened little man with a shock of white hair standing straight up as if electrified, an even shorter roly-poly woman with equally short white hair, and a pretty girl with spiked black hair, her buff midriff bare over tight pants, a swagger to her walk. That had to be the stepsister. They were introduced by Blake: "My father, Si Ackerman. My mother, Nadine Ackerman. My sister, Sara. This is my girlfriend, Melissa. Don't bite her."

Everyone greeted her, making no attempt to disguise their curiosity. They were all looking her over and examining her quite openly until she felt like hiding behind Blake. She was so nervous she didn't even listen to where they were going. It turned out to be a Chinese restaurant where students often ate with parents.

"There's a law that must be federal, since it applies in every state," Si said as they looked at the menu. "No Chinese restaurant more than twenty miles from a major urban center can be trusted, and no good food can be served within two miles of any college or university."

"So what are you studying, Melissa?"

"I think I'd like to go into journalism. Investigative journalism."

"A dying field," Si said glumly.

Blake squeezed her knee under the circular table. "Melissa has been working with Phil, Roger's son. Phil plans to follow in his father's foot-steps."

"Good footsteps." Si nodded at her. "I know Roger. I must have met Phil, but I don't recall him."

Nadine tilted her head to the side. "Is he the little guy who came to the house just after you got back from Washington? With funny red hair?"

Little guy, she thought. Nadine must be all of five two. Blake, Sara and she towered over his parents.

"So how'd you meet my bro?" Sara was playing with the chopsticks, arranging them in squares, Xs, outlines of houses.

"We had a writing class together our first semester."

"You're the first white girl Bro has gone out with," Sara said. "Must be something about you."

"His mother was white, Sara. And that girl Marietta was damned pos-sessive. I was glad Blake cut her loose." Si frowned at his daughter.

Marietta must be the girl who had visited him before they hooked up. How did Si know Blake's mother was white? Blake had told her nothing was known about his blood parents. Maybe the hospital had recorded that much. Unknown white woman.

"So where do your parents live?" Nadine pursued.

"In Washington, D.C."

His parents exchanged a look. "So much for the sudden interest in Russian." Nadine grinned broadly. "It all becomes clear."

"I wanted to learn Russian," Blake said. "And I did damned well in that course. You saw my evaluation. I just didn't see why I couldn't do it in Washington and have fun with Melissa at the same time."

"So how long have you been going out?" Si asked.

"Quite the interrogation you two have going," Blake said. "Pity you can't double-team like this in court."

"Honey, we're just interested. How could we not be curious and want to know as much as we can about your friend?" Nadine turned to Melissa. "Do you have brothers and sisters?"

"An older and younger brother and an older sister."

She saw Blake dig Sara in the ribs. "Hey, I'm starving," she said. "I'll pass out on the floor if we don't order. Does anybody know if the Buddha's Delight is edible here?"

Ordering was not like being in a restaurant with her parents. It was a fast hard negotiation. I won't get the too-hot tempeh dish if you don't get the peanut chicken I hate. "No, Sara, you can't impose vegetarianism on us tonight," Nadine said. "You did it at Thanksgiving, but not again. You don't eat what you don't want, but you can't keep us from eating what we want. If it grosses you out, go sit in a booth by yourself."

"But, Mom, Melissa hasn't got to choose anything," Blake complained. Somehow with his parents he was younger. His voice often rose closer to treble. She thought, Everybody stays a helpless kid with their parents. She certainly went on the defensive with hers. She should not be judgmental because the Blake who interacted with his adoptive parents was far less commanding and far less in charge than her Blake. Her Blake was the real Blake, escaped from his family, as this was the real Melissa, having gotten away from hers.

"I like most things," she said. "What you're ordering is fine with me."

Everyone looked at her as if she had made a faux pas. Apparently insisting on something was what this family expected and admired, while the bland go-with-anything air her parents cultivated was dismissed as wishy-washy here. Well, she could recover. She could play their game. "I do really like mu shi pork . . . or chicken," she added, remembering they were Jewish. "With pancakes."

"Extra pancakes," Sara said. "So what attracted you to my gangly brother? His bike?"

"Didn't know he had one until I'd gone out with him." She could hardly say that it was the feeling they both were outcasts. She kept watching for signs of his lower status in his family, but she could not find them. Perhaps the Ackermans were so different in manners, habits, decibel level from her parents that she read them poorly. "I liked the essays he wrote for class." She thought that was a politic answer and the parents seemed to like it, although Sara shot her a look that said she knew bullshit when she heard it.

"Blake started out having trouble in school. But he's become an exceptional student. Largely because he wanted to," Si said.

"More because I got into computers. I hadn't cared about school before that."

"How did you happen to name him Blake? Is it a family name?"

"Oh, he was named that by his father," Nadine said. "I think it was in honor of the poet Blake and his stand against superstition and oppression."

How did they know about his father? She was very confused, but she did not want to make a point of questioning them in front of Blake, who had immediately changed the subject to what he was hoping to get out of his classes this fall. If both his parents were unknown, as he had told her, how come they knew his mother was white and his father admired Blake, the English poet? "Tyger! Tyger! burning bright/In the forests of the night. . . ." That was the one. She had been reading him at Miss Porter's for a paper. She shivered suddenly.

"Somebody walked over your grave," Sara said. They were sitting side by side in the booth and Sara had felt her reaction. "That's what my bubba always says."

"The air-conditioning is a little high," Melissa said defensively.

"I hate air-conditioning," Nadine said. "My body's thermostat is set too low and I'm always chilly. I'm the only woman I ever knew who enjoyed her hot flashes."

"Mother!" Sara said. "Don't be gross. Who wants the last dumpling?"

Melissa didn't think she was scoring high with them. If only she could think of something brilliant to say that would win them over. But startling statements were not her forte. She was a plodder, excelling, when she did, by simple stubborn persistence and remembering to cross every *t* and dot every *i*.

"So what does your father do?" Si asked.

The question she had dreaded. She did not see how, when asked directly, she could lie. "He's in the government," she said softly.

"What does he do in the government?" Nadine persisted.

Blake threw her a warning look, but what good could it do to lie now, when they would surely find out. "He's a senator."

"Dickinson," Nadine said. "Oh my god, your father is Dick Dickinson?"

She nodded.

Everyone looked at her and at Blake.

"My old enemy," Si said. "Well, this is a surprise."

"She didn't ask for him to be her father," Blake said. "She's a good person. You can't hold her father against her."

"But don't you see?" Nadine said. "It's the Capulets and the Montagues. You can't hope that who your families are won't enter into it."

Sara was grinning as if she had known all along. Had Blake told her? Was that why she had come along? To see the fireworks.

"I'd prefer, I'd really very much prefer that you don't talk about her father until you know Melissa better. Then we can discuss him."

"Why didn't you warn us?" Nadine laid her chopsticks in an X across her plate as if to forbid herself to eat more.

"Exactly because of how you're reacting. I didn't want her father to be the focus. I didn't want her to end up having to defend him just because he's her father when she doesn't agree with him ninety percent of the time. I wanted—I still want—you to get to know Melissa for herself. I won't even discuss her father now and I won't let her discuss him." Blake half rose in his seat.

Sara pushed him down. "Let's not go there. Enough with the Actors Studio scene. So you guys don't like her father. Blake's not fucking the Senator. Let's cool it. I like Melissa—what I've seen of her—and Blake's crazy about her. Why not give him credit for knowing her better than we do?"

No, Melissa decided, Sara had come along because Blake had asked her to. She was on his side. Whatever might be his real position in the Ackerman family, he had a loyal supporter, and that he had never told her. Maybe he just took his adopted sister's support for granted. Melissa was confused by the family dynamics. They were warmer than her own family, more argumentative. She could not say she felt comfortable with them. She could not tell herself she had won them over. She didn't understand Blake's relationship with the older Ackermans, with his sister, with this entire densely populated and very involved clan. She had dozens of questions to ask him, and a queasy suspicion that he wasn't going to answer them readily. That he would, when she began to question him, pull that number of starting an argument and scaring her into apologies. He knew where her buttons were, and he knew how to push them. But she had to be proud that he had finally introduced her to his family; and maybe the worst was over on that front. Maybe the worst was over.

Melissa decided that on the whole Blake's parents had behaved better than hers. They had stopped their interrogation when Blake demanded they do so. He must wield a little more power in his family than she did in here. They hadn't made a scene about her not being Jewish. Further, Blake's parents knew they were involved, whereas her parents had made all that fuss about someone who as far as they knew was just an acquaintance from school. Yes, in the congeniality contest, his parents won hands down, although the evening had been tense.

She waited to see if there would be any negative reaction in Blake's attitude toward her, but instead he complimented her on not losing her cool under questioning. "They're not happy, but they're prepared to act civilized. They'll tell each other it's just a passing thing, and they'll wait for it to pass."

"I wanted them to like me. I wanted that so bad."

"Sara liked you."

"Yeah, but she's in Texas. A lot of good that does us."

"Oh, she can make her opinions felt, don't doubt that. Besides, I think she'll break up with her boyfriend and come back. She's getting tired of his fuck-ups. He went out to L.A. with the grand scheme of being a screenwriter, but he's a bartender in a sleazy bar in Austin."

She frowned, sitting on his bed against the wall with a pillow behind her. "I know your parents are supposed to be crack lawyers, but I have trouble imagining that. Especially Nadine."

He grinned at her, shaking his head. "Many a prosecutor has thought the same and gone down in flames. She comes on grandmotherly. She charms the jury. Then she goes for the jugular, always with an air of just cleaning things up. Don't let the little pigeon body and sweet smiles fool you. She has a serrated mind. And Si is one of the top ten in the country at what he does. Criminal cases and a lot of appeals."

An e-mail message was waiting for her from Rosemary that evening, although it wasn't Friday, only Wednesday.

That rather strange young man whom you brought into the house while we were in Maine turns out to be the son of Simon Ackerman. As you may recall, Ackerman and your father were at odds for years over the trial, conviction and execution of a man who killed a Philadelphia policeman, Toussaint Parker. Ackerman was a real thorn in your father's side. They also clashed around another less publicized case involving a convicted felon, Atticus Jones. Ackerman openly supported your father's opponent in both gubernatorial and the recent senatorial elections. I feel that his son is not the best companion for you, and we certainly do not welcome him into our home. Please keep this in mind. You must choose your companions less unwisely. I have often told you that people judge you as much for the company you keep as on what you yourself may do or say.

College in some ways is preparation for life, but in other ways, it *is* your life. Your father made friends in college who are his backers to this day. While in some ways the college environment is protected and not quite real, the friends and acquaintances, the enemies, the contacts you make there can help you or haunt you long after you have been graduated.

Blake would also be reading this message, since he monitored Rosemary's e-mail. She was furious. How dare they essentially forbid her to bring a friend into the house because of what his father had done in previous elections? Was she supposed to befriend only descendants of people who had laid money on Dick?

A message came from Blake almost immediately:

> Don't answer in anger. Let it stew for two days. Then we'll compose
> an answer together.

She e-mailed him back:

> I'm too pissed off to answer tonight anyhow. Let her worry for a
> change.

"Rosemary is so condescending it gives me heartburn," she said to Emily. "She addresses me as if I'm an idiot."

"It's just her manner. She talks to me the same way, and we're not even related."

"She never talks like that to men. She doesn't talk that way to Dick or Rich."

"How many women talk to women and men the same way? Get real." Emily was riding high because, standing in line at registration, she had met a guy she had a good time with, in and out of bed. She had seen him twice already. Besides, she liked the gang he hung out with better than her old group from the year before. "You hear me on the phone with Mitch. Do I sound like an idiot, or what? I hear my voice going up into baby treble and I hear myself giggling the way I never do, right?"

"I know I talk to Blake just the same as I do with you, Em."

"Yes, honey, yes, baby, yes, sugar. You don't *yes* me all the time that way. We're all a little tainted when we're with a guy we need to impress with how soft and sweet and sexy we are."

"Anyhow, I'm ripshit with her. She has no respect for me."

"She's your mother. Mothers have no respect. They just have rules." Emily had got a car finally from her parents, a five-year-old Honda—not what she wanted, but it had wheels and an engine. Last Sunday the girls had gone for a drive, Em and her and Fern and Fern's new almost-girlfriend, Tammy, from the Ultimate Frisbee team, to the state park and back.

"At least they gave you a car. I couldn't even get a motorcycle out of Rosemary."

"This car is just about embarrassing."

"Yeah, but Em, it goes. We have wheels finally."

"Training wheels. Even tricycles have wheels."

"We could trade parents."

Emily snorted. "No thanks. I may be fed up with mine, but yours are worse. If my mother wrote me the kind of letter Rosemary just sent you, I'd file for divorce. At least my parents don't ride me. I'm beginning to think that's cool."

That evening, Blake wanted to show her the stuff he had been working on, proof, he called it, that King Richard had played fast and loose with campaign finances. Dick was using money he had raised for campaigns to pay for his attempts to get close to powerful members of the Senate. "That's illegal. That could cause something of a stink."

"Really? It just seems a technicality. I mean, who could get excited about that? So he's friendly with guys he sees at work. Big deal."

"The media. The Senate. They care about technicalities. Paying attention to technicalities keeps them away from the real corruption, the buying of legislation through contributions. That's legal, but taking money out of the till for any use that could be construed as personal, that's dirty pool."

"So what are you going to do with this?" She perched on a chair. She knew better than to pick up anything on his desk. He went ballistic if she touched his computer or his discs or his peripherals. It was one of the least endearing things about him.

"Get it to Roger via Phil. We'll establish a relationship so we can feed him things."

She felt a little queasy about what he was planning to do, but frankly it all seemed too esoteric to matter. Besides, her parents had been nasty. They'd arrived without warning, without a polite little phone call saying, Here we come, ready or not. Instead they'd barged in and then Rosemary was furious that she actually had a life. They had been rude to Blake. In fact, they had been rude to her. "You're going to set things up so you can give information directly to Roger eventually—cutting Phil out of the loop."

"It'd be simpler that way, unless Phil starts coming up with goodies he dug up on his own. He's been useful—but you don't find him easy to get along with."

"I don't. You've met his father? Roger?"

Blake nodded. "But we need to establish our reliability first." He put the materials together and tucked them into his backpack. "We should meet Phil tonight and pass on this stuff."

"*You* can give it to him."

"Are you nervous about it? Cold feet?" He took her chin in his hand.

"This is a long way from trying to influence my father, isn't it? Giving stuff to some reporter who has it in for my dad."

"This should come from both of us. And this does move you into a position of power—when the time comes, he'll be more likely to listen. A spot of tiny blackmail. Besides, I thought you were pissed at them."

It could help her to stir up a tiny fuss, to pull Rosemary's scrutiny away from her and Blake. Her mother went into a dither whenever Dick was criticized. Rosemary would be mounting a countercampaign and too busy to bother with her. It would prove only a passing nuisance, but her parents' attention would be elsewhere. Plus she was really angry with them. Phrases from Rosemary's message kept bobbing up to jab her.

By the next day, she felt she had mulled over her response quite enough. She was not going to wait for Blake to compose an answer. Rosemary was her problem, so she should crank up her courage and deal with her.

I thought one of the purposes of going away to college was to meet different kinds of people and broaden my horizons. If the sins of the fathers are to be visited on their sons and daughters, I'd be quite the outcast here, wouldn't I? At least half the kids on campus wouldn't speak to me. And don't tell me I shouldn't speak to them. Our home environment is quite controlled enough. It's time I learned there are other kinds of people and other opinions. Isn't that part of growing up?

As for Blake, I like him. I have been seeing him since I got back to school. I find him pleasant, not pushy or aggressive, but intelligent and thoughtful. I think judging him by his father or grandfather or uncle is silly. It's him, not his family, that I go to the movies with. Eat lunch with occasionally. Are you going to vet everyone in my classes whom I decide to see now and then? Some of them are probably Democrats!

She was pleased by her reply. She read it to Emily, and then she sent it, before she lost her moment's courage to stand up to Rosemary. She had never been good at fighting back. She wasn't being that courageous. Describing Blake as if he were a casual date was a calumny on their love. It belittled him. But it was a beginning. If she wrote honestly that she loved him, was deeply involved with him, wanted eventually to marry him, then her mother would be up in Middletown tomorrow to drag her out of school and take her home, she was sure of that.

Out of idle curiosity, she told herself, she went online and checked Connecticut's laws on marriage. She was old enough to marry without parental consent. Not that she was really about to run off with Blake and get hitched, but it made her feel stronger to know that legally she could, that her parents couldn't stop her. It was a little fantasy she could use to prop up her courage and keep in the back of her mind as a secret weapon against them. Yes, she would wear her blue Tencel dress, her favorite. Or she could wear the bridesmaid's dress she had dyed black last summer. She'd never had an occasion to wear it since. They were bathed in golden light and a tall, distinguished-looking . . . what? Would Blake want a rabbi? She had never been to a Jewish wedding. Emily had. She'd ask her what they were like. Blake would be utterly handsome.

She and her parents were engaged in war, and the prize was her identity, her life as she wanted to live it. Merilee was back at George Washington law school for her last year, and Rosemary was again monitoring her social life. Merilee had given in and gone up to Maine. Melissa had not. She was stronger than her golden picture-perfect sister. She suspected that Merilee too wanted more autonomy and that was why she had taken the summer job in New York. Now she was back, and Melissa did not think her older sister would ever truly break free. But she would. No matter what the cost, she would be her own person and free.

A reply from Rosemary was waiting on her e-mail when she got back from class:

I think you are making a foolish mistake. I explained to you previously that the people you mix with in college, whether friends or simply acquaintances, form others' judgment of you as well as your own accomplishments or lack of them. The young man you were dining with in our kitchen is obviously not of your kind. People seeing him with you would always notice, not favorably, and wonder why you had resorted to someone so different from yourself.

I ask you to reconsider your contact with this young man. No matter how innocuous he may appear to you, he may not appear so to others. A person may appeal because they are exotic, the very reason that a companion may prove to be completely unsuitable. I want you to know that your father has expressed his concern over your associations at Wesleyan. We both feel this connection could be quite damaging. He is extremely busy this week, or he would communicate with you himself—he is that concerned. However, he asked me to convey to you his desire that you stop seeing this young man at once. Any connection with Simon Ackerman is unacceptable to him—and to me—and should be to any loyal daughter.

Furious, she erased the message, hoping she had been quick enough so that Blake would not read it. It was so insulting, so condescending, so bigoted, she felt smeared with shame as if it were a sticky substance plastering her. How could Rosemary presume to judge Blake at first glance? How superficial could her mother be? It wasn't superficiality: it was racism, blunt, pervasive and unashamed.

She asked Blake that evening as they were standing in line to see a Czech film, "Did Roger get the material on Dick's use of contributions?"

"He liked it, but he's checking into it. I hope he's preparing an exposé."

"I hope so," she said bitterly. "I hope so more than anything else!"

"You've been having it out with your mother?"

"I can't stand them!"

"At least they're up front about their racism. Maybe that's easier to deal with than someone who talks the talk and then does what he pleases. You know what you're dealing with."

Blake never talked during movies, so it was not until afterward when they stopped for ice cream in the student center that she could ask him, "Have you had fallout from your folks?"

"Not much. They trust me more than your people trust you. And I'm a guy. Parents tend to meddle less with guys."

"Because you can't get pregnant?"

"Maybe that's at the core. Or just that men are expected to see a certain number of females when they're younger. Si and Nadine are more laid-back with us kids. They've always given us a lot of rope. If my grades dipped, they'd sit up, but I have close to a four-point average."

"Because you're brilliant."

"Long as you think so, I've got it made." He stretched. Her fingers traced his biceps through his black tee. He liked to wear black, and he looked good in it. It brought out the warmth, the hidden sun in his skin.

ROGER'S FIRST ARTICLE appeared within a week. She did not hear from Rosemary with any pointed exhortations to dump Blake that week, and the Friday e-mail was marked by brevity:

> The enemies of your father are up in arms against him. We will
> prevail, of course, and the dirt they are throwing at him will
> rebound on them. Still, it is a difficult time for all of us. I know your
> prayers are with us. I will let you know how the battle is going.

Melissa went online and checked the *Philadelphia Inquirer* Web site. There was Roger's piece with the information they had fed him through Phil and more besides he must have found himself. We did that, she thought, and felt a quiver of triumph. It was a strange new sensation. She was playing a chess game against Rosemary and, for once, she was winning. It was an extraordinary rush. This must be what power felt like,

Rosemary and Dick's true high, their vice. She had never understood it. What she had wanted was love, to be held in a shimmer of affection. She had that now, but not from them. Having love, for the first time she tasted power. She had the capacity to rivet their attention on something. She had the capacity to hurt them, as they had so often hurt her. She felt large and strong. She was becoming herself, not the weak, wobbly, sorry little girl she had been. She was turning into someone to be reckoned with. If she had to proceed in secrecy, well, Rosemary always worked behind the scenes. That was how things got done. But she was actually making things happen, and that was a new sensation, one she rather liked.

"You'll never guess where we're going this weekend," Blake said over lunch, a private lunch for once outside on the grass. Now that they were sophomores, they could eat sometimes out of Moron, could use one of the fast-food places in the student center.

"To New York?"

"Not nearly that far."

"What's closer than New York? Boston!"

"Not that far, and that's the wrong direction."

"Hartford? Why would we want to go to Hartford?"

"We wouldn't. Ever."

"New Haven? Like, Yale?"

"Nothing like Yale. Not New Haven."

"Providence?" She had never been there, but she knew Brown was there.

"Wrong, again. You're never going to win a prize this way. But you get one anyhow."

"So where are we going?" She loved him teasing her, she loved the mystery. This was the kind of day they had first hooked up last year, a bright blue day when the sun made everything shimmer as if lit from within, the golden trees, the red vines. They had been together for a year and they were tighter than ever. She tossed her hair, feeling special, feeling attractive and joined. Maybe he meant he was taking her up to the ledge where they'd first made it.

"To Foxwoods."

"The gambling place? What for?" Disappointment swamped her.

"We're gambling that the guy we're meeting will give us some good documentation."

"But why there?"

"Hard to find a more anonymous place. Nobody is surprised when you go there. We'll be among crowds of people who don't know each other, aren't interested in each other, never will see each other again. He suggested it."

"Who is he?"

He took her face between his hands and smiled into her eyes, very pleased with himself. "A disgruntled ex-staffer of King Richard's. Through some old connection, Karen told me about him—"

"When did you talk with Karen?"

"We talk maybe every couple weeks. I told you, I like her. She has good politics."

She should be happy that Karen and Blake liked each other, but she felt left out. That was oftener than she talked with her aunt. "So what's with this guy?"

"Might have information. We talked and finally set up a meet."

"Why can't we just go see him?"

"He's afraid of your father. He doesn't want any link to us or to Roger. He doesn't know who you are, so don't tip him. That would scare him off."

"But maybe I know him."

Blake shrugged, a graceful shiver of his shoulders. "I doubt it. He never met the family, far as I can tell, except for Rosemary. He doesn't want trouble, but I suspect he wants payback."

"And we're his tool?" That made her feel queasy. She did not like the idea of being anybody's shortcut to revenge against her father.

"He has information, and we want to understand Dick. So Saturday, we go on a date to a casino. Don't say I never take you anyplace." He squeezed her shoulder. "Maybe we'll like it and become addicted gamblers and waste our lives."

"I so don't think that!"

"Me neither. We're serious types, Lissa mine." He radiated a beam of pure joy that made her happy against her will. But she still felt dubious about this ex-staffer who might actually recognize her. What kind of devious turd would turn against someone they worked for? She did not like that. It felt unclean. But then she quizzed herself. If any dirt on the place she worked last summer had come into her hands, would she have felt loyalty to them? Not likely. This guy had probably held down some menial job in her father's organization. Someone incompetent who had a grudge because he didn't feel his talents had been sufficiently recognized or recompensed. Rosemary and Dick were clever at using people, and their staff members were passionately loyal. Probably he had been far down the hierarchy and thus bereft of that eye-beam of approval that so enchanted most underlings. Loyalty was important to her parents, and generally they commanded it successfully. She did not look forward to meeting this little worm who had turned, but it would be fun to go off with Blake. She was still furious with Rosemary. Anything that happened served them right.

"Do you believe in loyalty to an employer?" she asked Fern and Emily over breakfast. They were sharing a table in Mocon, where the roar around them even this early would cover their conversation. Even though Melissa did not intend to tip anything about what she and Blake were doing, she felt safer if no one else listened.

"No!" Fern said immediately. "When I think of all the crappy jobs my mother has held down or that have held her down, I'd like to throttle her bosses. The restaurant she works in now, the guy is always juggling their hours and cutting back on help so she has to work more tables and then gets less tips because she can't give as good service. It's backbreaking work."

Melissa was glad Tammy wasn't along. She often skipped breakfast, providing Melissa an opportunity to see Fern without her. Melissa felt as if Tammy disapproved of her in some undefined way. She was a big girl, as tall as Fern but blockier, pretty features or maybe she should say handsome. When Tammy was around, Fern was paying attention to her and not to Melissa.

Emily, whose parents didn't believe in her wasting time on menial jobs, just nodded at Fern. "My parents' receptionists come and go every year. It isn't like a relationship. It's just a convenience on both sides."

"But if you believed in what they were doing," Melissa said tentatively.

Both of them looked at her blankly. "You mean, like believe in Italian food? I don't get it, I hereby swear allegiance to overcooked lasagna." Fern had more confidence these days. She stood straighter and her voice was firmer. She and Tammy had quickly moved into a relationship.

"I mean, I believe in chiropractic, if like your back is out," Em said. "My parents get into fads, like this month it's heat and next month it's cold, and all sorts of extracts of bark and weird herbs, but if you're in pain, they can help you, for sure. I don't get where you're going with this? Does this have something to do with Rosemary dumping on you?"

"Indirectly," Melissa said. "Forget it. I wasn't going anywhere with it." But she was. To Foxwoods on Saturday. Even Emily felt some loyalty to her parents. As the day approached, she was increasingly nervous about what they were doing. It felt like a silly game, the way she used to play with Billy. It was all unreal, she told herself, but she remembered how real that article on the Internet *Inquirer* site had felt. She no longer felt powerful; she felt out of her depth. She wished she could just tell Blake to cool it and forget about her parents. She wished she could just run away with him and come back in five years with two kids, say, and her parents would have to accept them. Somehow everything was tied into knots and she felt coerced and tangled. My bad, she thought, my bad and things are just getting worse.

CHAPTER NINETEEN

Now Melissa had a leather jacket she'd bought to break the wind as she clung to him on his Honda. The trip was along back roads. The leaves were beginning to turn. By the bank of a creek, aspens rustled golden, leaves like bright pirates' coins. One lone red maple stood in a field of stubbled corn. The poison ivy and Virginia creeper twined scarlet. Big puffy clouds scudded over them. He braked abruptly as a flock of red-winged blackbirds stormed just a few feet above the road, thousands of them passing for two minutes going south. She was happy, a high plateau she had never before visited. They belonged together. They were a conspiracy, a good family of two. Her cheek rested against his shoulder, the engine roared into her, the sun beat on her head and arm in the cool whoosh of the wind of their riding. The machine thrummed up into her body. She did not really care where they were going and whether the mysterious contact was worth the bother. It was going off together that mattered, not their arrival anyplace. She had the sense as she clung to him that never again in her entire life would she, could she, be as happy. It was an uncanny nostalgia for something still occurring, as if she were in the moment and yet high above it, looking down and back and already missing the intensity and the joy. That pumped a vein of melancholy through the joy, making it even more intense.

She had seen the ads for the casino on TV—who in New England hadn't?—but she considered that image an artist's sketch. The reality was as much a fantasy as the ads, mammoth structures rising out of a forest. However, they did not go directly to the casino. "We're not meeting our contact till four," he said, chaining the bike.

"So why are we here at one? Like, you don't expect me to gamble. Do you gamble?" She wondered suddenly if he had a secret vice. Ever since he had suggested going to Foxwoods, she had been a little apprehensive.

"This is the museum. Come on. State-of-the-art archeology."

It was modern, sleek and very light, a pleasant, even elegant building, as opposed to the huge casino and hotel complex. He acted giddy as they roamed through the Ice Age past a giant beaver and an outsize wolf, both extinct but looking quite real, and cases of artifacts. "You like that wolf," she said. "I didn't know you were so interested in archeology."

"I was really into paleontology when I was a kid. I loved dinosaurs. I had all these models and I could tell you everything known about each of them."

"How come?" She'd never seen the appeal. Just big nasty lizards who would probably try to eat you.

"I guess because they were so big. I felt if I was a dino, nobody could bother me. I'd be able to defend anyone I loved. Kids like me dig those horny hides and scales and big teeth."

They strolled into the 1600 village. All around the room were representative groups of figures in daily activities, while the sound boxes they'd picked up on the way in told them what they were looking at. If she wanted to know more about any of the exhibits, she simply pressed a button for details. The figures were well done, not as stiff as most mannequins and very individual. She commented on that to Blake.

"Yeah, they're each modeled after someone in the tribe. I read that."

"You think you might be part Native American?"

"Could be. . . . But isn't it great? Imagine soaking all that money from gambling and setting up a museum. I love it."

One of the figures in the village did look something like Blake. If she could see the guy it was modeled after, would he resemble Blake? She tried to decide how she would feel if Blake were Native American. Actually it would be kind of cool. A couple were setting up housekeeping together, building a wigwam. "Imagine, we could build something like that in the woods. . . ."

"Doesn't look that hard." He slipped his arm around her waist. "Want to? The hell with dormitories."

It looked cozy, just the round space and most time spent outside. The couple had been given blissful expressions. Instead of classes and grades and her parents ranting at her, there they'd be in the woods fishing and hunting and growing their food. "No housework. And I bet their weddings didn't require making plans a year in advance and spending forty thousand dollars."

"Is that what your brother's wedding cost?"

"I just made up that number. The bride's family paid."

"Do you have fantasies about your wedding?"

"Only that it be over clean and quick, with just a couple of friends."

"You know, my sister, Sara, she ran off with this guy and eloped. He was a client of my dad's, a con man who was facing heavy charges. Dad got him off and he ran away with Sara. By the time my parents found her, in South Carolina, she was already sorry she'd done it. They had the marriage annulled. Dad was furious at the guy. Let's see, Sara was eighteen. I was just thirteen when it all came down. Turned out he planned to use Sara in some scam that had to do with bilking older men. She always falls for these abysmal losers."

They wandered through the museum holding hands, finding an occasional deserted corner where they could kiss. Finally it was three thirty and time to go.

He was less ecstatic when they entered the casino, where the air was heavy with smoke even in the elevators. It was jammed everywhere, the rows of stores, the gambling halls, the restaurants, the entertainment, the benches set up at regular intervals. Aunt Karen had described Las Vegas to her years before, flyers on whorehouses and call girls handed out on every corner. Here there were no visible hookers, although she assumed they must be around. Suburban people with kids in tow passed in droves. Everything was indoors, clean, neat, well tended, brightly lit. Buses disgorged the elderly with their fanny packs as Karen had described, but there were just as many kids on dates—like them. They didn't stand out.

Families ambled along as if in a mall, couples strolling past the huge rooms of intent gamblers parked at their machines. Even in the no-smoking casino, smoke hung heavy in the air, and there were ashtrays on the poker tables. Blake, who had asthma and suffered smoke badly, began to labor in his breathing. She hoped their contact, whoever he was, would be on time. Blake could get sick if they hung in here too long. He used his inhaler, but it wasn't enough.

It was better when they sat on a bench in the concourse in front of a shop selling Native American artifacts, watching people surge by in an endless procession. They had ice cream, then set out to find the location their contact had specified. Thousands of people were milling about, but the most interesting to her were those stuck in front of every slot machine grimly pushing in coins. Adrenaline hung in the air like sharp perfume. She was appalled and fascinated. "Do you understand gambling?" she asked him. "To me it's like throwing money down the toilet."

"It's a rush, obviously. Look at the people. They pull a lever and it presses a button in their head. I don't have that button, you don't—but some folks would say we're addicted to each other. That we have to have each other. That the pleasure we give each other is our weakness."

"You don't make me feel weak. You make me strong."

"He told me where to meet him, but I'm not figuring it out yet. Let me see that map they gave you." He frowned at it. She could feel anxiety coming off him in waves. "Okay, I think we're on the wrong level. Let's try going downstairs. Like it would be entirely stupid to come all this way and hang around and then miss him because we can't find where he meant for us to be."

They made their way to the high-limit slots and took up a position against one wall. She wondered if she would recognize this supposedly former assistant to her father. Blake had told her to say her name was Mary Jo. She had no idea where he'd plucked that name from, but she said it over to herself four or five times to get used to the sound. By ten after four, no one had approached them.

"We may have come all this way for nothing. Do you think he got scared?" She kept staring around them, hoping to find someone who looked likely.

"Could be. Or he's not as punctual as you are. You're the only person I know who says they will be ready in two minutes and means two minutes. Who says they will meet you at four, and is there at four exactly."

"Rosemary couldn't endure for us to be late. She runs on a tight schedule. I learned to have a precise sense of time. I can't help it now. I'm trained."

"I'm not that housebroken, and I don't want to be." He was forcing himself to look around as if idly. They were both wound tight.

"I think there's nothing I hate so much as just waiting. Maybe Rosemary feels that way and so she makes us run by the second hand." She remembered again that it was Karen who had put Blake in touch with this guy. "What do you talk about with Karen?"

"We're both interested in some of the same political problems. I really like her. I trust her instincts."

She knew she should be happy that someone in her family liked Blake, but she felt disregarded and jealous that they were communicating separately, making her unimportant. She knew she must not show that. "How does Karen know this guy? She was locked up for five years."

"She's in touch with people she knew when she was with Eve. People in Pennsylvania working to defeat King Richard. An old contact told her about him."

It was partly tedious standing against the wall, leaning on him. Yet it was also fascinating to watch the people. She discovered she could stare at individuals, the woman with the bright orange sweater and thin yellowish white hair and oversize plastic earrings in the form of tropical fish; the man with a trim goatee, sweating heavily in his tweed jacket, his tie askew; the tiny bald man who kept figuring something on the calculator he tried to hide. She could stare freely because they looked only at their machines and did not feel her gaze. There was an intensity to them she almost envied. If she could study like that, she would have a 4 point average instead of a 3.6. She would no longer be a B plus type but A all the way. She imagined that she could do a striptease where she stood, and they would never break their concentration to look up.

It was four thirty. "How long should we wait?"

"Till five. Then we'll get something to eat and take off. But we have to give him that long, because suppose he got stuck in traffic. Or had car trouble. Got lost."

"An idiot could find this place. You can see it for miles."

"Maybe he had to wait for a parking place. The lots are huge, but they're full. Just relax. You liked the museum, right?"

It felt stupid leaning against the wall in a room full of people all intent, passionately involved. Time oozed by. She kept looking at her watch and finding that only a minute had passed. She began to hope the guy would not turn up and they could just clear out.

Finally, twenty minutes later, a man who had been sitting at a machine came toward them. "Are you interested in politics?"

"Very much so," Blake said, and they shook hands.

"Sam? You're just a kid."

"I'm twenty-two. I look younger than I am."

"Who's she?"

"My girlfriend, Mary Jo. She's studying journalism. She does power structure research."

The guy was of middling height and weight with dark blond hair cut bristly short. His chin came almost to a point and his ears were like handles on a cookie jar. He wore a navy blazer with a striped blue and white shirt, khakis, tassel mocs. He was obviously uneasy, keeping his head and voice down. "I saved this stuff for two years. The bastard fired me."

"How come?"

"I worked like a dog for him. Nothing was too hard or too dirty for me. I worked for him from before his second gubernatorial run. Well into the Senate race. Then I had a situation with an undercover cop in a john. It didn't even hit the papers, it was so minor. But he fired me on the spot."

"That's terrible," Blake said. "No gratitude."

"Fuck gratitude. No severance pay, not even a letter of recommendation."

He must have meant he was gay and had tried to pick someone up. Dick and Rosemary went ballistic about gay people. Melissa realized she had seen him before: in Harrisburg, at the mansion. It was while she was at Miss Porter's. She was home for Christmas vacation and he had come in with the secretary of transportation and the attorney general. She was sitting on the steps waiting for a friend. She had her ice skates with her, yes. Hank, the oldest man, who was now secretary of commerce, asked if she was going skating outside or inside, and she had thought for a moment he meant was she going skating in the mansion. She felt foolish then. He meant in a rink or on a pond. Yes, this man had been with them, had stood uneasily while Hank teased her about skating down the steps, stood shifting from foot to foot carrying a leather attaché case and wearing a blue muffler wound around his neck, a muffler he had not removed any more than he had taken off his coat. Impatient? Nervous? His ears had stood out just as they did now, like handles.

She glanced at him uneasily, waiting for him to recognize her, but his gaze was fixed on Blake. He did not remember her, or maybe she just looked too different. She liked the latter explanation. She wanted to believe she had blossomed out of that chubby awkward miserable child into someone far more attractive.

"I've held on to this stuff since I was thrown out. Just kept it in a safe-deposit box."

"Now it's time to give it to someone who can use it, don't you think? It does no good sitting in a lockbox."

The man slipped a fat envelope from inside his blazer, but he seemed reluctant to hand it over. She could feel the tension in Blake's arm, his desire to grab the envelope and bolt before the man had time to change his mind. "What are you going to do with it?"

"We have contacts with investigative reporters on good newspapers. You let us worry about what to do with the information." Again Blake extended his hand, waiting.

Slowly the man put the envelope into Blake's hand, but he still did not let go. Melissa could feel her body clenching. Was he going to hand over whatever it was? Blake tried gently to pry the envelope loose. The man kept glancing around, looking in every direction including up, as if fearing surveillance. Finally the man released his grip and let Blake take the packet.

"Now you've got it all. It's yours."

"We want to thank you for your help. You won't regret it." Blake nodded, trying to reassure him.

"I hope you're right. I really hope so. Don't contact me again." Once again the man stared all around, turning in a tight circle. Then he spun on his heel and strode out of the room, dodging quickly among the aisles of machines. In a moment he was gone.

"What's in it?" she asked, peering at the envelope. "Let's see." She made a gesture toward the envelope.

"Not here. Not now." Blake stuck it inside his leather jacket. "Let's mosey on out." He looked carefully around. He was enjoying the cloak-and -dagger stuff. Well, let him enjoy it. She was curious about what the guy had made such a fuss about. Was he just a loser who wanted to feel important? Probably.

THEY WERE in his room at the dorm before Blake opened the envelope. She leaned forward to peer at the top page. "It's just a bunch of dates and names and then a column of numbers." She had expected something spectacular from all the secrecy and *Mission Impossible* atmosphere.

Blake was wheezing and feeling rotten. "It's going to take . . . some research to . . . figure out what this is." He put the papers down on his desk, next to his computer. "Tonight we can . . . start looking . . . for these names . . . on Internet . . . see who they are. I hope . . . that guy isn't nutcase . . . that really is dynamite . . . he was sitting on." It took him a couple of minutes to get a sentence out.

"Baby, do you need to go to health services? This isn't good." Lists of numbers? Too boring to do any damage. But Blake would enjoy a treasure hunt on the Internet. She took his boasts about her father as a kind of playing, like kids going on about their scores on hot video games. If Karen and Eve hadn't been able to do it, Blake and Phil and she certainly weren't about to. Still she felt a little queasy about that guy and his lists. She wished they could just forget the whole thing and have fun, go on trips without having to meet some shady guy to justify the time.

"I'll be fine . . . if lie down. Waiting for my meds . . . kick in."

"Then just be quiet. We can talk tomorrow. Should I stay with you?"

He shook his head no. "Better . . . don't talk." He kissed his hand to her and waved her out. She was exhausted anyhow. Trips on his bike were like exercise, really. She would tell Em all about the casino, leaving out the reason they went, of course. She would tell it like an adventure all over her floor. Guess what Blake and I did today! It would make a cool story. Ronnie would be jealous. Nobody else on the floor had ever gone to Foxwoods. She could even pretend they had gambled, lost some money playing the slots. That would sound like an adventure.

CHAPTER TWENTY

Melissa was walking back toward the dorm after her eleven o'clock political economy class. As she was crossing Andrus Field, skirting a Frisbee game, she saw Emily coming toward her. "Lissa, your mom called. She said it was urgent—an emergency. She sounded up the wall."

"Is something wrong? Somebody hurt?"

"She wouldn't tell me. You know she thinks I'm a ditz. She was pissed she couldn't reach your cell phone. I don't think she believed me when I tried to explain you can't leave them on in class. She discounts everything I say."

"You're lucky. The less attention she pays you, the better." She did not want to call her mother. "I'll tell you what. Let's have lunch first. I can take it better on a full stomach."

After lunch, she sat on the library steps and called Rosemary. She could not imagine anything her mother would want to say to her that she would want to hear. It could only be bad news or trouble. She hoped not to get through or to have a conversation with Alison instead, but Alison put her mother on right away.

"Melissa, are you still seeing that boy? The Ackerman boy?"

What point was there in denying Blake? "Yeah, Mother, I see him. So what? He's not responsible for his father's courtroom activities."

"We've learned more about him, information that is relevant to our family and to your own safety. Si Ackerman isn't his father—"

"I know all that, Mother. He's adopted. He doesn't know who his mother or his father were."

"Yes, he does. It's a poorly kept secret. His father was a murderer."

"A murderer? I don't believe you. He doesn't know who his father is, I'm telling you. What does it matter?"

"He knows who his father was—a cop killer. Your father prosecuted him. Toussaint Parker. He was executed soon after your father became governor. You must remember the execution? There was an enormous fuss in the media and picketers outside the mansion, chaos that night."

"I remember." She could see the candles bobbing. "What makes you think that man was Blake's father?"

"His son was called Blake. After his mother died in a drug-induced car wreck, the Ackermans adopted the boy. Ackerman was Parker's lawyer and caused us no end of nuisance, taking a hopeless case up through appeal after appeal. It cost the Commonwealth of Pennsylvania millions to finally mete out justice to him and avenge the death of that policeman. The officer had three children and now you're dating his killer's son? If you have any sense of loyalty to the family and any sense of self-preservation, you will never speak with him again. I'm demanding this."

"He can't be the same boy. He can't be! He would have told me."

"He's probably ashamed of who he is. He's been lying to you, obviously, and to everyone else. I can't imagine a good college would have let him in otherwise. The Ackermans have colluded with him to conceal his identity."

"Where did you get your information? Why do you believe this story?"

"We had your father's speechwriter Eric look into it—he's a whiz at research. It wasn't difficult to find out who this boy really is—and there is no doubt, Melissa. The adoption wasn't a secret. The boy was seven. He knows who he is, and now you do. End this ridiculous flirtation at once, for your own good and for ours. He could prove dangerous."

Melissa found herself weeping. "I can't talk."

"It's meaningless to cry about it. I'm considering taking you out of school and bringing you back here. It might be safer for all of us. You must see that he has only been pursuing you to hurt us in some way. I'm sorry if it upsets you, but I tried to warn you that this association was undesirable—in the extreme."

"I can't talk any longer." Melissa broke the connection and shut off her phone. She was stunned, as if an electric current blasted through her mind. She had believed in Blake absolutely, that he loved her, that he was truthful with her. He was lying to her. Why? To get revenge on her father? Blake did not love her. He was using her and she had been a complete fool. She stumbled back to her dormitory shamelessly weeping. In her room, Emily came and put her arms around her. "What happened? What's wrong?"

When Melissa could speak, she told Emily.

"Maybe he really doesn't know whose son he is," Emily offered tentatively.

"He was seven. I remember lots of things from when I was seven. Don't you?"

"People suppress trauma, Lissa. Maybe he managed to repress the trial and everything. It has to be really traumatic to have your father accused of murder, arrested, carted off and tried and finally put to death, the whole thing all over the papers and TV. Maybe he doesn't want to know whose son he is. Maybe it was all just too awful and he never wants to think about it for the rest of his life."

"I don't believe that. He wants to bring my father down. He wants me to help him. That's why he's with me, that's the only reason."

"Lissa, I don't believe that. He's crazy about you. I see the way he looks at you. He's made you feel good about your body for the first time in your life."

"Maybe he was lying. It doesn't mean anything to him."

"You have to confront him. You can't just believe Rosemary and give up on him. You have to let him explain. You have to talk with him. Then if you want to break up with him, do it. If he's just using you, say bye-bye and walk out that door. But find out for yourself."

Melissa slid out of Emily's arms and flung herself on her bed. She wept and wept. Emily went off to class. Melissa cut hers. She lay there unable to move and, after half an hour of weeping, scarcely able to breathe. Emily was right. She had to confront Blake. But she did not want to see him. She felt hideously betrayed. She had loved him totally, and he had lied to her. Lied from the beginning. Lied all the way through their relationship. She had thought they had this perfect intimacy, and it was all made up. Of course no one could love her the way she had dreamed of being loved, and the belief that Blake did had been illusion and wishful thinking. She had simply willed herself to be blind, she had wanted to be fooled into submission to his plans. Her anger at her parents had played into her willingness to believe. He had manipulated her beautifully. He had seen her weakness and used it. She had allowed him to play her. He was a liar and a manipulator, but she was the one who had made his schemes work. He had made his plans when he heard her read that ridiculous essay about her parents.

Finally she got up and sent him a brief e-mail. "I have to talk with you. I'll be over at seven thirty. This is very, very important." She did not sign Love. Would he guess something was wrong? What did it matter? It was over, the lie of their relationship, the farce of their great love.

She forced herself to wash her face and stumble off to her three o'clock French class, where she would find Emily and they could sit together. To be with Emily, who knew how she was torn open and bleeding, gave her comfort. Among all these indifferent students, Emily, her only real friend, was there with her, helping her to hold on. She sat through the class, she even answered the questions the instructor put to her, while all the time she felt numb. She had no hope. Nothing awaited her but pain and after pain, boredom forever, to the grim grey horizon.

After picking at her supper, she trekked over to his dorm, rehearsing speeches in her head. This was the breakup she had dreaded, and now it was happening. She would never love anyone the way she had loved Blake. She would start off, she decided, saying, "I know now you have lied to me. That our whole relationship was a lie. That you care nothing about me and were just using me to get to my father, because your father was a murderer and my father brought him to justice. So let's say good-bye and end this sorry farce."

She thought that said it all with dignity. Then she would leave immediately, before she did something humiliating like cry. She was sure her face was still puffy from the afternoon, but what did it matter if she was ugly? It was over.

He was waiting for her, standing in the middle of his room. "Your mother told you who my father was, and you think you know something about me you didn't know last night."

Of course. He was reading Rosemary's e-mail, so he had expected this. She must have been communicating with Rich and Merilee about her discovery before she called her third child. She began her speech. "I know now you have lied to me. That our whole relationship was a lie—"

"No!" He leapt toward her, putting his hands on either side of her face. "We belong to each other, and nothing about our parents can change that."

"Why did you lie to me?"

"If I'd told you right off what your father had done to mine, you would have been terrified. You would have walked away."

"I should have."

"No. You don't believe that."

His familiar scent. Leather. His lemon verbena aftershave. A tinge of sweat. A smell like gingerbread that emanated from his skin. The scent of his body had always excited and comforted her. "Why didn't you ever tell me the truth during all these months?"

"I was afraid. Afraid to lose you. Have I lost you?"

She meant to say yes, but now she was clinging to him and the words would not come. She could not let go of him. "Make me understand. I can't endure this. It hurts too much!"

"It's a whole world of pain, Lissa. This is at the core of me. If I let you in, will you be able to endure what I endure? Or will you run away?"

"Tell me. Talk to me. I'm so confused I don't know what to do, what to think, what to believe."

"Believe me. I'm the one who loves you." He led her to his bed and they sat there against the wall. He looked as haggard and exhausted as she felt. "So you want to hear my story?"

She nodded, swiping at her eyes.

He gave her one of his big white handkerchiefs. "My father was Toussaint Parker. Named by his own father for Toussaint L'Ouverture, who emancipated the slaves of Haiti in war against several armies and made a free black state—whatever came down the pike later. Anyhow, my father took his name seriously. He was in the Black Panthers when he was sixteen. He was a community organizer all his life. He was not, in his later life, a violent man. I don't know what he was like at sixteen, but at forty he was a determined but nonviolent organizer. He was a powerful speaker and he could move people." He reached into his desk drawer, leaning forward and then immediately sliding back to put his arm around her, holding her tightly against him. He put a photo in her hand, the careworn face of a man who had been handsome, prematurely grizzled, his arm around his little grinning son. "He cared for people and he stood up for them. He was not popular with the city administration, and the police hated him. He put tremendous pressure on them, about how they policed African-American neighborhoods."

"But he killed a cop."

"No, he didn't."

"You still believe he didn't? He was convicted and all his appeals rejected."

"Melissa, I know he didn't. I was with him when he was supposed to have done it. They wouldn't let me testify—a child just turned five. He was home with me. It was my birthday, and we were waiting for Mama to come home from the hospital."

"Your mother was sick?"

"She was a nurse. An RN. She was white. Theirs was not an easy marriage, but it was a love match. She was as political as he was. She served as a medic in demonstrations and was gassed I don't know how many times, even though she had asthma and could easily have begged off. The riot police often target medics in demonstrations."

"So your mother was working and you were home alone with your father."

"My grandma had been there earlier, but she left."

"You could have fallen asleep."

"On my birthday? I was too excited. We were waiting for my mother to come home when we'd have cake and ice cream. My father had hung bright blue balloons from the lamps. We lived on the ground floor of a town house with all these plants my mother grew. She loved begonias and scented geraniums. I remember geraniums that smelled like roses, like cinnamon, like lemon. We had a big chocolate cake my grandma made, but we hadn't even cut it because we were waiting for Mama. Instead the police came. They never listened to me. They never believed me. They didn't want to. My father would never have shot that cop, but besides that, he couldn't have. He was with me the whole evening. He would never go out and leave me alone, and he didn't. He was playing with me and reading to me all that evening, until they came."

"You remember all of it?"

"Of course. It was my birthday. And it was the night the world of my childhood ended. Ended cold."

She tried to imagine what that would feel like. To know something but never to be listened to, never to be believed because you were a child, because they thought you couldn't remember. To know that if they listened to you, you and you alone could save your father—but they wouldn't listen. "So you knew he was innocent, but you couldn't make them hear you."

"It was a nightmare that just kept getting worse. He was treated badly in jail and then in prison. They did their best to keep him away from the other prisoners—they knew he was a hero to many of them. They wouldn't let him have his books. They kept him in solitary for months at a time." Blake was sitting with his long legs pulled up to his chest, his voice slightly muffled as he pushed his face into his knees.

"That's why you won't celebrate your birthday. Why you won't let me give you presents."

"It's nothing to celebrate for me. It's when everything went wrong."

"How did your father's lawyer come to adopt you? What happened to your mother?"

"It was tremendously hard for her. She was involved in the early appeals, and she kept going off to see him whenever she could. All the plants died. She began doing drugs. You know, nurses and doctors, they can get drugs as easily as I can buy a packet of gum. I don't actually know what she was doing—some kind of downers. It kept her going. Now, my father was in a prison way in the corner of the state farthest from

Philadelphia. It was a four-and-a-half-hour drive in the best of circumstances. She generally had to drive both ways in a day, in order to get back to me and to go to work the next day. She was driving back late at night, as usual. She got in an accident on the Pennsy Turnpike. A truck that veered. She was killed instantly. I remember, I was sleeping at my grandma's and the phone rang in the middle of the night."

"How long was this after your father was arrested?"

"Two years. I was seven. That's when Si and Nadine adopted me. My grandma wanted me, but she was too weak to take care of me. She had crippling arthritis. I knew the Ackermans, from my father's trial and all his appeals. They had tried to make things easier for my mom, but nothing could really help. So I became theirs. They've been very good to me—but you see, I'm not their son and I never can be . . ."

"But why didn't you tell me? I keep coming back to that." Seven. She had been crazy about horses and dogs, and her father still made a fuss over her. Her worst fear came from a video of *Snow White,* all the grasping trees. She played Mommy to Billy and pretended to spank him when he was bad, although none of them had ever been spanked. Where did she get that? TV, probably. She was happy then, adoring her parents, with her little brother as playmate.

"For years I haven't told anyone. Si said I shouldn't—that it would cause me trouble. That the authorities—principals, teachers, administrators, bosses—would expect the worst from me, and I'd be having to prove myself all the time. So I haven't told. Not friends, not girlfriends, nobody. I thought of telling you, but it seemed such a big thing—at first, I wanted you to know me before I spoiled everything. Then I kept thinking it wasn't the right time yet. And then I'd waited too long to suddenly say, Oh, by the way, actually I do know who my parents were. Guess who."

"But you didn't get involved with me to get back at my father?"

"I was watching you from the first day of class, don't you know that? At first, who your father was put me off. That's why I waited so long after we spoke the first time to make a move. I didn't know if I could handle your family being who they are. Then I decided, it's not your fault. You didn't choose them."

And he hadn't chosen his birth parents. She had almost broken up with him because of them. She put her arms around him, huddled as he was with his knees drawn up, and tried to hug him. "Neither of us had a choice. We got what we got."

"I'm not ashamed. Don't think that. But it's still an open sore. My father was killed for something he never did. I've always known that, and there isn't a fucking thing I can do about it. I've always been powerless."

"And now you aren't? Because of me."

He put his knees down finally and turned on the bed, pulling her against him. They lay side by side with the length of their bodies pressed together. "I can't lose you," he said into her hair. "I can't. You're the first, you're the only woman I ever loved. We're supposed to be together. It's our fate to find each other and be together."

Tears ran slowly down her face again, and she clutched him. "We are together," she promised. "It doesn't matter what I know now. Rosemary can't pull us apart. No matter how hard she tries." He was hers, he really was. She was not a fool. What she had learned made no difference between them except to give her an understanding of what he had gone through, the pain inside him. She did not love him less for that. She loved him more.

He was pushing his prick at her. She helped him pull her panties down, and then he thrust into her. They weren't even undressed. But she felt the same dumb compulsion to couple, to push themselves into each other and hold on, to move together like frightened children rocking themselves to sleep. They were proving to each other and to themselves that they were still joined. He needed to feel that and so did she. It was not pleasure, not desire but the compulsion to know they had each other that drove them, with him pounding into her and her thrusting up at him, on and on because for a long time neither could come. Finally, sore already, she shivered with her orgasm and shortly afterward, as she bit the insides of her cheeks because it hurt, he came with a loud groan.

"Together we'll set things right," he said. "Together."

CHAPTER TWENTY-ONE

Melissa was on the telephone with Rosemary. "I won't leave school just seven weeks into the semester. I won't!"

"We've decided it's better for you to return home. Alison has checked, and we can get you into American University in January."

"Better for whom?" She articulated carefully, putting on the *m* as she never would with anyone else. "Not for me. I have friends here. I'm doing well in school, and you want to yank me out. No, thank you. You've paid my tuition and my room and board for the year, and I'm staying."

"Melissa, you've behaved irresponsibly and you must accept the cost."

"Of seeing a boy whose parents you don't like? He didn't choose his father. He didn't choose who adopted him. Why blame me? Why blame him, for that matter? I think you should just chill out. He's one of three guys I've been seeing. You only met him because I ran into him in Washington. I've gone out far more with Jed—whom you'd really like. But he's also seeing another girl. . . . Blake's just a student here. He has a better grade point average than I do."

"Your father is under attack now and we need to circle the wagons. Seeing that boy is potentially embarrassing, and could prove dangerous. Ridiculous stories the *Inquirer* is running could hurt Rich's campaign, as well as potentially damaging your father."

"I don't see what newspaper stories have to do with occasionally dating a boy here. He's not a reporter. He doesn't work for a newspaper. He's just a student, like me."

"He's nothing like you, and don't forget that for a moment. Why are you being so stubborn about this? Are you sleeping with him?"

"Absolutely not! But I have to be free to choose my own friends in college. As I told you, he's not even the guy I'm most interested in."

"You can never be free to make poor choices, Melissa. It reflects badly on your father, and we are a public family."

"If I dumped him because of who his dead father is, wouldn't that reflect really badly on me?"

"Melissa, this is not negotiable. This is not a request. We will not allow you to see that boy any longer, for your own good and for the good of your family. A modicum of loyalty, please."

"I will consider what you have said. Carefully."

"Do more than 'consider' it. Implement it."

When she hung up, Melissa was quivering with anger. Rosemary was not the least bit concerned with her well-being but only too willing to sacrifice her desires and her happiness to Dick, to Rich, to Rosemary's own considerable ambitions. Could they really pull her out of school? Her tuition was paid, her dormitory was paid through January. She had to talk to Blake right away.

She caught him just after his web design class. "Blake, my parents are putting tremendous pressure on me to break up with you. They're talking about pulling me out of school."

"We won't let them do that." He started to head toward the student center, then spun around. "Let's go to my room. We can talk there."

They sat cross-legged, facing each other on his bed. "I've been saying that we just see each other casually, but they may guess that isn't true. Rosemary's adamant about getting you out of my life. She's afraid of you, I think."

"I can tell from her correspondence with Rich that she means business. He advised her to pull you out of school, and she's ready to do so."

"I won't go! I'd feel humiliated. Like someone sent home from camp for wetting the bed. I won't break up with you at her command. I won't!"

"We have to stop them." He rose to pace the room. "Do you have any money?"

"Not much. But everything's paid through January."

"I have some money. Friends of my father put it into a trust that Si arranged after my mother died. I mean, it's not a lot, but it's mine. It was in trust until my eighteenth birthday so I could go to college no matter what. It could pay for you if your parents won't—there's enough I think."

"You'd just give it to me?"

"I know if we were married I could." He was still pacing, turning on his heel, running his hands roughly over his close-cropped hair. "Maybe it's time we do that."

"Get married? Like, for real?"

"We'll do it eventually anyway."

"I always hoped we would."

"If we marry, your parents can't touch us."

"So are you asking me, Blake?"

"Sure. Why not? We'll be safer."

"How do we do it? I mean, so it's legal and all." See, she was right and Rosemary was wrong. Not only did he really love her, he was ready for them to get married. She was so excited she jumped up and hugged him, hard. She would be married way ahead of Merilee. She was loved and she would have her own family, away from them.

"I'm not sure. I think we get a license and a blood test—like to tell if we have syphilis. I don't think they test for AIDS. But whatever."

"When should we do it?"

"As soon as possible, to head your mother off at the pass. I'll go online and get the facts for Connecticut. We have lots of states to choose from in New England if there's a problem. I'll get on it right now." He headed to his computer and booted up.

She almost said that she'd checked Connecticut law, but she was afraid to sound as if she had already been thinking about marriage. "Should I, like, go home and get packed?"

"Don't do that until I see if we have to leave. I mean, we don't require a honeymoon. We just need to make it legal. I have a test in web design Friday, so I don't want to be away then. But we could get married in the morning and still get back in time for me to ace that test."

She giggled. "It sounds so unreal. Getting married in the morning and going back to class in the afternoon."

"We're mated already. It's just a legal thing, so they can't push you around, you know?" He stood up and came around his chair to put his hands on her shoulders. "This is okay with you, right?"

"More than okay. I want to."

She ran back to her room. She was delighted to see Emily at her desk with her laptop on, writing a paper. "Em, guess what? No, don't. You'll never guess in a hundred years."

"Must be something good. You're all lit up."

"Blake asked me to marry him!"

"Jesus. Are you real? Was he kidding around?"

"He meant it. And I said yes."

Emily backed out of her file and shut down her laptop. "Lissa, what is this? We're just sophomores. He's only like the second guy you ever bonked."

"But my mother is threatening to pull me out of school. If Blake and I were man and wife, they couldn't touch us."

"They could try to get the marriage annulled."

"It would be a scandal if they did. Because the two of us would be screaming and kicking and fighting."

Emily straddled her desk chair, staring. "But how come you want to get married so quick? I mean, it seems crazy to me. We're still kids. We don't need to think about pairing off permanently for years. We have lots of time to meet guys and get to know them and find out what we really, really want. It's time for fun, not for settling down in a condo with some guy you only met last year."

"But I love him, Em. How much can you love someone? That's the way I love him. It can't get better than that. What would I be waiting for? A rock star? A millionaire? I just want someone to love me the way I love them."

"So can't you just go along loving him for a couple of years until you know for sure what you want to do with your life?"

"I don't have a couple of years. Rosemary's threatening to pull me out of school."

"That would be so uncool. You couldn't get into a good school in the middle of the year."

Melissa snorted. "That's what I told her. She doesn't care. She'll always sacrifice me to my father or Rich. Everybody's more important than me."

"You just can't let them pull you out of school! You have to talk to her."

"She's not interested in what I want. Only what's good for Dick. What's good for Rich. What's good for her."

"So if you got married, you could stay in school?" Emily frowned, trying to puzzle it out.

"I wouldn't even tell her unless she tried to make me go home. Then that would be my trump card. You see?"

"Sort of. But it just seems like such a drastic step. Although I suppose you could always get a divorce if it doesn't work out."

They both laughed. "Me, a divorcée at twenty." Melissa felt close to Emily again. "It seems like I'll wake up and it's just a game or a fantasy, something you play around with imagining when you're bored. But it's the only way I can be sure of being with him, of staying in school. The only way to keep them from just eating me up to satisfy themselves. And it isn't like I never thought of marrying him. When the two of us stayed in my parents' house last summer, while they were up in Maine, we pretended like we were married."

Melissa wished that Emily could enter into her plans more enthusiastically. She tried to imagine how she would feel if Emily came barging in one evening and announced she was getting married. Probably her first thought would be that she would have to get another roommate and she would not see nearly as much of her friend. "Em, it'll be a secret. We'll just have the ceremony and come back here and resume. I'll be living here, we'll go to classes and do each other's hair and borrow clothes and everything will be the same. But I'll just have an insurance policy against my mother."

About an hour later, she checked her e-mail and found a message from Blake. "Wow, do you believe this? Above eighteen, no parental permission is needed." Melissa turned to Emily, waving her hands like wings. "It costs thirty-five dollars and we need to get a blood test and I need a rubella vaccination. What's that?"

"Measles," Emily said. "You must have had it. We all did in grade school or earlier."

"How can I prove it?"

"Go get another one. Who cares if you get revaccinated?" Emily laughed. "Thirty-five bucks. At that price, we could afford to get married every week."

"Tomorrow morning we're going to pick out rings."

It was the weekend before they had everything organized. Emily would be a witness. Blake had not told his parents, but he had let his sister know. Sara flew in from Austin to Logan in Boston, where Emily drove them to pick her up the night before. Emily was agreeable about driving back and forth. She also drove everybody to the justice of the peace Saturday morning.

"Do you mind doing it like this?" Blake asked Melissa in the backseat of Emily's car.

"I hate big weddings. They're gross and humiliating. I've always said if I ever got married, I'd do it quickly, quietly and no fuss."

"Well, what you wanted is what you're getting. Quick, quiet and sans fuss. So here we go."

Sara leaned over the seat. "Never understood big weddings. Unless you could have an orgy. That would be cool. Did you remember to buy rings?"

The jeweler had tried to talk them into ordering fancy rings, engraved, platinum, part of a set with a diamond. They bought the plainest gold bands in stock. Blake put them on his Visa. Now he jingled his jacket pocket. "Right here."

They had an appointment but they still had to wait. A couple was ahead of them and another couple came in while they were sitting around the little waiting room—sort of like a doctor's office: vinyl chairs, a small sofa and coffee tables covered with *House & Garden* and *People* magazines she was too nervous to pick up. She almost expected her parents to rush in. She half expected Blake to jump up and say it was all a joke. But the other couple came out, looking dazed, and the justice's wife waved them in. "The Ackermans? Come this way, please."

"That's us."

"Are you going to take his name?" Sara nudged her. "It's not a great last name."

"I don't want to keep my father's name. I've never been a proper Dickinson." The idea of getting rid of the whole family at once was exciting.

The justice of the peace was a heavyset white-haired man with a silver-tipped cane leaning against his mahogany desk. On two walls were shiny leather-bound legal books she suspected were not real, they looked so untouched. She imagined opening one of them, and nothing but blank pages riffling past. How did somebody get to be a justice of the peace? A strange phrase. Was there a justice of the wars? He made a joke she smiled at without hearing. Then he asked for the license and the blood tests.

"Everything seems to be in order. Shall we proceed?" A rhetorical question. "You're sure you want to enter the holy state of matrimony?"

She felt a little sick to her stomach—apprehension? Fear that something would go wrong, someone would burst in and stop them before they could marry.

She was trying to imagine what she would say to Rosemary if she suddenly appeared, when the justice said, "I now pronounce you man and wife. You may kiss the bride."

"Are we married?"

"Absolutely," the justice said.

His wife added, "I hope you'll be as happy and loving to each other as we are."

"Married forty-four years," said the justice, rubbing his cheek absently. "You can pay my wife in the outer office. Send the next couple in, Betty."

She could not remember the ceremony. She knew she had spoken on cue, but it was a blur. She felt as if she had missed her own wedding. But what did it matter? Emily and Sara took turns photographing them on the sidewalk. As they crammed back into Emily's little blue Honda, Melissa said, "It's hard to believe it's legal. It's like a game we played. Like a rehearsal. When I was a little girl and we played wedding, it took much longer than that."

"It's real." Blake was looking moody. She wondered if he regretted marrying her, if he already had qualms. She was afraid to ask. She turned the ring on her finger round and round. Finally she asked softly, "Are you okay?"

"Did you see the way that fat pig looked at me? And the way he asked you twice if you really took me in matrimony?"

She hadn't noticed a thing, lost in a fog of anxiety. "Yeah, he was a loser. But who cares? The ceremony is just as legal. It's like we stuck a couple of twenties in a Coke machine. We put the money in, and five minutes later, a marriage comes out."

"You're right. That pig doesn't matter. We're legal." He clutched her hand. "We did it."

Sara knelt backwards on the front seat, grinning at them. "So when are you telling the folks?"

"I'm not in a hurry." Blake shook his head.

"I think you better before they find out accidentally."

Blake grabbed her by the shoulder. "You won't tell them."

"No way. They don't even know I'm here. . . . But I'm serious, you better carry the news yourself." She turned to Melissa. "What about you? When are you breaking the news?"

"My aunt Karen will be the first to know. I trust her. But I'll tell my mother only when I have to. Not before."

"Bunch of cowards. What are you afraid of?"

Emily said, "You don't know her mother. She's to be afraid of, believe me."

"Yeah? What could she do?"

"Call out the National Guard," Melissa said. "Send me to Devil's Island. Cut off my head."

"Seriously, what can anybody do except yell and moan?"

"She could try to have the wedding annulled," Emily said. "Right, Lissa?"

Sara shook her spiked black hair. "Wouldn't that cause a great big scandal? As I understand it, your mother would do anything to avoid that. Besides, you've consummated it."

"Not in the last five minutes," Blake said. "Maybe it doesn't count before. Could you pull the car over? We can do it now. You all shut your eyes."

"He's so romantic," Emily said. "I see why you fell for him."

"My husband," Melissa said, trying out the words. "He's my husband."

"It sounds so weird," Emily said. "I know every girl is supposed to want one, but I think I'll stick to dogs for pets, no offense meant, Blake."

"Arf!" He was sunny again. "I can do any trick your dog can. And more! I'm a bargain."

"If Rosemary was thinking straight," Emily said, "she'd thank you profusely. Your brother's wedding must have cost twenty-five, thirty thousand minimum. I can't even guess. You saved her a bundle."

"I'll be sure to tell her that when she goes ballistic." Melissa shuddered, not bothering to say that the bride's family had paid that bill. She could scarcely believe how everything had changed. She was a real grown-up, a married lady like friends of Rosemary's. Who would ever have expected it? She felt as if she had done something totally clever, that eventually would show them all how mistaken they had been about her. One, a handsome brilliant man had married her. Two, she had married before her older sister. Three, she had brought it all off secretly and they couldn't touch her. She had escaped for good and forever from Rosemary and Dick and them all. She was somebody else now, somebody much better. She almost wished she could call them up and tell them and hear their reaction, but *almost* wasn't enough to jump into the shark's mouth. Her own satisfaction with herself would do her just fine.

elissa decided that she would confide in Karen first. She called her Monday night. "That was a huge step," Karen said. "What prompted you?"

"Rosemary and Dick walked in on us, I told you. They know I've been seeing him."

"But you said you were just eating supper. They didn't walk in on a sex scene or anything they could wax heavy about, right?"

"Blake isn't white. That's all they saw. And then they found out who his adopted father is—Si Ackerman, an attorney—"

"I know who he is. A top-notch defense lawyer, does a lot of appeals on capital cases. He's the genuine article, Melissa. No wonder Dick can't stand him. They've gone head-to-head since Dick was a prosecutor."

"It gets worse." She told Karen about Toussaint Parker.

"How come you didn't tell me all this before? Did you think it would scare me? Come on. You should trust me more."

"Well, Blake didn't tell you either when you were talking, did he?" She couldn't bring herself to admit to Karen that she had not known. "I didn't think it was terribly relevant. I wanted you to meet him, not to be thinking about his father."

"Still, you could have told me after I'd met him, when we were talking about him together."

"I'm sorry. I just didn't think of it. After all, his father isn't very real to me. I was just a kid when he was executed."

"It was a cause célèbre for a lot of us. We thought he was innocent and that he was framed and railroaded."

"Do you still think so?"

"Nothing ever came up to change my mind."

"Blake knows his father didn't kill that cop." She told Karen the story.

"That's enough to drive anyone crazy. Knowing the truth and not being able to do anything about it. It's scary, kiddo, really scary." Karen was silent for a moment. Melissa waited her out. She was disappointed in Karen's reaction. It seemed as if no one was going to rejoice with her. Karen finally continued, "It just seems like too much of a coincidence, the two of you getting together."

"We had the same writing class. It wasn't like we hit it off right away, but we liked what each other wrote."

"I have never been a great fan of coincidence, that's all."

"Okay, the truth is out. Blake went to Wesleyan just because I was enrolled there. Somehow he found out. Then he bribed the registration people to put us in the same class. Actually maybe I went there because he did, since he was accepted way before me. He got better grades in high school."

"I guess I'm being paranoid."

"I guess you are."

"Melissa, did he know about your family before you started going out?"

"Of course not." She was getting used to lying, because she was beginning to understand she was going to have trouble getting others to accept their union. "It was a shock to him. He didn't actually know till we were both in Washington last summer."

"I want to be happy for you, kiddo. You're both just a bit young to get married. And it's bound to cause a huge flap."

"For now, it's a secret. I'm not going to tell anybody else, except maybe Billy, I haven't decided. You can't say a word to anyone, drop a hint, anything."

"I don't have much communication with the rest of the Dickinsons. I'm the black sheep. The lavender sheep, whatever. Unless somebody dies, I never see them. And I sure don't call them up to chat."

"Anyhow, I wanted you to know." Melissa wished someone would say, How wonderful, you have married the man of your dreams. She had.

"IT'S LIKE *Romeo and Juliet*," Emily said. "Star-crossed lovers who secretly marry."

"I never read it." Melissa was sitting cross-legged on her bed brushing her hair. She was startled every time she looked at her roommate. Emily had dyed her hair red—not reddish like Karen's had been or Billy's was, but bright garish red. She decided she wasn't interesting enough looking to attract interesting men, and this was her solution.

"Maybe you should," Emily said. "It's so much apropos."

"Didn't they end up badly?"

"Well, it's a tragedy. Shakespeare's tragedies all end with body counts."

MELISSA WENT to see Fern, who was home in the room she shared with her girlfriend Harriet, a short slim girl with light brown hair worn in a single pigtail. Harriet was sitting cross-legged on the double bed. Fern sat straddling her desk chair. Tammy had proven to be a kind of lesbian predator, who brought out young women and then moved on, but Fern had not remained alone long. She had been seeing Harriet for a month and they seemed tight.

Harriet said, "It's heterosexual privilege, you know. Like we couldn't get married, no matter how much we wanted to." She was glaring, her forehead creased in a frown.

But Fern squeezed Melissa's hand. "I know what this means to you. You're crazy about him. I hope it all works out. No matter what, you have what you want. My mother never got to marry my father before he was killed, and she always regretted that."

"I always assumed your parents were divorced?"

"He's the only soldier I ever heard of who got killed on a training mission. He drowned. She was mad at him for enlisting, and she didn't even tell him she was pregnant. . . . So at least, no matter what happens, you get to be together now, and that's what matters."

Melissa felt at least slightly congratulated. Jeez, marry him now before he drops dead. Nobody was going to cheer, so she had to settle for being glad herself. She walked from Fern's through the streets of Middletown past the Victorian houses, the trees dropping their leaves in huge drifts in the gutters and on lawns students didn't bother raking, onto campus itself and past College Row, with its nineteenth-century brownstone buildings that always struck her as gloomy and even more so today. Why didn't anyone understand?

HE SENT HER an e-mail:

My own, great news, too hot to send. Come by me ASAP.

He was pacing, sparking energy. Like a great cat, he covered his little room in three strides, turned and strode back, again and again. "I deciphered the papers that we were handed. I finally figured out at least part of it."

"So what is it? More contributions."

"There are two lists." He handed her the lists from the guy who had met them at Foxwoods. "One of them has numbers beside it that I bet are contributions. But the other list had me stumped. I chased these names down through database after database."

She shook his shoulder impatiently. "So cut to the chase."

"This is the chase, babe-aroni. I finally found them. They're all convicted of crimes in Pennsylvania."

"Crimes? I don't get it. He's getting contributions from prisoners?"

"That's what the guy was giving us. Lists of contributors and lists of convicted criminals. And the link between at least some of them—gubernatorial pardons or releases from the parole board he appointed. I've only begun to work through the list, but I can link pardons and early paroles to contributions to a special fund by family members, business partners, whatever. He was selling pardons and paroles, Melissa. Is that corrupt or what?"

"Like he was letting people out of prison for money? That's hard to swallow. He's always been so over the top about punishing criminals, locking them up forever and throwing away the key."

"We're not talking about petty criminals, your mule caught with cocaine in her tummy, the guy peddling smoke in the 'hood, guys boosting cars. We're talking white-collar criminals."

"Like what? I still don't get it."

"Like the guy embezzling old ladies out of their savings, the guy with his hand in the till at the corporation, the assistant principal who gets paybacks from contractors. The savings and loan officer who lent himself a bundle. Real estate scams. Second mortgage scams. Contractors caught using second-rate material when the bridge or the roof collapses. I've just begun digging. That guy gave us gold, Lissa, solid gold."

"That's hard to believe—that my father would just sell pardons or early paroles. It just seems too gross. I can't imagine Rosemary letting him get involved with anything so shady."

"It's oblique. The funds come roundabout. You have to follow the computer trail to get back to King Richard. I'm still trying to sort it out."

She closed her eyes and considered her parents, trying to imagine them from outside of the box of family. They certainly always needed money. Dick had family and connections; Rosemary had brains. Neither of them had brought cash to the table. Rosemary had invested shrewdly and obviously nowadays there was a lot more money than when she was little. But Rosemary hated to use their own investments to subsidize campaigns. Politics ran on money, Melissa had known that as far back as she could remember. Backers, supporters were the people who had to be pleased, whose desires ruled the city, the state, the nation. The corporations that spent money on a candidate bought the official's votes. That was simple enough; she had always understood those facts. But selling pardons seemed worse—if he really had done that. Briefly she wondered if they could not use this information to blackmail Dick and Rosemary into letting her stay in school. But they could not "let" or "refuse" any longer. She was a married woman. That was hard to believe while she was still living in her dorm and he, in his. Nonetheless they were legally married, meaning her parents could no longer coerce her. She finally had someone to stand between her and their power over her. She could see that Blake was really excited by what he had uncovered, and she could recognize that it looked as if her father had engaged in underhanded practices. The discovery was something that potentially could hurt him, although he had weathered many considerable scandals during his years in office. She supposed, in an ideal world, Dick would be punished for his abuse of public office, but this world was a mess anyhow.

Why wasn't she more excited? Perhaps because she no longer needed to fight her parents to kick free. She had put herself beyond their reach. She was safe from their meddling. Safe from the swift, lethally sharp blade of their decisions that had always whacked through her life whenever they chose. Blake was not the first person they had decided she could not consort with. Boyfriends, girlfriends, families of whom they did not approve, the Korean-American boy Mark. "No, you may *not* go to Rosalia's birthday party." "We don't want you seeing that Levin boy again." "No, you may not," again and again. They had done the same thing to Merilee; they were still doing the same thing to Merilee. She, who was supposed to be the weak one, had dared what her golden brilliant sister could not: she had set a barrier between herself and Dick and Rosemary's ability to control.

He was still going on about his discovery. "We have to work our way down this whole list to prove our case. I thought we'd split the names. I've noted the ones I was able to get the details on so far. I'll print it out for you."

"Why not just e-mail it to me? Then I'd have it right on my computer. Easier."

"Because e-mail is never secure, and I don't want them getting one of their jazzy research assistants to hack into our e-mail and find out what we know."

She didn't much feel like traipsing back to her dorm and sitting at the computer until the wee hours running down meaningless names. "You know, I can't just hack into databases the way you can. It's not my expertise."

"I'll help you. At some point you have to learn how to do it anyhow. It's a necessary skill."

She put her hand on his knee. "Blake, we're together now. We're in it for life. How much longer do we have to go on bothering with my father? When do we just say good-bye to them and get on with our lives?"

"When I've got justice at last. And this *is* my life." His tone was cold. He was disappointed, she could tell, that she wasn't more enthusiastic.

"Did you ever really want to dig up stuff on him so I could influence him? Or was that just to get me involved?"

"I never knew your father personally. I thought you might be able to approach him. I even thought by and by he might issue a posthumous pardon for my father, to clear his name. As I've gotten to know your parents, I've begun to doubt that either of us could ever persuade your father to change his mind or his course. But I still need justice, and if we have to blackmail him to get it, so be it. Right now, we need to make them back off. I don't think you want a showdown with them just yet. We can distract them with some bad publicity, maybe, and get them off your back."

To please him, she sat down beside him at his computer and tried to follow what he was doing. In the end, however, he decided that it would take more time than he was willing to spend to teach her some of his tricks. Now she was disappointed too, because he was clearly going to spend the whole evening at his computer. He did not really care if she stayed or went back to the room she shared with Emily. She decided she might as well return and catch up on classwork.

She had to take an interest in his crusade, she told herself as she walked across the path to her dorm through the bleak chilly night. After all, investigating Dick was something they could share. Her father wielded great power as a senator. The reasons she had agreed to investigate him still held, in spite of her own feelings that she had escaped them. Blake had liberated her, but she could not therefore decide that she was indifferent to her father's errors. She would do better next time Blake approached her with the results of his research. She would force out enthusiasm. Since investigating Dick was so important to Blake, she would try to make it important to herself. But she was beginning to feel caught between her husband and her parents.

The next day she did not hear from him at all. They had taken care to enroll in the same European history class, but he was not there. She took careful notes so she could share them with him. Finally, on Thursday, she rushed over to see him in the late afternoon. She was determined to heal the little rift her lack of enthusiasm had caused.

He was sitting at his computer, as she had guessed. His eyes were bloodshot. His clothes looked as if he had not changed them since yesterday at least. The dregs of old coffee sat in paper cups on the floor, the desk. Remnants of pizza lay in the box it had arrived in, on his bed, in which he clearly had not spent the night. He had not shaved, and his black beard with coppery glints shadowed his cheeks and chin. His room was usually so neat, the chaos and the litter were almost shocking.

"How is it going?" she asked cautiously, moving the pizza box to perch on the edge of his bed.

"I've found all but two of the names on the list," he said, his voice rough with lack of use. "I don't think it's worth trying to find out what happened with the last two. Maybe they got off on appeal, whatever."

"But how many does that make, that you've verified were pardoned or paroled?"

"Eighteen. Now I'm trying to run down the contributors and see what their interest was. Sometimes it's easy—a wife, a brother, a father, an uncle, a business partner. Sometimes it's harder to dig up, but then I can ferret out the connection—business or financial. Some I can't trace yet."

"How many have you been able to connect?"

"I'm not sure." He called up a new computer screen and counted out loud. "Thirteen."

"That's two thirds. Isn't that enough to prove your case?" She stepped up beside him and read the screen. "Blackstone. I remember him. He actually came to dinner at the mansion."

"For twenty thousand, I'd imagine Blackstone rated a dinner."

"I remember him because I'd been reading a children's book about a magician with the same name. Blackstone the magician. I asked him if he did magic tricks, and Rosemary looked annoyed, then said, You might say that he does have a talent for making things disappear. Then my father looked annoyed in his turn. He almost never gets angry at Rosemary, but

I think he was angry right then. Obviously she couldn't resist a crack. Maybe she didn't like what was going on."

"Clearly, however, she had to have known about the scheme. Blackstone. . . . His brother was a lawyer who embezzled money and valuables from estates of his clients."

"No wonder Rosemary thought my question was awkward."

"After all, it wasn't her money." Blake leaned way back in his chair, his eyelids drooping. "So you actually saw him with them. He's the earliest name on this list."

"My father had only been governor for a year or so."

"You know, I'm wiped. Totally. It just hit me. I'm hungry, I'm tired, I can't think. My eyeballs feel boiled. I've downed so much black coffee, I don't have a stomach lining."

She put her arms around him, holding his head to her breasts. "Come lie down. Take a nap. You'll feel better. Come on, baby."

"I can't sleep yet. I'll take a shower. Then let's get something decent to eat. Chicken. I think I want chicken. Real chicken."

"Whatever you want. And change your clothes. Just stand them in the corner and let them air out."

"I must be a little ripe." Mischievously he rubbed his stubbled chin across her neck. "Let me clean up."

They went off on his bike to find supper—not one of the fast-food places where they usually ate but what he defined as a real restaurant. He did in fact have chicken, roasted on a spit. He was happy and the wound was sealed.

"After college, do you want to live in Philadelphia?" she asked.

He shrugged. "I'd kind of like to try the West Coast. The Bay Area or maybe Seattle. It's early to make plans. I might have to go where jobs are."

But she needed plans. She needed something concrete to believe in. "I've been to L.A. but I've never been in San Francisco. I love the idea of California."

He was frowning. "I really would like to run down those last five names."

"Seth on my floor comes from Orinda. He says it's in the hills above

Berkeley. His web site has photos of his family's house, and it looks, like, beautiful—all on a steep hill and with exotic trees." She was on a coed floor this year.

"I'm going to check out possibilities—that maybe those guys died or something."

When they had eaten and ridden around in the clear crisp night air for half an hour, they went back to his room and made love. He fell asleep immediately after. Careful not to wake him, she extricated herself from the tangle of his long limbs. She was tempted to stay, but she had an early class. Out she tiptoed, greatly relieved. Her Blake was sensitive and needed constant encouragement—and why not, didn't she need the same thing? They were both insecure at the core, lonely. That was why they could understand each other so intensely.

To Emily she said, "I think I'm, like, a much more selfish person than Blake is. He cares about justice. He cares about the larger picture. I care about my own freedom and my own happiness. That's a difference between us. But I can become a better person too, if I try."

Emily just gazed at her, her chin down against her chest. Finally she said, "That's just so much BS. You're a good person. Blake's not pure. He's manipulative. He gets what he wants from you."

"Not as often as he should. I mean to be really good for him. I do."

"Let's hope it's mutual, Melissa." Emily shook her head slowly. "I'm not always sure about him. He has a lot of agenda. Sometimes I trust him, and sometimes I really, really don't."

CHAPTER TWENTY-THREE

Melissa and Blake were having a picnic on the floor of his dorm room. They had planned to take the bike up into the hills, but the weather had shut them down. The day was dank and cold, with a wet fierce wind that bashed the dead leaves against the buildings. He was on a chicken jag, so they ate take-out chicken, coleslaw and french fries on a blanket, sitting cross-legged with a new Khaled record blasting from his speakers.

"So how come you aren't racist?" he asked her. "Everyone else in your family seems to be."

She frowned. She did not want to answer off the top of her head. Finally she offered, tentatively, "I think it's because of how hard it is to get in college these days. Like it isn't enough to have the grades and the money. You have to rack up all these extracurricular activities and community service. I was volunteering in Hartford. People think like it's all insurance companies and glass buildings. Sure, the suburbs are rich, but the city is a great big slum."

"So that turned you off, or what?"

"I was working with these kids, an after-school program tutoring them. I liked them. About two thirds of them were African-American, and most of the rest were Latino. It wasn't like I expected. They wanted the after-school stuff as long as I made it interesting, and they made it interesting for me. It was the first time in my life I ever dealt a lot with kids who weren't white—this is going to make me to so sound like a simp—but I just liked being with them. I felt better with them than I did with the girls at Miss Porter's. I liked myself when I was with them. We laughed a lot. Oh, they would put me on. But I didn't mind. It was, I guess, a big escape from my life."

"So that changed your attitudes?"

"It made me think about them. Oh, in school, we talked about racism and I was against it, in theory, you know. But this wasn't theory. They were real kids and I got to know a lot about them—tutoring them in English, having them write about their lives and their dreams."

"I couldn't hate whites because my mother was white and I loved her like crazy. Then the Ackermans took me in. I knew how hard Si tried to save my father. I'll always love him for that, besides how good they are to me."

"But you told me you felt like an outsider."

"I *am*. I'm my father's only son, his only child. I have a duty to him. I can never forget that. I'm not Si and Nadine's kid, I'm Toussaint and Anne's. I'm a Parker. I was born an outsider, and I became ten times more of an outsider the moment the cops broke in and busted my father. I'm the son of a man the state murdered—not because of anything bad he did, but because of his strength, because of the good he did. I never forget. If I ever forgot it, I would die inside. Everything that's strong and real in me would dry up."

"Maybe you should change your name back to Parker and we should both be Parker."

"I couldn't do that to Si and Nadine. It would be like slapping them down. And it would raise all the questions I've skirted around with the authorities about who I really am." He leaned over to caress her cheek. "But it's sweet of you to suggest that. Maybe someday I'll take my father's name back. When I've earned it. Then we can share it."

A party was getting going on his floor. His friend Jamal came knocking on the door. "Time to shake it, bro. I got to run the music, so it will be loud and fat."

At once Blake jumped to his feet, forgetting their conversation she had so wanted to continue. "Coming!"

She forgot her disappointment when they started to dance. She wasn't the world's coolest dancer, but she did okay. At least she followed the music. Blake danced well, although there were far fancier steps being laid down. The hall was jammed with moving bodies, and she had to watch out not to get slammed or elbowed. She forgot to mind the interruption and lived in her body.

HE CAUGHT HER after class the next afternoon. They sat on a bench facing across the green downhill into the town, much more visible now that the leaves had fallen. "Well, the shit hit the fan. Sara told Si and Nadine I had something important to spill. So Nadine called me last night with Si on the extension. So what's up?" He imitated her way of speaking. "So what do you have to tell us?"

"What did you tell them?"

"I couldn't see any reason to lie."

"What did they say?"

He shrugged. "What you'd expect. Anyhow, they're coming up Saturday, so we had better be prepared to defend ourselves."

EMILY SAID, "Two lawyers for in-laws. That could be brutal." She was dressing slutty. Mitch had dumped her so she was on the prowl to hook up with someone new. "My hair looks like shit. Maybe I should go blond."

"You look fine. Just brush it up the way you do, to give it some body. Whose party is this?"

"Some girl Ronnie knows. It's a Halloween party." She eased on a pair of fishnet stockings. "I'm going as a whore. I thought that would get attention."

"But the kind you want?" Melissa thought she would never have the guts to wear something like that, with a huge midriff, a skirt more like a Band-Aid than a real piece of clothing.

"Exactly the kind I want." Emily was applying makeup, including mascara and dark red lipstick, twice as heavily as usual. "Do you think Blake's parents will try to get the marriage annulled?"

"I have to persuade them not to." She must convince them they wanted to welcome her into their family. They would be fine protection. What she wanted more than anything else was to be free of her parents and safe from their interference. All her longing now was for the approval of the Ackermans. She would show them what a wonderful daughter-in-law she could be, if only she knew the rules of their game.

"How should I be with them?" she'd asked Blake.

"Be yourself."

"What part of myself? Nobody's ever themselves with another person, especially someone who has power over them."

"Just be natural. Don't be coy or afraid. Let them see you as you are."

That was not useful advice. How was she? With Blake usually she wanted to get into bed. Often she felt she was nobody. The third Dickinson child. The younger, less pretty, less bright, less accomplished sister. Blake made her someone special. Blake loved her; and he had also fashioned her into a weapon against her own parents. Who was she, then? The young Mrs. Ackerman? Blake's wife? She sought for herself, but she felt as if she were grasping at something slippery in running water. She was just a minnow evading her own grasp, escaping into vagueness as she so often had throughout her childhood and adolescence. Her favorite answer to Rosemary since she entered adolescence: *I don't know*. Duh.

SI AND NADINE said they would arrive at five thirty, and they were within five minutes—which impressed her, since they had driven from Philadelphia. She was waiting with Blake. He did not want to face them alone, he said; he wanted them to present a united front.

They went to the same Chinese restaurant, and all climbed into a booth, without Sara, who was in Austin with her bartender boyfriend.

Nadine leaned over the table toward Melissa, her eyes bright, almost beady with intent. "Are you pregnant, dearie?"

"No!" Melissa said loudly.

"Well, that's good," Nadine said, and Si rolled his eyes. "So why all the hurry? Are you planning to quit school?" She poked at her white hair absentmindedly until it stood out around her head like a lopsided Shasta daisy.

"Of course we aren't," Blake said. "That was part of the idea. Her parents were threatening to pull her out of school to keep her away from me."

"What do they have against you?" Si asked. "Never mind, I can guess. We don't have to run through the messy parts." He rubbed his nose as if the thought embarrassed him.

"They didn't like him the minute they saw him in Washington," Melissa said. "But they first got really upset when they learned that you were the people who had adopted him. Then when they learned he was Toussaint Parker's son, they exploded. They're threatening to pull me out of school. . . . I don't have any money of my own, except a little from my summer job."

"You told them his parentage?" Si asked, head propped on chin, eyes resting on her from under his brows.

"No. They had one of their aides investigate."

"Why didn't you tell them?"

Instinctively she knew she shouldn't let them know that she had been ignorant herself. "I tell them as little as possible. Whatever I really want to do, they disapprove of."

"Give me an example."

"Like seeing Blake. Like demonstrating with the African-American students against the firing of the only teacher who really knew about Africa. Like the research we've been doing on my father."

"What sort of research?"

Both Blake and Melissa were silent. Si looked from one to the other. "Someone has been feeding information on Dickinson to a reporter at the *Philadelphia Inquirer*. The same reporter you mentioned when you told me that Melissa was working with his son? Unless I'm mistaken."

"You're not mistaken," Blake said. "I don't think we should talk about this."

Both Si and Nadine put down their chopsticks and stared from one to the other. Nadine said, "This is something you're doing together?"

"I don't see any reason to talk about it," Blake said. "It's our project. It doesn't involve you."

"You're getting the information on your father?" Si kept his gaze on her now.

She did not answer, letting Blake say whatever he chose to.

"Why?" Nadine asked, leaning so far forward her dress brushed her food. "Because you love Blake, you're doing this? Because of his father?"

Now she had to answer. "Partly. Partly I feel my father is wrong. If I know and do nothing, I'm an accessory—aren't I?"

"Interesting," Si said. "And you've been applying your computer skills, I suspect." He was talking to Blake now. "That could get you in legal trouble."

"Melissa is the only witness to whatever I've done."

"And she can't be forced to testify because she's your wife now. It all begins to make a certain insane sense."

She wanted Blake to assure his parents they had not married for legal reasons, but he was silent. Maybe that was the kind of answer that made sense to them. Give a lawyer a legal reason. Still, she felt a little burned.

Blake sat back. "I don't want to talk about this. We're engaged in a project together. We're not about to stop. We're not about to turn back. We know a lot that had never been put together, and we have a way to use it. That's all you need to know."

Nadine said, "This could be dangerous for you both. Have you thought of that?"

"Dangerous, how?" Melissa asked. "You mean like we could get into legal trouble?"

"Things have happened to people who have gone up against your father. Don't you know that?"

"I know my aunt was put in an institution for five years because she was doing the same thing we are."

"I met her," Blake said. "She's a good person. Cool. She was Eve Kalman's lover, if you remember her."

"Sure I remember Eve," Nadine said. "A fervent and very political woman. And she died in a plane crash some people said was arranged."

"That's a rumor without foundation," Si said. "I don't want to scare you unnecessarily."

Blake snorted. "What's our quotient of necessary scaring?"

Nadine patted Melissa's hand. "I'm beginning to get the picture. Do your parents know you're married?"

"My god, no," Melissa said.

"Are you planning to let them know?"

"When I have to," Melissa said firmly. "When we have to."

"What do you think they'll do?" Nadine was still holding her hand. Nadine's hand was very warm.

"Call out the National Guard. I can't imagine. But it will be loud and long."

"I think you should tell them, but I understand your reluctance." Nadine sighed. "They're your parents. We won't interfere. But when you tell them or they find out, I would like to know at once. I have to say we're not thrilled at having them as in-laws, any more than this development is going to warm their cockles, whatever cockles are."

"I think they mean valves," Si said wearily. "Well, this isn't what I expected in the way of the first marriage in the family. David is gay, Sara— Whoops, I forgot, she did marry that jackass. But it only lasted five weeks. I hardly think that should count. I hope you both understand the choice you've made."

Blake said, "We're committed to each other. We belong together."

"Thousands would say differently," Si intoned. "But what the hell, we wish you the best and we'll do what we can to help out. But I don't think you've chosen an easy road, nor one I would have picked out for you."

"Do you remember a Yiddish word you taught me when I asked you about how you and Nadine got together?" Blake was working on Si to charm him; she knew the voice. "You said Nadine was your *bashert*. Your intended one. Your destiny. Well, I know that Melissa is my *bashert*."

"I hope so," Nadine said. "I hope, for both your sakes, it's so."

When they were leaving, Si drew Blake aside and they spoke

earnestly. Nadine was chatting with Melissa, and she had to answer and keep up her end, but she really wanted to overhear what they were saying to each other. Still, it had gone far, far better than she had imagined beforehand. They had accepted her. They had accepted the marriage. They were on her side now.

MELISSA SLEPT in Blake's room, in his narrow bed. She was too exhausted to make her way home, and she desperately needed to feel him beside her. This was one night she had to spend with him as the married couple they were supposed to be. The conversation with his parents had ended well, but it had shaken her. Everyone thought they were crazy. Everyone thought they had acted rashly. And had Blake really married her to protect himself because of how he had hacked into her mother's and father's computers? Maybe she would never know. Maybe it was better if she didn't know. She had to believe he loved her; after all, it would be kind of drastic for him to marry her if he did not. He'd used that word, *bashert,* and more than once he had told her that they were each other's destiny. She must believe. She asked him what Si had been saying to him so vehemently as they were leaving the restaurant.

"Warning me to be careful. He's worried about us."

"Are you worried?"

"Some risks are worth taking." He rested his chin on her shoulder as they made spoons in the bed. "Like being with you. Like us being man and wife. Like fighting the good fight together."

"Together," she echoed. This night they were truly together. The day after tomorrow, she had to make a presentation in French Philosophical Lit on Robbe-Grillet. A year ago, she would have been frantic; now it seemed like a minor blip in her life. If she could face Blake's parents, she could face her French class and her French professor and overcome, in French and in spades.

elissa read Rosemary's latest e-mail, appalled but also relieved. Rosemary wrote:

> I am delighted you have come to your senses and stopped seeing Toussaint Parker's son. Even to be in a group with such an individual can reflect upon you in the eyes of people whom you would like to respect you.
>
> Breeding is an unpopular term, although the owners of racehorses are paid huge sums for the genes of winners. Breeding can mean two things: the genes that an individual receives from his ancestors. Your father is the product of fine bloodlines as truly as any Triple Crown winner. Generation after generation has produced winners, generals, leaders of men.

Melissa paused, wondering about the sudden influx of horse-racing terminology into her mother's vocabulary. Was Rosemary buttering up some important Washington player who was crazy about the races? Melissa made a bet with herself that she was right. Fine bloodlines. She thought of her crotchety grandfather, with his fondness for cows and disgust with people. What had he ever accomplished besides making terrible cheese? It infuriated her that Rosemary was going on about horses when she had never let Melissa have her own, something she had passionately begged for from ten on.

> The second meaning of breeding is that indefinable polish that those who have grown up in a home of refinement, who have attended culturally rich schools, who have associated with the best people,

exhibit in private and in public—an aura of quality to which even voters respond.

Surely we have not failed you to the degree that you do not appreciate the second, for we blessed you with the first criterion of breeding.

Melissa read the message to Emily. "You never met my mother's family, because she has absolutely nothing to do with them. And they don't bug her, because they're scared of her. They don't know how she happened to them."

"Are they, like, gross?"

"They're nice—much nicer than my father's dad was. They're like meek church mice. They're quite religious in a low Protestant style, a lot of hymn singing and an occasional wham-bang shouting tent revival where everybody gets saved for the seventeenth time. Her father taught shop in a technical high school. Her mother worked part-time in the same accountant's office for thirty years. Now they're retired and living in a cottage on a lake in Michigan. They're quiet people who are active in their communities and their church, who live within their tight incomes and tried to give her and her sister everything they could. Their culture is TV and tuna sandwiches, but they mean well. I used to like visiting them, especially at the lake. I think of strawberry shortcake Grandma Higgins made and raspberry cobbler. They grew black raspberries at the lake, and I was allowed to pick them. . . . I haven't seen them since I was eleven."

"Did your parents have a fight with them?"

"Not that I know of. But they were inconvenient. Rosemary gives the impression of being, as she would say, wellborn. Born to culture and money. Anybody meeting her parents would know it's an act, one she's good at, but her going on about our breeding as if we were royalty in exile is a bit much."

Emily yawned, stretching luxuriously. "Getting laid is so good for the muscles, even when the guy can't do you right. . . . Aren't you going to read the rest of the message?"

"I suppose I better."

You contradict everything you have ever been taught, or that we
have tried to teach you when you consort with the son of a
murderer, raised, once his father was brought to justice by your own
father, by two shysters who have done everything within their power
to send criminals back on the streets to continue abusing and
terrorizing innocent citizens.

We are under scurrilous attack in the press, particularly our old
bête noire, the *Inquirer.* We are trying very hard to learn where
these unfounded but potentially damaging accusations are coming
from and on what they are purportedly based. These are dangerous
times for our family, and we must circle the wagons. This is as
important for your future as it is for the future of your father, Rich
Junior and all of us. It's ironic that these attacks should come just
as your father is about to score his first major triumph as a senator,
passage of the interstate transportation legislation he cowrote.

We will be gone this weekend to Kentucky, where the chairman of
the Rules Committee has invited us to visit with him on his lovely
farm in the bluegrass country. He's having a get-together of certain
senators and industrialists and important CEOs. Your father and I
are thrilled to be invited.

"Oh, there are the horsies," Emily said as Melissa got that far in her
reading aloud. "I'll bet it's a horse farm."

Rosemary continued:

I'm sure it's no accident that these attempts to undermine your
father come just as he is beginning to achieve some well-deserved
visibility and influence even in his freshman term in the Senate.
After only two years in office, he has made friends and begun to
garner influence.

It is more than ever important you watch your associations and
also what you may say about your father or your family. Enemies are
all around. I can't believe you could have told this boy anything
while you were seeing him that could cause us trouble, but you

should think back on what you might have said or implied. Let me know if you remember anything.

Melissa reminded herself that Emily had no idea what she had been doing with Blake that was causing Dick problems. She was not about to confide in her roommate. After all, the less people knew, the less likely she and Blake were to get into trouble and the less likely they were to be uncovered as the source of the information Rosemary was lamenting.

"Yeah, when I first met you at Miss Porter's, I thought, Wow, it must be great to be a governor's daughter. I mean, you got picked up a couple of times in a limo. You got to live in a mansion—"

"Where I wasn't allowed to make holes in the walls by hanging anything, where my mother fussed constantly we would break something valuable, where three quarters of the house was offices and visiting backers and dignitaries and camera crews and constituents and state reps, all wanting something. Where you never could, like, go downstairs in your bathrobe and put your feet up and get away with smoking a joint with your friends or drinking beer somebody's older brother bought."

"I get it by now. It was a bad deal for you. You got nothing out of your father's fame, except your mother on your back all the time telling you how to behave. As if adolescence isn't a bitch anyhow until you get away from home."

"I didn't think yours was. I mean, they left you pretty free."

"My folks are cool as folks go, but like you, I never felt I lived up to their weird expectations. I eat meat, I'm no beauty, I have sex with strangers—"

"They don't know that."

"I think they kind of do. But they don't want the facts so they pretend they don't see what's obvious."

"Everybody else's folks look better from the outside. But I still think you got the better deal."

"I won't fight you on that one." Emily got up and began to dress. She was seeing Mitch again. He'd turned up in their dorm room a couple of evenings ago and acted sorry and cute. Since Emily didn't like sex with the guy she'd picked up at the Halloween party and she really liked it with Mitch, she'd decided to give him another chance.

"Will you be back?"

"No idea. If it doesn't go well, sure. Wish me luck."

"I wish you a great lay, Em. You deserve it."

"You bet I do."

It struck her she would never go out with anybody else in her life again, never have sex with anybody else. So what? Her other experience had been depressing. Dating had never been her forte. She had always felt awkward and as if she were dressed wrong, saying the wrong things, liking the wrong music or films or food. It was a relief to have it all behind her, but still she felt a little startled, as if it had not occurred to her that part of her life was finished. She was, alone among her friends, a married woman.

ON FRIDAY, Blake said to her, "Let's take tonight and get done what we have to for class. I want to take a little trip Saturday."

"Are we meeting that guy again?"

"This is something completely different. Be prepared for a longish trip. Dress warm enough. We might stay in a motel overnight, or not."

He loved to surprise her, and even more, he loved control. Most of the time that didn't bother her. At worst, she felt he was preparing a maze for her to run correctly or badly. She would be judged. At best, she felt planned for, cared for, supremely important, as she had never before been to anyone.

They headed toward Philadelphia, but when they got to I-80, he turned west. They stopped for lunch in Stroudsburg in the Delaware Water Gap, as much to warm up as to toss down chili and a hamburger, then stopped a couple of times more just to stretch and use the facilities. Why should she be so happy? But she was. When they rode off together, she held tight to him and wanted to grin or whoop with joy. She felt as if everyone they passed could glance at them and see a couple, mates, the real thing. Love seemed to her much rarer than it was supposed to be.

Once upon a time she had loved her mother and her father passionately. Her mother loved her as someone with many dogs might love the runt of the litter, the one she could not sell but had to keep around. Her mother approved of her most when she was quiet. Rosemary would have preferred her mute and stuffed. Gradually, she admitted it to herself, she had stopped loving them. Quiet and obedient, a dog successfully put through its training by someone paid to do just that, that was the only time she pleased Rosemary. Dick had lost interest when she grew out of her early girlish cuteness.

In her classes, among her friends, she heard much about dysfunctional families—parents who fought wars over or around their children, fathers who drank, mothers who did drugs, bitter divorce and custody battles. But privately she sometimes wondered if the worst luck wasn't being the child of parents who doted on each other, who loved passionately and found each other fascinating. Yet Rich had done just fine. Merilee had enjoyed fulsome attention from both of them. Melissa was the superfluous one. Perhaps if she were gorgeous, like Billy, they would have forgiven her for coming along unwanted, untimely. But she was just herself, pleasant looking but no beauty. Nothing spectacular that Rosemary could feel was worthy of them. But Blake found her special and he made her special. She still felt a shiver of shock every time she remembered that he was her husband. She was his wife. Sometimes she felt she had dreamed the whole thing, or that it was just a hoax. No real wedding could slip by the bride's attention, could it? Were they really married?

He left I-80 heading south, along the river. They came to an old industrial town, grimy and depressed, downtown mostly boarded-up stores. He handed her an envelope with an address and instructions scrawled on it in his scarcely legible handwriting.

"Turn right on Elm," she read off. After three more turns, climbing up from the river, they arrived at a double-barreled frame house that had perhaps once been white. It listed visibly downhill in a line of elderly houses the color of smoke and rust straggling around the corner wedged against the granite of a mountain. All had tiny dark backyards tucked under an overhanging ledge that almost hit the houses. It had been a while since the trash had been collected. A man sat on the stoop smoking and staring at nothing. He glanced at them and away, then his gaze returned to Blake and he glowered. He did not move aside for them and they had to step around him.

The doorbells did not look functional, hanging on exposed wires. Blake found the name he was looking for, Grabowski, and they climbed to the third-floor right front apartment. "I hope she's expecting us," Blake said. "I've been in contact with her."

She was Sharon Grabowski, a harried-looking woman Melissa judged to be forty. She opened the door perhaps an inch on its chain. There were grey streaks in her dark blond hair. "Mrs. Grabowski? Karen put us in touch with you, if you remember. Karen Dickinson."

"I remember Karen." She stood aside, opening the door for them. They walked into a cluttered livingroom. A fat child was sitting on the floor banging on an empty tomato juice can. "That's Bobbie. He's seven now."

"Seven?" Melissa repeated. He didn't look nearly that old.

"Down's syndrome they call it," Sharon said. "He's a sweetheart, full of love. He's just so good!"

"You've lived on the river all your life?" Blake asked.

"My father worked at the plant. My mother sold bait. She used to have these metal rods that gave a shock in the ground, and the night crawlers would come right up so we could catch them in cans like that one." She pointed to the big can that had held tomato juice. "She liked to fish too."

"In the river?"

"Yeah, the river." Sharon waved at the couch. "Sit down. Would you like some coffee?"

"I'd love some," Melissa said. She was still cold through and through.

"No, thank you," Blake said. "I don't drink coffee. Lissa, are you sure you want coffee? It makes you jittery."

That was weird. Of course he drank coffee. Gallons of it.

"Tell us about your mother," Blake went on.

"She was a good woman. She never hit any of us. She did her best for us. After all the fish died off in the river, she took up hooking rugs. She was always collecting rags and making these rugs with big fish on them. People liked them." She pointed to her feet. "That there's one of hers."

Melissa looked down to see a braided rug of concentric ovals with a big bloated-looking blue fish filling the center. "It's wonderful," she said lamely.

"Is she still around?" Blake asked.

Sharon shook her head wearily, passing her hand across her forehead and eyes. "She died of kidney failure two years ago. She was fifty-one."

Melissa was startled. So then Sharon could no way be forty herself. "Fifty-one?" Melissa repeated, to make sure she'd heard right.

"A lot of people around here die pretty young. The cancer gets them."

"And your father?"

"He's in the hospital. Lung cancer."

"Sharon, maybe you could talk a little about what happened in your marriage. Melissa wants to write about all this, what's happened to the people here. I would really appreciate it if you could explain."

"My husband and I, we moved up the mountain. He liked woods and he hunted a lot. In and out of season, like guys do around here, you understand. It's what they've always done. We weren't that far from town. We planned to have a family. My husband, his name was Broderick but everybody called him Brud.

"Brud and I, we planned a big family like we came from, both of us. So when I got pregnant just two months after our wedding, we were glad. But I lost the baby in the fourth month. Six months later, I got pregnant again. That one I carried to term, meaning the whole nine months. But the baby, a little girl, she was born dead. The doctor, he goes, It was a mercy because something was wrong with her. Her intestines didn't reach all the way. She would have starved to death."

Sharon did not look at either of them but into her lap as she related the next three miscarriages. "Finally, Bobbie was born to us. It's true, he's got problems, and the doctor says maybe he won't live so long, but he's a real kid and he's alive now. . . ."

Sharon was quiet so long, Melissa was trying to put together a sentence of condolence when she spoke again. "It was too much for Brud. He just took off. He said our luck was rotten and there was no use trying to go on."

"Did the doctors ever tell you what caused all these problems?"

"PCBs in the river water. We been drinking it all our lives. The doctor who spoke to us said it was from eating the fish. I saw him on local cable. The governor said they were cleaning up the river, they were going to make it right for us. But people go on dying. It hasn't stopped."

Melissa almost dropped the coffee she had been sipping. Carefully, as if it might blow up, she put the cup down on the coffee table. That was why Blake had tried to warn her.

"I really want to thank you for talking with us, Mrs. Grabowski. I know it's hard for you to speak about it."

"We don't talk about it to each other, you know? We see those movies about pollution and justice and such, but there's no way out for us. So it's kind of a relief when somebody from outside comes and acts interested. We just stew in our own juices and we can't do anything about it."

When they left, the guy was still sitting on the steps. He ignored them until they had stepped around him. Then he spat.

Before they got on the Honda, Blake said, "That was what Karen was investigating when they locked her up in the loony bin. There's a lot of horror here. Pain and misery."

"But my father didn't pollute the river."

"Neither did he clean it up as promised. He ended up giving the polluters the right to go on polluting and charged the minor cleanup to the taxpayers."

She clung to him as they roared off downhill and then upriver to the interstate. She was glad they could not talk. That poor woman. She wished she could bring her father to meet Sharon, but it would never happen. Would he say she was sentimental? That was Rosemary's insult. Rosemary would say, How can you prove it's the water? It's probably genetic. Inbreeding. She wanted to believe that, but she couldn't. This was what political decisions turned into, a woman with five miscarriages and a little boy with Down's syndrome.

When they stopped for coffee a couple of hours into the trip, she said to him: "You're educating me, that's what you're doing. Right?"

"I'm reminding you why we began this project. What it means in human terms."

"I feel so ashamed sometimes. I resented my parents because of the way they treated me. I wonder, if they'd been warmer to me, would I just go along with what they do in the world? Would I agree, because it was them? I ignored the politics, because I was so focused on myself."

"That's what growing up is all about, Lissa. Understanding the bigger picture. Looking farther than the ends of our noses."

"And you're worried now that I have a secret weapon against them, that we're actually married, I will just walk off and forget everything."

"I suspected it wasn't feeling as urgent to you."

"Well, the bottom line goes that I want to please you. I want you to get what you need too. So I won't ever walk away." She put her hand over his on the tabletop beside the remains of not very good cherry pie.

"I want it to matter to you too. Come on, let's see how far we can get. You don't mind traveling in the dark, do you?"

"With you, I don't mind it at all."

elissa found several messages upon her return. A phone call from a classmate who had missed Friday's French was easy to deal with. An e-mail from Rosemary said,

We tried to reach you Saturday. Where were you? We tried as late as midnight. This is alarming.

She e-mailed back,

I went to New York with two new friends from my Sociology of Politics class, Heather Grimes and Lindsey Rockingham. Merilee knows Lindsey's brother Stu. We went to a rock performance and then dancing. We had a wonderful time.

Both the women she mentioned were in her sociology class, but she had never done more than share a cup of coffee with Lindsey and talk about doing a project together for class, maybe in a local mall.

She tried twice to return Karen's call, but Karen did not yet have an answering machine. Finally on the third try, she caught her in.

"Listen, Melissa. Tom has been busted. And the FBI is somehow involved."

"Tom?"

"The gay guy I put Blake in touch with. Who used to work for your father?"

"Busted for what?" She remembered he had been arrested in a men's room once. "Was he caught trying to have sex?"

"No, it has something to do with being accused of stealing your father's papers and selling them. Because Dick was governor, and the papers crossed state lines, it's more serious."

"He never knew who I was," Melissa said. She had an instant stomachache, pulsating.

"But he could describe you both. Blake is rather distinctive-looking. Ask Blake what he said when he made contact with Tom, because if he talks, you could be in serious trouble."

She ran to Blake at once, for he had long since taught her to say nothing that could hurt them in e-mail or on the telephone. He frowned, straddling his desk chair. In that position, he looked all arms and legs. "I'm trying to remember what I told him. I knew him as Tom, no last name. I told him my name was Sam."

"Why Sam?"

"It was the first name that came to mind when he asked me. Do I know any Sams? Yeah, Si had a cousin in Baltimore named Sam. But he's dead."

"No Sams in my family. Quick thinking."

"I can't remember what I said to him. I'll concentrate and see if I can bring it back." He dug at his scalp, frowning still. "Let's hope he doesn't get chatty."

"What could they actually charge him with?"

"I don't know. At some point I should ask Si. I hate to involve him, but he's the only person who can answer questions like that."

Blake brought up various newspapers on the Internet. The *Inquirer* had a photo. "That's him," Melissa said. "He has a cap in front of his face, but his ears are memorable."

"I better call my dad," Blake said grimly.

When he said "father" or "dad," she always had a moment of disorientation, wondering which of the two men he was referring to. It made her feel alienated, remembering all he had not told her until she found out from Rosemary. It surprised her how much she resented that withholding, even now, even after so much else had happened between them. She still resented that he had not trusted her. It was a sore that would not heal. She sat with her knees drawn up to her chest and her arms clutching her legs, chilly in the too-warm dorm. At first she tried to follow the conversation, but Si was doing most of the talking. She tuned out. Blake would tell her what was going on when he hung up. All the news seemed to be bad, so why be in a hurry to hear it?

He turned to face her, crossing his arms as if he too needed protection from something dangerous in the air. "He says Burt Sandoval is taking Tom's case. He's going to use the Pentagon Papers defense."

"What Pentagon Papers? I don't know what you're talking about."

"Before our time. The *Times* published secret papers about the Vietnam war. Some guy—Daniel Ellsberg—who had access stole them, because there was a lot of information about how the government had lied. The *Times* knew they were stolen and printed them anyhow. A judge finally ruled that it was in the public interest and a newspaper had the right to print such material. . . ."

"I don't get what's happening, who's after who."

"Your father is after the *Inquirer* for publishing the stuff we leaked to Roger. Tom's in trouble for stealing papers from your father's office."

"I thought my father would claim they were bogus."

"He did at first. But there's too much info that can be checked. He's trying to bottle it up at the source by going after Tom, who took the stuff and passed it on, and the *Inquirer,* that published it, and Roger, who wrote it. They haven't found out we were the middlemen—yet. I hear Mexico's nice this time of year."

"Could we run away?"

His laugh was more like a cough. "Not really. For the moment, I say we go with the flow and watch."

"Why can't we run away?" She looked out his window on a bleak November day with pellets of snow circling aimlessly, vanishing as they hit the ground. A day without sun or color. A warm place far from her family had strong appeal: palm trees, a blue-green tropical sea swishing lazily at their feet.

"And live on what? It's premature to break and run." He stretched languidly. "Besides, Mexico has extradition laws. And we'd have to be picking up checks from Si and Nadine to survive. We'd be easy to trace."

"Aren't there other places? Places that don't have treaties?"

"Like China?"

"People disappear in the U.S. all the time."

"We're kind of striking, babes. People notice us. You could dye your hair, but I can't dye my skin. We should just sit tight and see what happens. We're not on the spot yet."

"In Mexico there are a lot of mixed-race people, Blake."

"How well do you speak Spanish? I sound American, and I bet you do too."

In bed they clutched each other, even more passionate than usual. "After college, we'll have children, won't we?"

He smiled into her eyes from two inches away. "One at a time, I hope. Yes. We have to have children. They will be absolutely gorgeous. Like us."

"I never thought of myself as gorgeous."

"You aren't patrician looking like your mother. But you *are* beautiful in your own way, my girl. You're built. You've got curves where you ought to. You're the right height for me and you feel good. Oh how you feel good. You're made of cream and velvet."

"I want to know we'll be together for years and years, to get old together like my mother's parents. They actually love each other still, you can tell, even though they're really old, like seventy. I don't know if I want to live to be that old, but if I do, I want it to be with you."

He held her face between his palms. "I want that too. I want to be a great-grandfather with a tribe of descendants. Multicolored like a quilt, some with your hair, some with mine, all of them strong and confident of belonging and being loved."

"I think that's like beautiful."

"But we should wait to make babies till we're graduated and we have a place to live and some money. I don't want you to get pregnant too soon. I've seen what that does to people."

"I'm in no hurry, believe me. I just need to know we have a future we care about. Making plans even if they're just pretend makes me feel good."

"They're not pretend. We can do it. Why not? It's not like we want to be President, the way your old man does, or want to be rock stars or basketball millionaires. What we want is simple enough, so why can't we have it? Each other and a decent life together."

She held him, she held him tight, her cheek pressed to his chest, the sparse wiry hairs tickling her.

THREE WEEKS passed, exams came and went, papers were due, and it seemed as if nothing was happening. The first snowstorm of the season muffled everything in puffy white globules, a wet snow that bowed branches and striped tree trunks. Andrus Field was studded with kids throwing snowballs. Snowmen, snowwomen, a big dog of snow stood here and there on campus. By the end of the week everything was drooping and grey. She was delighted with a thaw on Sunday, even though it made the world a soggy mass of dead leaves and choked gutters.

Monday everything froze and campus was a sheet of bumpy ice. They were going to class when Emily slipped and landed on her butt. Now she was hobbling. Melissa was already worrying about Thanksgiving. She was nervous about going home. The farther she stayed from her parents, the better for her. She did not want them questioning her, she did not want to have to lie, to be afraid all the time she would let something slip. She was worried too that if she went home, they might somehow keep her there.

"It might be a good idea to go and scout them out," Blake said, rubbing his chin thoughtfully. "You could find out what they know."

"I doubt it. I've never been great at getting stuff out of Rosemary. I'm not her confidante."

"But Merilee is. Maybe you could get her to talk."

"Blake, I'm ten times likelier to spill something by accident than to learn anything useful."

Tuesday started off as an ordinary day of classes and bad weather, sleet on top of ice. She got the results of her tests and found she had done uniformly well. Marriage must be good for her studying. Maybe feeling more secure with Blake improved her concentration. She was set to see him after supper, but he appeared outside her Sociology of Politics class, waiting for her.

"Roger has been subpoenaed to appear before a grand jury investigating the theft of documents from the governor's office."

"Oh, shit! You still don't want to run?"

"Roger's going to plead First Amendment, freedom of the press, the right of a journalist to protect his sources. We're his source, and he promised he'd protect us. There's a lot of precedents for a journalist refusing to testify. Besides, the papers went through Phil, and Roger sure doesn't want to implicate his own son. Right now I'm off-the-wall glad we didn't bypass Phil."

Still they were scared. They sat drinking coffee in the student center, not saying much. She felt years older than the kids around her, some from her classes, some she knew from the dorm or previous classes. She was married already, she had adult worries. She was in danger. She might even be arrested. It was not like she was still worrying about boyfriends or grades or her complexion, like them, like Emily even.

They watched the evening news together. Of course there was nothing on the local, but on the national news, there was Roger, who only faintly resembled his son, being ushered into a courthouse surrounded by a clicking rustle of cameras—the sound of a horde of insects—and reporters sticking mikes in his face. He drew himself up and spoke resonantly: "I'm defending the freedom of the press. I'm fighting for all of you as well as myself. If I have to go to jail to protect my sources, then I'll go to jail. We have to stand firm or we can't do investigative journalism any longer. A free country must preserve its free press."

"I thought he was pretty persuasive," Melissa said.

"It's a question the grand jury and judge will decide. He's our hero. He may not be theirs. Maybe the judge who will hear him was appointed by Dick."

She put her head into her hands. "It's not a game anymore."

"It never was a game, babes. You ask your aunt."

"But it felt like one. I mean, we were just harassing him. Nipping at him. Playing tricks. Finding things that were hidden. Now it feels so heavy, so serious. Like we could maybe go to jail."

He looked at her for a long time. "Of course we could. Or at least, I could. After all, you're King Richard's daughter."

"That's not fair. I've done everything you've done. Except the computer stuff. I don't know how to do that. I'm your wife. We share everything, the good and the bad. That's what getting married means."

"We'll just hold on and see what happens. . . ."

They learned that Roger's papers and computer had been confiscated along with his phone records. The *Inquirer* had stopped running the articles. That seemed to upset Blake more than anything else. "If they turn coward over those articles, then it was all for nothing."

"Maybe they're just waiting to see what happens in the courts."

"But the news is now. It's a hot story. If they wait six months, it'll just be a little story in the back of the paper. This is our chance."

The next weekend Blake disappeared with two of the guys from the African-American caucus who had been in the demonstration with them last year. He didn't tell her where he was going or how long he would be gone. She was worried sick, and furious too because he wasn't confiding in her. It wasn't fair! If she was his wife, he had to tell her things. It just wasn't right to treat her like this. All of a sudden, he trusted these two guys he had hardly said boo to for weeks, and she was left hanging, waiting on him, not knowing where he was or why he was there or when he was coming back. Could he have fled, the way she suggested? Had he abandoned her? She was terrified. Maybe he had listened to her advice and run off to Mexico. He said that the two of them together were too striking, too visible; maybe he really meant that, and he had taken off on his own, leaving her to face her parents and the law and the government and everything.

In desperation she went in search of Florette, finding her at the table her group usually occupied. "How the hell would I know where Blake is?" Florette glared at her. "You been seeing far more of him than we do. I hear you really hooked up. Why you suppose I know where his ass is at?

You think he's getting some on the side? Don't come running to me, white girl. I don't keep tabs on him. That's your job."

She believed Florette. So where was he? She was embarrassed she had bothered Florette; Blake would be annoyed. But she did not know what to do with herself. Oh, she studied, she worked on a paper, she did her laundry, she trimmed Emily's ends, she answered Rosemary's weekly e-mail, but all of the time like a sore tooth she probed his absence. Could he have abandoned her?

Emily was less than sympathetic. She was painting her toenails, using shiny black polish. "So he's gone off with a couple of guy friends. Do you want him to stop having friends? Marriage isn't supposed to be a box. You got married way too young, and now you think you own him body and soul so he can't sneeze without your permission. Lissa, you're dead wrong."

"But I don't even know where he is. He could have told me."

"He probably needed to feel he still has a life. The two of you spend so much time together, maybe he just had to take a breather."

There was no way she could make Emily understand her anxiety, because she could not tell Emily what she had been doing with Blake. Things were closing in on them. How dangerous their project had turned out to be. She imagined Emily's surprise when the police came to haul her away. Maybe the FBI? Then Emily would see she had not been frightened without cause. It came down to her wondering again if Blake really, truly loved her. Maybe someday she would be free from the underlying fear that he was conning her, using her, but when she was frightened, that old worry surfaced. Ultimately, could she trust him? Was he really *for* her, as well as with her?

She called Karen. "Go out to a pay phone and call me collect," Karen said. "They could be tapping your phone."

She felt more than ever like someone in a thriller, a film about spies and secret documents. She obeyed Karen and called her collect from the only working pay phone she could find on campus, in the student center. Most everybody used cell phones, so there were fewer and fewer pay phones around. Blake had told her that cell phones were even less secure than regular phones, or she would have used hers.

Karen, like Emily, did not see it as terribly important that Blake had gone off without telling her where. "Guys will be guys, whether you marry them or not. Probably he's just pushing against the bars. Wanting to prove to himself he's still one of the pack and not always accountable."

"But I'm afraid of getting busted for giving that information to the reporter."

"Now *that's* something to worry about. I don't think you're about to go to jail. It would be too much scandal for your father. More likely they'd get you committed for general nuttiness. But being married should be some help."

"If he's around."

"Melissa, you trust him or you don't. If you don't trust him, you should never have married him. If you do trust him, stop climbing the walls. You have to assume he had some errand he didn't think you needed to be involved in. Maybe he went to consult his father on the legal situation. Hasn't he ever gone off without you?"

"When he was meeting hackers to get programs."

"There you go. He's probably trying to find a program to erase every trace of what you've been doing from both your computers."

She thanked Karen profusely. That was the first thing anyone had said to her that made sense. "That must be it."

"I bet he'll be back Monday. Don't get all worked up—it's not fair to yourself or to him. This hysteria about him being gone overnight is not becoming. Put a lid on it."

She nodded, even though Karen could not see her. "Okay. I will."

She felt much better. She went back to her room and apologized to Emily for making a fuss. But she felt she could not sleep or draw a deep relaxed breath until Blake was back with her and she knew they were still together.

When her cell phone rang Sunday at nine, Melissa was sure it was Blake.

Alison spoke earnestly. "I wanted to tell you, Melissa, that your mother is much relieved that you've stopped consorting with the son of that murderer. I have to say that you troubled Rosemary greatly. She's a splendid person, Melissa, and you should be more careful in future. She was beside herself, such as I've seldom seen her."

"Did Mother ask you to talk to me?"

"She doesn't know about this call. I want you to understand how troubled you made her. Your mother is the most brilliant woman I have ever had the privilege of knowing. I would do anything for her, and I'd expect you to feel the same way. But you put her through a difficult time."

Melissa felt like hanging up, but she suspected Rosemary might be listening on an extension. "Well, I'm sorry, I'm very sorry for upsetting her, but I need to live my own life too."

"She gave you life. . . ."

Melissa tuned out. She had always hated that phrase. She had always thought it meant, She gave you life and she could take it back. And Rosemary did try to take it back. Control.

". . . make sure that you understand these are rocky times. I find it hard to see her so besieged. We all have to pull together. They've given you so much that it's a small thing to ask that you do nothing to aggravate her further. . . ."

"I think it's wonderful how loyal you are to her," Melissa said carefully.

"As you must be."

"Shit," Melissa said to Emily afterward. "Alison's given up her life to Mother and she expects me to. She's pitiful."

"She probably thinks the same of you, not appreciating the great and glorious Rosemary." Emily had just had a haircut at a local salon, and she kept fiddling with her suddenly very short very blond hair. "What did she want?"

"To continue the campaign. They think I've stopped seeing Blake, and they want it to stay that way. They don't trust me." And they shouldn't.

BLAKE SHOWED UP outside her eleven o'clock Public Opinion and Electoral Politics class on Monday as Melissa was leaving. "Lunch?" he greeted her.

"No, I'm not lunch. I'm your wife. I've been worried about you."

"Yeah? Those rumors of man-eating lions on the Jersey Turnpike are not true, I can tell you. All the rest stops looked safe to me."

"You were in Philadelphia?"

"The same dirty old town." He slid his arm around her as they walked.

"Did you see Si and Nadine?"

"They give you their love."

"I wish they would. I really like them."

"You impressed them much more favorably last time. You're winning that battle. What have you heard from your folks?"

"I managed to convince Rosemary I've stopped seeing you, and she has bigger problems now than me, or so she thinks." She watched him to see if he would be angry and pull that bit about being ashamed of her pet darky, but he seemed not to take offense.

"Good, good. Now I am starving. I got back here late this morning, and I've had nothing to eat but a stale doughnut, so let's mosey toward food."

When they were seated in the student center with plates of tacos, she asked, "So what were you doing that was so important?"

"Just things I needed."

"Programs from your hacker friends?"

"I wanted to talk with Si face-to-face. It seemed like a good idea."

He hadn't answered her about the programs. That was usually New York.

"Did you get a chance to stop in New York?"

"Not this time. God, am I tired. I'm going to sleep through my afternoon classes after missing my morning classes. Tonight I want to hit the sack early and pile up some z's."

"You don't want to get together?"

"Sure I do." He patted her hand. "Couldn't do without it. But I'm going to throw you out by nine thirty."

"That's fine. I have a paper to write for sociology. That project I'm doing with Lindsey in the mall."

"Sounds thrilling. If you were named Lindsey, we'd never have hooked up. That name gives me hives. I bet her family is loaded."

"Good guess. But it thrills my mother to hear I am hanging with her. Merilee knows her brother Stu."

"Then mall away. It should help keep Rosemary off our tracks."

He was in an oddly jolly mood, although he kept rubbing his bloodshot eyes and yawning. Maybe Si had given him more hope than he had left with. But why wouldn't he share any good news with her? She could use some cheering up.

That evening he was more forthcoming. "Si had me talk to a guy, without naming any names, somebody he got off who's a flaming computer genius. He advised me to stop monitoring Rosemary's e-mail. It's possible if she brings somebody in who knows their shit they could find out what I've been doing. So, sadly, my girl, we're going to have to forgo reading her communications. I'll miss it and I know you will."

"I don't care, really. I know how she writes to each of us now. I know where I stand with her—down at the bottom of the list, the way I always thought."

He rubbed his sore eyes. "When you go home at Thanksgiving, see if you can sneak in and get on her computer. I'll give you her passwords."

"I so don't want to go back there Thanksgiving."

"If you don't, babes, she'll be suspicious. Business as usual, that's the way to go. Maybe you'll learn something."

"Suppose they don't want to let me come back to Wesleyan?"

"You said she'd dropped that. She's too worried about what's going on with the exposé to worry about your love life. Just stick to the story that you're not seeing me any longer, and talk up Lindsey the Mall Girl. Tell her nothing and keep your ears open and your eyes peeled for a chance to get into her stuff."

"Yeah, like that's going to happen."

"Don't be so down. You might grab a break. They go out a lot, right?"

"Thanksgiving they have the multitudes in." She sighed. "Will we ever, ever have a holiday together?"

"The rest of our lives. Every single holiday. Christmas, Chanukah, Kwanzaa, New Year's, Halloween, Thanksgiving, Labor Day, Arbor Day, the works. We're still in school, babes, and we have to not freak out the elder folks."

SHE DEVELOPED a stomachache the night before she was to leave, but she didn't see how that would absolve her from going. Alison drove up to get her. "I could have taken the train, easy," Melissa said. "How come she made you drive all this way?"

"We decided it was safer. Your parents are feeling quite vulnerable right now, and they want you protected. You said you aren't well?"

"Just a stomach virus. Or something I ate in the food hall."

"Right before Thanksgiving, that's so sad." Alison shook her head. "If you reach into the backseat and look in my bag, you're find several remedies. Why don't you try one of them, and if that doesn't work, try another in an hour or so. We want you in fine shape for tomorrow's feast."

Melissa entertained the fantasy of staying in bed, then sneaking down later and helping herself to leftovers. But Blake had severely warned her to act normal at all times, and skipping Thanksgiving was not her usual behavior. Besides, Rosemary would never grill her in front of guests. She was probably safer at dinner. If she were alone, Rosemary might well come upstairs on the pretext of commiserating with her sick daughter and begin to ask all the questions that Melissa feared.

"Who's coming?" she asked Alison.

"Let me see, Tony and Kurt, of course; then the Senator's interns . . ."

"Did you ever notice," Melissa said slyly, "that my father always has male interns?"

"Of course," Alison said. "With all that's gone on in Washington in recent years, the Senator wants to avoid even the possibility of impropriety. Rosemary vets them. We had one project manager in the Senator's campaign who was gay, and he turned out to be a renegade. He stole papers from the office and tried to discredit your father. You must have seen something in the papers?"

"Yeah." Melissa grimaced. "I think I saw something on TV."

Alison cautiously approached the subject of Blake. "So are you still seeing that young man who so upset your mother?"

"I told her I wasn't." Literal truth.

"You broke off with him, then?"

"It wasn't a big deal, until Mother made it one. He was just a guy I saw sometimes. I told him I had gotten involved with somebody else, and he believed me. I wasn't his only interest either, so it was nothing to fuss over."

"It was quite a bit to fuss over for us, believe me, Melissa. Even having contact with such a person is dangerous."

"Bullshit! He's just another student at Wesleyan. He doesn't remember his father. The last time he saw him he was just five, so it's a much bigger deal to you people than it ever was to him. The sins of the fathers. You were all paranoid."

"Your parents were truly, truly disturbed. Causing them such worry is nothing you should take lightly. They're important people, Melissa, good people, special people. We have to help them, not cause them distractions."

Melissa turned on the radio. "Let's get the news and weather. By the way, you never told me who else was coming to Thanksgiving."

"Let's see," Alison said as if having to remember with difficulty, although Melissa knew perfectly well that Alison's mind was organized and could call up any of her hundred current lists at will. "Rich, Laura, Merilee, Billy and some friend of his—"

"Male or female?"

"An exchange student on his hockey team—from Norway, I think? But Billy swears he speaks English."

"And?"

"Senators Dawes and Nottingham and Mrs. N., Audrey and her little girl. Eric. The representative from District Eight, Angus Spears. He's recently divorced, and your father has taken him under his wing. He's quite good looking."

"Does Rosemary intend him for Merilee or for me?"

"Rosemary is simply being nice to him. . . . It's possible Merilee might like him, and he's certainly both available and suitable."

"Then he's not for me."

"Unless Merilee and he do not strike it off, and he and you do. You might try being a little forthcoming at table."

"I'll try." Should she flirt with him outrageously to throw her mother off the scent? Could she pull that off? She had never been a practiced flirt. Neither Merilee nor she had picked up Rosemary's almost professional skill.

IT FELT STRANGE to be back in the house in Washington, where Blake and she had cohabited so merrily and pretended to be married. Now that was no longer pretense but fact, yet she felt less married to him now than she had those precious weeks of August. She did not want to be here, in the cement-hard bosom of her family. She could not escape a flush of guilt whenever she heard Rosemary discussing the *Inquirer* attacks. She repeated to herself the litany of Dick's sins in office, but she still cringed. She began to study herself in mirrors, not from vanity but from fear of what her face might be giving away. Fortunately, the house was overrun with people, so that Alison and Rosemary were tied up with Thanksgiving plans—not only dinner but, on Sunday afternoon, a reception Melissa hoped she could avoid.

Merilee, in her last year of law school, was busy until that night when she arrived with a backpack at ten, tossing it down in the room they shared. Merilee flung herself on her single bed—exactly like Melissa's, with a matching Ralph Lauren spread—and closed her eyes.

"Wiped?"

"Totally." Merilee did not open her eyes. "I hate law school and yet I wouldn't be anyplace else. It's absorbing—a constant challenge."

"I hear that a recently divorced rep from Pennsylvania is being served to you at Thanksgiving."

"Damn." That was strong language for Merilee, who had never learned to swear. "Or am I being served to him?"

"You're not interested?"

"It's been lovely to have Mother off my case for a couple of months while they've been stewing about your déclassé boyfriend from the 'hood."

"He's not from the 'hood, Merilee. He was raised by two affluent lawyers."

"The Ackermans. They're both brilliant, by the way. I've read some of his appeals, and they are both ingenious and profound."

Melissa tried to imagine what an ingenious and profound brief would be like. She had glanced through Merilee's law books and had yet to find anything remotely interesting.

"Is that young man going into law?"

"No. He's into computers." She felt a stab of fear. Blake had carefully not mentioned that to her parents when they had walked in that night. She had carefully not mentioned it since.

But Merilee had lost interest. Her lids slowly lowered. "Um."

ALISON HAD GONE shopping and bought dresses for Merilee and Melissa at a boutique recommended by someone with taste Melissa found appalling. This was as bad as the thing she had worn at Rich and Laura's wedding. Laura at any rate was allowed to wear something comfortable, a velvet maternity dress that made her look like an upholstered easy chair but had to be ten times gentler on the body than the blue sheath she had to struggle into. Merilee's dress was black with spaghetti straps. Melissa guessed it was supposed to make Merilee look older and more sophisticated, presumably to appeal to Angus. Her dress seemed designed to keep her from eating too much. She wondered if it might not simply pop open in the middle of dinner, spilling her out onto her plate.

She winced when she saw her father coming down the steps to the diningroom with Rosemary on his arm. He was so handsome it was unfair. He seemed to radiate confidence like heat. He looked presidential greeting everyone with a special smile, a special hand squeeze, that gaze into the eyes that seemed to shine with sincerity. He loved to work a roomful of people almost as much as he loved to work a crowd. Some politicians seemed to suffer the public gaze; he gathered it into himself and beamed it back, intensified. She had trouble meeting his eyes—if he knew what she had done, he would be so hurt and furious. She wanted to slink away and hide.

Since she could scarcely breathe in the dress, she did not talk much at table. Nobody seemed to notice, although Billy's friend Torval tried to engage her. He spoke English quite well, with a charming accent, but the interchanges were awkward. Besides he was two years younger, so she wouldn't have been interested even if she weren't married. It would be wonderful when she was allowed to put on her ring. She usually wore it around her neck, but Blake had vetoed that idea for Washington. It would be too easy to notice and too hard to explain, he said. But she missed it. Usually it was right there between her breasts, making her new condition real to her with its slight metallic pressure.

Merilee did look spectacular in black. Merilee was slender with small breasts, but Alison had provided one of those push-up bras that could give cleavage to a cutting board. Her blond hair glistened. The representative was seated next to her, and after a while they fell into animated and almost private conversation. Rosemary smiled approvingly and concentrated on her favorite, Senator Dawes, and the elderly Republican Senator Nottingham from Mississippi. Nottingham had been elected so many times he scarcely bothered to return to his district on holidays. Washington said that after he died, he would be stuffed and continue to represent his state, still winning election after election, and no one would notice the difference. Rosemary had obviously been working on him for some project of Dick's. Mrs. N. ate steadily without speaking. Melissa could tell from her glances that she did not like Rosemary. She was probably here under protest.

Sometimes Melissa looked at her mother and was startled by how beautiful she was. Would her own life be better if she looked like that? But Blake liked her the way she was. He liked the breasts and hips and ass she had been trained to be ashamed of. All she could think of was how many hours she had to go before she could rip off this iron maiden of a dress.

The representative—Angus—was tall and bony with a neatly trimmed thatch of reddish hair. He was freckled, which was kind of endearing, and he had a deep bass voice that made her think perhaps he sang, like in a choir. He seemed an improvement on most of the politicians her father brought home as protégés. But he was about as sexy as an Irish setter. The conversation at table was mostly in-group Washington gossip: who had done what to whom, who had attended or snubbed what hostess, who was rumored to be divorcing over what, who was about to retire from the House or Senate or the bench. The interns were showing off their knowledge, glancing surreptitiously at Dick to see if he was impressed. He listened as if fascinated. He always encouraged his staff to pick up gossip. He knew how to be the center of everything without saying a word. Melissa was bored. She did not belong here, she did not belong to them.

It was Saturday afternoon before Rosemary had the leisure to call her into her tidy office. Melissa had gone out with Jessica earlier, shopping for CDs. Jessica had to be back at her parents' house by five, so Melissa had reluctantly come home. She had hoped to avoid this conversation, but short of running out into the street, she was stuck.

"I was wondering with whom you've been socializing at school lately?"

"I've been seeing a lot of Lindsey. We're actually working together on a project for sociology."

"And boys?" Rosemary propped her sharp chin on her steepled hands, her light brown eyes fixed on Melissa, who was thinking idly that at least she had her mother's eyes, if nothing else.

"I haven't really met anyone I'm interested in. . . ." She had a quick idea that might throw her mother off stride. "But I really liked the guy at Thanksgiving, Angus. He seemed really cool. Very sophisticated."

"He's a little old for you, Melissa. He's been married and divorced. He's thirty-seven."

"I liked him. I thought he was bright and articulate and really good looking."

"I believe your sister is interested in him, and he's far more suitable for her. You need someone much younger and less . . . experienced."

"I don't know," Melissa said airily. "I like older men. In a way he reminded me of Daddy. His politics. His way of expressing himself."

"He's a protégé of your father's, yes, but not what you should be considering at this stage in your development."

"I don't see why not. He could teach me a great deal."

Rosemary grimaced. "This is silly. But, yes, he is a more respectable and responsible sort than you were interested in earlier this year. Perhaps your taste is improving. But don't get the idea of going head-to-head with your sister, if she does turn out to be interested in Angus. . . . Where did you and Jessica go?"

BLAKE E-MAILED her around ten that night:

Hope you had a chance to look around.

She answered at once.

No way. The house is teeming. Billy's here with a Norwegian exchange student and they're playing video games all the time. Bang bang. Alison hasn't stopped hovering. Dick has been working on a speech about estate taxes with his writers in his downstairs office. Rosemary has been closeted with Senator Dawes or playing bridge with Mrs. Senator Nottingham and two administration wives. Rich is

on the phone nonstop with the producer who did my father's video
for the last campaign. Laura's lying around reading baby magazines
and ordering things.

She had not tried, because she just knew she would be caught if she
did. He didn't understand the situation. She thought she was doing pretty
well fending off Rosemary's attention, but she had to be cautious. She
could scarcely wait until Sunday afternoon finally came and she could
return to school and safety. And Blake, her secret husband.

Melissa was waiting for Blake. He said he had big news, and from his voice she figured it was good. Well, they could use some. She felt as if she had been living with tension for so many weeks that she was almost used to that tightness in her belly, in her chest, that anxiety that seeped through her dreams and woke her sweating. She wished she could just forget about the danger for a week, even for a day. Doing work for her classes was some kind of relief, because it took her mind off the fear. She was afraid of the FBI, afraid of the police, afraid of her parents. It was hard for her to remember that she had lived much of her life worrying about nothing more than being laughed at by other girls, dreading only her mother's disapproval.

Soon she would have to go home for Christmas. It had been relatively easy to avoid Rosemary during Thanksgiving, but Christmas they would spend in Philadelphia, in the much smaller town house, without all the bustle of staff and interns and assistants and secretaries coming and going. There would be people passing through, sure, but she would be stuck there with them for much longer, and inevitably, Rosemary would have more time to spend quizzing her, turning her inside out like the pockets of a pair of jeans going into the washer.

She wished she could just announce she was married, let the whole family thing blow up and spend Christmas with Blake as a couple. After all, his family knew. When were they going public? It was time for honesty. Why was she so reluctant to bring that up with Blake? Maybe she did not want to hear his equivocations, his always good but never quite good enough reasons for procrastinating. Maybe she was afraid to push him too hard. Why? After all, they were legally married. Emily was tired of hearing about the situation. She was over at Mitch's house tonight. Their off-again, on-again thing was hot and heavy at the moment. Em had gone through a pregnancy scare, and Mitch hadn't bailed, so Em was feeling close to him.

Blake arrived finally, carrying a paper bag. In it was a bottle of California champagne. "Got something we can drink this in?"

"A couple of water glasses."

"It'll taste just as good."

"What's the occasion?" She clutched herself across her breasts, wishing he would explain already. What she did not know made her nervous.

"I talked with Si. His friend who's representing Roger passed on some information. Tom gave the FBI a description of the guy he met at Foxwoods."

"Why should we celebrate that? And what about me?"

"His description is that I was a very tall Hispanic named Sam in his middle twenties with a goatee. As for you, all he could remember is that you were a blonde wearing a leather jacket."

"Blonde? Don't I wish. Plus, where did the goatee come from?"

"Damned if I know. Either he's protecting us or he just didn't look at us carefully. Maybe he was too nervous. Maybe he thought that's what I should look like." He popped the cork and poured. "Anyhow, let's celebrate our freedom. With that description, they don't have a trail leading to us in fifty years."

She lifted her water glass full of bubbly. "Here's to Sam. Long may he wave."

"My sentiments exactly. We may never know if Tom was protecting us or just unable to focus." He was leaning back on his crooked elbows on her floor.

"Blake, when are we going to reveal our marriage?"

"What's the hurry? Once you do, you can't go home again, and we're cut off from a great source of info."

"Why do we need more? We've dug up plenty."

"The public has a right to know about their officials and what kind of shit they're into." He sat up on one elbow, fixing her with his large luminous eyes. "Until we have King Richard nailed, we've done nothing. Nothing at all."

Nailed? What was that supposed to mean? "Suppose the voters don't give a damn. I've heard the word *affable* used about him five hundred times. Face it, Blake: people like him. He comes across on television. He's handsome in a nonthreatening Yankee way. He's a patrician who knows how to put on the just-us-folks voice. He's weathered dozens of scandals over the years."

"It's different now. He's in the Senate. The appearance of propriety and operating by the rules counts there."

"Oh, sure. He's got appearance to burn."

"Lissa, I have to have justice. It's our mission. I owe it to my father. I can't live my own life till I've brought justice to the man responsible for my father's execution. We simply can't fail." He took her cold hand in his warm dry hands and stroked it as if he could rub courage and conviction into her like hand lotion. "It's like a sign that this guy Tom didn't turn us in, that he protected us."

"Did he protect us, or was he too flustered to look at us? He certainly paid no attention to me."

"We'll probably never know, but it comes out the same in the end." He sat up and poured more champagne. "Let's toast ourselves."

"To us. Our future together," she said, clinking her water glass against his.

"I'll drink to that. To the rest of our lives, together."

ALISON CALLED on her cell phone as she was having lunch. "I tried your room. I spoke with your roommate—Emily?"

"Is something wrong?" Melissa asked warily. Blake was right across the table from her. She motioned for him to be quiet, mouthing "Alison" at him.

"It's good news. Laura finally had her baby, two weeks overdue. It's a healthy bouncing boy! She was in labor for eighteen hours."

"Wow. That sounds grueling. Is she okay?"

"She's fine, and the baby is wonderful. He weighs nine pounds, two ounces. We're waiting to see him now. Rich and your mother think you should fly to Philly for photographs. This is a great time for Rich and good publicity."

"I can't go now. It's exam time."

"Just explain to your professors."

"That my sister-in-law had a baby and my brother wants me in the background of a couple of photos to aid his campaign? I can't do it. Besides, I have a huge zit on my nose."

"Makeup will take care of that."

"Alison, I'm in school. That matters to me, even if it's of no discernible importance to my mother or my brother. I look forward to seeing the baby over Christmas." She hung up and turned off her cell phone.

"The dynasty continues," she said sourly and filled Blake in.

"They really don't take your college career seriously, do they?"

"They don't take anything I do seriously." She let the corners of her mouth turn down. "That's their mistake."

"Absolutely. But I take you very seriously, don't I, babes? You're my Bible. My compass. My heart."

"I'm your wife, which is more important."

"You sure are. So, what will they name the baby?"

"Richard, of course. That's what they call the firstborn boys nowadays. Richard the Fifth. Quintus."

"She told you all that? I didn't even hear you ask the baby's name."

"I don't need to ask. I know how it works. The new king is born. I can just imagine the fuss, and it makes me want to vomit."

"It's not the baby's fault. Maybe he'll grow up to be a jazz musician or a horse trainer."

"Never. He'll draw himself up to the public trough. They'll start grooming him before he's five."

Rosemary called next to issue her edict: Melissa had to go to Philadelphia. She flew down Saturday morning with a return ticket for Sunday night. It felt really lame to have given in, but the whole gang was there; even Karen had been summoned. This was the birth of the heir to whatever.

She walked into a hospital room crammed with flowers from local politicians, supporters, friends of Rich or Laura, friends of Dick. Her father was in a corner talking on his cell phone. Rich was outside in the hall in earnest conversation with his campaign manager, an oversize man who had played football for Notre Dame but carefully retained his South Philly accent. Actually she had heard him switch accents from phone call to phone call—like Blake, who could make his voice and language whiter, blacker, more streetwise, academic, hackerese. She barely fit in the room, but she had to make herself visible so that Rosemary would cross her off a mental list. See, I showed up. Give me one credit. The baby, red faced and crying, was clasped in Laura's arms. Probably he needed to be fed, but there were just too many people.

"How come they made you come?" she asked Karen in the hall when she had a chance to get her out of earshot.

"Since Father left me the farm, I have a certain position. If they want to use it now and then in the summer or fall, they have to stay on my good side. But then I also have to pretend to be a member of the Dickinson mafia." Karen glanced around. "So where's Blake? Have you made your big announcement?"

"Not yet. I want to. But because so much is up in the air with your friend being busted, we're hanging back and waiting to see what happens." Melissa looked around nervously to make sure they couldn't be overheard.

"He's a cute little bugger—the baby, not Blake. Have you seen him yet?"

"Me and half of Rich's constituents. I hate coronations. So is Rosemary enjoying being a grandmother? I'd think it would freak her out."

Karen pursed her lips. "The line has to continue. But she isn't going to do a lot of diaper changing. She's found a nanny already, and she's lending Rich and Laura her assistant Alison for a week. . . . It must be funny to be lent out like a lawn mower. Here, take her, she's useful."

"I don't think Rosemary can do anything wrong in Alison's eyes. But she'll suffer, being away from Washington and Rosemary."

"So Rosemary's going back?" Karen glanced over her shoulder.

"Monday morning. She said, 'The Senator has an important committee hearing.' " She imitated her mother's voice referring to her husband as "the Senator," as she so often did.

They were called in to view the baby. Melissa never understood what people meant by a cute baby, all red and squally. She supposed that if they had everything they were supposed to, the standard equipment and all functioning, that made them beautiful in the eyes of those who had spent so many months producing the kids. She wanted children, she wanted them badly, but she still couldn't see that babies were cute. She was sure, however, when she had her first baby with Blake, she would change her mind. She would think that baby shone like a little sun. Not that she was in a desperate hurry to reproduce yet. Mostly she just wanted them to live together as husband and wife and be recognized by everyone as married. Then other girls would stop flirting with Blake and behave themselves. Then she would be free to show off her pride in her handsome brilliant husband.

Laura looked worn out but pleased with herself. She mostly concerned herself with little Dickey. Richard Potts Lee Dickinson. He would be wealthy and spoiled. He would go to the best schools, and trainers would be purchased to teach him whatever he needed to know to excel in sports. Why was she so jealous? Well, she just was. It was the same scene replicated. Rich Junior, heir apparent to the Dickinson political dynasty, now had his own crown prince. God help the girls who came along later. Blake was right: the dynasty would roll on and on unless someone threw up a roadblock. After all, she wasn't dynastic. She was superfluous.

Dick took a moment to put his arm around her shoulders and smile into her eyes. "I'm glad you came to your senses about that Ackerman boy. He simply won't do for you. You have to mistrust someone like that."

"He's just a student, Dad."

"And you're my girl. My little honeybee. We're a family and we have to stick together. Strength comes from unity, you understand?"

She tried to wait him out, but he was not about to let her go without a response. "I understand what you mean." Oh, did she.

"That's my sweetheart." He gave her shoulder a squeeze before letting go. His blue eyes looked into hers until she just had to look away. She could not help the surge of guilt that swept through her, until she was afraid she was sweating it through every pore. "We're all in the public eye, and we have to be conscious of our responsibilities—to ourselves and to each other. I know I can depend on you, the way I always have."

Finally they went out to supper in a restaurant where Philadelphia politicians and bureaucrats ate, where her father was greeted even by the Democrats with unctuous goodwill and hearty backslapping. He strode among the tables like a conquering hero, Rich in his wake, and they both received congratulations as they passed out cigars and showed off photos from the afternoon. While Rosemary had insisted she attend, Melissa was left pretty much alone. Rosemary was running over arrangements with Alison, who was making lists and notes on her PalmPilot. Their two heads almost touched, sleek blond and cropped auburn, as they created a zone of intensity and concentration. Melissa could not stifle a pang of jealousy for their closeness, but she suppressed it quickly. To be as close to Rosemary as Alison was, it would only be necessary to relinquish any pretense of her own life. Abandon Hope All Ye Who Enter Here.

Afterward, they adjourned to the town house, except for Laura, who was at home with the baby and the new nanny. Merilee had been called back from interviews in Boston. She was busy already being interviewed in various cities. Melissa was surprised that her older sister wasn't going to return as a matter of course to the firm in which she had interned the previous summer. Perhaps, Melissa speculated, the men who ran that firm were too close to Dick, and Merilee wanted a little more independence. Perhaps her sister hadn't done as well as everyone expected and they didn't want her back. Melissa was sure she'd never find out, unless she could get Alison talking. Sometimes Alison let things slip—but so rarely it was hardly worth the investment of effort. "So how did it work out with you and Angus?"

"Who?"

Rosemary heard that, her third and fourth ears pricking up. "That charming young man serving in the House. You got on so well with him at Thanksgiving."

"Oh, him. What about him?"

"Have you seen him again? You seemed to hit it off."

"Mother! I don't have time for that." Merilee sounded exhausted. "I'm on the Law Review. I'm trying to keep my grades up. I'm interviewing. I don't have time to do my laundry, let alone worry about some representative who lost a wife and needs a replacement."

"You have more time now than you'll have when you're practicing law as an associate in some huge firm, working an eighty-hour week," Rosemary said in a gentle, reasonable tone. "So now is the time to put some effort into finding a suitable mate. Angus is eminently suitable."

"I'm not ready to 'mate.' I'm not going through all the hassle and bone-breaking work of law school to throw it all away on a mommy track position married to some guy who needs an acceptable photogenic wife to further his career. I want my own career, and I want it fifty miles away from politics."

Oh, it was such fun when Rosemary and Merilee disagreed. She had to root for Merilee, but mainly she was delighted when Rosemary focused her annoyance on her older daughter. Melissa was about to escape back to school, back to Blake, back to Emily, back to her half-written sociology paper. Back to freedom, and none too soon.

elissa and Blake had been studying together in the library. It was nine and they were just collecting their books to head for his room when Phil came up to them. "I got to talk with you, man."

"You can talk in front of Melissa." Blake's forehead furrowed in annoyance. "What's wrong?"

"This is personal."

"Lissa, babes, want to go back to my room and wait? Do you mind?"

Of course she minded, but she didn't see how she could tell Phil to fuck off when he was obviously upset. "I'll wait for you there—until eleven. If you aren't back by then, I'll head for my dorm."

She found herself in Blake's room alone. Suddenly she wasn't annoyed. She had been given a secret, rather shameful gift, one she relished. This was her lover, her husband, and all his private things were open to her careful inspection. She felt a buzz of arousal, as if this were his body. First she opened his top drawer, much neater than hers. All his socks were individually balled and sorted by color and type, all his sports socks together on the right, all his dress socks on the left. His underwear drawer was equally neat, with a couple of ties folded to one side for the rare occasion when he needed one.

The third drawer was sweaters, each one folded. She buried her nose in them and smelled his gingery body odor lightly clinging to the wool and cotton. Then she felt something hard underneath. A box. She carefully drew out what she was feeling: a box of .38 shells. She stared at them, confused. Why would Blake have shells? Unless he also had a gun. Carefully she returned the shells and more quickly but equally carefully went through his other drawers. She found nothing but clothing and sports gear. She rushed to his closet. His shirts were grouped by color; his pants suspended from pants hangers; his jackets and coats occupied the far end. No gun. Why would he have shells without a gun? There had to be a gun someplace—unless he was keeping them for someone else. Just as cautiously she explored his desk drawers. Normally she would have taken her time and prowled through everything, but she was on a mission. She perched on his bed, terrified he would walk in and catch her snooping. Then on impulse she squatted and felt under his bed. Something was taped to the underside of the box spring. She ran her fingers over it, heart pounding. She could feel the outlines of a gun. Why did he have a gun? She could scarcely ask him. She checked that she had returned every object to its rightful place. It frightened her that he had a gun. It felt out of character. It felt all wrong.

She was sorry she had looked. Now she had an upsetting mystery she could not solve by asking. She would have to find some roundabout way to learn why he had a gun and where he had acquired it. And when? Had he always owned a gun? She found herself shamefully remembering the way Rosemary always described Blake as the son of a murderer. His father too must have had a gun. She simply could not face him. Although only forty minutes had passed, she scribbled a note saying that she had gone home to get a good night's sleep, since she hadn't been getting enough z's all week. "Love, XXXX," she scrawled, but she felt funny. She hoped she wouldn't run into him on the way out of his building. Nervously she kept glancing around, but he must still be with Phil. Of course, she had grown up with guns. Her father collected guns. But that was her father, champion of the NRA. Why did Blake have a gun? Maybe he too had grown up around guns. Maybe Si kept guns for self-defense. After all, a lawyer who dealt with murderers must have a sense of personal danger sometimes. But Blake had never said anything about it to her. Of course, neither had she ever brought up her father's gun cabinets. Blake had seen them in Washington but never showed any interest. Maybe because they were old hat to him, as to her.

The excuse she gave him proved ironic, because she did not sleep at all. She tried to tell herself that a lot of guys had guns, but she didn't believe it. Not at Wesleyan. Not Blake. It frightened her. It made her doubt him. At the same time, she could not, absolutely could not, let him guess that she had been going through his drawers. He had such a developed sense of privacy, he would never forgive her. It would be too sleazy a confession. She deserved her punishment because she had been snooping. It was a character flaw, the same curiosity and love of secrets that gave her a thrill when they were uncovering information about Dick and Rosemary. But she had to trust Blake. He was her husband. He was the center of her life. She had to trust him. What choice did she have?

HE CAUGHT UP to her at noon. "Babes, I was surprised you didn't wait for me. Are you feeling okay?"

"I was wiped. I've been having trouble sleeping."

"You're worried."

"Yeah, a bit. You know?" She shook her hair back, not used to the new heft of it. "What did Phil want?"

"He's nervous. He's feeling guilty about feeding his dad stuff that got him in legal trouble. Basically he wanted reassurance."

"Well, his father isn't about to turn him in."

"He needed hand-holding. . . . Oh, Nadine and Si are coming up this weekend. They want to know how we're doing. They'll take us out to dinner Saturday night, okay? They want to see you too."

"Really? That's sweet. But didn't you just see them last weekend?" If he hadn't gone home, then where had he gone?

"Things are happening fast, and he probably knows something he doesn't want to talk about on the phone. We'll find out Saturday. Feeling better?"

Yes, somehow she did. Nadine and Si seemed so normal, so much parents, so caring and affectionate that they made things feel almost safe. "I'm glad they're coming. I like them. And I want them to like me."

"They do. As they get to know you, they'll like you even better. I promise."

In the women's room at the restaurant, she approached Nadine. "How well did you know Blake's father?"

Nadine was renewing her lipstick, brushing at her halo of lamb's-wool white hair. "We knew him even before the frame-up. He was a good man. A really good man. We tried like hell to save him. It was an awful defeat."

"Are you so sure it was a frame-up?"

"Absolutely. As sure as I'm standing here. He wasn't a thug, Melissa. He was an intellectual. A sensitive man. An organizer. He was charismatic. He had a voice like hot chocolate. He even had a fine singing voice. He wasn't religious but he was a deeply ethical man. He might have killed in self-defense or in defense of his family, but he would never go out and shoot down a cop." Nadine turned from the mirror to search Melissa's face. "Why are you asking about him?"

"Because he's Blake's biological father, because he means so much to Blake, I want to understand who he was. My parents demonized him, so I have a lot of mental rewriting to do."

Nadine seemed satisfied by her answer. "You should talk to Si. After all, he was Toussaint's lawyer all through the appeals. He ran the defense team. Si knew Toussaint even better than I did, because of seeing him through all the stress and hope and loss of hope, to the bitter end."

"Just to be safe, I've brought you a new computer," Si was saying. "Transfer what you absolutely need to it and junk your old one. Don't give it away. Don't play around. Smash it with a crowbar and take it to the dump."

"A new computer?" Blake was startled, she could see. "You think things might get really hairy."

"They might. I want you on this right away." Si turned to her. "Now, is there anything on your computer that might cause problems?"

"I don't think so. . . ."

"Please check it over. I can FedEx you a new computer tomorrow if you call me. Don't think because you've erased things that they can't be restored."

"Even e-mail?"

"Sure," Nadine said. "I've had two cases where erased e-mails were restored and used against clients."

As they stood outside around the Ackermans' car, awkwardly she gave them each a peck on the cheek. Her family wasn't much for kissing, but she had noticed the Ackermans went in for that. "I'll go check my computer. Actually, there's all the family e-mails. Blake was reading them. I never thought about that."

"Tomorrow I'll FedEx you a new one, overnight. Transfer what you need and destroy the old computer. Tell me what you have, and I'll get something that looks enough like it so perhaps no one will notice and you won't have to give any lengthy explanations."

The men had opened the trunk and were looking at the computer Si had brought with him. "Nadine"—she clutched her mother-in-law's hand—"would it be good, would it help, if I converted?"

"Converted what?" Nadine was watching the men deep in argument.

"To Judaism."

That got Nadine's attention. "Oh, Melissa, we aren't religious really. We're what they call bagels and lox Jews. We identify, but we only go to a synagogue for High Holy Days and bar and bat mitzvot. It's a long and complicated and not very pleasant process to formally convert."

"But would you like it?"

"We pretty much take intermarriage for granted, there's been so much of it. I wouldn't like it if you raised the grandchildren Christian, frankly, but until you have children, it's not a pressing issue—and you have enough troubles."

"I don't have any religion. My parents are Episcopalian, but it never had a pull on me. It seemed a matter of social importance and social class. . . . I just want you to know how happy I am to be part of your family and how much I want to be part."

"That's very sweet, but let's not deal with religion right now. We have enough to worry about."

When she was in bed that night back in her dormitory room, with Emily mumbling in sleep and sighing heavily, she realized she had forgotten entirely about the gun. Sometime she would find a way to bring it up, but it felt less urgent. Being around Nadine and Si made everything seem normal. She was particularly grateful to them for treating her as if she were really and truly married to their adopted son. Actually they were very good to him. When she thought about it critically, it seemed to her that he had greatly exaggerated his alienation in his adopted family. She only wished she had ever felt as doted on as he seemed to be. But of course if she brought that up, he would go on about his executed father. Well, she could hardly complain about his being treated well, because they were also treating her kindly. That seemed to be part of the family package.

The computer arrived, and she promptly switched over her few programs to the new computer and lugged the old one out to the trash. Emily was at a game cheering on Fern, but Melissa had begged off.

Melissa did not look forward to Christmas vacation, when she would be in Philadelphia for weeks under Rosemary's scrutiny. By now, she simply hated to go "home"—she put it in quotation marks in her head. Blake was home to her. The Ackermans seemed to have accepted her, if only provisionally. She was part of a different family from her own, one that she liked better. She even got on with Blake's sister. Still, she knew she would not feel grown up after a few hours in the town house. She would feel years younger and infinitely less capable and in control. Why did she have to go and give a performance? She wanted to declare her loyalty, her union with Blake. She wanted the battle to be in the open. They would cast her out and only gradually come to accept her marriage, if ever. Maybe she would even get in touch with Rosemary's mother and father, her grandparents.

ON MONDAY, Jamal was waiting for her outside her eleven o'clock, at the time and place Blake usually met her. "I been trying to call you on your cell phone," he said accusingly.

"Professor James makes us keep them off. If one goes off in class, you get thrown out and are not allowed back in for a week." She shrugged. "What's up?"

"It's what's coming down. The feds raided Blake's room. They grabbed both his computers and a lot of other stuff."

Blake had spent part of Sunday downloading stuff from one computer to the other, but he hadn't had time to finish. She remembered the gun instantly. "Do you know what else they took?"

"Looked like papers mostly. I heard them barge in, and I went into the hall to see what was happening. Blake signaled me to tell you."

She realized she was clutching herself across her breasts. She didn't want anyone else overhearing them, so she started slowly walking down the hall and then outside into the cold. "They didn't get anything from his drawers . . . I mean . . . or under his bed?"

"You thinking about his piece. He could tell somebody been going through his stuff maybe a week ago, so he laid it on me to keep for him."

"That's good," she said, letting her breath out and making herself try to breathe normally. "So they didn't find it."

"He got that in Philly, like he must've told you. Hadn't had it but maybe a week when he was sure somebody messing with his stuff."

And she had tried to be so careful. "I thought he was being paranoid. . . . Did they arrest him?"

"They took him away for questioning."

"I'm going to call his father right now."

"Good thinking. You stay cool, girl. I don't know what this about, but don't freak and don't talk to no one yet—except his daddy, one bad lawyer. Course you know they always after him because of his real daddy."

"You knew about that?" She was mortified. Had Blake trusted everyone in the world except her?

"I come from the 'hood. Course I know. Everybody in the old crew knew about Blake and Toussaint. It's like he had Malcolm X for his daddy."

Her hands were sweating so badly she could hardly get her gloves off to use her cell phone. She retreated to a bench beside one of the sidewalks through campus. She called the Ackerman house immediately and got the answering machine. However, it gave office numbers for Nadine and Si. She tried Si first.

"He's in a meeting. Would you like to leave your name and number?"

"This is an emergency. It's about his son, Blake."

"Hold, please."

As she expected, Si came on within a minute. "What is this?"

"It's Melissa—"

"I figured it was. What's so important?"

"I just heard that Blake's room in the dormitory was raided this morning." She filled him in with what little she knew.

"Call Nadine and tell her. I'm going to get right on finding out where they took him and what's going on. Had he gotten rid of his old computer?"

"He was still transferring programs and stuff. I'm sure this has to do with the pardons and the paroles."

"Don't say anything more. Call Nadine."

She obeyed his instructions and called Nadine. "Oh shit," Nadine said. "I've been afraid of something like this. What's Si doing?"

"He's going to try to find out where the feds took Blake."

"Sit tight." Nadine was silent for a moment. Melissa could imagine her scratching her head, setting her white hair on end. "If they haven't come after you yet, you might be safe for the time being. Don't do or say anything to call attention to yourself. One of you in custody is one too many. I'll be back in touch when we know more. Leave your cell phone on."

She was too nervous to go to class that afternoon. Emily had not got back for lunch, but they ate supper together. "Emily, don't answer any questions about me. You don't know anything. Don't even let on you know we're married."

"I won't. But what's this about?"

"You don't want to know, believe me. You know Blake's into hacking sometimes. I figure he hacked into someplace sensitive and they've caught him."

"What's that got to do with being married to you?"

"I didn't do any hacking into databases or whatever, but what would that matter if my name came up? My parents would kill me if I got involved." She hated lying to Emily, but it would be a disservice to tell her the truth.

Melissa was so frightened, she felt icy. She seemed capable of operating as if normally, speaking in a calm voice, shoveling food into her mouth and chewing it, nodding and greeting acquaintances and classmates. She had reached a state of numbness. She was so frightened, her nerves had cut off. She knew she was afraid, but she could not feel a thing. It was as if fear were sequestered in some bony box deep in her body and held there, radiating a deep and deadly chill quietly in the background of consciousness.

Why didn't Si or Nadine call her? Why didn't they let her know what was happening? She was Blake's wife, she had a right to know. But she could not come forward as his wife. Sometimes she simply could not remember why. She could not remember why they had been carrying on this dangerous game of spying on her father. She should simply break off with her family, try to forget them and let them forget her. Let them pretend she was dead. She should have pried herself loose and just walked away. Why had she let Blake talk her into concealing their marriage? So he could continue his vendetta against her father. What did that matter now? Being together mattered, building a life, making their own way in the world and forgetting about his father and hers. Letting go of the past. Why hadn't she insisted?

Emily was talking. Her lips were moving and words dribbled out. Melissa nodded and made noises in her throat that seemed sufficient to satisfy Emily. Melissa had not insisted, she realized, because she had so much anger toward Rosemary and Dick and her older siblings. She wanted her father's attention, yes, but perhaps even more she had wanted to punish them for their long disregard of her, for their neglect and disrespect, for always putting her dead last. She would be first now if only through hurting them. That was what she had wanted, she realized in the clarity of her fear, even more than she wanted Blake. Her anger toward them had been the spine of her being for years and years. It was an essential part of who she was: that was why she had not insisted on being truthful with them. That was why she had not walked away. Her anger at them was greater than her love for him. She had pretended he was the instigator, but after demurring and dragging her feet, she always joined in. She had never thrown her energy or the weight of her attachment and feelings into resisting him, because she was too spiteful.

"Hey, kid. Are you here?" Emily was tapping her arm.

"I'm sorry. I'm so worried and confused, I just spaced. What were you saying?"

"I was wondering how we could find out where they took Blake. And maybe you should go over to his room. Maybe there's some clue to what they wanted."

She didn't believe that for a minute, but she wanted to go there anyhow. She had a silly hope that she would go to his room as she so often did, and Blake would be there, grinning at her. "All a mistake," he would say. "Just a big fuck-up. No problema. My babes was worried for nothing."

No, she didn't believe there was no problem, but she had to go, now that Emily had put the idea in her head. "Come with me. Let's go see what happened over there."

"Sure, but can I finish my ice cream first? Aren't you going to eat yours?"

Melissa could not remember eating anything, but indeed there was a dish of strawberry ice cream melting in front of her. "You take it. I'm too nervous."

Blake's room was torn apart. His computers were missing, and the papers on his desk were gone. His drawers had been dumped out, both in his desk and in his dresser. The skim of thick ice over her fear cracked and she could taste it like blood in her mouth. Her hands were shaking. She thought she might throw up, but she managed not to.

Jamal came to the door. "Heard anything?"

"I'm hoping his parents will find out what's going on."

"You called them, right?"

"Both of them. You haven't learned anything else?"

"They were asking questions about him. But nobody wanted to give them anything. Blake hangs to himself a lot but people like him. He never has a bad word for anybody. You know what this is about, don't you?"

"Maybe," she said.

"But you don't want to talk about it?"

She shook her head.

"Cool," Jamal said. "Later."

Emily cleared her throat behind her. Melissa realized with a start that she had forgotten to introduce them, so she quickly did. Then Emily and she went back to their dorm.

"What did he mean, You know what this is about?" Emily asked.

"Well, I didn't want to sound like a dweeb. I don't know a thing. . . . He must have hacked into something sensitive. I'm going to call his parents again."

Only the answering machine seemed to be home. Phil appeared at her door and immediately started blurting out his fears. "We're all going down! It's Blake's fault. I don't know what to do!"

She seized him by the elbow, walking him to the stairwell and pushing him down on a step. "Shhhh. Don't go around telling people what they don't need to know."

"How did they track Blake down? How did they know to grab him?"

"How do I know? I've spoken with Blake's parents, and they're in a much better position to find out the facts."

"Are they going to let us know?"

"I assume they'll call me as soon as they can."

He gave her his card, with his cell phone number and e-mail address. She thought it pretentious of him to have a card. She did not know anyone else in college who had cards printed and handed them to people.

"Call me as soon as you know anything."

"Sure." She was glad to get rid of him.

She went on calling the house regularly, but she got only the answering machine until nine. Then Nadine answered. "It's that guy, Tom Belle-fontaine. They subpoenaed his phone records and they've been making their way through them. He called Blake, and Blake called him from his cell phone at least twice. That much we know. It's a question of what they'll get off Blake's computers. After all, talking to someone on a cell phone is not in itself a crime, as we have been yelling all afternoon."

"You found out where he's being held?"

"Sure. Now what could they have found in his room?"

"I'll call you back."

To Emily she said, "They've located him, and it sounds like it's all a big mistake. Anyhow, I'll call back tomorrow and find out what's going on. Both his parents are lawyers and they're on it."

She took her towel and toothbrush and went down the hall, but instead of heading into the showers, she slipped into the stairwell and called Nadine back on her cell phone. "It's me again." She explained her maneuver. "I don't see any reason to get Emily more involved. She has no idea what we've been doing, and I think it should stay that way."

"Smart choice. The fewer people who know, the better for both of you."

"Can I see Blake?"

"He doesn't want you to—"

"Oh!"

"Not like that, sweetie. He wants to protect you. It's better for you to stay out of it, at least for now. You can communicate through me."

"But I want to see him, I need to see him."

"You need to do what's best for both of you, and right now, Blake feels strongly that means staying away from him. He doesn't want the two of you connected. He doesn't want anyone to know about the marriage yet. You have to wait to hear from one of us, Melissa, and just stay put."

"On his computer, he was monitoring my mother's e-mail."

"Did he erase it?"

"I think so. But maybe they can reconstruct the stuff."

Nadine sighed. "This just gets worse and worse. I'll talk with him tomorrow. At least as his lawyers, we can have private conversations with him."

"I know he did have on his computer all that information about paroles and pardons. He was correlating the names of contributors with instances of prisoners being paroled or pardoned. I doubt if he erased that."

"That would absolutely link him to Bellefontaine. Not good."

"It's all unbelievably bad."

"Hang on, Melissa. I'll be in touch when we learn something relevant. In the meantime, try to act normally and behave as you always do."

"That doesn't make sense. I'm with Blake most of the time I'm not in class."

"Well, carry on as normally as you can and don't call attention to yourself."

She sat on in the echoing stairwell, clutching herself. What would happen to them? Would they both go to prison? They didn't put married couples into prison together. How serious a crime was this? She tried to imagine prison. Images from old B movies and sensational made-for-cable movies swam through her head. She would take a shower. She would take a long, very hot shower and try to settle herself. How could she go to classes, how could she stagger zombielike through what was left of her daily routine? She could hear a score of competing records playing rap, rock, hip-hop, fusion, jazz from the rooms on her corridor. She could hear two girlish voices in an argument about who tore whose sweater. She could hear a hockey game on some TV. She could hear canned laughter and she could hear real laughter. A woman came up the steps, tears rolling down her face, and pushed past without looking at her. Melissa could not cry. Fear had dried her tear ducts. She could only clutch herself and shudder, wondering what lay ahead for Blake and for her, separately or together.

CHAPTER TWENTY-NINE

B lake was back and in her arms. They lay grasping each other in his room. They had fallen into bed and made love in a trance of desperation, digging at each other, thrusting as if they could totally interpenetrate and fuse. Now they were spent but still entwined. She felt sore and on the verge of tears.

"I should have made you stop this months ago. I feel so guilty. I feel as if I sacrificed you to my anger against my parents."

"That's nonsense, babes. I have my own agenda, and it involves my father. All my life since his death, I've carried the burden of needing to clear his name and avenge him. I would have tried to do that even if I'd never met you."

"But I got you in much deeper than you could have gone on your own."

"You've been a big help, but I'd have done it anyhow. It would have taken me longer to get the same information, but I would have kept at it." With a hand under her chin, he lifted her head to stare into her with his large luminous dark eyes. "I'm sorry I got caught, but I'm not sorry we tried to do what we did. Maybe it'll still do some damage."

"Did they hurt you?"

"They were rough at first, but nothing serious. After Si and Nadine showed up, they were careful with me."

"Is it over?"

"Not nearly. They took my old computer."

"You erased everything damaging, didn't you?"

"Of course. I downloaded onto zip disc everything hot, and I gave it to Jamal for safekeeping. I trust him more than Phil—"

"Phil's pissing himself with fear."

He snorted. "I'm not surprised. Anyhow, Jamal's cool with keeping stuff."

"What kind of stuff?"

"My zip discs. My backups. Printouts."

"How do you know Jamal will cover for you?"

"I've covered for him."

Maybe the gun was Jamal's. She wanted to think so. "So what are you worried about?"

"I ran a good erasure program over my hard drive, but I think a hacker type could still find my data. But I would have to ask my hacker friends in Williamsburg, and I'm nervous about calling. I'd have to go out of town a ways and use a pay phone to be safe. And you can't tell if they're under surveillance."

"Can't you ask them without being specific?"

"I'll try."

"Will they know who you are if you don't say your name?"

"I'm Caped Crusader." He grinned. Strangely enough, she thought, he seemed less frightened than she was. Maybe things would be all right. Maybe his parents could get him out of trouble.

"If we do get through all this safely"—she touched his cheek—"then we should retire from the spy business. We should work on our lives instead. We should get on with school and just be married and together."

He smiled, a crooked, almost aloof grimace. "That would be pleasant, wouldn't it?"

"I hope you think so."

"Sure. A quiet student life together worrying only about what should we eat for supper? Sounds like paradise. But we have to get through this battle first."

"The timing just sucks. I'm supposed to go to Philadelphia next Friday."

"We have to figure out how to turn that into a way to help us."

"They wouldn't help you if you were drowning and they were standing there with a life preserver."

"They might not help me. But they might help your husband. They might want to prevent a big scandal."

She sat up, rubbing her scalp and setting the hair on end. She felt a stirring of hope that had not visited her since Jamal had brought her news of the raid. "That's possible. That's really and truly a possibility. Rosemary hates scandal. . . ."

"How much does she hate it?" He stared at his joined hands. "More than she hates me? Doubt it."

"There's a chance we could reach a compromise where they would drop charges and do a neat cover-up if we agree to stop going after my father. That they would agree to in order to keep things quiet."

They were sitting cross-legged on his unmade bed, facing each other. "Is that what you want to do?" Now he was staring into her eyes again.

"I want you not to go to jail. I don't fancy going myself. I think we do have some leverage if we play it just right with them. I can't promise anything. They might let us both swing."

"So how would we play this?" His head was cocked to one side.

She could tell she had not convinced him, but she was surprised and pleased he was willing to listen. Maybe they would come out of this mess right side up. "I'll go there for Christmas like always. In Philadelphia while he mends fences and butters up backers and makes a show for his constituents . . ."

"And I'll be there with Si and Nadine. So what's the plan?"

"It's a better place than Washington for pulling something off, because there's less staff to shield them. Alison, of course. We'd have to pick a time when they're not putting on an event or a party because Rosemary just won't pay attention. 'Oh, you're married, fine, did the flowers come yet?' "

"We'll have to play it by ear. So you'll make your big announcement."

"That's the idea." She shuddered. "All hell will break loose."

"Look, let's modify a bit. You let me in. I hide somewhere like your room until you've raised the subject. Then I appear and we both plead for our lives."

"Would you do that?"

"If we have to. I want to hang loose about this until I know what the feds have been able to extract from my computer."

"Maybe we won't have to do anything. Maybe this will blow over."

"Maybe John Lennon and John Coltrane and John and John-John Kennedy will all rise from the dead and do a circle dance around the Washington Monument. Or maybe not."

"You don't think you managed to erase enough?"

"I have no idea. Tomorrow I'll get an estimate from my hacker buds."

"Don't you just feel exhausted with all the being afraid and all the waiting and the tension? I'm just overstretched and like I'm going to snap."

He pulled her toward him, turned her around and began to knead her neck and shoulder muscles. "Got to keep it under wraps, babes. No use in combusting. We need all our smarts to get through this one."

THEY RODE OUT in midday on his motorcycle to a mall on the edge of Middletown, where they found a pay phone. She waited, perched on the edge of a planter filled with frozen earth and dead chrysanthemums. Someone, maybe Alison, had told her that the chrysanthemum was the flower of death. Alison sometimes said strange things like that. She read a lot. Melissa remembered gladiolus being the common flower at funerals of her childhood, and now people seemed to go for roses or lilies.

When he got off the phone, he was looking worried. "They say it's likely that someone who knew what he was doing could reconstruct my data. That would pretty much do me in. They aren't sure how much could be reconstructed, because the parts of the hard drive that were erased and then recorded over would be cool. But the parts that were erased and not recorded over, someone who knew what he was doing might get a fair amount of data off the drive."

She wrung her hands. "It just gets worse and worse."

He smiled at her, a forced smile, but still he looked so handsome standing there it seemed impossible that anyone could bring him down, that anyone would want to. Even when she dreamed of him in her sleep a couple of times a week, he had a radiance. It was different from that glow that surrounded her parents in public. It was not so much a glittering surface as something that shone through his skin from within. She had tried to explain that to Emily, who said, "Girl, you are in love. He's a guy, not a saint. Come off it."

Now he could be taken from her. Locked up for years. Brutalized. Tortured. Men got raped in prison. There his handsome face and lithe body would work against him. He could not go to prison. She had to stop the process, but only Dick and Rosemary could do that. Did she have any leverage with them? She frankly did not know.

"I have to go Christmas shopping," she said.

"We do a little of that, not much," he said. "There are real advantages to being Jewish. We give each other one present and quit while we're ahead. Grandma calls it Chanukah gifts, but it's really just a nod to the rest of society."

"I have to get presents they'll like, as if I could afford anything that Rosemary would really want. But it's a way of ingratiating myself." Strangely enough, Rosemary actually did care for presents. Melissa imagined that in the lower-middle-class family in which her mother had been raised, presents had been severely practical. Mittens, gloves, scarves, socks. Rosemary loved jewelry. How could she find something her mother would feel was a worthy present? Rosemary wasn't the sort of mother who cooed over her children's lopsided bowls made in pottery class or their daubs from art class. Back when she had been in a Brownie troop, she had given her mother an apron she had sewn out of blue calico for a merit badge. Rosemary had barely been able to hide her displeasure. An apron! Melissa had been crushed.

She had to find something to give each of them that would put them in a good mood. She tried to explain the problem to Blake, but he didn't understand. He tended to give his parents books he was sure they'd find interesting. She couldn't imagine giving Rosemary or Dick a book. Or Rich or Laura or Billy. Perhaps Merilee. No, she had to come up with something that would curry favor. It was going to be a big project.

It was going to empty the cash reserve she had, but she could put expensive items on her credit card. By the time the bills came in, the crisis would have been resolved one way or the other, one way or the other.

Emily could understand. Melissa enlisted her and her car in the search. In an antiques barn two towns away, they found a necklace that Melissa thought Rosemary would approve of. She also found a World War II cartridge box she thought Dick would like. For Rich she got cuff links; for Laura, earrings; and for the baby, a stuffed toy. Her credit card was going to be maxed out. Billy was easy. She got him some CDs. Merilee would receive a burned-out-velvet scarf. What about Alison? She had to get her something. Every year Alison joined their Christmas. She ended up getting her a scarf too. A Middletown woman made pretty ones. She was out of ideas as well as money. It was bribery, but she needed every bit of goodwill she could muster from her family.

BLAKE JUST DIDN'T get it. "You think giving your mother a necklace from the twenties is going to fix marrying me, you're thinking upside down."

"I think we need every bit of edge we can find. It's going to be murder."

He was sitting on a bench next to her, kneading a snowball in his gloves. Then he let it fly against an oak, stripped for the winter to a few raggedy leaves still clinging like torn paper bags to its hefty limbs. He hit the oak trunk dead center.

"Good shot," she said, trying to defuse things.

"You really think we're going to get someplace with your parents? By suddenly persuading them how nice we are?"

"I think a combination of polite blackmail about scandal and trying to persuade them how cute and puppylike we are is the only way to go."

"The case has dropped out of the papers. Nothing. I think King Richard's going to get away with it. We had him dead center, and nobody cares."

"Blake, we've got to let that drop. We must! You don't want to go to prison. I don't want you to go to prison. I sure don't want to go. We took it as far as we could. We're just a couple of college kids, not detectives, not investigative reporters with a national newspaper behind us hiring lawyers."

He did not answer. He scooped up more snow, shaped it hard and let fly again, hitting the same oak.

"Promise me, Blake, that you'll try to let this go, at least for a while."

Another snowball hit the oak. "I gave it my best shot. I thought we had him. I thought we did."

"Blake, if you try to continue, we'll end up in worse trouble."

"You really want to try throwing ourselves on their tender mercies?"

"I don't see another way to go. They *are* my parents."

"We'll be in Philadelphia, the whole cast assembled. You, me, Phil and his father, Dick and Rosemary, your siblings, Si and Nadine, all of us. All there gathered round full of holiday spirit. What a cozy thing to look forward to."

"If we end up getting through this free and together, it will be. We just have to feel our way very carefully."

"Careful," he repeated. "Full of care. That's how I feel. Really over-stuffed and loaded with care. Four more days and we all go to the City of Brotherly Love."

She looked sideways at his guarded face, praying that she had got through to him and he wasn't going to persist in a mad scheme of exposure and revenge. She could imagine an afterward when they were free just to be who they were, husband and wife together, openly. If this was close to hell, that looked to her close to heaven.

CHAPTER THIRTY

Melissa found the household in a very different mood than they had exhibited at Thanksgiving. Dick and Rosemary were upbeat. "I think we've weathered this little storm," Rosemary said. "The leak has been stopped and the attacks staved off." She was sitting in her office, at a small desk with a bouquet of Persian lilies to her left. She was wearing a pale blue suit and her hair was slightly lighter than usual. Nobody seemed to be around, not even Alison. The office was crowded with two desks, one for Rosemary and one for Dick, but his real office in Philadelphia was downtown, where his local staff worked.

"Did they catch anyone?" Melissa stood before her mother wondering if she should take a seat or stay prepared for a hasty retreat.

"We don't feel it behooves us to look over the shoulders of the police and the FBI. They're holding that homosexual campaign worker who stole and altered papers. I imagine he'll go to prison eventually. These things take time, and that's just as well. The longer the process takes, the more the situation is defused."

"So they're proceeding against the reporter from the *Inquirer* and the campaign worker." Melissa noted that, even with contempt edging her voice, Rosemary would say "homosexual" and never "fag" or "queer." She did not use slur words she considered vulgar. "Did they catch anybody else?"

"They are still looking for the conduit between that man and Roger. I think they have someone likely, but as I said, I have been letting them do their work. I'm expecting to be brought up-to-date shortly after Christmas."

That's when the shit would likely hit the fan. Melissa tried to keep a blandly interested expression on her face. "So you're feeling better?"

"Your father has been getting some good press lately. The *Washington Times* ran a piece calling him one of the rising stars of the Senate. Someone who has quickly established his presence and is being mentored by powerful senators. We also had a small but favorable mention in the *Wall Street Journal* last week."

"Great. So how's everyone else?"

"We fired Yolanda in Georgetown. We caught her taking home food—"

"Leftovers?"

"More than that." Rosemary's mouth thinned. "I can't abide thievery. We have to be able to trust anyone who comes into the house here or in Washington. Too many sensitive things. Besides, someone who steals a steak one day might help themselves to the silverware tomorrow and a watch the day after that."

Melissa sighed. "But she sure was a good cook."

"Cooks are plentiful. Honesty is what I value above all. Loyalty."

"So how's Alison? I haven't seen her today."

"She's at the doctor's."

"Is something wrong with her?" Melissa felt she should pretend an interest in Alison she had never actually experienced. Yolanda made the kitchen smell like paradise. Alison was just a busy extension of Rosemary.

"We had a scare." Rosemary steepled her fingers on the ebony surface. "She had a bad Pap smear. Her results came back with a possible problem this November, right after Thanksgiving."

"What kind of a problem?"

"There seemed a possibility of cervical cancer—not often fatal these days. Still, cancer is cancer, and we were very concerned." Rosemary sighed, her forehead creasing. "Fortunately, she had her ultrasound Wednesday, and everything is normal. A great relief! I couldn't do without my Alison."

Melissa felt a pang of jealousy. Rosemary had actually been worried about Alison. She cared about Alison, she really did. "You've had other assistants."

"But never one so loyal, so devoted. And bright. She's almost perfect, Melissa. She does the job of a secretary, an administrative assistant, a general all-around helper, a researcher, a computer person. No one has ever taken such good care of me."

Enough of that. "Is Billy home yet? Merilee? The house feels empty."

"You arrived at an off time. Alison should return in forty-five minutes, depending on traffic. Merilee is still in Foggy Bottom, but she'll arrive tomorrow. Billy got in last night, but he's off ice-skating."

"And how are Rich and Laura and little Dickey doing?"

"Fine." Rosemary's gaze flickered.

Something wrong there. Something off. "The baby's all right?"

"Spectacular," Rosemary said, beaming now. "Cutest little boy. He's going to be big, you can tell already. Laura is a first-rate mother, I will give her that."

"Is Rich's campaign going well?"

"He's gathering support." The phone rang. Rosemary looked at her caller ID and picked up at once. "Frank!" It was her geisha voice, and she waved Melissa out. Frank was Senator Dawes. He seemed to call daily. Melissa supposed he was lonely and probably bored back in North Dakota: she would be, she was sure.

Melissa could not help but wonder what was wrong in the Rich sector, where any trouble that would attract Rosemary's attention and divert it from her could only be helpful. She would keep her ears open and listen at doors. Usually she had to acquire information by stealth—one reason she used to go snooping, long before she met Blake. It was time to go upstairs and use her temporary privacy to call him.

Her room here she had actually come to prefer to her larger room in Washington. It was too small to share with Merilee. Up at the top of the house, she had a measure of privacy. Here, Alison was the only staff on a regular basis. Meals in were catered, but the caterers brought the food in and, after setting up the meal, departed, a discreet service that required little contact. A cleaning service appeared twice a week for the downstairs. They stormed through the upstairs every Friday, so Melissa was forewarned to clear out. Almost as many people came through the downstairs as in Washington, but she could generally keep out of their way. The town house had a narrow back stairway, probably intended for servants who had lived up in the attic, where she had her room. She could slip down and out without interference. Blake suggested she get herself out to the Ackerman house in Mount Airy, and she planned to do that once she figured out the holiday schedule. Emily expected her on the twenty-ninth, but she would just have to see how things went and when the best window of opportunity might open to approach Rosemary and Dick about Blake.

The next morning, she could hear from the thump of rap music from the floor below that Billy was in. Maybe she could feel out her younger brother to see if he would ally himself with her. Down the back stairs she went to knock on his door. At first there was no response. She banged again and yelled, "Billy! It's me, Lissa." She tried to open the door but it was locked.

After maybe three minutes, she heard the lock turning over and he opened the door, looking tousled and a little wary. "If you don't want them to know you've been smoking, open the window. It reeks," she said, shutting the door behind her.

"Window's stuck."

"Let's see if we can get it open together." Using the end of a hanger, she picked at the sill. The window had been painted shut. Finally they pried it open.

She sat on his desk chair, wondering if he had grown since Thanksgiving or if he just looked taller in the small room. All the upstairs rooms were small. He had a room on the second floor, as did her parents and Alison. Alison's room was just a daybed in her office. Her mother and father shared an office downstairs, where otherwise the ground floor had been opened up into one large living-diningroom beside the narrow kitchen, running from the street to the tiny yard paved over for parking. "How has it been going for you? I heard your hockey team only lost one game so far."

"We're doing okay. Think we might take our division."

"You've made a lot of friends at school." This was not a question.

He shrugged. "Mom said you were dating a Black dude."

"Yeah. Sort of Black."

"You can't be sort of Black."

"He is. His adopted parents are white."

"I thought they were Jewish."

"So's he."

"Shit, Lissa, were you just trying to stir them up? See how mad you could make them?" He grimaced at her, sitting on his bed's edge. A magazine was sticking out from under the rumpled bedspread. Probably *Penthouse*. He was always hiding girlie 'zines from Rosemary.

"I like him. He's bright, he's buff, he's good looking and really sweet to me. He rides a Honda motorcycle. You'd like him."

"Lissa, you just can't do that. If there's anything I've learned, it's that we do best hanging with our own type people. It works out better. You can communicate. You just know the same things." He was talking to her with grim seriousness, explaining the world to his ditzy sister.

"Why would I want to go out with somebody who knows exactly what I know? Sounds dull to me." She drew herself up, feeling suddenly chilly. Was this her old coconspirator? "Getting more conservative, are we?"

"Just realistic. I've been with Black girls a couple of times, whores, just for the hell of it with some of the other guys. It's no big deal." He raked his hand through his strawberry blond hair, making it stand up in the cowlick he always tried to control. "But I wouldn't date one of them. Obviously."

"Blake gets better grades than I do, and he has more money, frankly."

"Those shysters are probably rolling in it."

"How can you assume what he is? I'm ashamed of you, Billy. I thought you'd want to meet him and see for yourself. All of a sudden you're on their side?"

"You sound like you're still hooked up with him."

"And if I am?"

"You better dump him fast. Or you'll be in real trouble."

"You going to tell on me?"

"No way. You're deluded on this one, but I don't want all the yelling. It'll fuck up the holidays if they find out."

"Good. Keep quiet about it and I won't tell on you."

"Tell what?"

"Smoking. *Penthouse.* And a few other things." She smiled, trying to give the impression she knew far more than she was saying. "Let's just help each other through this so-called vacation."

"Everybody smokes."

"Then why aren't you smoking downstairs?"

"Besides, why should I tell them about your Black boy? I don't want any trouble, Lissa. I got a problem you don't want to know about. Let's just keep cool and stay under their radar."

"Fine with me." She found she had nothing more to say to Billy. Nothing at all.

IT WAS ALISON who told her what was up with Rich and Laura. "I know your mother was planning to tell you, or I wouldn't say anything. She wanted to fill you in, so you wouldn't put your foot in it."

"What am I not supposed to put my foot in?" She did not like Alison in her room, but she was too curious to try to ease her out.

"Rich is having an affair with one of his campaign workers. A divorcée five years older than Rich, a publicist who's been helping him. I'm sure Rich got in deeper than he intended, but it could really hurt him."

"Does Laura know?"

"She doesn't have a clue, and that condition should remain intact." Alison touched her own cheek with her fingertips, a gesture she had borrowed from Rosemary—a flick of the wrist, the hand remaining in the air for a moment, gracefully.

"Nobody thinks she should know what's going on?"

They both understood that *nobody* really encompassed only Rosemary.

"It would be best for her marriage if she didn't find out. . . . After all, she's so involved with her baby that she's been practically ignoring Rich. It's partly her fault if he's strayed. She isn't giving him what he needs."

This sounded very like what Rosemary would say. She was a husband-first sort of wife, and that was the marriage she wanted for Rich. Perhaps what Rich himself wanted. "That seems a little harsh. She's just being a good mother."

"And an inadequate wife." Alison, who had never, as far as Melissa knew, had a boyfriend, pursed her lips in scorn. "She knew what she was getting into, marrying a politician. She has to put Rich first or things like this will happen."

"That's rather Rich's responsibility, isn't it? He wanted a son."

"Of course. But he's thrown in the way of temptation constantly. That's how it is with powerful men."

"But not my father."

"Every man experiences temptation, Melissa. You're too young to understand how it is with men. But your mother gives him what he needs from a wife, and they love each other. She's kept that alive between them, no small undertaking. Your mother is very wise, and you could do a lot worse than to study her and learn from her."

Learn to play geisha? Learn to flatter and charm and dangle? Learn to manipulate and sacrifice others? "Well, I want to thank you for filling me in. . . . I'm kind of surprised."

"Your mother feels it's time for you to pull your weight in the family. You made a serious mistake this year. They've forgiven you, but you need to prove you can behave responsibly. Your mother's giving you a chance to show your loyalty to the family. She may want you to distract Laura so she can have a conversation with Rich. He's been keeping himself unavailable, but he'll be here during the holidays. She plans to corner him and set him straight before there's a bigger problem."

"I understand." Rich's affair would seem microscopic when she made her announcements. Her hands grew cold just thinking of what she had to do.

"So if required, you will occupy Laura?" Alison was watching her carefully, her eyes almost beady. "You agree to do that if I signal you?"

"Sure. . . . Uh, I hardly know her. What does she care about?"

"Her baby. If you get her started on him, she'll go on for hours. Got that?"

Melissa nodded. Alison really thought she was stupid. Repeat instructions three times, because Melissa is a dim bulb. Rosemary had always underrated her, and she supposed that Alison picked up attitudes straight from her idol's mouth.

"Now the signal," Alison said, "will be if I say, 'I wonder if the weather is going to improve tomorrow.' Whenever I say that, you go into action."

"Weather improving tomorrow. Got it."

Alison looked a little dubious. "You won't forget."

"I'll write it down." Melissa used her most sarcastic voice, but Alison just nodded and collected herself to leave.

"Good idea. Write it down." Alison descended the narrow back stairs.

Dick was in an expansive mood at supper. "Everybody was congratulating me on the *Wall Street Journal* mention. Even Senator Whitehead called this morning and asked after you." He was talking of course to Rosemary. "My visibility is increasing, and the fuss around those scurrilous pieces in the *Inquirer* has died down. We're over the hump." His bright blue eyes glinted like faceted stones. He winked merrily, cutting into his fillet of salmon. "Time to enjoy the holidays." Suddenly he turned to Melissa. "You had us worried there for a while, my girl. I hope you learned a lesson about choosing your associates." He leaned over to pat her hand. How warm his hands always were. "I know you meant well, but you didn't behave with due thought for the consequences. But I hope my little girl is back on course. Now give us a smile."

"I still think you both made a big fuss about nothing."

"Letting someone that dangerous near you is something to pay attention to," he said, taking more wild rice. "Even beside the possible risk to you, you're a member of a highly visible family, and that makes everything you do a matter of public interest, if not now then down the pike."

"When you're running for President."

Dick paused and his gaze grew intense. He could not seem to decide whether to take that as flattery or to be annoyed. In the end, he chose to ignore it. "Just learn to be more careful. What you do reflects on all of us. We must constantly watch appearances as well as realities. That whole nonsense in the *Inquirer* proves that—if nothing else. But we're on track now, right?" He turned to smile at his wife. "These little storms come and go in public life."

"Is supper satisfactory?" Rosemary asked him, leaning on her elbow and toying, as always, with her food.

"Delicious. As always you've done well with the arrangements."

Dick, however, ate with a good appetite. He truly did not care much what he ate. He would eat hot dogs at a county fair or three rubber chickens in a row at functions with the same relish as he dined at the most expensive restaurants. It was not an act. He seemed to enjoy any food put in front of him so long as the occasion required eating it. He was looking healthy, gleaming. He carried himself with that air of invincibility and utter confidence that always cowed her. How could she and Blake ever have thought they could influence him or even slow him down? He was rolling along, and they were in danger. That was the way it always went with him. Troubles enveloped him, then dissipated like a cloud of steam. The accusations, the scandals, the revelations vanished, and he stood there taller than ever and stronger. He was who he was, a man made for the public, a man made for power. She did not want her supper. She never wanted to eat anything again. She felt sick and very small. What on earth had they imagined they were doing? She had been an idiot to go along with Blake. She should have just told him to stop when things started getting bad. They had failed, they had been foolish, they had brought the law down on themselves. Of course.

CHAPTER THIRTY-ONE

Melissa escaped from the house on Monday. Rosemary, Alison and Dick had picked up their tempo, trying to get as much done as they could before the holiday, trying to cram a week's work into two days. No one had extra energy to spend overseeing her. Billy was out most of the time. Their special closeness had eroded. She felt a void where her younger brother had always been. Merilee was off with a classmate studying. Melissa simply said she had last-minute shopping and slipped out. Blake picked her up with his bike on a corner of Rittenhouse Square.

"So where are we going?" She rested her cheek against the cold leather.

"A long way. Out to Mount Airy. Are you cold?"

"It's not that cold today." It was, and she was, but she didn't care. It was such a relief to hold him. Such a relief to be out of the house, to be for a few hours who she really was, not who she was supposed to be. Still, her ears might drop off. She clutched him tight and wished they could ride off the edge of visibility, into a magical sunset beyond their families and their troubles.

"How has it been going?" he asked when he was stopped for a red light.

"Better than I expected. They haven't had time to third-degree me."

"So what exactly is happening with them?" The light changed.

His neighborhood was made up of mostly turn-of-the-century big rambling houses with a few newer ones interspersed, some clapboard, some brick, most of the grey stone she associated with rural eastern Pennsylvania, a sense here of space and comfort. Houses stood among bosomy trees, rolling lawns. Some of the kids she saw on the street were white, some African-American, some other. It seemed to be an integrated neighborhood, a wonder in Philadelphia. It reminded her a bit of the suburb where they had lived before Dick was elected governor, but there everything was newer—the houses, the streets, the trees—and everybody was white. A lady in an SUV was unloading three boys with hockey gear. An African-American girl with a white boy just behind her whizzed past on their bikes in spite of the snow and ice. A portly man with a grey-streaked beard was knocking icicles off his gutter with a rake. Two little kids were building a snow fort on the corner lot while an older woman bundled up till she was round as a beach ball sat on the steps clutching herself and watching them. An aide helped an old lady down the steps to the street, where a van was waiting.

Si was at his office, but Nadine was home to greet her at the door and kiss her on both cheeks. "Don't you look blooming. Cold weather must agree with you."

Nadine was affectionate and friendly, but Melissa felt she was being judged. Blake would deny it if she said anything, but she knew they did not consider her quite worthy of him. We'll put up with you cheerfully because we recognize a fait accompli, and because we are too smart to risk antagonizing Blake. But we will watch and wait. This too is likely to pass.

The house reminded her a little of Emily's. It was big and well furnished, a turn-of-the-century grey-stone house with pillars on the porch and a sizable yard with its own stone garage. NPR had been on when she came in, but Nadine shut off the radio at once. A big bushy black cat lay on the sofa in a patch of wintry sun. An Egyptian-looking dark orange kitten perched on the mantelpiece with its oversize pinkish ears pricked toward her. Blake tossed his leather jacket over a chair and nobody rushed to hang it. He swooped up the black cat, who began purring loudly as he flung himself on the couch with the cat on his chest. "Hey, Rasputin, how's it going?" Then to her, "From a shelter, but how he grew." Yesterday's *Philadelphia Inquirer* and *New York Times* were scattered around the livingroom. Here and there books lay open. The fireplace had recently been used, but nobody had swept out the ashes. They did not have a

Christmas tree, but a large bay tree stood in the diningroom in a Mexican earthenware pot.

The livingroom and diningroom had warm red-toned Oriental rugs on the floor and art on the walls in a variety of styles from abstract to landscape to African. Still, the house was not intended to be looked at, to serve as a backdrop. It was a place several people lived and left their activities scattered about like clothes they had dropped. It was not dirty, but it was not neat. She liked the feel of it. Her own home was always as perfect as Rosemary could manage to keep it. Nothing was left out for long. Everything had a proper placement in the scheme of things. Before she was ten, she had learned never to walk in and toss her coat or jacket over a chair. She had been trained to hang anything she removed at once. Maybe that was why she threw her clothes into vast multicolored drifts all over her dorm room and Blake tidily folded his.

She was surprised she was hungry enough to eat any of the lunch spread out on the diningroom table. Sara came down the stairs to join them, yawning. "Hi, kid. How's the bride? My brother treating you right?"

"You came back for the holidays?"

"Dad got me a job. I gave up on my skanky boyfriend. I'm thinking of going back to school, but in the meantime . . . I need to make enough money for my own apartment. I am just too old to move back in." She had grown out her hair since Melissa had seen her last. A wild combination of black and brown, most of it braided, it resembled a field partly burned over. Still, Sara was pretty enough to get away with the mess on her head.

Lunch was smoked fish, sliced tomatoes, sliced red onions, hard-boiled eggs and rye bread. Melissa found the sturgeon and the nova fine, but the whitefish with their heads still attached made her queasy.

"So how are you holding up?" Nadine asked her. "Are you pregnant yet?"

"No!"

"Don't be in a hurry. You want to finish school first, both of you."

"I'm in no hurry. Although I want to have children before I'm too old."

"What's too old nowadays?" Nadine waved her fork. "Grandmothers have babies. Not that I could have gone through that. It's best to do it when you're too young to have any idea what you're getting into. But not yet! Not yet."

"So are you glad to be back here, in Philadelphia?" Melissa asked Sara, frantic to change the subject.

"I have friends here, but I want to be in New York. Once I get the money together."

"She has romantic notions about being poor in New York," Nadine said. "This is our resident romantic."

"I was in film school when I met Nick. We were going to shoot a film in Joshua Tree. That was the idea when we went west."

"What happened to the film? Can I see it?"

"We never finished it. . . . Hell, we barely started it." Suddenly a large tear rolled down Sara's cheek.

"That's too bad," Melissa said hastily. "Do you want to go back to film school?"

"It was his fault. He smoked the money. He was a loser, just like Mother said. But he could be so sweet!" Now tears were trickling from both eyes. Her black eye makeup began to run.

Nadine patted her daughter's shoulder. "Don't cry, sweetie. He isn't worth the tears."

"But I loved him! You never understood. He had a horrible childhood with an alcoholic mother. He loved films and ice cream and just being outside in a pretty place and lying in the grass. He liked so many things."

"A guy can be really likcable and still not be someone you want to hitch up with. I've known some really charming murderers and the sweetest bank robber you ever could meet." Nadine took one of the whitefish and slit it neatly along the belly, separating the fine bones from the flesh.

Sara snorted. "He wasn't a murderer or a bank robber."

"Just a pothead," Nadine said. "Is that how you want to spend your life?"

"Better than robbing banks, I guess." But Sara had stopped crying. She scrubbed at her eyes, blew her nose and went back to her lunch. "Anyhow, it's over and dead, so bury it."

"Sweetie, I didn't bring him up. I'm glad to drop the subject."

Everybody had trouble with their parents, everybody. It was a law of nature. Even a nice warm mother like Nadine could stick her nose in it. Blake had kept quiet, but now he carefully changed the subject, asking Nadine about a client she was representing. Sara cast him a grateful look, but Nadine took the bait and launched into a description of her defense of a thief she was convinced the cops had framed.

After lunch, Nadine drove to her office, where she was meeting a new client. Sara looked at them. "I'm retiring to my room and turning on my music. So I won't hear you and I don't want to see you, and have a good time."

"Thanks." Blake kissed her on the cheek. "See you at supper."

Blake's room was on the second floor. It was twice the size of hers, well furnished with electronic gear plus state-of-the-art player and amps. "It's soundproofed." Blake waved at the room, papered with posters of rock stars and some old flyers about his father, declaring his innocence, calling for rallies in his defense. Melissa remembered the candlelight vigil outside the governor's mansion in Harrisburg that Noreen had let them peek at, to Rosemary's displeasure. She examined all the flyers and posters. "His case must have generated a lot of interest."

Blake unfolded himself onto the bed, covered with a bright pieced quilt. "A lot of people believed in him. They knew he was innocent. The way I did."

"Did that help? That others believed in him too?"

"I was a kid. Nothing helped. Maybe nothing ever will. I knew he was innocent, and I was powerless to save him." Blake lay staring at the ceiling.

"At some point you have to let go of it. He's dead, unfairly, yes, but your anger and pain can't help him." She wanted him to look at her, not the ceiling; she wanted to be able to reach him. "You have to get on with your life."

"He couldn't get on with his. We were robbed of him. My mother never got over it."

"But you have to, Blake. For us to have a life together, you have to begin to let go of your anger and your desire for revenge. Otherwise it will poison you. Otherwise it will destroy us. Your mother and your father are dead and you can't help them, but you can help or hurt us."

He lay staring, his anthracite eyes fixed on nothing. She took his limp hand in hers, perching on the bed's edge. She felt like throwing herself on him to bring him back, but she did not want to make things worse by seeming to ignore his mood or by making a demand he pay attention to her. She simply held his hand and waited. It felt as if an hour passed without Blake responding, but she saw from her watch that only ten minutes went by.

Finally he sat up and squeezed her hand back. "Of course you're right. The sensible thing to do is to let things go. . . . You said your parents were in high spirits?"

"Things are going well. He's been getting good press. He's viewed in his party as up-and-coming. He's made friends with powerful senators. The legislation he's pushing to loosen gun laws is popular in his party and stands a good chance of passing. Other senators have been signing on as sponsors. It eliminates the Brady Bill provisions, whatever they are."

He shrugged. "It's not that hard to get a gun now." He was frowning into space again.

She wanted to ask him if that gun that had been in his room had been Jamal's, but she did not dare admit she had looked through his things. It would remain a mystery until someday he told her. She was seventy-five percent convinced Blake had been keeping it for someone else, the way Jamal had kept Blake's zip discs for him. He had never said anything about owning a gun, and as far as she knew, he had no more idea than she did what to do with one. Her father, Rich and Alison were the only people she knew besides bodyguards who would actually be able to use a gun successfully. Grandpa had kept a shotgun, to kill varmints, he said. She remembered it in the passageway between the kitchen and the barn. She had been forbidden to touch it. When he had been younger, Grandpa had gone hunting, but he had given that up by the time she was old enough to pay attention. Her father took part in duck or deer hunting on occasion as a political act, but she knew he found it boring, because she had heard him confessing that to Rosemary. He had tried to talk his wife into going with him just once. It was one of the few times Melissa was aware of that Rosemary had disappointed Dick, but she said she wasn't about to tramp around in the woods all day in a hideous orange outfit trying to blow holes in some animal she had no desire to eat. Dick agreed with her, but he had to keep up his credentials with hunters and the NRA. Hunting was big in Pennsylvania. She remembered mothers of friends complaining that it seemed to go on for months, making the roads unsafe to drive in the country.

Melissa had volunteered to go with him instead. She was thirteen, still trying to please. Dick had agreed, although when they arrived, she could tell the other men were annoyed. It had been horrible. They had tramped around for hours in the woods. She had to pee and kept trying to fall back to get behind a bush, but her father was afraid she would get lost and made her stay close. Finally her father and his press secretary Mac—he had not come to Washington with Dick—climbed onto a platform in a tree and the others made noises down the valley until they drove a deer toward the blind. The press secretary shot the deer. It died spurting blood near where she was standing uselessly. It had beautiful brown eyes that looked into hers. She had shamed Dick by crying and the men had called her Bambi. She knew she had screwed up, making her father sorry he had brought her. She was ashamed of disappointing him, yet that night and the next, whenever she thought of the beautiful deer bleeding to death, she cried again. Although Mac had shot the deer, the photo in the paper was of Dick standing over the carcass. She would never be able to attack a deer or any other animal, except maybe a mouse. Even mice were kind of cute. She wanted to be at peace with the animal kingdom. She wasn't a vegetarian, but she wasn't about to go out and start killing things either. She almost said something aloud to Blake but realized she was miles from his thoughts at the moment. She stared at him, wondering how to break through. This was not developing into one of their more intimate afternoons.

"Blake, I'll have to go home about four. I don't know when I can get away again."

That got his attention. He swung around to look at his VCR clock. "Sorry. I have a lot on my mind. My lawyer tells me he thinks my case is going to a grand jury soon. They've probably managed to extract enough data from my computer to get me into real trouble."

"Oh, baby, you didn't tell me. That's terrifying." She clutched his hand hard.

He put his arms around her and drew her down on the bed with him. "It sure is. . . . So your father got away with everything we uncovered?"

"He doesn't seem to feel threatened any longer."

"So he ought to be in a pretty good mood?"

"I think they're both enjoying the holidays. More than we are, so far."

His mouth moved over hers and he began to kiss her, passionately, fervently, as if drinking life itself from her. They kissed and kissed until she felt molten, all her bones turning to flaming jelly. She felt if anyone had been looking at them, they would have shone with a blinding light, would have left spots on any observer's eyes. They were burning together. They fumbled out of their clothes and, for once, he let his drop on the floor. His hands fastened on her breasts, danced on her spine, slid between her legs teasing her, withdrawing, slipping back into the grove of her swollen labia. Finally when she was clawing at his back, they came together. She forgot everything in the rush of pleasure. Afterward she dozed for perhaps fifteen minutes. Then he was ready to start again. They were lost in each other, making love until they were sated and then showering in his own bathroom. Most males' bathrooms she had been in—her old boyfriend Jonah's, her brothers'—had been untidy, the basins littered with stubble from shaving, a smell of piss around the toilets. Not Blake's. His bathroom smelled of verbena aftershave, of spicy soap. He took a clean towel from the closet for her. After they showered, rubbing soap into each other, lathering, joining again under the spray, she dried herself and reluctantly dressed. "I have to go."

"We haven't figured out what we're going to do. Okay, sit down and draw me a picture of the layout of your house, floor by floor." He pulled a tee shirt over his wet head and groped for his jeans on the floor.

"Why?"

"So I have a notion what I'm walking into."

She thought it was silly, but she understood he was nervous about finally meeting her parents as her lover, her husband. She drew diagrams as he asked.

He studied them, scratching his head with his nails. "Okay. Can you get me in the back door?"

"It opens onto a little parking area and then a street that's really a big alley."

"What's the best time to catch your parents together, with a minimum of other people around?"

"Usually early evening. But it varies. What I can do is call you each day when I know my parents' schedule. Say I call you at ten in the morning and give you the latest information. But I don't understand what you're planning."

"Look, I've got to do something. They're closing in on me. By now, they've probably reconstituted what I was doing on my computer—or they will have all they need very soon." He was pacing the length of his room, from his long dresser with the posters and flyers of his father papering the wall above it to the windows with their blinds closed. Outside, it was growing dark. "You let me in. I throw myself on their mercy. Only after that, you tell them we're married. Leave most of the talking to me."

"Why should they help us?"

"To avoid scandal. Maybe they'll try to buy me off. I have no idea—and you don't either. So we'll just wing it. It's the only chance we have."

"I wish we had a better plan. Maybe I should talk to them first."

"No! Don't give them time to put up their defenses. We'll spring it on them and see if we can persuade them that the scandal is worse than what we did." He stopped pacing and put his hands hard on her shoulders. "Don't say anything. I can be eloquent. Just get me in there without announcing me, without warning them I'm coming, and let me talk to them. You stand by and keep quiet until I signal you to join in. Okay? Agreed?"

"Why do you think you can get through to them if I can't?"

"You're their daughter. They have you pigeonholed. They don't know me. I have a chance of getting through. If it doesn't work, we're no worse off than we are now, right?"

"I guess so," she said, although she really wasn't sure that was so. Now her parents had no idea of their relationship.

He stared into her face. "Are you sure that what we did, what we revealed has had no consequences? Are you sure of that?"

"Yeah, I'm sure. He's flying high. Why does it matter now?"

He sat on the bed's edge to pull on his socks and his boots. "Because if there are consequences, if his career is in jeopardy, if there is any chance of prosecution or even just political fallout, he'll be less apt to hear us out, right?"

"Of course."

"Let's roll." He grabbed his jacket. "I've got to take you home. I think we can risk dropping you at your corner this time. And stay in touch. We'll talk every morning. Every afternoon. Every evening."

"I'm scared of telling them, you know. But in a way, it will be a relief."

"It'll be something, anyhow." He smiled thinly. "It will be some kind of a change."

CHAPTER THIRTY-TWO

Melissa was having trouble sleeping. She would fall asleep all right, but then at two or three a.m. she would come bolt awake and her mind would begin to churn. She simply could not make herself stop thinking about what was going to happen with Blake and her parents. It felt hopeless. His plan was weak and unlikely to prove effective, but she could not come up with anything better.

Several times she resolved to break her agreement with Blake and talk to them, but each time she faced them, she could not imagine the words that would make them understand. What she had done was foreign to them. How to make them comprehend that marrying Blake had not been an act aimed at them but something she passionately wanted; that she had married him not out of defiance but with love. They might not care about her motives. Would her love for Blake weigh more than a feather with them? Ultimately, she lacked the courage to take them on by herself. She submitted to Blake's wish that she remain silent, because doing nothing was easier than approaching her parents. If only Blake and she had not gotten involved in that stupid attempt to discredit her father, then their marriage would not seem, perhaps, such an attack.

Still every night she woke and played out endless scenarios in her head; none came out the way she wanted. Even in her imagination, she could not force her parents to acquiesce. They remained adamant and punitive. No matter how she pleaded and how she imagined Blake pleading with them, she could not believe in a happy ending. It was only a question of whether Blake went to jail alone or whether their anger would prove stronger than their fear of scandal. Perhaps if she agreed to have the marriage annulled, they would not prosecute Blake. That was the only bargaining chip she could imagine producing. However, she would not share that idea with him. She would keep it in reserve for the time right after his best efforts deflated.

In the livingroom stood a bushy Douglas fir Alison had bought and erected. They had trimmed it on the obligatory home evening, with Alison taking photos for publicity and next year's Christmas cards; she had finished sending off the six thousand and fifty-second card the previous weekend. The chairman of the state party dropped by. "I still think you should have a dog. You could borrow one for the shoot."

"No dogs," Rosemary said with a sweet smile. "The children are all allergic."

The vacation crept along like a slug leaving a slime trail of fear, of deceit, of constant anxiety.

"You're not eating," Alison said.

They were at supper on Christmas Eve. A supporter had sent Dick a pheasant, and the caterers had agreed to prepare it. Melissa wouldn't have been excited about eating a pheasant any time, but she simply did not want anything tonight. Why did Alison notice everything? Rosemary hadn't observed her lack of appetite. "I'm on a diet."

Rosemary turned to her. "That's an excellent idea, but it is the holidays. You could eat less than usual, but have a bite of everything. I find that works beautifully. You just taste a forkful or two and then put the fork down. That way you don't feel deprived, but you definitely see results."

Rosemary always thought there was too much of Melissa. Melissa used to worry about her size, but Blake liked her body just the way it was. Still, her appetite shrank as her anxiety grew. She chewed each bite over and over until, when she tried to swallow, it stuck in her throat like a stone. No matter how little she ate, the food turned to a brick in her stomach. All she wanted was water. Her thirst was endless. She kept refilling her water glass from the silver carafe frosted with condensation. How cool it felt in her hand. She longed to roll it against her forehead.

Her parents were euphoric. They had been invited to a party at the house of a CEO in pharmaceuticals, a possible backer. Rosemary and Alison were researching his family, his wife's habits, everything they could learn. Rosemary was feeding Dick information about the needs of the pharmaceutical industry, the kind of legislation that benefited them, the kind they feared, the kind they desired but had not yet managed to buy. Dick would be well prepared. He could learn his lines quickly. He would have been an excellent actor, she thought, except that he played only himself—but himself with a difference depending on the company. He would shape his approach, his manner, his ideas, his likes and dislikes to fit the contours of the backer he was wooing. All her life since she had been old enough to overhear, to eavesdrop, she had wondered at her father's ability to remain Dick and yet alter his coloration, his tone, his demeanor, his opinions to suit the occasion.

Every day, Blake and she spoke or e-mailed several times. Blake was asking for an optimum time for his surprise appearance, and always she had to explain that there were too many people around. Finally on Christmas, she saw an opening. Her parents were going to a cocktail party, a formal dinner and then they would drop in to the local Republican soiree. But nothing was scheduled before five. Merilee was meeting a colleague from the Law Review. Billy was going to watch a game at the house of a friend who had a giant wall TV—something Billy had been lobbying for all vacation with no perceptible results. Her parents scarcely watched network television; they were not about to give over a wall to it. All they ever had on was omnipresent CNN or an occasional football game.

"Can you get away?" She sat in the bathroom running water to cover her voice.

"Sure. No problem."

"Si and Nadine won't mind if you disappear for a couple of hours?"

"Remember, it's no holiday here. Nadine's working on a brief. Si's on the phone with a client who just got busted. He'll probably have to go down to the station. Business as usual. They won't miss me."

"Then come to the back door at two. I think that's the best time. Everybody but Rosemary and Dick should be out of the house."

"Let's synchronize our watches." He was playing spy again. He did sound lighter, less banked in with anxiety.

"I have eleven twenty . . . seven?" She looked at her new watch, that Rich and Laura had given her. It was fancy, all silver, but it had no numerals, making it hard to read.

"You're fast, but I'll change my watch to match yours, so we both know the time you have to slip down and let me in."

"Are you sure you don't want me to talk with them first? Prepare them?"

"Absolutely not. You're just as surprised as they are to see me. . . . Things are still upbeat there? Everybody wearing a happy face and letting the money drop in their laps?"

"They're in a good mood. Dick gave my mother diamond earrings for Christmas. He even gave Alison a gold necklace. They must feel flush and up."

"Does Alison actually live there?"

"She sleeps in her office. She has a daybed."

"Is she going to be around?"

"She's out now. I think she went to church. Blake, it doesn't really matter if she's in the house. She'll be up in her office diddling around with her computer. She would never interfere. Never!"

"I'd rather they be alone."

"She's Mother's shadow, but I don't see why she matters."

"Don't be superelitist. She may be your mother's lackey, but she is a person."

"If you say so. I've never been convinced."

"Is there any time you can think of when she wouldn't be there, when your parents would be all alone? Except for you, I mean."

"Maybe if she got hit by a truck or developed appendicitis. Not otherwise."

She heard him sigh. He was silent then for what felt like forever before he said, "Okay, we'll proceed. I'll be there at two sharp."

"See you. . . . And bring your best luck. We're going to need it."

"I think we ran out of that a while back, babes."

She wished she could throw herself on her bed and sleep until just before two. With so few people in the house, they did not eat a formal lunch, just grazed. There were plenty of leftovers, and Rosemary would scarcely eat, with so many dinners to attend during the holidays. Rosemary would always say in public when complimented on her slender figure that it must just be genetic, that she never went on a diet. That was true. Her normal eating was confined to such small quantities, it wouldn't put fat on a Chihuahua.

They gathered briefly in the kitchen, standing around nibbling a cucumber (Rosemary), a roast beef sandwich (Dick) and yogurt (Melissa), then wandering off. Her parents had spent the morning in their bathrobes, but just before what passed for lunch, they dressed. She guessed it was in case someone should unexpectedly drop in—as was going to happen, if all went well. Dick was in cashmere sweats. Not that Rosemary was wearing jeans or sweats; her casual was a wool jumper over a silk shirt, with only stud earrings, a designer scarf at her throat. The girls she had gone to Miss Porter's with would have identified the designer in thirty seconds, but she had never cared. If Alison did not take her shopping and buy her straight preppy gear, then she went with Emily, who always knew what was cool. Oddly enough, Rosemary, who cared passionately about the impression she presented, never did her own shopping—unless she was hanging around a boutique to meet some senator's wife she wanted to befriend.

Rosemary and Dick had retired, presumably to make love, right after lunch. Melissa became increasingly worried that Blake would come and they would still be closeted. Fortunately, Dick wanted to watch the Eagles. By one thirty, he was lying on the sofa facing the TV and Rosemary curled up in a facing chair. She was reading an apologia on Kissinger, a thick tome she had been carting around the house. Rosemary had the ability to read through anything. Her grandma had told her, not in admiring tones, that Rosemary could be reading and her baby crying right at her elbow, and she would not hear. Whenever she turned a page, she glanced at the TV so that she could partake of enough of the game to be able to answer Dick's comments on the loutishness of the opposing quarterback, the stupidity of the coach, the ineptness of the wide receiver. Melissa had never been able to figure out if her mother liked sports or simply endured televised games as she would a society function with people who bored her.

Melissa had put on a blouse she felt sure her mother would approve of, a plaid skirt, nylons, flats. She was creating the image of the proper schoolgirl, although once the revelations commenced, that wasn't going to help. She had brushed her hair until it glinted. She put on lipstick and light makeup. She examined her teeth and gave them a brush. Then she went downstairs and took a seat as if to watch the game. She observed the score and thirty seconds later could not remember it. Her brain felt scrambled. Her hands were clammy. Her stomach ached with apprehension. She stared into her own lap. How many colors were actually in the plaid? Navy, dark green, a skinny thread of yellow . . .

Alison appeared in the hall shedding her coat, looking in on her parents. Damn it! Why did she have to come back so soon? Didn't she have any friends? Alison did not bother to pretend interest in the game but asked Rosemary how she was finding the biography. Rosemary said it was fascinating and she would lend it to Alison as soon as she finished it, for there was much to learn from the career of a great man. She compared him to Richelieu. Alison nodded. Melissa wondered if Alison knew who Richelieu was; she certainly didn't. Finally Alison climbed the steps to her office-bedroom. Melissa heard the door shut. Good. Now if Alison would only stay out of the way.

At five to two, Melissa got to her feet and slipped out of the room. Dick's gaze was fixed on the TV. Rosemary was deep in her book. Neither of them glanced at her as she went into the kitchen. As silently as she could, she crept down the narrow back staircase. Below was the small dank basement she liked to imagine held a corpse buried under the floor. A skeleton from 1812, say. She unlocked the door and carefully, an inch at a time so they would not overhear, opened it and then the storm door. Blake was not in the yard. Her precautions were silly, since the roar of the crowd and the excited monologue of the announcer would have drowned out almost anything she did, short of clog dancing. She was almost relieved the yard was empty. She hoped Blake had abandoned his feeble scheme. Still, she slipped the bolt of the lock so it would not shut her out and walked into the small yard, paved over for parking, and glanced up and down the alley. She clutched her elbows against the cold.

The row houses were similar, almost matching on the street out front, but in back they were eccentric and individual. One had a tiny backyard where a dog was chained. Another had a makeshift garage. Some yards, like this one, were paved over. One house had a funny sort of caboose sticking out to the alley. A couple of yards, had been turned into miniature gardens or play areas.

She stood in the cold, almost enjoying it. It was above freezing today, barely. The ice against the house had not melted, but on the two cars it evaporated in the faint sun that trickled over the high slanted rooftops of the town houses in the block behind them. The sun was pale and watery, reminding her of food service custard. She wished Blake would call her. Her cell phone was turned on in her pocket. She was pecking out his number when she heard a motorcycle in the alley. She took a few uncertain steps forward. She did not see anyone until Blake climbed the alley fence and dropped into the yard.

"I thought maybe you weren't coming."

"Why? I'm on time."

She looked at her stupid watch again. He wasn't late enough to make an issue of; she was just nervous. "I'm scared. What should I say?"

"Just let me do the talking."

Slowly she walked up the steps to the kitchen. In her mind was an image from some movie, maybe a Western, of some guy mounting a platform to be hanged by the neck until dead. Why couldn't she just turn and run? Why couldn't she get on the back of his motorcycle and they would take off for parts unknown? Who would finally care? She would disappear. In a few years, she'd get in touch. They could make a living, somehow. Probably Si and Nadine would forgive them and send money. She turned back toward him at the head of the steps, but he was already looking past her. His face was set, a grim mask of hardened intent. Maybe if it didn't work, and it wouldn't, they could take off at once while her parents were still stunned. But was Rosemary ever stunned into inaction?

In a tiny pocket of old unresolved anger and misery, she realized, she nurtured the ridiculous wish that what was going to happen, whatever it was, would show Rosemary and Dick that they had always underestimated her, always considered her far less than she was capable of being. Even if they hated her, at least they might respect her, might admit surprise at what she had done. Perhaps that was the best that could be hoped for. To astonish them.

Blake gave her a prod forward. "Move," he whispered in her ear. "Someone could come in. Let's do it."

She saw herself walking forever toward the livingroom of the narrow row house, moving in ever slower motion and never arriving, like Zeno's paradox from philosophy class. But she did not live in Zenoland; she lived here and now. Time would not stop for her or linger in ever smaller fractions. She must arrive in the doorway, and she did, pausing there and imagining herself suddenly transported away, teleported into some other, more friendly dimension. Blake moved into the doorway slightly behind and to the side. Nothing happened for a couple of minutes. Rosemary turned a page of her tome. Dick groaned and cursed mildly as the Eagles' quarterback was sacked. Then somehow their presence registered. Rosemary looked up first and stared, freezing. Her response caused Dick to turn his head.

He got to his feet, hitting the mute button on the remote so that the house was suddenly still. She could hear the refrigerator running and Alison walking around upstairs. No one said anything for what felt like an hour but was, she guessed, perhaps one minute, perhaps two.

Blake broke the silence. "Mr. Dickinson, Mrs. Dickinson, we've met before in Washington, in your house there, when I was visiting your daughter."

"What are you doing here? How did you get in?" Dick was drawing himself up to a dignified stance, smoothing down his cashmere sweats.

"Melissa let me in." Blake stepped past her. He stood just in front of her and to the side, his hands loosely balled at his sides, his head slightly lowered. She guessed he was trying not to look confrontational but failing.

"Melissa, are you crazy? Why did you let him in?"

"I asked her to," Blake said simply. "She knew I wanted to talk with both of you."

"You've been stalking our daughter." Rosemary sat upright now, her eyes glittering. "I know you hacked into her e-mail and you've been reading it."

"I have a right to read her mail," Blake said. "She's my wife."

"We're married." Melissa's voice emerged almost as a squeak. She tried to regain control, lowering it into her throat so she would sound less of a ninny. "We've been married for a couple of months. We love each other."

"Married?" Rosemary shook her head in disgust. "We'll have it annulled."

"You're going to prison," Dick said. "Don't imagine manipulating Melissa into believing herself bound to you is going to change that."

"We're bound up regardless. That's how it is. We got married because we wanted to be together. We've been keeping it a secret from you because Melissa was waiting for a good time to tell you—"

"For instance, after you finished feeding all those lies to that scandalmonger on the *Inquirer*? Was that when you planned to tell us?" Dick rolled his eyes. "Or when you decided to confess to hacking into our e-mail?"

"I wanted to tell you," Melissa began, but Blake overrode her.

"Those weren't lies. Yes, I tried to damage you. I couldn't forgive you for my father's death. I was with him that night and I know he was innocent, and I suspect you do too. But it was politically useful to you to kill my father, and you think it would be politically useful to put me in prison."

"If he goes, I go," Melissa said. "We were both involved."

"You don't know what you're saying." Rosemary rose neatly unfolding herself. "You're mesmerized by him. But we'll protect you. You've been a foolish and willful girl, but we'll take care of you, no matter what. You, however, are in real trouble." She nodded at Blake.

"Judge, jury and executioner, the two of you." Blake took a step forward, his hands clenched now to fists. "Nothing we gave the *Inquirer* was a lie. But we'll shut up. We just want to live in peace together. We'll go off to California or Ireland or Mexico or anyplace. You won't have to see us. You won't have to have anything to do with us. We'll just vanish."

"I wouldn't let my daughter go off with scum like you," Dick said.

"She may be foolish, she may be stupid, but she's still my daughter. Get out of here and leave her alone, now!"

"I love him." Melissa wrung her hands. "He's my husband and I love him."

"Oh, shut up," Rosemary said. "You're an idiot. He was using you to get at us. I told you what he was up to, but you were too silly to pay attention—"

"Melissa is mine, not yours. You can't just take her back like an umbrella you left in a restaurant. We're legally married, the marriage has been consummated, and other people know we're married. You can't make it go away."

"Oh, can't we?" Rosemary smiled tightly. "We could offer to buy you off, of course, and I think you'd leap at the chance. But we can't trust you. I'm afraid we can't trust Melissa right now, either. She's besotted. But she'll be helped to grow out of it."

Dick said, "She'll come to her senses once we've got her away from you. We can still help her. I don't think any help would rescue you from your doomed obsession with your father. A criminal found guilty by a jury, remember, who went through seven years of appeals refused by every court he pestered. He was guilty and he was properly sentenced and properly executed. I had no contact with him and no personal grudge."

"You used him politically, to get elected and reelected."

Dick shook his finger, taking two steps toward Blake. "You had little to complain of. You were adopted by rich lawyers and spoiled rotten. If you insist on destroying your life, you have only yourself to blame." Dick was no taller than Blake, but he seemed much, much larger. "I'll protect my daughter from you. You've tried to ruin her and you've tried to ruin my family, but I want you to know you've failed. You've ruined only yourself."

Blake took another step forward. "If you think you could ever, ever buy me off so that I'd leave Melissa, you're the crazy ones. You don't under- stand her. You have no idea who I am. We belong together. We're one. She is my wife and she'll stay my wife, no matter what happens to me."

"Anyone can talk a good game." Rosemary shook her head gently.

"Where you're going is prison. Unless you flee, of course, you'll be picked up before the week is out." She crossed her legs and waited, head cocked, as if eager to hear what Blake would say next.

"Mother, Father, do you want this scandal?" Melissa moved to stand beside Blake. "Think how it's going to look. It's not as if you could keep our marriage a secret. Won't it look as if you're putting him in prison because he's African-American and I married him? Listen to me. You've been making a place for yourself in Washington. This won't help. I love Blake. If you let him go, I'll agree to an annulment and you can keep me at home for a year or until you're satisfied. I'll do whatever you want, if you let him go."

"That's sweet, dear, but unnecessary. We will get you an annulment and we will keep you out of trouble. But this young man is dangerous. He has an obsession." Rosemary wagged a long elegant purple-tipped finger. "He wants to get us. He's obsessed by visions of revenge. We can't afford to let him go. Frankly, he causes too much trouble."

Blake was standing more loosely now, smiling slightly. "Melissa, are you ready to walk out of here with me?" They had overridden him, they had almost vanquished him, but he wasn't ready to give up, she thought.

"Of course." She moved closer to him. She could almost feel herself on the bike behind him, holding on. "Let's go!"

"You don't care about her," Blake said as Alison appeared in the doorway behind Rosemary. She stood there a moment and then drew back into Rosemary's office. Good. She had decided not to get involved. Blake was saying, "You never loved her. You made her feel inferior. She wasn't up to your perverted standards. But I love her the way she is, and she loves me, and that doesn't mean a thing to you—that for the first time in her life she feels secure. She feels cared for."

"You attached yourself to her as a way to get to us. Let's be a trifle honest here," Rosemary said.

"I was curious about her because she's your daughter. But she's a woman in her own right, and it's her I love and it's her I married—not you people. I don't want her family. I have a better one of my own. One she likes being a part of."

"Oh, so your adopted parents were in on this," Dick said with a sense of aha.

"My sister let it slip we're married, so we had a scene with them. But they accepted Melissa. They do that."

"I'm sure they do," Rosemary said.

"I'm taking Melissa out of here. Now! If you ever want to see her again, you'll call off your dogs and let us be." He took Melissa's arm and started to turn toward the kitchen.

"You will not. Alison!" Rosemary spun around. "Time for a little help here."

Alison came out of Rosemary's office carrying their Smith & Wesson nine-millimeter semiautomatic, one of her favorites, held before her in both hands, properly fixed against her body. Her face was grim. "Stand perfectly still. Don't move," she said. "Step away from Melissa now or I will shoot."

Dick picked up the phone. "Sixty seconds and you're out of here, or I call the police. Alison . . ."

"What, you're going to shoot us? Father, Mother, are you crazy?"

"You can't do this!" Blake was sputtering with anger. "She's my wife. You have no right! Stop trying to push me around."

"Get out of my house!" Dick yelled, openly furious now, phone still gripped in his hand. "I want him out of here. Now, Alison!"

"Don't threaten us! You think I came empty-handed?" Blake let go of her and pulled something from his jacket pocket. "Did you think I was stupid enough to trust you? You killed my father and now you want to kill me." It was the gun she had found under his bed in November, she knew it was.

"Blake, no!" She grabbed at his arm. A noise filled her head and deafened her for a moment so that she saw Dick's mouth open but could not tell what he was saying. Then he was clutching his chest. "Daddy, no!" she screamed, and turned and struck at Blake, grabbing him. She could see Blake firing again and again, but because she was holding on to his arm, the shots went wildly around the room, hitting a vase, the wall, the couch where her father had been sprawled watching the football game.

Alison came forward with the semiautomatic in front of her, both hands steadying the gun propped against her body as she was always showing Rosemary how to pose. She moved deliberately, ignoring the wild bullets careening around the room. Then Blake fell and there was blood all over his head. Melissa knelt over Blake calling his name, and she saw her mother flinging herself on her father. She stared from one to the other and the minutes gelled into something heavy and thick and she knew suddenly that they were dead, Blake and her father, both. Everybody was dead. She could hear again now. Her mother was weeping hysterically, yelling for Alison to call an ambulance.

Alison leaned over her. "I'd love to shoot you too, you murderous traitor, you stupid little bitch! But it would kill your mother." She turned and picked up the phone where it had dropped. "I'll call an ambulance."

"Yes, hurry! I can still feel a pulse." Rosemary looked up at Alison, her face streaked with tears. She was incredibly pale, her shoulders shaking. Blood had spattered all over her silk blouse and jumper, Dick's blood. There was so much blood every place, so much.

Melissa knelt over Blake's body. She could not cry yet. She was too frozen. She was stunned. What did Blake think he was doing? Now everyone would say he was a murderer, son of a murderer. Why had he done that? He was supposed to help her reach her father, that was what he was supposed to do. She wanted to shake sense into him. But his head was all smashed and she could not even hold him. He was gone from her. He had vanished and left her with bits of bone and brain and blood, with the mess of her splattered life and a mother who would hate her always. No one would ever understand them now. Never. She knelt there, dead herself over his broken body.

M elissa put her hand over Karen's on the table, among the plain white crockery and stainless steel cutlery of the little restaurant where Karen had taken her for lunch. The food was better than Mountain View Rehabilitation Center's bland cuisine, but the thrill was getting out for a few hours. "I know you hate coming near the place, but I really appreciate it. And eating real food."

"Oh, the cooking in the bin—right. They feel that any flavor—herbs or spices—might excite the residents, cause a riot."

"I wonder if Dr. Baines or Dr. Hildebrand has ever failed to diagnose anybody as being whatever their families were willing to pay to have them described as. I mean, do they ever turn anybody away and say, But this kid is normal? Or, There's nothing whatsoever wrong with Mrs. Zilch?"

"They wouldn't get paid then, would they? But they do turn people away—if they think they're too much trouble. Too violent. Uncontrollable." Karen frowned. "Do you know your diagnosis?"

"Borderline."

Karen waved her hand. "BPD—Borderline Personality Disorder."

"You know about it?"

"A Dr. Krotkey originally defined borderline for the *DSM*—the bible of psychiatry, but they keep revising it. They mostly apply borderline to women and young people—impulsive, unstable, bad self-image. Standard adolescence, in other words."

"How do you know all this?"

"I studied up. I wanted to know what I was dealing with. A friend smuggled photocopies in for me—patients aren't supposed to know about illnesses." She nodded at Melissa's empty plate. "Would you like something more?"

"Maybe dessert?"

"How are you bearing up?"

"I scrape along the bottom. I hate Dr. Hildebrand. He tries to manipulate me."

"You didn't hate Blake for that."

"Blake didn't manipulate me. He loved me. He was pursuing justice."

"Through you, Melissa. You have to see that."

"Are you on their side now?"

"Of course not." Karen sighed. "I just thought you might have a few ideas about responsibility and taking control of your choices by now."

"How can I take control of anything while I'm locked up?"

"Don't get upset. Let's have dessert."

She was especially grateful for Karen's visits, because she knew how her aunt dreaded entering the gates and sitting in the waiting room with its air of stodgy disuse, chairs never sat in, couches never sprawled upon. It was in the main house, where the alcoholics and addicts were, upstairs. Karen always sat by the floor-length windows as if to provide herself an escape. The residents never entered that room unless summoned by an approved guest. Karen had only gotten on the list by managing to persuade Rosemary it would be more of a nuisance to keep her off than to put her on. An attendant would escort Melissa from Ryder, the young people's house, to the main house, the old robber baron's mansion, called a camp.

The facility was in the Adirondacks, occupying what had once been an estate, then a school for rich girls whom their families did not wish to send to a normal college, and now storage of those over fourteen who had caused or threatened to cause their wealthy and powerful families some kind of annoyance. The view from the windows was beautiful, mountains all around their cloistered valley, blue today with autumn haze, patches of brilliant red and gold. But the mountains might as well have been painted on a wall. Her friend Boo, daughter of a tire family, called it the Mountain View but Don't Touch. Boo had an affair with her gym teacher. The teacher was fired and Boo was shipped here.

Melissa had been in Mountain View for over three months before Karen was allowed to see her. Very hard time. Now she was on milder tranquilizers than the heavy stuff they had first given her, that kept her woozy and detached, as if her head had floated loose of everything down below. She still felt lethargic, but at least her head was back on her shoulders and she could manage two consecutive thoughts without losing her way in a drug-induced soggy haze. She was slow, but she no longer shuffled.

All she had wanted was to weep, to be unconscious, to die, but she could not even manage that. She had tried and failed in Philadelphia, with a combination of sleeping pills and antihistamines. Then she had tried a razor blade. While she was heavily drugged, her emotions had sunk deep below. In between was a thick layer of smog that choked her so she could not cry and scream, so words were fish shapes that escaped into the grey-ness and she was left groping for herself. Now she felt empty, but she knew how and why she hurt. She knew.

"Have you heard from Merilee lately?" Karen was motioning for the waitress. Karen drove from Vermont to the Adirondacks to see her every two weeks. They had, after experimenting, decided on the Bear Trap as a place with big portions, comfort food and waitresses who let them sit at the table for a couple of hours without hassle. This waitress was called Freddie, short for Winifred, a name she told them she detested. She had blonded hair worn in straggle curls, a great gap-toothed grin, a sandpapery voice and an infectious giggle that Melissa could never resist no matter how depressed she was. Freddie was bringing black coffee for Karen, who would have to drive back to Vermont, and a big slice of blueberry pie for Melissa, who would be returned to Ryder House.

"She's not good at writing, but she tries. She's the only family besides you I have contact with. If only they'd let me have e-mail, I could really communicate with her. They let me have a laptop now to do my home-work, but I have to send everything by snail mail." Merilee was working for a firm out in L.A. that specialized in environmental law. Rosemary did not approve. Rosemary had visited Melissa twice, the second time on the occasion of her marriage to Senator Frank Dawes, the senior senator from North Dakota. He was hardly dashing, older than Dick had been, but a force in the Senate. He had both money and power. Rosemary would never forgive Melissa but was too busy to bother with her. Alison had waited in the car. Emily was not allowed to visit Mountain View.

When Karen arrived, Melissa always gave her letters for Emily and received at least one she could hide away, read, reread.

When Karen had to return her, her suicidal friend Jon was waiting. "So, she fed you up?"

"Stuffed. Almost happy."

"Don't ever get happy here. Keep fighting." He put his arm around her waist. She shied away. He might be interested, but she wasn't. She didn't think she'd ever be interested in a guy again. There were quite a few young people stored here—in residence, as they said—and they hung out in little gangs, the ones who were fairly functional and not in lockup for some rebellion or infringement of the Byzantine rules. Many residents in the other houses were middle-aged, and some were quite old. Families had diverse reasons for wishing to stow members safely and silently away. There were addicts, alcoholics, kleptomaniacs, those whose sexuality had represented a problem—they liked the wrong sex or those too young to be legal. There were some genuine crazies too, stored in Clifton. Schizophrenics, mostly.

"But I am a widow," she repeatedly told her psychiatrist.

"You weren't really married, and you were manipulated into an unhealthy and abusive relationship. You won't improve until you accept that."

"I knew him far better than you ever could. And I loved him. And he loved me. Those are the facts."

"Your delusions are standing in the way of your improvement." Dr. Hildebrand was extremely tall, extremely thin and grey all over. Grey hair, grey eyes, greyish skin—except in ski season or once when he took off to the Caribbean for two weeks, when his face turned paprika red. They detested each other. She guessed she represented something that irritated him, maybe a daughter? He had two, she could tell from a photo on his desk. She knew why she detested him: he was trying to force her to revise her life, to turn against Blake, to forget she had been for a time really loved. He considered her attempt at suicide a sickness; she thought it common sense.

She glanced at the fading scars on her wrists. She liked to wear sweaters with sleeves short enough so she could see her razor cuts. If they ever faded completely, she would feel she had lost her last link with Blake and the visible proof of her suffering, her shame. They would not let her wear her wedding ring—it had been taken from her.

At first when she was shut up here, she fantasized about escaping so she could finish the job. That would prove to everyone that she had really loved Blake, that they had been meant to be together, that she saw herself as the outlaw she was and that she knew she was doomed. As time passed, she thought about suicide less, but it was still a scenario she cherished when she was more than usually bored. Karen promised that when she finally got out, she could live on the farm in Vermont. Melissa appreciated the invitation, but what would she do there? What would she do any-place? It would not be fair to kill herself on Karen's farm—her aunt would suffer and be blamed—but she had not come up with a better idea of where to go and what to do with herself. Not that the decision was imminent. She was not getting free soon. If she could go anyplace she chose, then she wanted to be with Emily. Emily was in her senior year, but they could still live together after Emily's commencement.

No one, not even Karen, would understand that her life was over. She had lived it all in a year and a half—meeting Blake, falling in love, getting married, losing him, burying him. She had done it all. She was really much older than the others her age in Mountain View. How could Jon interest her? He was just a kid from Cambridge, Massachusetts, who had taken too much Ecstasy and freaked out his parents, both college profes-sors. He had kissed her once when she was too surprised to stop him, but he had no idea how thrilling that wasn't.

She dreamed about Blake often, and when she woke up, she recalled the dreams in as vivid detail as she could, over and over, until she had memorized them. After a while, she was not sure whether a memory that surfaced was from her life before the institution or her dream life here. Last night she had been with Blake in a forest with tall evergreens, needles underfoot like carpeting. They had been lost, but it had not mattered. If she was with Blake, how could she be lost? She was only lost without him. She wished they would let her have a photo of him, but that too was forbidden, as if she didn't have a right to a picture of her own husband. He had loved her, no matter how much they all wanted to deny it.

At some point, Dr. Hildebrand told her, she must face what she had done and come to terms with it. He was a fool. She had been done to. Her husband had been shot in front of her and died in her arms. She did not think about the other stuff. She had nothing to do with that. Sometimes she saw her father lying on the floor bleeding from his chest, with Rosemary holding him, but she veered from it at once. Twice when she had not pushed it away quickly enough, she had thrown up. No, she had done nothing wrong but try to bring her husband and her family together. It was like Romeo and Juliet, the Montagues and the Capulets, the way Emily and Nadine had said. And she, like Juliet, was supposed to die. She saw that clearly, saw her own death before her like a stage play she could watch over and over again, the way she replayed her favorite videos like *My Little Pony* when she was a child. If they caught her talking to Blake, they would increase her meds again till she was a zombie. She was on four different meds anyhow. She was numb sexually and she hadn't had a period in three months. She had briefly hoped she was pregnant, but no such luck. She so did not need any heavier meds. She had known she could not be pregnant after so long, but she hoped for a miracle, as if her body might have secreted some of Blake and hidden him within.

In the meantime, she had five minutes to get ready for the attendants to march them to food service. She brushed her hair hard and reapplied lipstick and checked herself out in the mirror. She always sat with Jon and Boo, so she wanted to look good. She'd heard too that there was a new guy just out of the preliminary solitary where they kept new "residents" for the first weeks. Then they'd watch MTV together and maybe dance. She was getting to be a better dancer. Blake and she used to dance together. She would imagine him watching her. Jon and the new guy would eye her, because she and Boo had worked out this new step that was really sexy. There wasn't much else to do in here, except work out new ways to wear her hair, new ways to dance, try to bring up memories so vivid that she wept, secretly. Study with the lame tutor who was supposed to be teaching her history or something. She had been coaching tennis, thanks to all the lessons she'd had from Karen when she was growing up, but soon it would be too cold to play. They had a tiny indoor pool reeking of chlorine, but she wasn't allowed in it. They thought she might try to drown herself. It looked about as exciting as swimming in a sewer.

Death and trivia, she said to herself, as she gave her hair a last brush. That's all we have. But at least she had her gang of friends here and that was something. They were all in rebellion from their parents, so she wasn't an outcast, no matter how bad Rosemary and Dr. Hildebrand tried to make her feel. Everything had gone wrong, but she had only wanted to bring her two families together. That was all she had wanted. It wasn't her fault, that terrible dying, the blood, the two of them suddenly gone and never to be again, even if sometimes, when she woke up at night, she shook with the pain of it. Maybe it was better she was on all those drugs. They kept bad things a little distance away, even if they didn't always work. She brushed her hair harder. Guilt was like a slimy pit, but she would not fall into it. No. She would go downstairs and eat with her friends and then dance and maybe watch TV later. That would be okay. Guilt was outside pushing in, but she would not let it in. Not yet.